BETRAYAL

NOEL PRIMROSE

Content

Dedication

For my wife Lynda, whose unstinting patience, encouragement, and insightful editing enabled me to complete this novel.

About the Author

Noel was born in Glasgow but now lives in an East Sussex village with his wife, Lynda.

He began his career with British Railways but spent most of his career at board level in the NHS. His main interest is his family and being outdoors where walking and gardening are his main pursuits. In the past, he was passionate about running, especially marathons. Noel is a keen football and rugby fan

THE BEGINNINGS

Chapter One

Three men stood in the dock, three youngish men, the oldest 29. None of them had previous convictions, and this was a big crime for a first offence; it had made it in the Press and Television. They had all pled guilty a month earlier at a Pre-Trial Hearing and were about to be sentenced; the Trial itself had only lasted two days.

One stood apart from the other two, Edward Phillips, the oldest of the three. Dressed in a blazer and flannels, white shirt and striped tie, you would have guessed him to be a university type and been right. His whole demeanour suggested anxiety as he made involuntary little drumming movements with his fingers on the dock rail. Then, seemingly becoming aware of what he was doing, he would grip the rail tightly from time to time to stop his hands from shaking. Face pale, lips tight, eyes blinking frequently; he looked the nervous wreck he had become. One hand lifted yet again to brush his untidy shock of brown hair away from his eyes.

Not for the first time Phillips looked over his shoulder at the blonde seated two rows behind him, searching for a response. She was his wife, but she made no effort to meet his eyes and offered no smile of comfort; if anything, she seemed to be watching one of the other two men.

The Judge, Justice Jean Walsh, was preparing to address the trio, having adjourned the court for just over an hour to consider sentencing.

The youngest man, Craig Murray, 26 years old, regarded the Judge impassively. He showed no emotion, willing her to get on with it, wanting it all to be over; his eyes were on the Judge. She was young, with dark, flashing eyes set in a striking bone structure. She was, indisputably, an attractive woman. The traditional white judicial wig covered her hair, which he guessed would be black and cut short.

She began to speak. *Here it comes, thought Murray, she's going to hammer me, but I bet that bastard Phillips gets off with a smacked wrist. It was his fault they'd been caught, stupid bastard that he was.*

He looked at Phillips momentarily and then beyond him to the blonde seated amongst the packed public gallery. By chance, in that brief second, they caught each other's eyes. She seemed sad or perhaps just resigned to the inevitable. Before he could react, she had bowed her head, and the moment of connection was gone. He turned back to face the Judge, but his thoughts stayed with the young woman. *Sam, oh Sam, however, did you come to marry a prick like Eddie Phillips.*

'Edward Phillips,' Judge Walsh's voice brought Murray out of his thoughts. 'Have you anything to say before I pass sentence?'

Phillips, ashen faced, shook his head.

'Please answer properly, Mr Phillips. The Court has to hear your reply.'

'No, your Honour.' Phillips responded, licking his lips nervously; he looked like he was going to burst into tears.

'Very well, Mr Phillips.' Justice Walsh fixed her best sentencing stare upon him and went on, 'You have pleaded guilty to the offence, and there is no doubt that you had a key role in the crime committed. In fact, it was your direct actions that resulted in immeasurable distress and panic and caused untold disruption to public and private services alike. I am, however, cognisant of the fact that you co-operated fully with the police following your arrest, confessed freely to your guilt and, importantly, have returned the proceeds of your crime to their rightful owners. You have also expressed great remorse in respect of your actions.

The moment had come; Murray watched Phillips stiffen visibly, his face strained and fearful, so pale he would have looked more at home in a coffin.

'I am therefore sentencing you to a suspended prison sentence of one year. The terms governing this sentence will be explained to you later.'

Phillips breathed a sigh of relief, almost smiling as he mumbled, 'Thank you, thank you, your Honour.'

Murray looked at Phillips disdainfully. *Thank you, Your Honour, three bags full, Your Honour; you fucking creep.*

The Judge addressed the second man, Richard Henry Connor, age 28.

'Mr. Connor, do you have anything to say before I deliver sentence?'

Harry Connor shuffled forward in the dock. He was of farming stock, not tall at 1.7 metres, his barrel chest making him look shorter than he was. His round, ruddy-complexioned face was topped with close-cropped jet-black hair. Whatever his internal feelings were, he displayed no anxiety as he faced Justice Walsh.

'Yes, your Honour. I truly regret everything that has occurred and promise never to get involved in any criminal activity ever again. It was a one-off episode of madness where I allowed a misguided sense of adventure and excitement to overcome my natural honesty and common sense. I beg you to consider my wife and young family when you determine my punishment.'

Behind him, Anne Connor nodded support for her husband, fighting back tears as she waited to hear the sentence. She hadn't told her two children, Abigail, aged four and Ian, barely two, about the mess their father had got himself into.

'Mr Connor once charged and the evidence placed before you, you too co-operated fully with the police. I am aware that you were not the ringleader, a point confirmed by both of your co-defendants, and you have also returned your share of the proceeds of the crime to their owners. You have asked me to take into account the fact that you are married with a young family, although this is something that you singularly failed to do when you embarked on this crime. Your family has my profound sympathies, but you must, however, be punished for your wrongdoing, and I am therefore committing you to a custodial sentence of three years.'

Justice Walsh was interrupted as Anne Connor gasped and began to sob, murmuring repeatedly, 'No, no, no…'

'Mrs Connor,' Justice Walsh spoke firmly, 'I understand what you are going through, but I must ask you to compose yourself or leave the Court.'

Connor turned away from his wife to face the Judge, pain wracking his face.

'Mr Connor, I will be recommending that you be detained in an Open Prison and that you are considered for parole after a period of twelve months, provided your behaviour is satisfactory.'

Harry Connor nodded, visibly relieved, 'Thank you, your Honour.'

Craig Murray steeled himself, determined to show no emotion and to avoid any reaction no matter what punishment was imposed upon him.

'Craig Murray, have you anything to say before I pass sentence upon you?' *Was it his imagination, or was her voice colder, more remote; it sounded almost menacing?*

Murray spoke clearly, unfalteringly, 'Your Honour, I would only re-iterate that there was never any intention that anyone would get hurt as a result of our actions. I apologise unreservedly and sincerely for the unfortunate and unacceptable consequences of my actions. I assure you that these were unforeseen.'

He knew he was doing himself no favours; knew that he should at least give the appearance of being repentant, look crestfallen or scared or something, but that wasn't his style. What was done was done, and that was an end to it. In any case, he was sure she would see through any act he put on at this late stage.

'Very well, Mr Murray; you have admitted your guilt and acknowledged your role as ringleader, but your admission was made in light of the irrefutable evidence that the police were able to put before you. Had this not been the case, I doubt if you would have been so co-operative. Hitherto, you have expressed no remorse regarding your crime whatsoever; only now, at the last minute, claiming that it was not your intention anyone would get hurt. It is quite clear to me that you gave no thought in the slightest to the ramifications of your actions. Had you had any regard for the community in which you have lived hitherto, you could have quite easily envisaged the dire consequences of your actions. This eleventh-hour minimal apology that you now offer the Court is, to my mind, wholly ingenuous.

Yeah, yeah, up yours too, dear, get on with it.

Moreover, you have refused to return your share of the proceeds of the crime probably in the hope that you will benefit from these at some future date.'

You're spot on, Justice Walsh, that's exactly what I intend to do.

He held her gaze unflinchingly as she went on. 'I hope the authorities will take steps to recover the proceeds and ensure that you in no way benefit from your criminal act. You are hereby sentenced to a term of imprisonment of four years.' Justice Walsh then motioned to the attending police officers, 'Take them down.'

Murray let out the breath he'd been holding. *At last, it was over. Four years; hopefully, if he behaved himself, he would be eligible for parole after two.*

Phillips was led away promptly; the officers knew that there was no love lost between him and the other two. His wife didn't even glance at him as he disappeared down the stairs to a custody room where the terms of his sentence would be fully explained to him. His eyes didn't leave her, but she kept her head down, avoiding his gaze; his hoped-for sign of forgiveness or slightest hint of reconciliation failed to transpire. He knew now that whatever they had shared was over.

Harry Connor turned to leave the dock, looking across to his wife. She stretched out her arms to him, although the distance between them prevented any contact. 'I love you, Frank. It'll be OK, we'll get through this, I promise.'

Connor fought back his tears and forced a smile, 'I love you, Anne. I'm sorry, darling. Tell the kids…,' he hesitated, searching for words, 'tell the kids I love them.'

Craig Murray followed, stopping to face Anne Connor. 'Sorry Anne, I'm truly sorry.'

Tears were running down her cheeks, but her face became a mask of venom. 'Fuck you, Craig, fuck you. Don't ever come near us again.'

He nodded, pained by the vitriol in her voice, but understood her anger.

Murray turned away, looking for Sam Phillips but her head was bent with her face buried in her hands; then the officer's hand on his back pushing him on, and his chance of any kind of contact was gone.

There was no sign of Eddie Phillips when Harry and Craig reached the corridor leading to the custody rooms.

'In here, Murray.' The officer pointed to a door.

'Just a minute, please.' Craig looked appealingly at his escort, nodding towards Connor. 'Can we have a word?'

The officer nodded, 'Stay where you are and make it quick.'

The two friends looked at each other. 'I'm sorry, Harry, really sorry for you, for Anne, for the kids. I've really fucked you all up.'

Connor shook his head, 'We all made our own decisions, Craig, it's not your fault. Any one of us could have pulled out at any time; we were all greedy. That's all there is to it. As the French say 'C'est la vie.'

'Thanks for that, Harry, I feel so bad. We'll meet up when we get out.'

'Don't think so, mate, it wouldn't work, what with the way Anne feels about you. This is it, I'm afraid.'

Craig nodded grimly, 'I understand. I just hope time brings a change of heart.'

'OK, Murray, that's it, in you go.' The guard pointed into the sparsely furnished room, two uncomfortable wooden chairs and a small, scarred, stained table was all it held.

And that was how I, Craig Murray, began the next phase of my life.

I chose a chair facing the door and started to think about what lay ahead. *What would prison be like? What did the future hold?* I shook my head, answering my own questions; there was no good thinking about it, there were no answers. Four years, that would be March 1969, or maybe 1967 if I got lucky and was offered parole.

I was barely settled when the door was pushed open, 'Let's go, Murray.'

I rose immediately and made my way into the corridor, following my two escorts outside.

'Over there.' One of my escorts pointed to a plain white van, its rear door open, ready for departure. 'Can you tell me where I'm going?'

The guard, an old-stager, smiled wickedly. 'They don't like you, Sonny Jim, you're headed to Westmoor.' It meant nothing to me, so it was easy to look indifferent, 'I guess once you're inside, they're all much the same.'

The guard leered, 'That's where you're wrong, Murray. If prisons were graded like hotels, it would be a one-star; there are some very nasty people in Westmoor. Here's a bit of advice for you: do what you're told, keep your head down and don't upset anybody, neither guard nor inmate. And one more thing, seeing as you're a good-looking young man, best watch your arse as well.'

The guard laughed heartily at his own warped humour; I doubted if it was the first time he'd taken a delight in issuing such a warning.

Chapter Two

I was the van's sole occupant as it pulled away; it was going to be a lonely journey to Westmoor, wherever Westmoor was. I was left alone with my thoughts; there were no windows with landscapes and scenery to distract me. Thinking was going to be my sole preoccupation for however long the journey took. And so, I sat there, looking back to past events and forward to the future. I got so immersed that I became unaware of the progress of the van, except when the occasional hurried stop sent me sliding along the metal bench seat. I shouted a curse at the driver I couldn't see; if he heard, he didn't respond.

Looking to the future was easy; I knew exactly what path I wanted to take, but first, there was the little matter of four years in gaol, 'banged up' as they say. When my thoughts blackened, four years seemed like a lifetime, so I tried hard not to let my thoughts dwell on prison. Hopefully, if I toed the line with those in authority, I'd qualify for early parole.

'Christ, I wish I knew where Westmoor was.' I was talking aloud to myself. It was so frustrating not to be able to look out and get some idea of the direction we were headed from some passing road sign. Westmoor sounded remote, Cornwall perhaps, or Yorkshire, or Wales or, maybe even the country of my birth, Scotland? I hoped it wasn't Scotland; I didn't want to return as a failure and, worse still, as a convicted criminal. Not that it mattered, really; I doubted if anyone up there would know of my fate. There would be nobody visiting unless some prison charity, or the local vicar took pity on me. I had been orphaned when I was fourteen and brought up by my elderly aunt, a dear, kindly old lady who had passed away a few years ago. I did have relations abroad somewhere, but I'd never made the effort to get in touch with them, nor they me. I had allowed the friendships I had to lapse, allowed them to erode with the passage of time. Lapsing into philosophical mode, it seemed to me that if you were incarcerated behind four walls and locked doors, you could be anywhere, so roll on Westmoor, let's be having you.

My bum was already beginning to numb, but I made myself as comfortable as I could on the narrow bench seat and settled down to review the recent past, determined to be objective and not let bitterness colour my judgement. I remained convinced that it had been a good plan, simple easy to execute; we should have got away clean, but we hadn't. It was all too easy to put the blame on Eddie Phillips and leave it at that, but that wasn't the whole story, and I knew it. Where had it really started to go wrong? I started to pull together the strands of the past, encouraging pictures and memories to fill the stage I was now building in my mind.

I had moved from my job with the railways in Glasgow towards the end of 1961; electrification of the local rail system was approaching completion, and I had wanted a new challenge. Promotion and more money had been the prime motivators for relocating to England. It hadn't been easy to leave the city I loved; my roots were there and would always be there, but there were no close relatives to cling to. I'd known I would miss workmates and friends but had known too that there would be new friends to be made. So,

I'd upped stakes and headed for Crewe, that bastion of railway history and the lynchpin of main line electrification stretching south to London and north to Scotland. It had been towards the end of that migratory train journey to take up my new job that the first tiny step towards my current situation had been taken. I couldn't help but smile as I visualised the event, my head nodding in agreement. Yes, that's where this episode of my life had its genesis.

It had been a cold but bright, sunny November afternoon when the train had clanked, jolted and puffed to a halt in Warrington Station. I had been alone in the carriage since the train left Carlisle and was starting to get bored, staring vacantly out of a dirty window at the passing countryside.

The train had sat stationary for several minutes, and it had seemed that, yet again, no one would be joining me; but suddenly, a figure had dashed across the platform from the station building and was wrestling with the carriage door. I moved to help, but too late. The door had been pulled open, and a young woman had scrambled in, turning at once to slam it closed behind her. Even from the back, I could see that she had class: a good quality tailored wool suit cut a few inches above the knee, long, close-fitting leather boots, and a silk Liberty scarf round her neck.

She had reached up, placing something on the luggage rack, then turned back to flop down breathlessly on the seat opposite. To my eyes, she had been stunning, with her blonde shoulder-length hair, large hazel eyes and a smile you would find on the cover of Vogue. As far as I could tell, she was

13

slim but curvy and nicely proportioned; even now, I could imagine the delicate scent of the perfume she'd worn that day.

I had started our conversation. 'Looks like you've had a bit of a rush?'

She'd nodded, smiling brightly. 'Yes, I'm afraid I'm always a bit last-minute; never seem to allow enough time.'

'Going far?' I asked

'No, just to Crewe; I've been visiting relatives, keeping in touch, that kind of thing. What about you?'

'Same as you, Crewe; I'm starting a new job.'

'Really! That's where my husband works.'

I could still vividly recall the jab of disappointment I'd felt, even on that briefest of acquaintances, learning she was married.

'Who's he with?'

She'd waved her hands around, slender artistic hands, 'This lot, the Railways, he's involved with the electrification scheme.'

'No!' My surprise had been genuine. 'What a coincidence, me too. I start on Monday. What's your husband's name?'

'Eddie, Edward Phillips. And you are?'

'Craig Murray, pleased to meet you, Mrs Phillips.'

I'd extended my hand, holding onto hers briefly when she reached forward across the carriage to take mine.

'Samantha, but everybody calls me Sam, thank God. Going by your accent, you're a long way from home; it must be difficult leaving your roots.'

'Yes, I suppose so. There are lots of things I shall miss, but it was time to move on.'

'You're on your own?'

'Afraid so, still unattached; I haven't met a woman yet who'll have me.'

She had smiled broadly. 'Hmm, I'm not sure if I believe that, but if it's true, I suspect you won't be on your own for much longer.'

She had been easy to talk to; and we had rambled on about life in general, the local scene, holidays, all the usual conversation fodder. Time had flown, and all too soon, the train was pulling into Crewe Station.

We had said our goodbyes on the platform, both promising that our paths would cross soon courtesy of some work-related gathering or social event. And as time had gone on, we had indeed met regularly. I, for my part, had always sought her company on those occasions, and she had seemed to welcome my presence.

It had been easy to settle into the routine of my new job; it was a young office with about ten other blokes, all in their twenties, most of them very similar to myself. We had been supervised by an easy-going Londoner called Eric Bradshaw, not much older than ourselves. There had been an abundance of traditional male ribaldry and many fun times. I had got on well with everyone but had developed a close friendship with the only truly local guy, Harry Connor. I had really liked Connor, hard-working, honest, straightforward Harry with his feet-on-the-ground approach to life. I had readily identified with his directness and sense of humour. Harry, for his part, had literally taken me under his wing, and I had become a regular visitor to his home. As luck would have it, I had got on well with his wife Anne and their two children. Over time, they had become an adopted family.

The nature of our work had required Harry and me to work as a team, and our friendship had strengthened to the point where we trusted each other implicitly. Looking back now, I could see that without the bond that had developed between us, events might never have taken the direction they did.

One other person had played an important part in the lead-up to the robbery, busty Claire, as I'd called her. My landlady, Mrs Brown, a ruddy-cheeked, matronly-bosomed, elderly widow and motherly gem, had introduced us when Claire had called in to deliver a message from her mother.

'This is Claire, my next-door neighbour's daughter. You two should get together; I'm sure Claire can tell you where young folks spend their time in Crewe.'

Claire was a very curvy, if slightly plump, girl and the owner of a pretty face, covered with too much make-up, making her look older than she probably was.

'Well,' she'd said archly, looking me over, 'if he wants to ask me out some time, I dare say I'll think of somewhere to go.'

I hadn't been attracted to Claire, but I played the gentleman. 'Thanks, Claire, I'm honoured, I'll bear the offer in mind.'

In due course, I had asked her out and we had done the local pub circuit. I hadn't been seeking a relationship and didn't really fancy her, but she had proved to be bright and had a bubbly personality, so I'd stuck with her. I'd tried it on, of course, and she had seemed to enjoy my advances, but on one occasion, when my explorations had seemingly gone too far, she had rebuffed me firmly. 'That's far enough, Craig, I'm not the local bike. I don't mind a bit of fun, but I have my limits. It's not as if we've committed to each other or anything like that.'

I hadn't sought to persuade her otherwise; I had, in truth, been pondering on seeking pastures new. 'Fair enough, Claire, maybe I am rushing things. Sorry.' After that, I had drifted away, and she had seemed happy enough to let me go.'

Looking back now, I recalled the event that had made an indelible mark on my psyche, one that had made the town of Crewe headline news throughout the world. On 9th August 1963, the Great Train Robbery was carried out. In true Jesse James fashion, a gang had hijacked a train and

17

made off with £2.5 million in used notes, and for a while, it had seemed that the robbers had gotten clean away with the loot. True, they were all villains that couldn't be denied, but there had been a touch of romance and daring about the robbery that had stirred the public's imagination.

It had all seemed so perfect; a simple, well-executed plan leading to the theft of a fortune in used untraceable bank notes. The members of the gang would have been rich beyond my wildest dreams for what had seemed to me just a few hours work. However, a very determined police force had eventually caught the entire gang, or at least the underlings, though I was never sure how much of the money was recovered.

I had no doubt that the Great Train Robbery had been the catalyst for my entry into crime. Even now I had a clear recollection of one conversation I'd had with Harry Connor in the immediate aftermath of the robbery. We were out on the railway somewhere between Crewe and Stafford, taking levels and measurements, when I'd raised the subject. 'What a sweet job, Harry, make your fortune in a night's work.'

'Maybe, mate, but they'll all get caught, you'll see; just as soon as they start spending. And don't forget the driver, I hear he was badly injured.'

'Yes, it's a shame about the driver, I'll grant you that, but with used notes, there's no reason to get caught if you're sensible.'

'It's easy to say that mate, but they won't all be sensible; some idiot will do something daft and give the game away. Mark my words.'

'Time will tell Harry, but tell you what, I'd do a job like that given the chance. I wouldn't hesitate.'

He had looked at me intently, the tone of his voice revealing how concerned he was. 'You really do mean it, don't you, Craig?'

'Definitely, it's only lack of opportunity, not fear of getting caught, that stops me. I'd be quite happy to get rich at somebody else's expense.'

'In other words, if you knew what to do and knew you wouldn't get caught, you would rob some poor bastard.'

'No,' I'd protested 'not some 'poor bastard', some **rich** bastard or a bank; the same bank that's probably exploiting poor bastards like you and me this very minute.'

'I see,' Harry had summoned up his most sarcastic tone 'now you reckon you're a latter-day Robin Hood; taking from the rich and giving to the poor.'

'Not quite, mate, the only poor I have in mind is you and me.'

Harry had gone quiet at that point, then said quite deliberately. 'All right then, I'll tell you what; you identify the foolproof job and a foolproof plan to deliver a lucrative outcome, and maybe then I'll join in. Let's say a 60/40 split with you on the big end, seeing as how it'll be your idea.'

'If you're serious, Harry, I'll look for the opportunity, but it'll be 50/50, just you and me.'

He had laughed heartily, 'You're an idiot, Craig.' But he had proffered his hand on the non-existent deal.

I hadn't mentioned it to Harry at the time, but it hadn't been a totally theoretical concept; I did have a germ of an idea, an idea that involved busty Claire. Mrs Brown was forever urging me to take up with Claire again, determined that I should have a girlfriend. She reported on Claire's progress regularly, and the latest was that she had secured a very important new job, personal secretary to **the** Mr Fairweather. The name hadn't meant anything to me at the time, but it transpired that Mr Fairweather was the owner of Fairweather's, a large upmarket departmental store in Crewe. I'd visited it on occasion, taken in the hefty price labels and had mused on how much money passed through its tills every week. Other than banks and perhaps building societies, there was no doubt that it would have more cash on its premises than anywhere else in the Crewe area.

I think the latent criminal within me had always wondered what it would be like to rob a bank, maybe because I aspired to be rich and such a venture would provide a fast-track answer to my prayers. The complexity of bank security was way outside my scope, but I doubted if Fairweather's had any such safeguards. I had pursued my fanciful notion and wandered round the store, learning what I could, and soon figured out that the store's takings were held in an area designated STAFF ONLY. To advance this make-believe robbery, I would have to find out more about what went on behind that door. That's where Claire came in; if I was lucky, she might just be my passport to Fairweather's inner sanctums.

Chapter Three

'Hi Claire, how are you?'

I'd got back to Mrs. Brown's early and, for a boring fifteen minutes, had stood looking out onto the street, waiting for Claire to get home. I'd stepped outside, timing it so that we'd meet just as she reached her front door.

'Hi Claire, long time no see.' I smiled broadly and did my best to look pleased to see her.

'Hello Craig, I'm fine, thank you. You're home earlier than usual, aren't you?'

'Yeah, I've been out all day; didn't bother to go back into the office. Mrs Brown tells me you've got a new job, an important one by all accounts.'

Her face lit up. 'Yes, I'm Mr Fairweather's personal secretary; he relies on me for just about everything. Even went so far as to say he couldn't do without me.'

'Sounds to me like he fancies you, Claire.'

'I'll have you know, Craig Murray, that our relationship is strictly professional. Anyway, he's old enough to be my father.'

'That wouldn't stop him having the hots for you, and who could blame him? Anyway, I was only teasing; he's a lucky man to have you looking after him. Are you seeing anyone at the moment?'

'Nobody special, as it happens. What about you?'

'Same here, haven't come across anybody I fancy. Well, not till now anyway.'

'You can stop the teasing or the flattery, whichever it is, Craig. If you fancy me, there's only one thing on your mind.'

'OK, I confess, but you wouldn't like it if I thought you were unattractive, would you? And there might be more to it than that.'

She'd looked at me knowingly, 'Leopards don't change their spots, Craig.'

'Try me. How about the pictures this Friday?'

She studied me, making up her mind. 'Well, OK, I suppose, but you remember to behave yourself. What's on anyway?'

'Don't know, but doesn't matter, does it?'

It had turned out that Cleopatra was showing, and I had been on my best behaviour, venturing no further than holding her hand.

'Good looking woman, Elizabeth Taylor.' I'd observed as we walked home.

'Good looking man, Richard Burton,' she'd countered.

'I agree with you there, a real man's man. I bet he does more than holds hands.'

'Don't go getting ideas, Craig, you're not Richard Burton and just remember you're on trial.'

Come the moment, I had kissed her on her doorstep, brushing her lips with my tongue, waiting for some expression of disapproval. If she'd noticed, she made no comment.

'How's about on Saturday we go out for a drink and maybe a Chinese afterward?'

'You wouldn't be trying to soften me up with booze and a meal, would you, Craig?'

'You'll have to come along to find out. You can stick to orange juice if you like.'

'Not bloody likely. Pick me up at eight.'

I had known it would take time to gain her trust, do what I had to do and then get out of our relationship. We got together in May, and I had until December to do what I planned to do: seven months. I was using her, but it hadn't preyed on my conscience, and, I reasoned, if the situation hadn't been to her liking, she could have sent me packing any time she wanted. There had been a string of regular dates; pubs and clubs, pictures and dances, trips here and there, all attended with just the right amount of believable flattery. Good night clinches became increasingly steamy; I was getting there in more ways than one. There were times when I had wished that I owned a car, somewhere to cosy up in private, but I couldn't afford to buy one.

My opportunity came when she invited me to keep her company, babysitting for a neighbour. Alone in safe, comfortable surroundings, I had seduced her with little more than token resistance on her part, though as I was easing down her knickers, she had asked. 'What happens if the baby wakes?'

'We'll ignore it.' I didn't wait for further questions.

Afterwards, she had asked the question I knew would come, 'You do love me, Craig, don't you?'

'I'm sleeping with you now, aren't I?' I'd tried to keep it light, but she had pushed.

'You really do, don't you, Craig.'

'Of course, I do, darling.' The words had come out all too easily. 'Let's do it again just to be sure.' She didn't wait to be asked twice.

As we strolled home that evening, I had skirted round the future but said it would be nice if we had more time to ourselves. She hadn't missed the opportunity to show where her thoughts were leading.

'We will someday, Craig; when we're a proper couple.'

'I know what you mean, Claire, but we've got to be absolutely sure of each other before we make a commitment like that. I was wondering about Sundays when Mrs Brown goes off to church; it would be great to make love with you in bed, naked. We'd have a couple of hours to ourselves, what do you think.'

'Oh Craig, I couldn't; it would be so deceitful. I couldn't go behind Mrs Brown's back like that.'

'Think about it. Think of what we've just shared; Mrs Brown would never know.'

She'd shaken her head, 'I couldn't.'

'Think about it, darling, please; we'd be like a real couple.'

I would have bet a month's salary that she would overcome her concerns, and she had; come Sunday morning, she was there, knocking on the door.

Our lovemaking over, we had lain together talking, and I'd asked more about her job, flattering her, manoeuvring for an invitation to see her office, *'just so I could picture her at work.'*

'I don't know what Mr Fairweather would think about that.'

'I could pop in some lunchtime when he was out; he'd never know.'

'I'm not sure, Craig; I'll see what I can do, but no promises, mind.'

I had already elucidated from her that the busiest week of the year was the one before Christmas. 'We take in more money in that week than all the other stores in Crewe put together.'

'That's amazing, how much do you reckon they take?'

'Mr Fairweather showed me last year's accounts, and they took £450,000 last year; imagine all that money in just one week.'

'Gosh, I can't imagine what that much money looks like. I guess it gets banked daily, though?'

My heart had all but missed a beat when she'd shaken her head. 'No, the whole week's cash takings get banked on a Monday. Between you and me, Mr Fairweather likes to see it all piled up on his desk; makes a big thing of counting it. I swear his eyes light up when he sees money. He's a very nice man, and I really like him, but I think he's a bit of a miser; never happier than when he's talking about money, but at the same time very reluctant to spend much.'

'Surely all the counting up is done in Accounts? He would take ages to count that much money himself?'

'Well, it is counted up in Accounts for the books, but he likes to have all the cash, well, all the notes, brought to him at the end of the day, just as I'm leaving. He counts it right there on his desk, makes lots of little piles of notes in their different denominations.'

'No. I don't believe it. I just can't begin to imagine £450,000 right there in your office.'

'Well, it's only that much in the week leading up to Christmas and don't forget there's a lot of cheques involved. Cheques are kept in the Accounts Department safe along with all the coins. It's only the paper money that goes into the safe in his office; I'd say about £150,000. Only me and Mr Fairweather know the combination to be safe.' She had added proudly.

You don't mean to tell me that he's told you the combination? That settles it; I'll bet a week's wages the old bugger has got designs on you. Has he ever tried anything on?'

She had gone crimson and protested, 'Of course not; I told you he's old enough to be my father.'

'Then why are you blushing then? Just you watch yourself; I wouldn't put it past him.'

'Here, I reckon you're jealous, Craig Murray.'

I had lied, knowing it would please her, 'Well, maybe just a bit.'

'Well, believe me, there's no need; you're more than enough for me. Let's cut the chat for now and make better use of our time. It's me that's got the hots today.'

I wasn't alone in making manoeuvres. Whilst I was manipulating her, she, for her part, was doing her own angling; looking at rings in jewellers' windows, asking where I'd like to settle down, telling me about friends' babies. She was getting very serious, and I was already wondering how I was going to disentangle myself when the time came. I had needed to move things along.

I was jolted out of my memories and brought back to the present when the van turned sharply and came to a halt; I reckoned they'd been on the road for about an hour and a half. The rear door opened.

'Out Murray.' The two guards watched me closely as I climbed out; maybe they thought I was going to attempt an escape. They had stopped in a yard behind a brick-built two-storey building with no windows and one solitary door.

'Is this it, is this Westmoor?'

'Don't be stupid, dickhead; it's the local nick. We're about halfway there, and this is the only chance you'll get to have a piss.' He motioned to the door. 'Through there.'

'Where is Westmoor, by the way?'

'Cumbria, now get moving.'

'Will we be stopping to eat somewhere?' I was ravenous, not having eaten much that morning.

'No, we fucking won't, this isn't a fucking Sunday school outing; you go hungry till we get there.'

For some unfathomable reason, the thought of being in a prison in the Lake District had pleased me, not that I would be seeing much of it where I was headed. Back in the van, I settled down to my thoughts again. *'Now, where was I up to? Ah, yes, I was about to approach Harry Connor with my latest news.*

'Harry, you remember our conversation, the one after the train robbery, the one we shook hands on?'

'Sure, I do, but I had hoped you would go off the idea; you're not still pursuing that crazy dream, are you?'

'Just the opposite, mate, I've got an idea that will earn us a cool £150,000. Are you interested or not? £75,000 each, just think of it, £75,000?'

'I'm thinking of Anne and the kids, mate, with me locked up in the clink.'

'We won't get caught, this is foolproof, believe me.'

'Nothing is foolproof, Craig, but go on anyway, tell me about it. I'm shit-scared just thinking about it, but times are hard, so I'm interested.'

I had told him about Fairweather's and where I was up to with my plan.

He hadn't been overly impressed. 'And just how do we get into this place, how do we get past the alarm system and, having done that, how do we open this safe that may or may not contain £150,000?'

'All good questions and I confess I can't answer them yet, but I will be able to soon, I promise.'

'And just how can you promise all that, Craig?'

It was time to come clean, so I told him about Claire.

'You dark horse, how long has this been going on? Are you shagging her?'

'Regularly, mate, she thinks I love her.'

'And do you? Is she involved in this?'

'No to both questions. To be honest, I'm using her; once I find out what I need to know, I'll break free.'

'Not nice, Craig.' He had shaken his head in disapproval. 'There's a dark side to you, mate.'

'I'm not proud of myself, but I'll do what it takes to pull this off. Well, you know it all now. Are you in or out?'

'Don't know, mate, it's a big step. Can I sleep on it?'

'Sleep and dream of seventy-five thousand quid, Harry; dream about how you'll spend it. Talk to me when you're ready, and not a word to Anne about Claire, I don't want that link known.'

Two days later, Harry capitulated. 'OK, I'm in, provided everything stacks up at the end of the day. If at any time I'm in any doubt, I'll pull out, understood?'

'Everything will stack up, mate, I promise you.'

'When am I going to see this office of yours, sweetheart? I'm beginning to think you don't want me to see it.' It was Sunday, and we were lying on my bed again, me nuzzling at her ample breasts.

'I can't see why it's important to you, Craig.'

'Because it's a bit of you I don't know about; maybe you don't want me to see it for some reason. Maybe it's not as posh as you make out.'

She had taken the bait, as I had known she would. 'It's better than anything you've ever worked in, that's for sure, and I'll prove it. Come this Thursday at 1 o'clock, but if Mr Fairweather is there, you'll have to make out you've called in to leave a message from my Mum or something.'

'Don't worry darling, I'll think of something to say.'

So far, so good. It had all been going to plan except for one complication, one I had made no effort to avoid. I was becoming increasingly attracted to Sam Phillips. At office functions and parties, I found myself drawn to her and had taken every opportunity to get to know her better. I hadn't held her husband, Eddie, in much regard; as far as I was concerned, he was a bit of a fop. Whoever was to blame, from time to time, we had rubbed each other up the wrong way.

As time passed and I got to know her better, I had sensed that Sam wasn't entirely happy; she had lost some of her brightness and didn't smile as readily as she once had. I'd probed gently, but she hadn't revealed much and had never complained about her circumstances or Eddie. I had noted though, that she never enthused about things they did together either; it had seemed to me that their marriage was less than perfect.

I had been able to make her laugh, and she had seemed to enjoy my company, but it had never progressed beyond conversation. Just once, during a smoochy dance at a dimly lit party, I'd tested her and let my lips brush hers. She hadn't pulled away, just the tiniest shake of her head, but she'd snuggled closer and carried on dancing. I'd left the party not knowing if it had been the wrong moment, the wrong place or just wrong for her.

Chapter Four

Thursday arrived, and I had made my way up to the third floor of Fairweather's, walked purposefully to the door marked STAFF ONLY and pushed it open. Without hesitating, I walked straight ahead to the end of the short corridor, just as Claire had told me, passing a couple of offices on the way, one marked ACCOUNTS. The doors to both offices had been open, but I had just looked straight ahead, and nobody had challenged my presence. I remembered knocking on the door to Fairweather's office, holding my breath as I waited a reply. My wait had been short-lived; the door was opened almost immediately, and there was Claire, looking anxiously over my shoulder to make sure the corridor was clear. She wasted no time pulling me into the room.

'That was good timing. Mr Fairweather can't have been gone more than five minutes.'

I'd pulled her to me and kissed her, making an effort to get in her good books, 'You look gorgeous. I thought you would be dressed all prim and proper. No wonder the old boy has got designs on you.'

'Stop it, Craig. I told you he's old enough to be my father. I got dressed up nice for you.'

'Only kidding, sweetheart, I know you did. Still, I bet he was lingering round your desk all morning trying to catch an eyeful. Hmmm, speaking of which, I don't suppose you fancy a quickie.' I glanced across to the large antique desk.

'You're awful, Craig Murray, that's Mr Fairweather's desk.'

'Alright then, let's do it on yours.'

'No, someone might come in, behave yourself.'

'It's your own fault; you shouldn't wear such sexy outfits. Oh well, if nookie isn't on the agenda, I suppose I'll have to be satisfied with a tour of your office.'

I had taken in the details: the single window, high ceiling, wood-panelled walls, thick-piled carpet, a large four-shelf bookcase, and a door in one corner. There are two desks: Claire's on the left entering the room, and Fairweather's dominating the room in front of the window.

'Very impressive, Claire, very classy, not like mine, cramped and shared with ten other guys.'

She beamed, 'Well, Mr Fairweather is the owner after all, and I am his Personal Secretary.'

I'd continued looking round with feigned admiration, then expressed puzzlement. 'And where's this famous safe you told me about.'

Claire pointed to the door in the corner, 'Behind that door. It's always kept locked, and the lock is special, high security and all that.'

I did my best to look impressed. 'Hmm, I can understand why. I don't suppose I could see it? I've never seen a real safe, except in the pictures or on television.'

She had looked dubious, and for a worrying moment, I thought she was going to refuse, but in the end, she had agreed. 'I suppose it'll be alright.' She started across the room, then stopped, turning back to face me.

'You'll have to look away whilst I get the key.'

'Absolutely, of course, I will.' I tried to sound serious

I had turned away but immediately looked back over my shoulder. Claire was reaching up to the top shelf of the bookcase, third or fourth book along; the key was somewhere near there. I turned back quickly, making sure she didn't catch me spying on her.

'OK, you can look now.' She continued past me to the door of the safe cupboard. I could see that she had two keys and, on closer expression, that the door had two locks, a small but important detail I had missed. The incident underlined the need to be observant and to pay attention to detail; it had been a good lesson for me. I watched closely as she inserted both keys and turned the top one clockwise, the bottom anti-clockwise; then, leaving the keys in place, she turned the handle and pulled the door open.

It stood there, dark-grey steel, an inch or so taller than me and as wide as the entrance door. To my eyes, it was cold, forbidding, almost challenging. 'Wow, that's quite a beastie, isn't it? I moved closer, noting the numbered dial on the left-hand side above the lever handle. I reached forward to give it a twirl.

Her voice had rung out sharply, 'No, Craig, you mustn't touch it; I shouldn't even be showing it to you.'

'Sorry, sorry, can't see that it would do any harm though. It's bigger than I thought it would be. Still, it must hold a lot of loot.'

'Not just money, there are lots of documents and deeds as well.'

'Gosh!' I tried to sound suitably impressed. 'Imagine him letting you have the combination. That's quite a responsibility.'

'Mr Fairweather trusts me implicitly, Craig', she said proudly, 'now and again, I have to get papers for him when he's in the Board Room and can't leave a meeting.'

I shook my head admiringly. 'Gosh, I would probably forget the numbers, and I know you shouldn't write them down.'

'Of course not, but there are only six, made up of Mr Fairweather's birth date; they alternate left and right on the safe dial, it's quite easy, really. Anyway, Mr Fairweather says I've got a good head for figures.'

I'd taken it far enough; it was time to back off before she got suspicious of my curiosity. 'And talking about figures, I'd like to sample this one.'

I backed her up against the safe, but she'd wriggled away,

'Not here, Craig, you'll have to wait until Sunday.'

I put my disappointed look on. 'Spoil sport, but thanks for showing me round; I'll be able to visualise where you are now when I think about you. I guess I'd better go now before old Fairweather gets back.'

I'd left smiling. The pieces were falling into place; I knew where the safe was and, quite fortuitously, the existence and whereabouts of the two all-important keys. All I had to do now was figure out how to get into Fairweather's and find out those six vital numbers. Fairweather had used his birth date, and that was a real stroke of luck; I convinced myself that Dame Fortune was on my side.

Harry had seemed more relaxed about the robbery when I reported back on my visit to Claire's office and had even offered help in trying to find out the all-important birth date. 'I'm happy to go to the Registry and check out the records if you can find out what year he was born; it'll be slow, but there aren't that many births in Cheshire in a year.'

'That's a good fall-back position but I'd like to avoid doing that if I can, just in case someone remembers the guy that laboriously went through a year's registrations. I've got an idea; I reckon I can get Claire to cough up on that one.'

'Won't she remember telling you, Craig, she's bound to be questioned by the police if this does come off, especially when she's one of the only two people who know the combination?'

I nodded. 'I've thought of that, and with a bit of luck, I reckon she won't even know she's told me.'

When I explained what I had in mind Harry had chortled, nodding his head enthusiastically. 'Brilliant, it's worth a try; it might just work. So that leaves access and the alarm system. I was round the store last Saturday, and there is a large red bell on the rear wall, but that's all I could see.'

'Claire doesn't know anything about the security system, assuming there is one. I've alluded to the subject, but she just shrugged. I'm not sure what I could do to find out; that bell might just be a fire alarm. Leave it with me. I'll firm up on the access options and check out that bell this Saturday.'

Harry's enthusiasm for the robbery was growing fast. 'You know, when you first muted this idea, I thought you were mad, but now I can see it coming together; I'm getting a good feeling about the whole thing.' He had gotten serious then and asked me about Claire. 'When are you going to bid your fond farewells?'

'I have to do it soon, but I'm not sure how to go about it yet.'

Checking out the bell had been easy. I'd wandered into the store, found a fire alarm point in a quiet area and broken the glass to raise an alarm. Bells had gone off everywhere, and along with everyone else, I had evacuated the store immediately. Once outside, I made my way to the rear of the building and found the large red bell clanging loudly. The visit to the service yard had delivered an unexpected bonus; I came up with an idea for breaking into the building on the night of the robbery. The false alarm made the local newspaper where it had been referred to as *'an irresponsible act of lunacy.'* I didn't much care; I had found out what I wanted to know.

There had been one other happening that week, one that I could recall vividly, even now. I had quite literally bumped into Sam Phillips doing some window gazing in the local shopping precinct and had been taken aback by her appearance. Her trademark smile was missing, her eyes tired, her face strained; even her outfit somehow lacked its usual smartness. The words were out before I could control them, 'My God, Sam, whatever's wrong, you don't look very well?'

She'd bitten her lips and forced a small smile, 'Nothing really, nothing at all. I'm fine, honestly.'

I knew that just wasn't true. 'Sorry, Sam, I just don't believe you. I'm your friend; you can talk to me. Have you lost someone, had some bad news?'

'There's nothing wrong, Craig, at least nothing I can tell you about.'

I remembered reaching out and taking her hand, pleased when she hadn't pulled away. 'Come on, we're going for a coffee. I'm a good listener, and you know what they say, a trouble shared is a trouble halved.'

She hadn't wanted to talk, but I persisted, and slowly but surely, it had come out, 'Money problems, debt, mortgage in arrears; you name it, we have it.'

'But how Sam? Eddie does alright, and you've got a good part-time job; you should be reasonably comfortable.'

'You don't know him, Craig. Come to that, I didn't know this side of him. He spends money like water on his hi-fi equipment, on records, on clothes and on that bloody sports car of his. Always seems to be buying the latest thing then replacing it just as quickly. I pay the routine household bills, and he's supposed to attend to the big bills like the mortgage, but he hasn't for months, and we're in trouble.'

Tears had filled her eyes, 'I'm at my wit's end trying to make ends meet; it's only a matter of time till the Bank and Building Society serves notice on us. I reckon they're holding back because they know his family, but they won't wait forever. So, you see, it's not something you can help with, but thanks for listening anyway.'

'If I had money, I'd want to help you, honestly, I would.'

'Why on earth should you want to help Eddie and me?'

'I don't want to help him; it's you I'd want to help. You understand what I'm saying, **you,** not Eddie?'

She had looked at me, trying to search out my meaning, her eyes sad and weepy, 'I think so, Craig, but I can't see that…' She hadn't completed whatever she was going to say.

There had been an awkward silence which I had broken, 'What are you doing now?'

She had managed a wry smile, 'I think I'll go home, no point walking round the shops not being able to buy anything is there?'

'I guess not. Look, I can give you a lift home if you don't mind travelling in a Railway van.'

She'd shaken her head, 'No thanks, Craig, you've done enough listening to my problems; I'll get a bus.'

'I won't hear of it, come on, let's go.'

When we got to her place, she invited me for a coffee but then almost withdrew the offer. 'Maybe you've had enough coffee for one day.'

'I'd love one, and anyway, it gives me more time with you.'

She had given me that searching look again, hesitated but said nothing, then motioned me to go in.

I could remember clearly sitting in the lounge whilst she made the coffee, wondering about how to advance the genuine feelings I had for her. She put the tray down on a coffee table, and I patted the seat next to me on the sofa. An old saying had entered my thoughts as she sat down beside me. *'Faint heart never won fair lady.* It's now or never, Craig.' So, I'd taken the cup from her hand, put it down on the coffee table and leaned forward and kissed her, gently at first then passionately. She had responded willingly, almost eagerly, her lips working with mine to satisfy the emotion that was driving us both. Our lovemaking was over almost before it began; we climaxed all too quickly.

Afterwards, she'd shaken her head, 'I can't believe what I've just done; I promised myself that I'd never be unfaithful. You must think I'm cheap.'

I had held her close, nestling her head into my chest, whispering into her ear, 'You could never be cheap. Fate has thrown us together; no-one is to blame. I've wanted you from the moment you got on that train; wanted you a little bit more every time I was in your company. We're just fulfilling a destiny neither of us planned and neither of us can control. 'I pulled her to me, and we made love again, but this time tenderly and with love, not passion.

Afterwards, as we had our coffee, I told her I had fallen in love with her.

'Craig, we can't, we mustn't, I'm married; it's wrong, it's madness, there's no future for us.'

'Nothing as wonderful as what we've just shared can be wrong, Sam. Let's live in the moment and let the future take care of itself.'

'Being unfaithful can never be right, Craig.'

'Sometimes that's the only way it can be, to begin with at least. Let's see what time brings. I want to see you again, and again, and again.'

She'd shaken her head, tears filling her eyes. 'I can't.'

'Please don't shut me out now, not after what we've just shared. Let's leave it for now. I'll phone you; hang up on me if you don't want to talk.' I glanced at my watch. 'Oh God, I'm late. Darling, I don't want to, but I must go; I really must, honest. I'm so sorry; it's the last thing I want to do, believe me. They're expecting me back at the office. Try not to worry, something will turn up, you'll see.'

I remembered her smiling. 'Something already has turned up; this has been a happier day than I could ever have hoped for.'

As I drove back to the office, I had felt elated but guilty, too; she had been vulnerable, and maybe I had taken advantage of her. No, that wasn't true, I genuinely felt that I was in love.

I phoned the next day, and she hadn't hung up. After that, we met as often as we could, making love whenever possible trying not to take too many risks. Harry had covered for me back in the office, believing all the time that I was with Claire, never guessing I was with Sam Phillips. 'You lucky, rotten bastard; I'm slaving my guts out, and you're shagging away like a bull in the field. It's time you bailed out, though, Craig.'

Our love had deepened, and no matter how often we met, it was never enough. In the end, I asked her to leave Eddie. She had broken down, crying uncontrollably, 'I want to Craig, but I can't. I knew you would ask sooner or later, and I wanted you to ask, but I can't leave him, not while things are so bad. It would kill him. He might even take his own life; in fact, I'm sure he would. You don't know him like I do; he's always been neurotic; he's already receiving counselling for depression.'

I had begged her to be with me. 'But you can't go on living with him, Sam, he's not right for you, he'll drag you down. He's not the person you thought you married; you don't owe him a thing. You love me, I know you do; how can you stay with him?'

'I don't want to. You know I don't, but he's got to get out of this financial mess before I could tell him I'm leaving. I'm not having his suicide on my conscience. Please try to understand.'

I recalled our conversation word for word; it had meant so much to me. I remembered holding her at arms' length. 'Look at me, Sam. Are you saying that we can be together if he can get himself out of his financial mess?'

She'd nodded, 'I guess I am. I know that I love you, Craig, know that I want to be with you, but I just can't see how it's going to happen.'

I'd pulled her to me and whispered softly. 'We're going to find a way, Sam, I promise you.'

I sat back, even now savouring those recalled words; I could almost hear them. The prison van was speeding along now, no stops and starts, no turns being negotiated, lots of traffic noise. I guessed we were on the Motorway. Looking back, I could see now what a mess I had got myself into, stringing Claire along, falling in love with Sam, being untrue to both and not telling Eddie the whole story. I was a real shit, but despite everything, I had no regrets; it had been the right course at the time. There were lessons to be learned, and I promised myself I wouldn't make the same mistakes again.

Chapter Five

'You realise that if you were Chinese, you would be a Dog.'

Claire and I were lying on my bed at Mrs Brown's, naked, during one of our Sunday morning shagging sessions. Occasions that, for me, now produced minimal satisfaction; I couldn't get Sam out of my head no matter what I was doing. I had felt so disloyal to her that I had barely been able to go through the charade of what Claire called *our lovemaking*.

She had looked at me aghast, shock showing on her face, her voice indignant.

'What do you mean? That's not very nice, Craig; no girl wants to be referred to as a Dog.'

'You were born in 1946, and as far as the Chinese are concerned, that makes you a Dog, and, before you get ratty, Dogs are loyal, friendly, honest and generous.'

'Ah, that's all right then,' she had relaxed. 'I wouldn't quarrel with that. And what about you?'

'Well, I was born in 1944, so that makes me a monkey. Monkeys are very intelligent, enthusiastic and creative, but we're easily discouraged.'

'Hmm,' Claire sounded dubious, 'I'm not sure that all of that applies to you; can't say that you're easily discouraged. You tried to get me into bed from the day we first met. You're certainly not easily discouraged where sex is concerned. Still, you are a bit of a monkey, and I must say you've got a rather nice tail.' She had laughed out loud as she grabbed hold of my penis.

'I'm glad some part of me meets with your approval. Let's try it out on old Fairweather. What year is he?'

'He was born in 1899.'

'Christ, he is an old bugger, he must have known Queen Victoria. I'm not sure, but I think that would make him a Sheep. Sheep are elegant, creative and tend to be a bit shy.'

I hadn't the faintest idea what animal identified with 1899 or what the characteristics of Sheep were, but Claire knew no different. She nodded, 'I'd go along with that, though he's not shy once you get to know him. Do you really believe in this kind of thing? I'm not sure I do.'

'I quite believe in Astrology, though many say it's a lot of nonsense. I prefer the Western horoscope; I'm a real Capricorn.'

'That makes you a Goat. I won't argue with that,' she giggled.

'Just in case you don't know, Capricorns are sure-footed, ambitious, always trying to climb higher.'

'And what about me?'

'One thing's for sure, you're not a Virgo, well, not nowadays anyway. Let me think. You're Taurus, the Bull, thankfully without its traditional features, though, come to think of it, you can be quite horny. Your lot tend to be kind, passionate, and like to shag a lot.'

'That's not true, Craig Murray, you're making that up.'

'No, it's absolutely true, cross my heart.'

'I don't believe you.'

'Let's try it on old Fairweather; what's his star sign?'

'Don't know; his birthday is in July.'

'What date?'

'The second.'

'OK! He was born under the sign of Cancer. Now, I think he should be home-loving, considerate and very independent.'

'I suppose that's quite like him. You seem to know a lot about these things, Craig. Do you truly, truly believe in them?'

'Not really, but we Celts have a leaning towards the mystical side of Nature.'

She reached down between my legs, smiling. 'Mrs Brown will be back soon. Best we turn our attention to the more practical side of nature.'

'See what I mean about liking to shag a lot; up you get, it's your turn in the saddle.'

So that was it; much easier than I'd thought it would be. Fairweather's birthday all sorted out, 2nd July 1899, and Claire had said it was a six-number combination, so each number was used once giving a sequence of 271899. *'Christ, I just hope Fairweather has used them in order.'* Mission accomplished. All I had to do now was come up with a way of disengaging from Claire; one way or another, she had to be ditched and ditched soon.

My plan was taking shape, but there was one big change of direction that had to be agreed upon with Harry, and then there was the situation with Sam to be resolved. In my perfect scenario, Craig robs store, Sam leaves Eddie, tensions in the office follow, I do the decent thing and resign, and we go off together to live happily ever after. That had been the blue-sky version of my future. I had dreaded telling Harry about my latest idea, had known he wouldn't take it well, and he hadn't. I'd begun in true PR fashion with the positives, 'Things are going well mate, I know exactly how we are going to break into Fairweather's and even better, I know the old boy's exact birth date, so the safe will be a piece of cake.'

'Fucking great, well done. What a Christmas this is going to be. I can't wait.'

'Steady Harry, you won't be able to spend anything for at least six months, we agreed that.'

'I know, I know, but just the idea of having all that cash lying there waiting for me will be like a dream come true.'

'I've also been thinking about transport on the night, and as you know, I don't have a car.'

'I know that mate, we'll use mine.'

'We will if we must, but it would be better if we could use one of the office vans. Your car might just be noticed by some bystander, whereas a Railway vehicle probably wouldn't raise a second glance.'

'No problem with that; I'll make sure I get one booked out to me. It's not unusual for me to take one home, especially if I'm working the weekend, which, because I need the money, is every weekend. Leave it with me, that's something I can do when the time comes.'

'There is just one little problem left.' I had hesitated, knowing he would react badly, but I'd gone ahead and told him anyway. He had exploded as soon as he realised where I was headed. 'No way, no fucking way, it would be a disaster for all sorts of reasons. You must be off your trolley, Craig. Have you really thought it through? It's too much of a risk, forget it.'

But I'd persisted with my argument; one I'd thought out carefully and rehearsed a dozen times; I'd almost reached the point where I believed it myself. It had taken about an hour to wear him down, but eventually, Harry had come round.

'It'll tie in quite nicely with the Railway van, won't it?'

'Don't push it, Craig; I'll go along with it, but I don't like it one little bit.'

'Thanks, mate, it'll be OK, you'll see. I hesitate to ask since you're not entirely enthusiastic, but I wonder if you could follow up on this one?' I explained what I had in mind.

'Thanks, a fucking million, Craig; you really are pushing it, but I suppose I've got to do my fair share. Just how much are you prepared to invest in this little diversion?'

'I'll go along with whatever you decide; it can come out of my share.'

'It would serve you right if it did. We'll talk about it again.'

'Thanks, Harry, I owe you big time.'

That had left just Claire to be sorted out, and lady luck intervened on my behalf. I had offered to keep her company baby-sitting and nipped upstairs whilst she was in the loo to waken the kid from its slumber. The poor little bastard immediately started wailing and was in full flow by the time Claire put in an appearance.

I was well-primed and ready to act out my part. 'Here, he's all yours; take the little bugger.' I said crossly.

She had remonstrated with me. 'Oh, Craig, don't be so unkind. Toby can't help it; he's probably uncomfortable or frightened or something; you were no different when you were a baby. Probably needs his nappy changed. Don't you pet?'

'Yuk, not in front of me. I can't stand smelly nappies and crying babies.'

Claire had reacted just as I'd hoped she would. 'Well, you'll **have** to get used to them, Craig; all babies are the same.'

'No way, my house will be a baby-free zone.' I'd replied, scowling.

She had visibly stiffened, dismay showing on her face, eyes starting to fill, 'And what if I want babies, Craig? What then?'

'We'd be on opposite sides of the fence, darling.'

'Meaning?'

'Well, I can't see that we could have them, really, both of us would have to be in favour. We'll get along just fine on our own, like we have up to now.'

'You're not serious, are you, Craig?'

I had put on his best look of anguish, 'I'm sorry darling, but that's how it is.'

'You're telling me that you love me, but you don't want me to have your children. Is that it?' She had been near to tears, but there was no pulling back now.

'I guess that is what I'm saying, sweetheart. I'm sorry, I didn't realise it was so important to you.'

'And now that you know how important it is?'

'I'm sorry, darling, honestly.'

Our raised voices had added to Toby's distress; he was sobbing his little heart out in that insistent, repetitive way that only a baby can do.

'Don't 'darling' me. I've got to see to this baby then we'll talk some more.'

'It's no good, Claire. What would be the point? We could talk all night, but I won't change my mind, and it doesn't sound like you'll change yours. It's best we call it quits now rather than face a marriage breakdown later on.'

She had been absolutely dumbfounded when I said that. 'And that's it, is it, just like that, after all you've said to me? After all those lovey-dovey moments?'

I had tried to look distraught for her piece of mind; as I delivered my final line. 'I'm sorry Claire, I really am. I didn't count on the baby scenario. You don't deserve this, but it's for the best.' That said, I had turned and walked, ignoring her when she'd called after me.

Mrs Brown had looked surprised when I walked in on her.

'Hello Craig, you're home early. I thought you and Claire were baby-sitting.'

'We were Mrs Brown, but we've fallen out big-time.'

'Sit down, lad. I'll put the kettle on, and we'll have a chat. All couples have a fall out sooner or later.'

And so, we had talked about my split from Claire over the ubiquitous cup of tea, but despite her cajoling and counselling, I hadn't budged. 'At the end of the day, Mrs Brown, these things are best sorted out now; think of the heartache it would cause if we found out later on.'

'I suppose so, lad, but you make such a lovely couple. It's a real shame.'

I did my best to sound resigned to the situation so that she was convinced it really was all over. 'Yes, it's very sad, but that's how it is. If Claire does come round, please don't encourage her to think I might change my mind. I don't want to hurt her any more than I have already.' The deed was done; after that, Claire had barely spared me a glance when our paths crossed.

A couple of weeks later, during one of our trips out of the office, Harry reported back on his efforts. 'I've done it, mate, although it's against my better judgement.'

'Brilliant. It'll all be for the best, you'll see. No problems?'

'Not really; money overcomes most problems in my experience.'

'You're happy it can be done.'

'I'm certain it can be done. I still don't like it, but it'll work. Anyway, enough said; it's settled, but it's going to cost us twenty grand.'

'I'm happy with that; it can come off my cut.'

'It'll come off the top, then we split the rest.'

Dear old Harry, fair and generous as always. 'Thanks, mate, well done; now roll on December.'

In the months leading up to December I had gone over the plan time and time again, picking over it until it was perfect.

Chapter Six

The final weeks leading up to the robbery had gone slowly, the big day never seemed to get any nearer. All the planning had been done and gone over time after time; every conceivable angle had been covered and re-covered. A few acquisitions had been necessary and had served to relieve the long drag of anticipation; these were to be arranged early on to distance them from the main event. One acquisition had carried a high risk, but in the event, it had been like taking sweets from a baby.

Time alone had stood there like a barrier, somehow slowing to a crawl the nearer it got to that last shopping week before Christmas. Thankfully, there had been Sam, and we had met at every opportunity, but it had never been enough; meeting up had been a joy, but separation had plunged us both into despair. For my part, I had found it unbearable to think of her sleeping alongside another man. She had told me that she and Eddie never had sex, and I had wanted to believe her, but deep down, the thought had gnawed at me. I wondered if she was just trying to spare my feelings. What kind of guy was her husband if he didn't insist on sex from time to time? She had shared my frustration and unhappiness and had become more resolved to leave her husband. It had looked certain back then that we would begin a new life together.

Finally, the last grain of sand had run out of the hourglass, and the big day arrived, the last Saturday before Christmas, the biggest shopping day of the year. I smiled as I recalled going to Fairweather's that very day to do my shopping, laughing inwardly as I went round the store making my festive purchases in the knowledge that, in less than twelve hours, my money would be returned to me a thousand times over.

The prison van journeyed on, and I could recall every minute of that fateful day as though it had been yesterday. Vivid pictures and conversations flooded back to me. I'd stayed in that evening watching Mrs. Brown's small black and white television.

'Not often you stay in on a Saturday, lad, are you feeling all right?'

'I'm fine, Mrs Brown, it's just that we've got an emergency job on, tonight. We've got some repairs to carry out, so I'll be going out around eleven.'

Working weekends and late hours in the Railway was fairly common, and I'd done it before, so my excuse hadn't aroused any curiosity on her part.

'Poor you; still, overtime pays well, and I'm sure the extra money will come in handy at this time of year.'

'Yeah, it's not so bad, really; this won't be a long job. With luck, we'll be finished by two o'clock.'

'Well, see, you don't wake me up when you come back in, Craig.'

'I'll be as quiet as a church mouse, Mrs Brown, I promise.'

I had set out just after eleven, allowing half an hour to cover the mile or so to Harry's. The walk in the crisp night air had given me a final opportunity to go through the plan yet again. There I was, continuing to seek a flaw I hoped didn't exist. Once again, I had assured myself that it was perfect. If anything, I had worried that it all seemed so simple, so easy.

The Railway van stood parked in front of Harry's garage, a layer of frost glistening in the moonlight. I tapped gently on the lounge window, not wanting to waken the children with a noisy doorbell or banging knocker. Harry opened the door. 'Come on in, mate, you're a mite early, aren't you? Gives us time for a cup of tea before we go; no sense getting there too early; the Operating boys won't be ready for us.'

He winked at me and pointed upstairs. 'It's too bloody cold to hang about whilst they shunt trains about.'

'Well, as long as I'm not disturbing the household.'

'Not a problem, Craig; the kids have long since gone to bed, and Anne went about ten minutes ago; sends her love. Said you could come back with me when the job's done; said you could bed down in the lounge tonight.'

'Thank her, mate; I'd love to, but best not, Mrs Brown would worry if she got up in the morning and I wasn't there.'

We'd sat in the kitchen drinking tea, tension taking hold, scarcely a word being said.

'Everything alright, kiddo, you seem a bit quiet?' I broke the silence

'I'm fine, mate, no worries really, other than the one we both know about.'

'Relax, everything will go like clockwork, you'll see.'

'Sure. I'll be fine when we get going; in fact, it's nearly ten to twelve. Time we hit the road.'

Harry fired up the van and pulled onto the quiet estate road, heading along an avenue of Christmas-lit windows before turning onto the main drag leading to the centre of Crewe. It had been quiet, pubs and cinemas had long since emptied, and the chilly night ensured there were very few late-night revellers.

'Keep the speed down. The last thing we want is to give some officious copper a reason for flagging us down.' I was being super-cautious, and I knew it.

'Come off it, mate. I'm barely doing thirty-five.' But he had slowed down to less than thirty, nevertheless. 'Happy now, darling?' He'd blown me a kiss.

I checked the time as we approached the shopping centre: 11.58, not long now. The shop window displays had given warmth to the night chill, exuding Christmas spirit with their decorations and brightly lit bargains. The main street was bedecked with strings of coloured lights, flashing Xmas trees, nativity scenes and the ever-jolly, red-suited Santa.

'Looks good, doesn't it?'

Harry had given one of his disparaging grunts. 'Wouldn't describe it as good myself, waste of money Christmas if you ask me. Still, the kids enjoy it and thank God it doesn't last long.' He had looked at his watch, 'Dead on midnight.'

'Go round again, Scrooge; there's no rush; we can afford to hang on a bit.'

Unusually Harry's inner tension had spilled out, and he snapped at me, 'The more we drive round the town centre at midnight, the more fucking likely we are to be noticed.'

He had a point, but we didn't have to worry. The moment we were waiting for happened; just like a magician snapping his fingers or waving a wand, every streetlamp, every Christmas light, every shop window was suddenly plunged into darkness. It was two minutes past midnight.

I had punched the air with excitement, 'Game on, he's done it, he's done it. Eddie's pulled it off, the bugger's done it.'

'OK, no need to go mad; let's do our bit and get this over with.'

Even as he spoke, alarms were sounding all round us, activated by the electrical supply failure. It had felt like we were in the middle of a discordant electronic orchestra.

Like him or like him not, Eddie Phillips had pulled it off. The Emergency Authorities would have their hands full for hours. In the midst of what was happening, nobody would be interested in the welfare of a department store. Whatever his faults and inadequacies, the guy had delivered.

Looking back, I could see now how lucky I had been to attend that site liaison meeting where I had learned that the main electricity supply cables for the centre of Crewe passed across Railway land. In fact, the Electricity Board's Sub-Station for the locality was built on Railway land. Knowing that I had reasoned that if the two main transformers at the Sub-Station could be taken out of service, most of Crewe would be without electricity. Harry and I couldn't be in two places at once, and that was where Phillips had come to mind. The easiest way to inflict major damage on the transformers was with an explosive, but that would require a timer and a bit of electrical circuitry, and Phillips had the expertise.

Harry's opposition to Eddie's involvement was understandable, but knowing Phillips was in financial difficulties, I'd been pretty sure he'd grab the chance at earning a hefty sum no matter what was entailed. The arrangement suited my purposes in more ways than one. Phillips on board left one final problem: the little matter of dynamite and detonators. Phillips had told Harry that making a timer-operated device wouldn't be a problem; suitable batteries, a detonator and an alarm clock would do the job. He had also undertaken to put the device in place at around eleven on the night of the job and set it to go off at midnight.

I had been over the moon when Harry had reported back on his negotiation with Phillips; my prayers had been answered big time. Firstly, I would have agreed fifty grand, not the twenty he settled on. But more importantly, with Phillips in the money, the door would be open for Sam to leave him. I'd manoeuvred Harry into doing the negotiations in view of my relationship with Sam; I had been finding it hard to look the guy in the eye.

'Well done, mate, that's half the problem solved, but how the fuck are we going to get ourselves some dynamite, and how much do we need anyway?'

To my astonishment, Harry had said, 'I still don't like this, but I think I know how we can get our hands on some. My uncle works in the local quarry, and they're blasting rock to hell every week. It's all kept under lock and key in a building at the quarry, but I've seen the set-up and breaking in would be child's play.'

Later that week, we had gone to the quarry late at night and broken into the hut and stole two sticks of dynamite and two detonators. If the theft had been reported to the police, it had escaped the attentions of the Press, and we had heard nothing of the incident. I had insisted that Harry, not Phillips, obtained the batteries and clock. 'I'm not sure how discreet Eddie is, so best you get them, and don't hand them over until you have to; give him just enough time to do the job.'

I smiled wryly as my thoughts diverted as I recalled that Sam had been in touch just the day before the robbery to tell me that Eddie would be working late the following night, and I could come round for a couple of hours. It was the first and only time I had ever turned down an opportunity to see Sam. 'Sorry darling, I can't, I'm working that night as well, not with Eddie, I hasten to add.'

As we drove into the service yard behind Fairweather's we heard the wailing of emergency vehicle sirens sounding in the distance. The fire alarm bell on the store building was clanging fiercely, not that it mattered; it was one of dozens that were being ignored.

'Park over there,' I pointed to the spot I had chosen. 'Park parallel to the wall, directly below that window, and get in as close as you can; I'll get out your side.'

We'd got out and looked up at the window, thankful for the bright moon.

'It's a fair way up, mate.' Harry was gauging the distance to the first-floor window.

'You've brought the steps?' I regretted the question as soon as I voiced it; of course, he had brought the steps.

Harry had said nothing, just given me a withering stare.

'Sorry, put it down to nerves.' My stomach knotted as I followed his gaze; suddenly, the window seemed a long way up.

They're in the back of the van. I'll get them out. They're eight feet to the platform, should do the job easily,' he added reassuringly.

'Yeah, no problem. Get them out and onto the roof of the van; that should give us around fourteen feet, more than enough.'

I pulled on the tight leather gloves I had purchased earlier that day; I wouldn't be leaving any fingerprints inside or anywhere else, for that matter. Next, a large pair of socks over my shoes. I'd be leaving no footprints, either. It was a bit ironic that I'd bought them in the very store I was about to rob. Harry clambered onto the roof of the van and set up the steps.

'Be careful, Craig, they're a bit wobbly, but I'll keep a good hold on them. Time to go, mate; good luck, it's all down to you now.'

I remembered looking at my watch at that point, eight minutes after midnight. I had felt nervous but had been determined not to let it show. Strain shone through my voice as I made ready to make the climb. 'Right, I've got the bag for the loot, I've got the torch, two torches in fact, I've got the brick, I'm gloved up, have covers on my feet, I'm ready. I'm on my way.'

Harry clung onto the ladder, steadying it as I climbed the steps, but they still wobbled. I felt a wave of relief as I reached window level. My hand had shaken as I reached into the bag for the brick.

'Watch your eyes, Frank.' I swung the brick forward, flinching as it made contact with the window. Crash, it had sounded so loud; surely someone must have heard it. The large pane of glass shattered, pieces and splinters flying everywhere. I flicked on the torch, looking for jagged edges and any remaining shards, knocking them away with the brick where I found them, making sure it was safe to climb through. That done, I had lobbed the brick into the store, heard it strike something hard, then clatter onto the floor.

'On my way. I'll be about fifteen minutes if all goes well.'

'Good luck, mate. I'll keep watch.'

I climbed in, headfirst, and eased myself down onto the floor. Christ, it was dark in there; thank God I'd thought to bring a torch. I had taped over the head, leaving only a slit, cutting down on the spread of light to reduce any chance of it being seen by a passerby. I was on the first floor and had to get to the third, a journey I had made several times during my visits to the store. Even in the limited light afforded by the torch, the models cast eerie shadows as I made my way through the store; at times, they seemed to follow my progress. I reached the staircase leading to the third floor and began my climb.

Arriving at the top of the stairs, the staff area lay straight ahead. There were a few counters to negotiate, but finally, I was at the door to the corridor leading to Fairweather's office. I shone the torch on my watch. It showed thirteen minutes after twelve; just five minutes had gone since I put my foot on the ladder.

I reached forward, turned the handle and pushed, but the door was locked. No matter, I had expected it to be locked, and it wasn't a problem; I'd stolen Claire's key many weeks ago. She had reported the loss to Fairweather and had worried he would be angry, but it seemed he had been unconcerned and given her another. Poor Claire, I really had used her.

I turned the key in the lock, eased open the door and stepped into the room, shining the torch round to familiarise myself again with its layout.

Nothing had changed, and I went immediately to the bookcase, reaching up to the top shelf to the third book along.

I leafed it open, but there were no hidden compartments; books four, five and six followed, then seven and eight. Nothing, 'Fuck it, they've moved the fucking things.' *But why would they?* Then, it had dawned on me; the keys weren't in a book at all. There were no concealed compartments; I'd overcomplicated matters. I knew where they were. I took down books three and four again and explored the space vacated on the shelf. They were there, those two small, vital pieces of metal, the keys. My heart was pounding, and I took some deep breaths to calm myself before crossing to the cupboard holding the safe.

I inserted both keys, remembering to turn the top one clockwise and the bottom anti-clockwise, just as I'd seen Claire do all those months ago. I pushed the cupboard door open, my heart gathering pace again as I shone the torch over the final barrier to a small fortune; my watch showed seventeen minutes past midnight.

The second of July 1899 Fairweather's birth date. Two, seven, one, eight, nine, nine; six numbers that I knew by heart. They alternated left and right but which direction first? No matter; I zeroed the dial and went through the sequence, starting with two to the left through to the final nine and then pushed down on the lever handle. I had chosen wrong; it didn't budge.

My mouth was bone dry, my hand trembling as I reached forward to the dial again, this time starting with two to the right, alternating on through the numbers. I held my breath as I pushed down on the lever for the second time, dismay gripping me when it didn't budge. My heart raced; it felt like it would explode; I sucked in air, fighting to calm myself, wondering if I was really cut out for a life of crime. *Steady Craig don't panic. You knew this might happen; clever old Mr Fairweather has reversed the sequence. That makes it nine, nine, eight, one, seven, two.*

For the third time, I zeroed the dial then started to the left, alternating direction with each number, making sure I got them right. Disappointment again; the lever didn't budge.

Ah, well, it'll be fourth time lucky. I tried to reassure myself. *'Here goes'*

I zeroed the dial for the fourth time, starting to the right this time, drawing breath when I rotated the dial for that final nine. I could feel my heart hammering against my chest wall as I pushed down on the lever again, my stomach tightening when it didn't budge.

What now? I wasn't going to be beaten by a set of numbers; this couldn't be the end of the road. I would have tried a thousand sequences before going back to tell Harry I had failed. All those plans we'd made, all those dreams we'd shared, I couldn't let them come to nothing.

I looked at my watch: 12.26, eighteen minutes gone. *'Think, Craig, think; figure it out.'* I had almost shouted out the words, driving myself on. Then it came to me: I knew what Fairweather had done, or I hoped I knew what he'd done. He had reversed his birth date to make it easy to remember. It was obvious now that I had worked it out; at least, that's what I told myself in those desperate moments. For the fifth time, I zeroed the dial, deciding to start to the right, this time putting in the year first, one, eight, nine, nine, then the day two and finally the month seven. I had hesitated then and begged Fate to be kind to me before pressing down firmly on the lever. My mouth widened in its broadest-ever smile when the lever yielded. I enjoyed a moment of triumph as I pulled the safe door open and shone the torch on the shelves. It was there, thousands of pounds, huddling together in neat little stacks.

I couldn't believe it; I was rich. For a fleeting moment I had understood Fairweather's fixation with money; I could imagine how the man felt as he counted pile after pile of bank notes.

It was time to load up and get out; I raked bundle after bundle of notes into the bag, smiling as it got heavier. 'You lovely Christmas shoppers.' Every note loaded, I pulled the zip sealing the bag, then pushed the safe door closed and reset the dial to zero. I backed out into the office and pulled the door closed behind me. I then moved across to the bookshelf and replaced the keys in their hiding place. Finally, I put the four books back in order on the shelf. One last glance around the room to make sure that everything was as I found it, and it was time to go. I shone the torch on my watch again: 12.34; with luck, we'd earned £150,000 in just twenty-six minutes. Outside the office, I had leaned back on the door, cuddling the bag, feeling totally elated. Sometimes, crime did pay.

Back on the first floor, I made my way to the window and looked out, peering into the blackness of the yard. I could make out the van, but the steps were gone, and there was no sign of Harry. *'Christ, where was he?'*

'Harry, Harry, Harry, where are you?' There had been no reply. 'Harry, Harry, where are you?' I had shouted louder the second time, relieved when I heard the van door sliding open.

'Coming mate, I'm in the van; it's freezing out here. Hold on whilst I get the steps; would have taken a lot of explaining if somebody had turned up, so I put them away. Did everything go to plan?'

'Not quite, mate, but the important bit did. I'll tell you all about it when we're on the move. The main thing is, I've got the loot.'

Harry climbed onto the roof of the van and erected the stepladders, shivering as he grasped the cold metal to steady them. 'Promise me, Craig, if there's a next time, you'll make it a summer job.'

I descended the ladders more quickly than I went up, and seconds later, I was back down on good old terra firma. 'It's all here, Harry,' I said, patting the bag. 'One hundred and fifty thousand beauties. *We're in the money, we're in the money.'* I had sung a few words of the old song.

Harry beamed, teeth gleaming in the dark, 'Well done mate, let's get the hell out of here and save the celebrations for another day. The sooner we get back home and into bed, the better.'

We had one more job to do before heading back; the bag had to be hidden. We had all agreed that we shouldn't attempt to spend any of the money within six months, so a safe hiding place had been found and made ready just a few miles out into the country, in Delamere Forest, an area Harry knew like the back of his hand. He parked the van and led the ways to an abandoned woodcutter's cottage, where we put the bag containing the loot in a plastic sack along with the gloves, socks and torches. That done, we had buried it in the hole he had dug the day before. Frank had kissed the bag goodbye, 'See you in six months, baby.'

Well, that had been the plan.

Chapter Seven

'Craig, Craig, wake up, there's something wrong.' Mrs Brown was shouting, desperation in her voice, knocking on my bedroom door, breaking into my deep sleep. I'd slept fitfully for most of the night in the aftermath of the robbery, my mind grappling with the enormity of what I had done and how I was going to spend the small fortune that lay waiting for me. I had lain in much longer than I usually did, even for a Sunday. It wasn't like Mrs Brown to disturb me; she had never woken me up at weekends.

'Craig, Craig, answer me, please.'

'Coming, Mrs Brown; I'm just putting on my dressing gown.' I had pulled open the door and found myself looking into her anxious face.

'Whatever's wrong, Mrs Brown, you're in a real state?'

There's no electricity Craig, nothing works; I can't imagine what's wrong. The lights won't come on, the radio won't work; I'm sorry I've had to wake you, but I didn't know what else to do.'

I had known instantly what was wrong and, listening to the anxiety in her voice, had begun to realise the full consequences of last night's diversion. Hundreds, maybe thousands of homes all over Crewe without electricity, hundreds of elderly ladies like Mrs Brown at their wit's end. *Shit.* But what was done was done; I couldn't turn the clock back; I had to behave as I would normally.

'I'll take a look, Mrs Brown. Don't worry, it's probably just your main fuse gone.'

I had followed her downstairs to the kitchen and into the pantry, where the fuse board was located.

Conscious of Mrs Brown's watchful gaze I had pulled out the main fuse and looked at it studiously.

'No problem there, Mrs Brown; I'll look at the others.' One by one, I had checked the fuses shaking my head in puzzlement.

'They're all OK. Must be something wrong outside the house. Have you checked with next door? If they've lost power, it must be at the Electricity Board's end. I'll go and find out.'

To my relief, she had insisted on going; I really didn't want to encounter Claire whilst all this robbery was going on. There were too many links in that direction.

'I'll go, lad, it's cold out there, and you're in your dressing gown.'

She had returned minutes later looking crestfallen, 'It's terrible, Craig, I don't know what we're going to do.'

'Whatever's wrong, Mrs Brown?' I'd put my arm round her shoulders. 'It can't be that bad.'

'It is Craig, it's really awful. Mrs Hilton hasn't got any electricity either; in fact, the whole of Crewe hasn't got any electricity. And worse than that, she phoned the Electricity Board, and they told her there'll be no power for at least three days.'

'Oh dear, that is bad news. Did they say what the problem is?'

'Mrs Hilton didn't know. What am I going to do, Craig?'

She had seemed on the brink of tears, and I'd given her a cuddle; I felt lousy knowing that I was to blame. The scale of what I had done was becoming crystal clear.

I gave her a cheery smile. 'Well, for a start, we're going to look after each other; there's no good crying over spilt milk. We've got gas for cooking; we've got the coal fire, and I'll get us a supply of candles. It'll be really cosy, you'll see. You must have had times like this during the war.'

She had brightened up for a moment but almost as quickly gone back into despair.

'But what about the television? I'll miss all my programmes and my eyes aren't too good for reading by candlelight. I'll end up sitting around all day with nothing to do, and it gets dark early at this time of year.'

'Well, I can't help with the television, but I've got my transistor radio, and it can work with batteries, so you'll have that. There's lots of good stories and plays on the radio; music too if you want it; it won't be for long. Where's that wartime spirit you told me about? I'll go get my transistor right this minute, and we'll have something to listen to. And, maybe if I'm lucky, whilst I'm getting dressed, you'll make us something to eat; you've still got gas.'

As we ate breakfast together Mrs Brown's laments had been continuous. 'Poor Mrs This, poor Mrs That, how will they cope? What about the hospitals? What about the schools? How will the shops manage? Would the Post Office still issue her pension?'

I had tried to reassure her, but the full realisation of the previous night's act of destruction was becoming all too clear to me.

Even now, as the van bumped, swayed and rolled along, I could visualise the newspaper reports and headlines, particularly when the police had announced that they were firmly of the view that the Fairweather robbery and sabotage of Crewe's electricity supply were linked. I recalled that during that first week or so, feelings had run high in the area; the perpetrators had been variously branded as uncaring, unfeeling, irresponsible, unprincipled, inhuman, and greedy beyond belief. Every vestige of glamour and feeling of success I'd had enjoyed, had been stripped away and been replaced with guilt and remorse. At times, I felt quite depressed; nobody had been meant to suffer other than Fairweather and his insurers, and they could afford it. *Christ, I bet Jesse James and Robin Hood never felt like this.*

I had met up with Sam as soon after Christmas as her commitments allowed and satisfied our pent-up passion in her spare room.

'God, I needed that, Craig. I couldn't wait for Christmas to end. Sometimes, my body aches for yours.'

'I know how you felt, darling. It seemed to drag on and on, but this is the last one we'll spend apart.'

I had avoided the subject of the robbery, but even there with Sam, there had been no escape. She had raised it, and her criticism had stung me. 'Who would do such a thing, Craig? It's absolutely despicable, all just for money; sheer greed, that's all it is. They must have known that elderly people rely on electricity and that they would struggle to cope. It's completely disrupted the hospitals; I heard one poor woman who was in the middle of a tricky birth when the lights went out. She and her baby could have lost their lives. I hope they catch the bastards and cut their balls off.'

It was the only occasion I heard her swear, and I had barely been able to respond, 'Yes love, I know; it's been awful; poor Mrs Brown was miserable at times. What does Eddie think about it?'

'Oh, he hasn't said much other than whoever did it must have been well informed.'

I had prayed hard that day that she never found out that I was behind the robbery. Harry, Eddie and I had got together and held a post-mortem; all of us all felt bad about what had happened, especially Harry. I had tried hard to raise their morale. 'Look, guys, it's water under the bridge, and it's down to me; I came up with the idea in the first place. It'll soon blow over, but in the meantime, act normal and join in the general criticism; it's important that we behave like everybody else. Appear to be shocked by the whole business, and don't spare the condemnation. Six months from now, it'll all seem like a bad dream; only one thing will have changed…. we'll be rich.'

They hadn't been convinced by my words, and for that matter, neither was I.

Along the way, Mrs Brown had told me how *'poor Claire'* had been questioned by the police about the robbery.

'Why would they question Claire, Mrs Brown?'

'Well, it seems that Claire knew the combination to the safe, and that's how the thieves got into it. I think she feels that the Police suspect her of being involved.'

'Ridiculous idea. Claire would never do that. Old Fairweather might try it on though, then claim the cash back on insurance. It would be an easy way of doubling your money if you got away with it. There's no way would Claire get involved in anything like that.'

'Thieves never prosper, Craig, God sees to that.'

'Of course, He does, Mrs Brown, but they keep trying though, don't they?'

If Claire had mentioned our relationship to the police, there had been no follow-up, so all had seemed well in that direction.

About a month after the robbery, Phillips had asked to meet Harry and me somewhere private. We met up whilst we were out on a job, and he dropped a bombshell. 'I need my money, now, I'm desperate.'

Harry had exploded, 'Well, you can't fucking have it; we agreed on six months, and that's it. You'll get your £20,000 then and not before.'

To my surprise, Phillips had stood his ground, 'And that's another thing, the papers are saying that well over £100,000, some say near £160,000 was stolen. I reckon I should be getting more than £20,000.'

Harry had grabbed Phillips by the lapels, 'You listen to me, you fucking weasel, you get £20,000 and not a penny more. Do you understand me? You agreed £20,000, and £20,000 is what you get.'

Things were in danger of getting out of control, and I had intervened.

'Calm down, guys, we all know what happens when thieves fall out. Harry's right, Eddie, a deal is a deal. Most of the setting up was done before you got involved, and Harry and I took the greatest risk. You earned your share pretty easily. And remember this: we don't know how much money there is. Papers exaggerate, and who knows what story old Fairweather has spun the police so he can claim on insurance. The one thing you can be sure about is that you will get your agreed share no matter what we got away with.'

Phillips had backed off at that point. 'OK, £20,000 it is, but I need my money now.'

Harry had flared up again. 'Look dickhead, you can't go splashing cash about; you'll attract attention to yourself. We'll all end up in the clink if we're not careful.'

'I'm not going to splash it around. I just need a thousand or two to clear some debt. I'm desperate; I need the money, and I need it now. You don't know what it's like being in a hole.'

Harry wasn't sympathetic. 'If you had an ounce of common sense, you wouldn't have got into a hole in the first place.'

To his credit, Phillips hadn't argued that point. 'I fucking know that, but the fact is I am in a hole, and it's a big one; I'll have no roof over my head if I don't come up with the money. The Bank and Building Society are both after me, and Sam has said she wants to leave me. I'm desperate, at my wit's end. Maybe if I can get out of this mess, we might be able to patch things up.'

At the mention of Sam's name, I had weakened. It sounded like she was ready to leave Phillips, and it had seemed to me, helping him solve his problems meant she could leave him with a clear conscience.

'OK, Eddie, I'm halfway convinced. What about you, Harry? I guess you would feel the same if your marriage was under threat. I know I would.'

I had known that marriage and his home were nearest and dearest to Harry's heart and that in a similar circumstance, he would do anything to avoid losing Anne. For my own selfish reasons, I had preyed on his weak spot.

He shook his head emphatically, but he didn't sound adamant. 'I don't like it, don't like it at all, I just don't trust this dickhead. But it's your call, Craig; I'll go along with you.' He'd rounded on Phillips again. 'But mark my fucking words, Eddie, you muck this up, and I'll kick your head in, I mean it.'

I breathed a sigh of relief. 'That's agreed then. Just one more thing whilst we're all here, I'm going to suggest that we share out the cash so that each is responsible for his own. I've had a nagging worry since we hid it that some dog or walker might find it. Anybody got strong views on this?'

Harry shrugged, 'I wouldn't give him a penny more than we need to, but it doesn't seem to matter what I think.' Phillips, of course, hadn't dissented from the proposal.

'OK, we'll sort that out by the end of the week, but remember Eddie, once you've paid your Building Society and Bank what you owe, no more spending for another five months. Got it?' Phillips, of course, had readily agreed.

Frank and I had gone to Delamere Forest to retrieve the bag the following day and, with mounting enthusiasm, sat in Frank's car and gleefully counted out the notes.

'I make it £142,000, not quite the £150,000 we expected but not bad for a night's work. Christ, think of how much it would have been if it wasn't for cheques and buying on account. Will you give dickhead his share, or do you want me to do it?'

'I'm still not happy with this, Craig. I just don't trust the guy. He's been a plonker from the day and hour I met him.'

'I know he is; he's our very own loose cannon, but he's desperate, and God knows what he might do if we don't give him the money. He might try to borrow on the strength of it; worst-case scenario, he might try to negotiate a reward for turning us in; who knows. If we were a Chicago mob, we'd take him out and be done with it, but we're amateurs and must do it the easy way.'

Harry had looked really glum in spite of his newly acquired wealth. 'I guess so. Give it here; I'll hand it over, then I can put the fear of death up him just one more time.'

'I was hoping you would say that. You know, you've got a natural gift for that sort of thing; just watching you in action frightens me.'

He never did tell me about the handover, but whatever he said failed to have the desired effect; a month later Phillips turned up at the office one morning driving a nearly new E-Type Jaguar. Harry and I, like all the other guys from the office, had clustered around this wonderful machine in awe. It was every young man's dream to own an E-Type, but none of our lot could afford one; up to now, that was. Phillips had tried to keep space between himself and us. I could see that Harry was seething; I felt sick to the pit of my stomach.

One of the guys asked, 'How can you afford a machine like this, Eddie?'

He had dropped his eyes and stammered an unconvincing reply, 'I.. I.. I didn't really, it's a…. it's a…. it's a present from my father. He's…. he's had some unexpected luck with his stocks and shares, big gains.'

I could see Harry was livid, and I butted in. 'You're a very lucky guy to have such a generous Dad; I'd like a drive sometime. Hey, look at the time, guys; we'd better get back to the desks before Eric blows his top.'

The excitement was over, and the gang began to drift back to the office. Well, everybody except Phillips; Harry wasn't letting him go anywhere. I saw him grab Eddie by the arm and whisper something in his ear. Phillips paled visibly and tried to pull away, but Harry wasn't letting him go anywhere. I followed a step behind, making sure that we weren't being watched.

'In here dickhead.' Harry hauled Phillips into the Depot stationery cupboard. My thoughts were racing as I followed them in; whatever Harry was about to do; it was too late; the damage was done.

Harry spat out an instruction at me. 'Watch the door while I attend to this piece of shit.'

He had pinned Phillips against the wall, shaking him violently, kneeing him in the balls. He had offered no resistance and just looked like a rag doll being savaged by an errant child.

'Tell me how you got the car, Eddie.'

'I told you; my father bought it for me.'

Harry kneed him again. Phillips wilted and sunk to his knees, holding himself, groaning.

'Tell me again, Eddie.'

'Honest, I swear, my father bought it for me.'

Harry grabbed his hair and pulled Phillips to his feet, their faces just inches apart.

'You're a fucking liar, but I'll tell you what I'm going to do. I'm going to phone your father and tell him how much I admire the lovely car he's bought his son. I'm going to tell him I'm looking for one and ask him where he got it, cause his son doesn't know. And know what, Eddie? If I'm wrong, I'll apologise and buy you a coffee. On the other hand, if I'm right, this is going to be the worst day of your life.'

He turned to the door, 'Keep him here, Craig. I won't be long. A good kick in the balls will settle him down if he gets difficult.'

Phillips had cracked at that point, 'I'm sorry, I'm sorry, please don't phone my father. I bought the car. I'm sorry, don't hit me again.' He flinched, raising his hands to protect his face as Harry moved towards him.

I stepped between them, 'He's had enough, we can't turn the clock back.'

'How much did you spend, Eddie?' I kept my voice low, concealing the anger I felt; I wanted to know just how much damage had been done.

He looked at me like I was his saviour, his voice almost a whine. 'Not much, Craig, just a couple of thousand or so. I paid cash. Nobody knows. I won't spend any more. You can have the rest back if you want; keep it safe for me. It'll be alright, I'm sure.'

I snarled at him, 'You stupid fucking clown, of course people know. I fucking know, Harry knows, the office knows, the whole fucking Depot knows you've got one of the best cars on the market. Your neighbour knows, your whole fucking estate knows, and soon most of the town will know. And, of course, it's an everyday occurrence for somebody to wander in off the street and hand over cash for an expensive car. You're a fucking idiot.'

He'd burst into tears, a sorry wreck of a man. 'I'm sorry, I'm sorry, Craig, I couldn't resist it. You've seen it; it's beautiful. I had to have it.'

Phillips stood there, bent over, hands on his hips, gasping for breath, his face wracked with pain. I almost felt sorry for him, but Harry didn't. Before I could stop him, he had pummelled Phillips to the body till he collapsed onto the floor. His anger unsated, he grabbed Phillips by the hair, clenching his fist, ready to smash into his face.

'No, Harry!' I screamed at him in desperation. 'Don't mess up his face. Let's go; there's nothing else to be done here. It'll raise too many questions if he goes back to the office with his face bruised and bleeding.'

Harry had snarled one last threat at Phillips, 'If this goes wrong, if we get caught, I'll cripple you. If you get picked up, keep your mouth closed; leave us out of it for your own good. You squeal on us, and no matter how long it takes, I'll come looking for you.'

Harry hadn't pulled his punches when he got me outside; he had been venomous.

'I told you we couldn't trust him, Craig, told you over and over, but you, Mr Infallible, Craig Murray knew best. Well, you've blown it; it's only a matter of time till John Law knocks on the door. It's alright for you; you're single with no dependents. I've got Anne and the kids.'

He was right. I had made a real mess of it; I'd let my feelings for Sam get in the way of our venture, and now there was a good chance we'd all pay for it. Ironically, back in the office, I got a call from Sam later that day. 'Can't talk long, darling; Eddie's come home unexpectedly, he's in a state, says he's not well, so don't come round. I'll be in touch. Love you.'

Harry had been right, of course, it was only a matter of time; our fates were sealed the day Phillips had bought that car. Somebody, somewhere, had said something to somebody, about Eddie's new car and it had got to the ears of the police. They had tracked down the previous owner through the vehicle registration system, and he had told the police that Phillips had paid cash in used notes. After that, they had questioned Phillips. Where had he gotten the money from? *I saved it up.* Where had he been that Saturday night? *I was at home.* Unfortunately for him, the police had called in on Sam at the same time he was being questioned, and she had told them, quite innocently, that he had been at work. Caught out on that one lie, under further intensive questioning, he had broken down and admitted his guilt.

To his credit, he had initially refused to name his accomplices, probably because he was afraid of what Harry might do to him. But the police had offered him some kind of deal, and he'd put us in the frame. After questioning, he'd been released on bail and told not to say anything to anyone, including his wife, or the deal was off.

The police had been patient and smart, first checking that Harry and I hadn't been at work contrary to what Harry's wife and Mrs Brown told them when questioned. They had ascertained that Harry had booked the van that weekend, although he hadn't been working. They had contacted the quarry manager, who had confirmed that two sticks of dynamite couldn't be accounted for. Looking through the list of quarry personnel, they had found out that Harry's uncle worked there. He had innocently advised that he had once shown Harry round the site.

They knew from my address that I lived next to Claire, and on further questioning, she had confirmed that I had been her boyfriend a while back. She had told them that I had visited her in her office and that she had shown me the safe, though not the hiding place for the key. She hadn't told me the combination but admitted that she had let it slip that it was Mr Fairweather's birth date.

By the time the police pulled Harry and me in for questioning, they had built a cast iron case, and there was no point in denial. It was game over. Inspector Mark Hanley, a tall, dark-haired man from Yorkshire had very patiently, very succinctly laid out the evidence against us. We were all charged with the robbery; Phillips and Harry were given bail, having agreed to return their share of the proceeds. I was remanded in custody, having refused to return my share. I suppose they were afraid I might have run off, and they were right. I would have given half a chance. But no way were they getting my share of the loot back; I wanted a better souvenir of the robbery than a term of imprisonment. The money was safely hidden a long way from Crewe, and it would be there waiting for me when I got out of prison.

During that long journey to Cumbria, I had plenty of time to look back on events and learn from them. And just what had I learned? I had learned that if the plan is a good one, it will almost certainly work. I'd learned, too, that the main weakness in any plan is the people carrying it out. So, where did that leave me? I was convinced that crime could pay, and I knew that I was quite happy to break the law to make money. The thought of four years in prison hadn't put me off, and although I didn't know precisely what the future held, one thing was for sure: the Fairweather robbery wouldn't be my last.

The van slowed and came to a halt; I heard muffled voices. The van started again but didn't go far; more voices, then the van door opened.

'Out Murray. Welcome to Westmoor, your home for the next four years.'

LIFE IN PRISON

Chapter Eight

One thousand, two hundred and seventy-two days, otherwise three years and six months, I spent in Westmoor. In the end, they had given me six months' remission for good behaviour, and I'd probably earned it. My intention had been to be a model prisoner, maybe I had succeeded.

Parole had been on offer after eighteen months and every six months thereafter; I had applied but been turned down on each occasion. They had questioned me about my future intentions and whether I regretted my actions. Was I truly repentant, all that kind of stuff; I tried to sound sincere and come up with the assurances they sought, but I failed to convince them. I think they knew that my only regret was getting caught. Biggest fact against me was my refusal to return the money I had stolen; fuck them. Why should I; I had a criminal record, there was no changing that.

I hadn't wasted my time in prison; I had taken every opportunity to learn. I read about criminology, forensics, law and electronics, anything in fact that might be useful to my future ventures. They had drawn the line at my request for information on security systems, so I guess I wasn't entirely trusted. When I wasn't studying, I had involved myself in such sporting activities as were available and made good use of the gymnasium. A few of the inmates had been boxers or had an interest in the martial arts. A couple were happy to teach me the rudiments of self-defence, and I had proved to have an aptitude for boxing. By the end of my time, I felt that I was more than capable of giving a good account of myself if the need for fisticuffs arose. All in all, once I had established a routine, time had passed quickly.

Given the obvious restrictions, life in prison had been bearable, other than the void left by the absence of female company. I had missed Sam; her touch, her softness, her scent, her voice, her passion; there was nothing that could take her place. There had been many times in the early months when I longed for Sam, to hold her, to see her, to hear her voice, but there had been no contact. In the end, I had tried to write Sam out of my life.

I had been lucky with my cellmate; Dan Rawson was intelligent, well-spoken and pleasant, not the sort of prisoner I had expected to encounter at Westmoor. He was a fine-featured, tall, athletic guy and not much older than me. At first, I had wondered if he was gay; there were no female pictures on the wall, and he never mentioned women in any context. On the other hand, there were no male pin-ups either, and he hadn't made any unwelcome overtures. It soon became obvious that he had the respect of the other inmates and, more importantly, the ear of a few of Westmoor's heavyweights.

During the first month or so, Rawson hadn't shown any inclination to talk about his background, and I had steered clear of any personal questions till curiosity finally got the better of me, and I had asked outright, 'What are you in for?'

He had laughed and replied, 'Tax evasion.' before adding, 'A bit of advice, Craig, it's best not to get too nosy in here.'

We finally got to know each other better when we discovered we shared a mutual interest: chess. I had been very open and had told Dan all about myself and how I had ended up in one of Her Majesty's nicks.

'And what does the future hold for you now?' I had been surprised by the question, given that he had seemed genuinely interested.

'Who knows, Dan; I'll be looking for another opportunity to make another slice of easy money, that's for sure.'

'Easy money?' He'd raised an eyebrow. 'Sixty grand for four years of your life, and a criminal record, doesn't look like easy money to me. And you lost a woman you were crazy about.'

'The stakes will be higher next time, and I won't get caught; anyway, sixty grand is a lot of money by my standards.'

'Prisons are full of guys who thought they wouldn't get caught. Surely you realise that by now?'

'Of course, I do, but there are a lot of clever crooks who never get caught. I read somewhere that 80% of crime never gets solved.

He had nodded somewhat ruefully I thought, 'There are some, but not too many.'

'I know you don't like personal questions, Dan, but what will you be doing when you get out?'

'Let's just say I'm in the same line of business as you, Craig.'

'Maybe we could work together on a suitable venture?'

'I doubt it; with respect to yourself, you're not in my league.'

I didn't know what his league was, so I wasn't going to argue. 'Fair enough but keep me in mind just in case something crops up you can't handle. Anyway, I thought you were in here for evading income tax?'

'Tax evasion was what they pinned on me; they couldn't prove what they really wanted to get me for.'

'Which was?'

He gave me a warning look. 'Too many questions, Craig; let's play chess; I need the practice.'

We were both accomplished players and evenly matched; all our games were hard-fought. It had been through this media that our friendship had developed, though I learned very little more about Dan's background. It did emerge that he based himself in London and that he had lost touch with his family. He never spoke of any other attachments, not even those associated with business. Strangely, like me, he had no visitors.

'Any chance you'll be around tomorrow?' Dan had posed this question just before we bedded down for the night.

I laughed out loud, 'Afraid not, mate, I thought I'd pop into Carlisle and do a bit of shopping.'

'Ha, ha, very funny, smart arse; let me explain. Are you aware that Westmoor's two leading lights play chess?'

'I guess that's the Governor and you you're referring to.'

'Be serious, Craig. Every nick has some heavyweights, guys who call the shots, guys who can make your life a misery, guys that lay down the rules. Even the Governor has respect for them, provided they don't overstep the mark. That way, everybody is happy; in a way, it's a kind of partnership; they get some special privileges, and in turn, they keep the troublemakers in line.'

'And the point of this lesson on prison politics is what, Dan?'

'I'm getting to it. Our heavyweights are Peter Earl Cousins, who looks after the east block, our man, and Tony Razor Davenport, who heads up the west block. They both fancy themselves as chess players and they're competent as far as I tell. It seems that they've challenged each other to see who's best. Added to that, just to make it more interesting, there is a sizeable side stake. With me so far?'

'A sizeable side stake being?'

'Ten grand.'

'Jesus, ten grand. They are serious, aren't they? So why are you asking if I'm around? I don't think I'd want to referee those two.'

'Firstly, they play two games, so it could end up honours even, which would be a nice diplomatic outcome. Each game lasts a maximum of two hours, apparently, after which time it's deemed a draw. One starts at 10.00 am, the other at 2.00 pm; each player can request two five-minute breaks during a game, during which he can go for a pee or ask someone for advice. Earl has told me that I'm his advisor, and I don't want to let him down; we share certain connections on the outside. Understand me?'

'Sure, but where do I come in?'

'I was hoping you might be around to give me advice if I needed it.'

'Come off it, there isn't much between us.'

'That's true, but I think you play a better end game than me, so I'd like you to be around.'

'OK, count me in, always willing to help a mate. Just one thing, though; they're both good losers, I hope?'

'I hope so too, Craig.'

The first game started promptly at 10.00 am with both men playing cautiously, deliberating over each move. They both seemed to be playing to avoid defeat rather than fashion out a win. Standing to one side, Dan and the other nominated inmate followed the game, making identical moves on separate chessboards; these would be used to discuss tactics if one of the players called for a break. I studied both players closely, trying to assess their style looking for any weaknesses that could be exploited. Both were careful, but of the two, Tony Davenport was the more likely to take pieces and make things happen. Neither of them had called for a time-out, and at the end of two hours and with the game unresolved, a draw was agreed.

'What did you make of that, Craig?' Dan enquired.

'Boring, unimaginative, but it was a fair result. Hopefully, the afternoon's game will be more interesting. I can't say that there are any glaring strengths or weaknesses in either of their games; they're pretty average players.'

'That's how I saw it. I'll see you after lunch; I'm dining with Earl. Lucky old me has got to give him some words of encouragement and advice.'

Early play in the second game followed the morning's pattern, and nearly an hour passed without a reasonable attack being mounted. For whatever reason, at that point Davenport started to press forward and gain the upper hand. Dan heard me draw breath. 'What's up?'

'I think our man just made a bad move.'

Sure enough, after a few moves, Cousins was forced to concede a knight and a bishop for a knight and a pawn. Davenport now held an advantage, and he pressed forward to attack. Ten minutes later, Cousins gave away another knight and looked round to see if Dan was available.

'He's going to call a break. Any thoughts?'

'All he can do now is consolidate his defence; in his shoes, I'd castle out of trouble and try to regroup.'

'I'm not sure about that, Craig. Maybe it's time Earl did some attacking of his own.'

'Risky, Dan; he's not really a good enough player to attack from his current position.'

Cousins and Dan met at his parallel chessboard and engaged in earnest conversation as to what to do next. Judging by the look on Cousins' face, he wasn't happy with what Dan was suggesting. To my surprise, Dan signalled for me to come over, and I joined them. Dan didn't bother to introduce me.

'Tell Earl how you would handle this situation, Craig.'

'I reckon if you continue to defend, he'll wear you down, and sooner or later, he'll get checkmate. Your only chance is to go on the attack.'

Cousins interrupted me impatiently, 'We've only got a few minutes, cut to the chase.'

'As I was saying, you've got to go on the attack, and you've got to lay a trap for him.'

Cousins nodded, 'I'm listening; tell me more about this trap.'

I described to him what I thought he should do and waited for his reaction. After some thought, he pursed his lips and looked at Dan, 'What do you think, Dan?'

'It's risky, Earl, very risky; if he spots your move as a trap, you're finished.'

His brow furrowed. 'I can see that, but it's an option, and I do want to win this game. A draw leaves us all square, and it's all been a waste of time.' He looked at me. 'You can go now.'

That was that no thanks and no indication of how he was going to proceed. The two men conversed for a few seconds more, and then Dan joined me in the group of watchers, which had doubled since news got around that the contest might be about to end.

'Well?' I enquired.

'Don't know; he's undecided.'

The game resumed, and it wasn't long before Davenport began positioning his pieces for the end game. Cousins slowed the game down, taking undue care over his moves, but he was getting nowhere. Worse still, he lost his remaining bishop fending off a checkmate.

'That's it, he's blown it.' Dan sighed, shaking his head in disappointment.

'Looks bad, Dan; his only chance is to try what I suggested only maybe it's too late.'

Tony Davenport leaned back, smiling, sensing victory. 'Not long now, Earl, I'll take a cheque, by the way.'

'The shows not over till the fat lady sings, Tony. It's your move.'

'Resign Earl, it's over, and you know it.'

'Your move, Tony.'

Davenport shrugged and moved his Queen up the board. Cousins dithered, fingering his Queen, pondering which square it should occupy. Defence or attack seemed to be what he was considering.

Davenport muttered, 'Come on, Earl, or I'll start thinking you're trying to play out time.'

Cousins finally made his move, placing his Queen in a threatening position.

Davenport grinned and eagerly moved a defending Knight forward to remove the Queen. 'That's it, Earl, game over.'

Moving the Knight out of defence was Davenport's downfall; he gasped as Cousins swept forward with a Rook to place him in check. Davenport moved his King into the only square available, then watched dolefully as he realised his mistake when Cousins moved his second Rook across.

'I think that's checkmate, Tony. Well played, you nearly had me.'

'Nearly isn't fucking good enough, is it? What do you want, cash or cheque?'

'Send a cheque to the Prisoners Reform League.'

The two men shook hands, and that was it.

Earl Cousins strolled over to Dan, 'Thanks, Dan, a happy ending.'

Dan glanced at me meaningfully, 'Not really much to thank me for, Earl.'

Cousins nodded at me. 'I owe you one.'

I wondered if he even knew my name. I just shrugged, 'No problem, you had to make the moves.'

When Cousins had gone, Dan shook my shoulders. 'And I owe you one as well; I promise I won't forget.'

'Glad it worked out; I reckon we could beat both of them without trying too hard.'

'It wouldn't make for good politics, Craig. Now I've got something to tell you.' I could tell from his tone that he was going to announce something important.

'I've heard through my sources that I'm going to be given parole. The paperwork is being prepared as we speak. I'll probably be on my way by the end of the week.'

'I'm sorry to hear that. Fuck it, no, I mean, I'm sorry you're leaving; you know what I mean. I've been lucky having you as a cellmate; God knows who I'll get now.'

'Spare me the tears just yet, Craig; anyway, you've got less than a year to go.'

Dan checked out a week later. We shook hands, and I felt good when he handed me a small piece of paper, and I saw what was written on it. 'Keep this safe; it's my telephone number, something I don't give out too readily. Give me a bell when you get out, and we'll meet up in London.'

'I'll do that, I promise; and who knows, we might work together on something.'

'I'd like that, Craig, but I can't see it happening. I'm not entirely in control of my own destiny.'

'Meaning?'

'Meaning exactly that.' His reply was enigmatic, but he didn't add to it.

My new cellmate moved in later that day: a small Chinese guy by the name of Lee Sun Chow, or that's what it sounded like. His English was poor, and he evaded answering personal questions by exhibiting those blank looks of puzzlement. On the other hand, he didn't ask any questions, so our conversations had been brief and decidedly uninteresting.

Four months later, I was summoned unexpectedly to the Governor's office and stood there in front of him wondering what misdemeanour I had committed. He sat reading papers, ignoring me, leaving me like some naughty schoolboy up before the headmaster.

Hurry up, you prick. Didn't you read those before you sent for me?

Finally, he looked up, 'Seems to be all in order. We're letting you go six months early. They've accepted my recommendation for remission of sentence. They took a lot of persuading; they still haven't forgotten you haven't given back your ill-gotten gains. You should reconsider that; they'll be watching your every move.'

I felt elated, then guilty; I'd been bad-mouthing him, and all the time, he had been speaking up for me.

'Well, nothing to say, Murray?'

'Sorry sir, it's such a surprise, I'm gobsmacked. I guess I've got to thank you for your recommendation; it's not something I would have expected.'

'Your behaviour has been exemplary, Murray, but don't read too much into it; I've got a prison here that's nearly full. I need the space. Now, if you don't have any questions, off you go; report to the Duty Officer after lunch tomorrow. Keep your nose clean, Murray; I don't want to see you back here.'

'Thank you, Governor. Oh, sir, I'm quite happy to miss lunch and leave after breakfast.'

The old sod almost managed a smile. 'On your way, Murray.'

And so, Monday, 8th September 1969, had been the date of my release from Westmoor. I can remember how I felt as I left my cell for the last time and the excitement mounting in me when I got into the prison van that took me to Penrith. But it was only when I stepped out in Penrith that I really felt free.

A NEW BEGINNING

Chapter Nine

A chapter in my life came to an end; it was the beginning of a new life. My immediate future took care of itself; I knew exactly what I had to do next.

First off, I wandered aimlessly around Penrith for nearly two hours, just enjoying the sheer feeling of freedom, feeling the cool breeze on my face, looking up at a clear blue sky; for the first time in over three years, I could go wherever I pleased without restriction. The mini skirt was in fashion; girls were looking sexier than ever; just window-shopping brought me more pleasure than I could have ever imagined. I had to resist the compulsion to spend, to buy something. Not that I was in any position to buy much; my resources were limited to what I'd had with me at the time of my arrest, plus what I'd managed to accumulate in prison.

There was, of course, £60,000 waiting for me, but first, I had to retrieve it; hopefully, it would be where I had salted it away after the share-out. Panic filled me briefly at the very idea it might no longer be there; dire possibilities flooded my thoughts. I calmed down, telling myself that there was no reason why it shouldn't be there, but the lingering doubt remained, and I knew I wouldn't be happy till I had it in my hand. Governor Barker's warning words haunted me: *they'll be watching your every move* and I found myself looking around to see if I was being followed, but nobody seemed in the least interested. Christ, my first few hours of freedom and I'd already accumulated two worries.

I needed some clothes but wasn't sure how much I could spend; I had to sort out overnight accommodation, and I'd have travel costs. Back at Mrs Brown's, I had a wardrobe full of clothes, or did I? Quite likely, she would have thrown them out; she would hardly expect me to turn up on her doorstep. Anyway, I didn't want to go back there and face her. I didn't want to go back to Crewe at all; it was far too soon for people to have forgotten me and what I'd done to them. On the other hand, my bank was there, and I needed cash; I knew too that I should close my account or abandon it; cash movements were traceable. Then, the obvious occurred to me; I retraced my steps along the High Street to the local branch of the Westminster Bank and went in.

'I'd like to speak to the manager if I could please?' I asked the young woman behind the counter. She was pretty, with girl-next-door looks and an open smile; I realised that this was my first direct contact with a woman since Judge Walsh sentenced me and Anne harangued me in court.

'Do you have an appointment Mr…?'

'Murray, Craig Murray; no, I'm afraid I don't.'

'Might I be able to help you?'

Pent-up desires flowed through me. 'I'd rather speak to the manager if at all possible; please, it's important.'

'I'll see what I can do; he prefers clients to make an appointment.'

I gave her my very best smile but didn't push. 'Thank you.'

Seconds later, she was back and pointed towards a door. 'Mr. Carter will see you, but he has another appointment shortly.'

I nodded. 'Got the message. I won't keep him a second longer than necessary.'

Mr. Carter was a small, portly man with a somewhat reddish complexion. Formally dressed in a dark grey business suit with what looked like an old-school tie, he looked like the archetypal bank manager. He stood up when I entered, proffering his hand but remaining behind his expansive desk.

'Please, sit down; tell me how I can help you.'

'The young lady told me you had another appointment shortly, so I'll come straight to the point. Firstly, you should be aware that I was discharged from Westmoor a couple of hours ago.'

I paused, letting my words sink in, watching his eyes widen and his lips purse. He wasn't nervous, but he was no longer at his ease either. 'I want to withdraw the money I have on deposit with your bank and close the account. You'll appreciate that just having been released from prison, I'm desperately short of funds. The problem is, I'm here in Penrith, but my branch of your bank is in Crewe. I should add that my crime took place in Crewe, and I'm too ashamed to go back there.'

'Ah.' He relaxed, and his expression seemed sympathetic. 'Can I ask if you have any identification, Mr. Murray?'

'Yes, will these do?' I pulled my prison release papers and driving license from my inside pocket. I'm sure Governor Barker at Westmoor could vouch for me.'

'That won't be necessary.' He studied my license and papers then asked, 'Do you have your Passbook?'

'Sorry, it got lost along the way, but I know my account number.'

He pushed forward a biro and a sheet of paper, 'Write it down for me, and I'll need your address in Crewe. How much money are we talking about, by the way? I hope it's not too substantial?'

'Less than £200 if I remember rightly.'

'Not a problem; come back tomorrow morning around 10.00, and your money will be here.'

'You couldn't do it now, could you?'

'Sorry, Mr. Murray, there are certain formalities; tomorrow it is.'

'OK, thanks for your help; I'll see you tomorrow.' I shook his hand, thanked the young woman on my way out, and headed back along the High Street.

My next task was to purchase some casual clothes; I wandered round until I found one of those cheap outlets with an apparently never-ending sale. My limited funds ensured that it didn't take long to kit myself out. Next on the list was a sizeable cheap hold-all, the necessaries for daily hygiene, and finally, a newspaper.

Next stop was the local Information Office, where I sought advice on cheap B&Bs that provided evening meals and were within easy walking distance of the High Street. I chose the smallest one, reasoning that there would be fewer fellow guests with all the potential for unwelcome small talk. The helpful assistant, an elderly man, phoned Torr View to ensure there was a vacancy and gave me directions on how to get there.

The landlady of Torr View was a no-nonsense sort, as well built as some of Westmoor's male prison guards. She gave me a cursory look, wrinkled her nose and stared fixedly at me. 'You'll be the one they've just called about. I have a single; it's small, there's no view of the hills, and you'll share the bathroom and toilet on the landing.'

I shrugged, 'Sounds fine, I'll take it.'

She pushed a printed card forward, 'Fill this in, Mr?'

'Murray.' I started registering my details

'And how many nights will you be staying, Mr Murray?'

'Only two, tonight and tomorrow.'

She studied the registration card and looked askance at me. 'You haven't filled in your address.'

'I don't have one, I'm afraid.'

Her eyes drifted over me, nodding her head as she reached a conclusion. 'Hmm, I can put down Westmoor; I need to put something.'

'I don't mind if you don't. How did you know I'd been in Westmoor?'

'Nothing terribly clever, you don't have an address, you're very pale, your clothes are badly creased, and you've got a haircut that could only originate in the army or in prison. You'll have to pay in advance. That'll be twenty-five pounds.'

'I can just about manage that. Can I have an evening meal tonight and tomorrow?'

'Steak and kidney pudding followed by apple crumble; served at 6.30 prompt. That will be another five pounds for the two nights.'

'That sounds alright to me. Can I take a bath before dinner, please?

For a split second, she almost looked sympathetic. 'Of course, I expect it's some time since you had a relaxing bath. You'll find a towel in your room; top of the stairs, first on the right.'

I settled my account, leaving myself with just £10.

Later that night, as I settled down in what was a very comfortable bed, I looked back at the simple but satisfying events of the day: shopping, a hot leisurely bath, a good wholesome meal, and my freedom. I resolved yet again that I would never again be deprived of my liberty. I slept soundly, the quietness and cosiness of my room reminding me of my childhood home of long ago. Habits die hard, and I woke at six, the usual prison time, turned over and went back to sleep till near eight at which point I rose, shaved and showered and presented myself for breakfast, which proved to be in the best English tradition.

'That was superb, Mrs Skelton; you certainly know how to cook.'

She allowed herself the glimmer of a smile, 'Thank you, Mr Murray, I do try to look after my guests. Feel free to come and go as you please. If I don't see you in the meantime, I'll see you at dinner, six-thirty prompt.'

'Look forward to it.'

She had turned out to be not so bad after all, and I felt guilty when I went out next morning without saying goodbye. I never had any intention of spending two nights in Penrith; I was still harbouring Governor Barker's warning and being cautious. *They'll be watching you.* In all probability, I wasn't being watched, but why take chances? I went directly to the Westminster Bank, and it was just a few minutes after 10.00 when I was shown into Mr Carter's office. He welcomed me with a friendly smile and the news I wanted to hear. 'I've got your cash, Mr Murray: one hundred and eighty-five pounds, sixteen shillings and four pence. He proceeded to count it out for me, 'Mostly small notes. I thought you would prefer that.'

'Ideal, Mr Carter, I appreciate your help, I really do.'

'Are you sure you want to close your account? There's no need to.'

'I think it's best. I'm travelling back to Glasgow today to make a new start; I have some friends there who can help.' I wasn't going to Glasgow, but that's what he would tell anyone who asked.

'I understand. Good luck, Mr Murray.'

We shook hands, and I showed myself out, mission accomplished. I could feel the bundle of money in my pocket, annoyed that I hadn't thought to get myself a wallet. At Penrith Station, I purchased a single to Glasgow, maintaining my deception. The guy in the ticket office did the necessary. 'Next train is due in ten minutes; take it to Carlisle, where you can catch the train to Glasgow. He leafed through his timetable. 'It's due in from London at 12.14, goes through here but doesn't stop; platform 2 in Carlisle, I think, but check when you get there.'

There were around a dozen people waiting, and I studied them as I wandered, apparently aimlessly, up and down the platform, wondering if any of them was watching me. I was being paranoid; nobody showed the slightest interest, and I wondered if I was making too much of the Governor's warning. On the other hand, sixty grand was a lot of money, and surely John Law would make some effort to recover it.

The train pulled in, and everyone moved forward except me; I hung back and didn't board till the platform cleared. A woman with three kids looked irritated as I climbed into what they clearly regarded as their carriage. I sat down, offering a smile that wasn't reciprocated. Thirty-five minutes later, the train pulled into Carlisle, and I was happy to escape my noisy bickering companions. My pulse rate soared when I looked along the platform to the ticket gate and saw a policeman talking to the ticket collector. I broke out in a sweat. *Christ, why am I feeling guilty? I'm not doing anything illegal.*

The constable looked on as my ticket was checked, but I could see that he had no interest in me whatsoever. 'Platform 2 for Glasgow, 12.14; it's on time, I think, but check the board just in case.'

I made my way purposefully across the small station concourse, glancing over my shoulder to see if the policeman was watching, but he had his back to me. There were three taxis waiting outside on the road, and I signalled one forward.

'Where to?' If the taxi driver was grateful for my business, it didn't show in his expression.

'Lake Road, please.'

'What number?'

'Don't know, I'll tell you when I see it.'

Mr Happy sighed and sniffed but pulled away without comment. Fifteen minutes later, the cab turned into Lake Road. 'This will do; drop me here. How much?' I paid up, without a tip, my mini revenge for his surly attitude.

It was a ten-minute walk to Carlisle North Industrial Estate, and I enjoyed the warm sunshine, knowing that Cumbria got more than its fair share of rain. As I walked along, memories returned of my last visit to the area; so much had happened since I'd made a hurried trip there to hide away my share of the robbery. It wasn't much of an estate, ten or so boring steel-clad industrial units of various sizes; the building I sought was second on the right, Safehold Ltd. I pushed open the door and entered; not a soul to be seen, but a bell invited me to 'Ring for attention.'

A young man in a brown overall emerged from a door halfway down the long corridor ahead of me. 'Sorry to keep you waiting. How can I help?'

'I'd like to make a withdrawal, please.'

'Certainly, what name?'

'Coulter.'

'Follow me, please; I'll have to check your details.' He started back down the corridor with me in tow. 'In here, please. 'He pointed to a door to my right, and I followed him in.

Once in the room, he opened a drawer and removed the ledger, then flicked through it till he found the page he wanted.

'Let's see. Ah yes, here it is, Coulter.' He made an entry of some kind then looked up. 'You haven't been here for a while, Mr Coulter, over two years in fact.'

'I guess so; amazing how time passes. I made a deposit on my grandmother's behalf and promised not to touch it till she passed on.'

'Sorry to hear of your loss. Follow me; your locker is in Room 8. I assume you've got your key with you?'

I waved it in front of him. All the time I'd been in prison, I had worried about that key, just in case they got nosy and checked it out. Perhaps because it didn't have any identifying marks, it didn't seem to have aroused any interest.

'OK, follow me; it's three doors down on the right.'

I stood behind him as he made to open the door, my heart pounding in anticipation. He turned the key in the lock and stood back, motioning me in. 'It's all yours. You can remember which locker?'

I nodded. The room contained two banks of lockers about two metres high and four metres long. There were forty-eight in all, but I knew exactly which was mine: left-hand side, three along, two up from the ground. I strode to it and inserted my key in the lock; it was stiff, but it turned, and I pulled the door open.

The briefcase was there where I'd left it, the leather mildewed and no longer black and shiny; I reached in nervously and pulled it out. The guy stood there watching me, and I wondered whether to open it to check its contents. I decided not to; there was no point, I knew what it contained.

'Thanks, I'll be on my way.'

'Don't forget to lock up.' He pointed to the locker. 'You've still got over a year's rental left.'

I nodded and locked up. 'I wonder, could you phone for a taxi. I don't fancy the walk back.'

The guy did the necessary, and ten minutes later, I was sitting in a taxi, peering into a briefcase, relieved to see the cash was still there. I got back to Carlisle Station in ample time to purchase a one-way ticket on the next train to London, but before boarding the train, I made a trip to the gent's loo and decanted the money from the briefcase into the hold-all I'd bought in Penrith. I left the briefcase in one of the cubicles.

The destination board showed that the London-bound train was on time and due in ten minutes; if it maintained its schedule, I would arrive in the big city shortly after six.

Chapter Ten

'Hi Dan, it's Craig. I hope you don't mind me calling you?' I had booked into the Green Park Hotel just ten minutes previously and wasn't wasting any time pursuing the purpose of my visit. It was pure luck that I'd got hold of Dan Rawson at my first attempt; I had this image of him being involved in some nefarious activity.

'Craig. What a surprise; I thought you would be tied up for another six months. Of course, I don't mind you phoning; I'd be disappointed if you didn't get in touch. Where are you calling from?'

'I'm in London, mate.'

'Great! Where exactly?'

'I've booked into the Green Park Hotel for three nights.'

'I could have put you up; I've got plenty of room.'

'Thanks, Dan, but I've no intention of dumping myself on you.'

'Fair enough, but we must meet up. When are you free?'

'Hold on, I'll check my social diary. Let's see....... I'm free every moment from now on.'

He laughed, 'Still a joker. I'll pick you up in an hour, and we'll go somewhere for a meal.'

'Dan, I'm tidy but not too well kitted out yet, just back from holiday and all that. I'm planning to do some shopping tomorrow.'

'No worries, we'll go somewhere that's badly lit. Are you happy with a curry?'

'Perfect.'

'Are you in London for any particular reason?'

'Yip, to see you and catch up on old times.'

'OK. I'll be with you at eight.'

I settled myself into a comfortable armchair in the hotel's reception lounge ten minutes early, tucked away in a corner, still conscious about my attire. Not that anyone seemed bothered, and reception hadn't shown the least concern when I checked in. I'd made sure I got a room with a safe, and I'd felt relieved when I'd stowed away my £60,000. Just to conceal myself further, I picked up a copy of the Telegraph, spreading it wide, trying to look engrossed.

Dan spotted me before I saw him and strode forward, hand extended, 'Hi Craig, great to see you.' He gave me the once-over, then leaned forward, speaking in a whisper.

'You must tell me where you get your hair done. Come on, let's go.'

He put his arm round my shoulder, making small talk as we crossed the lounge to the revolving doors. Suddenly, I felt more relaxed; it was just like old times.

'Over there.' He pointed to a British racing green Morgan, double-parked in front of the hotel.'

I couldn't help but whistle in admiration. 'You lucky bugger; I've always fancied a Morgan.'

'I thought we'd go sporty tonight, sort of casual. It's my favourite really.'

'Sounds like you've got more than one car.'

He nodded, 'I've got a second-hand Roller for longer trips and when I want to impress.'

'Christ Dan, business must be good.'

'Not really, if I was an actor, I could be described as between engagements. Are you still happy with a curry?'

'I'd love a curry; it's over three years since I had a good one.'

We ended up in Veeraswamy's, just off Oxford Circus.

'Welcome, Mr Rawson. I have a quiet table for you, as requested.'

The manager, who was dressed in traditional Indian attire, as were all the staff, led us to a dimly lit alcove.

I could feel my feet sinking into the carpets; a glance round at the sumptuous surroundings made me feel out of place. Dan was wearing a casual light-grey linen suit, and his shirt and tie looked like they were genuine silk; everything about him suggested class and affluence.

'Happy here, Craig?'

'Poshest place I've ever been, to tell you the truth. I promise next time we meet I'll be more presentable.'

'Enough of that talk. I suggest that we have the fixed meal for two and skip all that pouring over menu business.'

'Suits me.'

'Wine, lager or water?'

'Lager, I think wine is wasted on a curry.'

He signalled to the waiter and gave him our order; the man bowed respectfully and headed off to the kitchen.

'Dan, I'm so impressed; this isn't your average curry house.'

He shrugged, 'Well, we're not average people, are we?'

'One of us certainly isn't, and he's not on this side of the table.'

We continued our small talk until the meal was set out. I did want to get down to business but took my cue from Dan and wasn't rushing things. I looked at the tableware, the silver service, the variety of Indian cuisine set before us and began to realise the gap between the haves and the have-nots.

'You know how to live, Dan.'

'We only get one shot at life, Craig; this isn't a rehearsal for another time.' He paused briefly before going on, choosing his words carefully, or so it seemed to me.

'Now, I know you came all this way to see an old mate, and I'm glad you did, but I suspect there's more to it than that. Am I right?' He eyed me closely, looking for my reaction, smiling when I nodded, confirming his assumption.

It was my turn to search for words; I wanted to get this right. 'You know what I aspire to, Dan; you know me better than anyone.'

He shook his head, genuine concern showing in his expression. 'You still want to operate on the wrong side of the line, Craig? I can't really advise you to go down that route; it's a high-risk environment.'

'You live in it, and you've done all right. Look at yourself. Your car, your clothes…this place, it all spells success. God knows what kind of flat you live in.'

'Maybe I've been lucky, but there are problems with this kind of life; it isn't all sunshine and roses, believe me.'

'Yeah, yeah, I can see that.' I made no attempt to conceal my sarcasm.

'Don't take it lightly, Craig, don't just brush off my advice; crime isn't a Sunday school picnic. Think about it carefully before you go down this road. I've got a flat, but I don't have a home. I work with people, but I have no real friends. I'm afraid to enter into a relationship in case I let my partner down; there have been no Sams in my life, ever. I have to get it right all the time. I've got the Justice system looking over my shoulder as and when it wants, and if I put a foot wrong, I'll be put away forever. Coppers don't like being outwitted, and they make bad enemies with long memories, believe me. Worse still, if I let my client down, and if his investment doesn't bear fruit, I might just end up floating in the Thames. Think about it; find another way of making your fortune. Now let's get back to our curry.'

I forced a smile, 'OK, I'll drop it.'

Dan raised an eyebrow; he wasn't totally convinced, but he relaxed and leaned back in his chair.

'I'll drop it till the coffee comes, then we'll talk some more. That's if it's all right with you?'

He gave me a look of resignation and shrugged. 'I didn't think you would give up that easily; just like a game of chess, I thought you would have an endgame.'

I breathed a little sigh of relief; at least he wasn't annoyed at my persistence.

For the next hour, we navigated our way through the exquisite Indian cuisine, looking back to our days at Westmoor, putting the world to rights, anything but crime. Finally, the meal was over; we leaned back replete, watching as coffee was poured. Mentally, I was rehearsing what I was going to say; I knew I'd only get one shot at this, and Dan Rawson was my gateway to the future I'd chosen.

I started by expressing my genuine feelings. 'Dan, no matter what, believe me, I would have come to London to see you; you were a good mate to me back there.'

'I don't need to be convinced, mate. I believe you, and whatever we say to each other tonight, I'd like to see you again before you leave London. Now, cut to the chase; you be straight, and so will I.'

'Well, first off, nothing you've said has changed my mind. I'd covered all the angles you've raised before I made my decision.'

He raised a disbelieving eyebrow, 'Really?'

'Well, not the Thames swimming lesson. That hadn't occurred to me.'

'It does happen, Craig; it's an occupational hazard.'

'It's still my choice, Dan.'

He pursed his lips, took a sip of coffee, then another. 'So, what do you want from me?'

'I'd like to work with you on a job; prove myself.'

He took another sip of coffee. 'That wouldn't be possible. How can I put it...I'm sort of retained, I guess you would say; I just can't open doors to any old acquaintance.'

'I'm not exactly unknown to you; fuck it, we lived together for three years.'

'Craig,' his voice took a harder edge, 'I'm trying to be gentle here; you've got to accept that you're a small-time operator with a track record of failure.'

Anger flared up in me instantly, 'I planned that job perfectly, carried it out perfectly; I did not fail.'

'Calm down and face the facts; you wouldn't have ended up in the nick if you hadn't failed. At the end of the day, you got caught because your judgement was faulty, and that's how my client would see it.'

'Your client needn't know that unless you tell him.'

Dan smiled ruefully, 'Once you're on his team, he'd make it his business to get to know everything there is to know about you. The people I deal with are meticulous; you're just not in this league.'

'I could play in any league given the chance, but it's your loss. However, I'm still looking for a favour from you for old times' sake.'

He nodded. 'I haven't forgotten that I owe you a favour. Just what are you looking for?'

'I've got sixty thousand to invest, and I need some contacts; I need an intro to your world. I'll put my money where my mouth is.'

Dan sighed, grimacing, searching for those how-do-I-tell-him words. 'Look, mate, I don't want to be hurtful; I know sixty grand is a tidy sum, but in this business, it wouldn't buy you a seat at the table. Setting up a job recruiting the right people costs big money, much more than sixty grand.

First and foremost, you've got to buy people you can trust; people who won't just take your cash up-front, pocket it, and walk away. They've got to be people who'll do exactly what you tell them, people who keep their mouths shut before, during, and after the event. Whatever the plan, you'll need information, and information is expensive. You'll need money upfront to source transport and equipment. Then you'll have to launder the loot, divide it up and hope you end up in profit.' He paused briefly, judging my reaction, waiting for my response. I didn't have one; he was right, and I knew it, but I said nothing.

'So how far do you think your money will go? I'll tell you; it'll buy some small-time thieves for a straightforward hit-and-run job, but it won't bring a big prize. It's a simple equation: big profit results from a big job, and they require big bucks up front. I'm sorry, Craig, but sixty grand just wouldn't be enough.'

I had one major card, one I hadn't wanted to play at this stage, but I was left with no alternative. 'I've got a big job in mind, a mega-job, but I can't do it without you.' I went on watching for a reaction, 'And it's bigger than anything you've ever done unless you did one that never made the papers.'

He was smiling, humouring me. 'I'm listening, Craig. What are you calling big?'

'Twenty million, maybe more.'

He whistled. 'Now I really am interested; tell me how I can get my hands on twenty million.'

'Another Great Train Robbery.' Disappointment cloaked his face; his eyes rolled upwards.

'Bear with me, Dan, please; they still transport used notes south from Scotland on a special train. There are fewer trains nowadays, and security has been tightened, but they carry ten times as much as they used to.'

'Forget it, Craig, it can't be done. We've already gone down that path; we know how much is involved, but the new security is too good. We can stop a train; that's easy, but it's the unloading time that's a problem. British Railways and the police work hand in hand each time a train runs; new rules operate now if a train makes an unscheduled stop. The area would be crawling with police within minutes. And we've heard rumours that there might even be a copper on some bridges along the route making sure the train goes through on time. It's an impossible task.'

'I'm impressed, Dan; everything you've said is true, but I've figured out a way round the security.'

'How come you know so much, Craig?'

'I worked in the railway before and after the robbery, and people are indiscreet; they say more than they should. It's the same in any organisation; people like to tell what they know. Over time, I picked up enough to figure out a way to beat the system.'

He sat there and stared at me for what felt like an eternity, his brain working overtime. A lifetime passed, but finally he spoke, quietly and deliberately. 'Prove to me that this scheme of yours can work, and I'll talk to my client.'

I was between a rock and a hard place; if I told him my plan, he could walk away with it. If I didn't tell him, he'd walk away anyway.

He read my thoughts, 'I know what you're thinking, Craig, but you've got to trust me.'

'You're asking me to trust you big time; this is all I've got.'

He shrugged, 'The choice is yours.'

I did trust Dan, but I didn't know those that he dealt with; in truth, though, I had no option, but I wasn't going to tell him everything.

'OK. I'll give you an outline, tell you how to deal with Rule Fifty-five of the Railway Operating Handbook and get away with it.'

He listened patiently as I went through my plan, asking questions and digesting answers. His eyes widening as he realised the possibilities.

'And that's about it, Dan; there are, of course, one or two little refinements I haven't offered up. I do trust you, but I don't know if I can trust your client, so I'm keeping a little bit of insurance.'

He nodded, smiling, 'You would be a fool not to; when my client says jump, I jump.'

'OK, put me out of my misery. Are you interested or not?'

'You know I am, and left to me I'd investigate further, but there are gaps to be filled, and this job will require a big investment. I'll have to discuss it with my client.'

'Definitely, but do you think your client will be interested?'

'Twenty million would interest anybody, though money isn't his sole motivation.'

'Meaning what exactly?'

'Now isn't the time for that kind of question.'

He looked around and signalled for the bill. 'I'm taking you back now, Craig; I've got some serious thinking to do.'

He didn't speak all the way back to the hotel, and even as he dropped me off just said, 'Sleep well; I'll be in touch when I have something to say, one way or the other.'

The Night Porter gave me my key, and I made my way slowly up the stairs to my room, reflecting on the evening; it was out of my hands now. I could only wait. The room was warm, the bed comfortable, but the combined effects of a late curry and a busy mind ensured that sleep didn't come easily.

I made my way down to a buffet breakfast next morning, still wearing the same clothes I had arrived in; I had showered and shaved, but I still felt grubby. It was time to purchase some new gear and see something of London. Selfridges would be my first stop; I had the cash, and I wanted good quality gear. I spent the morning in the store, feeling better and better as I transformed myself from scruff to toff. It was also pleasing to observe the respect that followed when you paid cash. I wondered if the day would come when they would ask, '*Shall I put it on your account, sir?*'

There was no news from Dan when I got back to the hotel, so I had time to kill and used some of it to answer my hunger pangs. Then, with nothing else to do, I decided to do the tourist thing and check out Tower Bridge and the Tower of London, two monumental icons that had always seemed to me to be the very essence of London. The sun was shining happily in the blue sky as I stepped out of the hotel and convinced me that I should walk the three or so miles along the Thames to my destination. The Tower thronged with visitors and was much more extensive than I anticipated, but I explored most of it. That done, footsore as I was, I walked back along the other side of the river, and it was six o'clock when I checked in with Reception.

'Do you have any messages for me, Murray, Room 218?'

The polite, somewhat effete young man looked behind him then shook his head. 'Sorry, sir.'

I felt disappointed and showed it.

'If one comes in, I'll see you get it right away, sir.'

'Thank you. If I'm not in my room, I'll probably be in the dining room having dinner.'

He nodded and scribbled something down on a pad.

The meal was pleasant, but I never quite found dining alone satisfying. For me, all my best meals had been in the company of a pretty woman. I promised myself that tomorrow night, I'd engage an escort, one that was totally accommodating. The remainder of the evening was spent watching television in my room, glancing at my watch a hundred times, waiting for a call that never came. Disappointment turned to concern. Concern turned to despair; Dan had failed me. Then optimism emerged from my gloom; he hadn't let me down at all. Mr Big was hard to contact, that was what the problem was. I was tired but doubted I would sleep soundly, so I downed a couple of whiskies from the mini bar just to help things along. Scotland's ubiquitous spirit did its stuff, and next thing I knew, it was morning, and my bedside telephone was buzzing. I grabbed at it, 'Craig Murray.'

'It's Dan with your not-so-early morning call.'

My spirits lifted instantly, 'What have you got for me? Is it a goer?'

'Meet me in St James Park on the Birdcage walk side at ten-thirty and don't be late.'

I pressed him for an answer. 'What's the scene, Dan?'

To my annoyance, he totally ignored me. 'See you at ten thirty.' He rang off, leaving me frustrated but hopeful.

A NEW LIFE BECKONS

Chapter Eleven

The young woman in Reception told me that St James Park lay just beyond Green Park, not much more than a ten-minute walk. It was coming up to 10-15am when I left the hotel; the weather was holding up, and a glance at the sky confirmed that another sunny day lay ahead. Early September, and the parks were still looking their best; trees in full leaf, flower and shrub beds alive with colour. I strode out, determined not to be late, punctuality and timing had always been important to me.

The Mall was quiet as I left Green Park and made my way around the pond in St James Park towards Birdcage Walk. There was the usual presence of tourists, chattering loudly and taking masses of photographs, most of which they'd probably bin when they got home. I walked the full extent of the park and back again, but there was no sign of Dan; it was still five minutes short of the half-hour, so I carried on strolling, trying to keep Birdcage walk in view. Just two minutes later, he came into view, saw me and waved, then waited for a lull in the traffic before crossing the road.

He looked serious and wasn't smiling. I was worried, but I tried to sound casual. 'No car today, Dan?'

'Easier to travel by Tube this time of day, and anyway, parking is horrendous in this area.' I could see he was appraising my new gear and approving it. 'Looks like you've had an upgrade. Pity about the hairstyle.'

'It'll grow, Dan, give it time. Well? I looked at him expectantly, 'Don't fuck about, let's have it.'

He wasn't going to be hustled. 'Let's take the weight off our feet.' He motioned to the nearest park bench; I checked it out for bird droppings, but he didn't seem to care. 'It's not been easy getting a hold of my client; he's always busy and not amenable to unscheduled contact, but eventually, I did get through to him, and when I told him what was on the agenda, he agreed to see me this morning. I've just come from him.'

'Great, that's great.' I couldn't stop myself from punching the air. 'He's interested, I knew he would be.'

'Hold it, Craig, don't get too carried away. It's not all plain sailing; I have good tidings and some not-so-good tidings. Good news first; he's very interested in the train robbery scheme, and if we can fill in the fine details, I think he might give it the go-ahead.'

I felt like giving Dan a hug but restrained myself. 'So where do we go from here? We've got loads of work to do.'

'Slow down, Craig; listen up to the not-so-good news

'Doesn't matter about that, it's game on.'

'You haven't got a green light, Craig; you won't been invited to join the team until you've proved yourself.'

I felt my adrenaline rush go into reverse, and the worry bug set to work. 'Meaning what exactly?'

'He wants your abilities tested on another scheme he's had his eye on.'

I relaxed again. 'No problem, I'm more than happy to prove my credentials; lead me to it. What's the target, what's the time frame?'

'I'll come to that in due course, but first, some news you won't like.'

I steeled myself for whatever was coming. 'Go on.' I felt tension take me in its grip and felt my mouth go dry.

'Put simply, you're only invited in if you take part in the job itself.'

I reacted instantly; this was a real no-no, totally opposed to what I'd promised myself. 'No way, Dan, you know that I won't involve myself directly; I just want to be a planner. I made that clear when we were banged up together.'

'You can walk away, Craig; it's your choice, but before you do, consider this. My client doesn't know you, and there's no reason why he should trust you. The only way he's going to let you in on his set-up is to test you. I can't see any other option open to him; you don't have any worthwhile history he can check out, quite the reverse, one job, one failure. You have until six tonight to think about it. There's nothing else I can say.'

I didn't need any time to think about it; I could see that the guy had a point. The facts weren't going to change in the next six hours; it was just a matter of how much I wanted to get on board, and there was nothing I wanted more.

'OK, you win.'

'It's not a matter of winning, as you put it, Craig, it's entirely your decision. You can still change your mind and opt out.'

I shook my head. 'I'm in.'

'Welcome to the team.' I was surprised when he offered me his hand, but I shook it anyway. 'It'll be like old times.'

'I suppose you'll be reporting back to your client now; I can't imagine I'll get to meet him?'

'No chance; I'm the only one he'll deal with; there's no need for you to meet him.'

I wondered what would happen if Dan got run over by a bus. But I knew better than to pose the question. 'So out with it, what's the job?'

'I'll brief you on that when you move in with me; you can check out of the hotel today.'

The idea didn't appeal to me; I valued my independence too much. 'I'm going to sound ungrateful, Dan, but I don't want to move in with you; I want my own place.'

'Don't panic. I'm not looking for a houseguest; it's purely a temporary arrangement until you settle down in London.'

Then it dawned on me. 'It's a requirement of your fucking Mr Big, isn't it? You've been told to keep an eye on me.'

'Your words, not mine.'

I was rapidly developing a dislike for Dan's client, but on the other hand, perhaps being cautious had brought him success.

'OK, I'll comply with the Big Man's orders, but not tonight, which brings me to two bits of advice I want from you.'

Dan had listened to me tight-lipped, and I could see he had something to say. 'Before we go on to that, here's a word of warning. It's best to be respectful about my client and learn to take orders with good grace; do that, and you might fit into his set-up. Now fire away with your questions.'

I nodded curtly; taking orders had never been my best attribute. 'I want some guidance as to where I should rent a flat; nice area, not too expensive.'

'I'll let you have details tomorrow. We should have some flats on our portfolio you can choose from; they're all legit and for you, bottom dollar. Next question?'

I wondered who the 'we' was that he was referring to, but I buried my curiosity. 'Reason I don't want to move in with you tonight is that I don't fancy you.' It was his turn to get worried.

'Only kidding, I think you're wonderful. Truth is, I want to spend tonight with a woman, and I wouldn't want you in the next bedroom. And that's where your advice comes in; I wouldn't have a clue where to look for a quality skirt.'

'No problem, leave it with me, and she'll be with you tonight. Shall we say eight o'clock, leaving at….?

'I want her there in the morning; she can join me for breakfast.'

'Not recommended; she'll leave when you go to breakfast. By the way, look on this encounter as my treat.'

'Won't say no; it'll be the best present I've ever had.'

'You'll have to leave the choice to me; it's short notice.'

'Frankly, I don't care as long as she has all the necessary attributes.'

Our meeting was at an end; he stood up, ready to go. 'Right, that concludes our business. Join me at my flat tomorrow after breakfast, say ten and try not to be too fatigued.' He handed me a card with his address.

I watched as he walked away, my thoughts racing; I knew very little about what I was getting into. But whatever, it hadn't done Dan any harm. In any event, the time for talking and dreaming was over; I had talked big, and now I had to deliver. My evening was taken care of, but a longish day lay ahead, and I decided to be a tourist again. I returned to the Tower of London and built on yesterday's introduction to history.

A few minutes before eight, I heard a light tap on the door; I was there in an instant. *Don't be too eager, Craig.* I sneaked a preview of my companion through the door peephole, not that I was bothered what she looked like; at that moment, any woman would have satisfied my need. First impressions were favourable; I could see that Dan had remembered that I favoured blondes, given my near worship of Sam. I opened the door, not sure what I was going to say. I needn't have worried. She greeted me with a smile and walked straight in like she had known me all my life.

'Hi, I'm Gail. Dan arranged for me to visit you.'

She had long blonde hair that flowed halfway down her back and light blue eyes that were giving me the once-over. *It must be tough for you, dear; you're stuck with Craig whether you fancy him or not.*

Her make-up was straight out of a magazine, overdone for my taste, but she was very attractive. She dressed expensively: white low-cut silk blouse and a pale blue cashmere suit that matched the colour of her eyes. Her mini skirt was short, very short.

'Come in, Gail. I bet you turned a few heads when you walked through reception.'

A well-practised smile acknowledged the compliment. 'Can't say I noticed.'

She looked round the room, her eyes lighting on the bed. 'It looks like we're going to be very comfortable.' She turned her attention back to me, seemingly waiting for me to say something, probably accustomed to men who planned their evening's entertainment. 'So how do you want to play this?' A smile flickered at the edge of her lips, her eyes widening with expectation.

Inside, I was floundering; I had never bought sex before. I knew my destination, but it was the route to get there I wasn't clear on. 'I thought we might begin by sharing a bottle of champagne, and you could tell me about yourself.'

Gail nodded appreciatively. 'Sounds good to me, bubbly is my favourite tipple.'

She turned towards the sofa, but I reached out, catching her arm, pulling her towards me. I needed that first kiss, needed to press her body to mine and release the head of steam that was building up inside me. She knew how to kiss, that was for sure; knew too how much of her body to give without seeming cheap. I broke free and took a deep breath to calm my emotions. 'Just testing; it's been a long time.'

She smiled as though she understood; perhaps Dan had briefed her about my enforced celibacy over the last three and a half years. But she made no comment, just turned away and plonked herself onto the sofa, making no attempt to smooth down her skirt, which had ridden up to tantalising heights. She caught me taking in the view and smiled; it was a smile that oozed confidence. For some reason, I felt like an embarrassed schoolboy, and I turned away quickly to pop the cork and pour some champagne. I swore inwardly to myself, admonishing my guilty feelings. *Fuck it, Craig, she's here to be looked at and shagged; she's not some reluctant virgin you're trying to bed.*

She leaned forward and clinked her glass against mine. 'To a good time.'

'To a good time.' I echoed her. 'Tell me about yourself, Gail.'

133

'Not much to tell, really, and to be honest, I don't give out much personal information.'

'How's about where you're from, what age you are, that kind of thing?'

'I'm a Londoner. I have a place in South Kensington. I'm 26 and, just in case you're wondering, I'm 36-22-36; that's what you're really interested in.'

I smiled and nodded. 'Got me in one. I'll test the cup size later. Is this your full-time occupation?'

'Sure is. I wasn't very academic at school, so I went down the beautician path, worked in Harrods for a couple of years.'

'And how long have you been in this game; what got you in?'

Gail frowned. 'It's not a game; it's my profession, and I'm good at it. Men, usually middle-aged and rich, were forever chatting me up for a date; most of them wanting sex and off home to the old lady afterwards. So, I decided to make them pay for it. It's been my life since I was 21.'

'Got a boyfriend?'

'Nope, it would complicate things. By the time I'm thirty, I'll own my flat and have a good bank balance; maybe then I'll look round for a partner. Who knows, I might start a new life abroad somewhere. Now that's enough of me, how's about another glass of that delicious champagne?' She ran her hand along my thigh. 'I've answered enough questions; let's enjoy the night; not many of my clients are young, virile and handsome.'

In my heart, I wanted her to be Sam, wanted to make love, but love wasn't on the agenda; it was just good old-fashioned sex. We had sex four times before midnight, then I'd had enough. 'I'm tired, Gail, time to go sleepies.'

If she was tired, she didn't sound it. 'As they say, you're in the driving seat, Craig, whatever you say goes.'

'Be there for me when I wake up.'

'You've got me until eight, lover boy.'

It was twenty past seven when I woke with a start, panicking, wondering what time it was. Gail was awake, propped up on her pillow, studying me as I rubbed the sleep out of my eyes.

'You look very peaceful when you're asleep.'

'How long have you been awake?'

''Long enough; I've had a shower, tidied up and made myself comfortable.'

'Talking of which.' I made to get up. 'Don't go away. I'll be back for one last curtain call.'

She smiled amiably, 'I expected as much. Do me a favour and have a shave while you're in there; I don't want you messing up my chin.'

We had sex one more time; it was good for me, but she was on autopilot; afterwards, she just slid out of bed and disappeared into the bathroom, emerging ten minutes later with every hair in place and make-up fully restored. I watched as she retrieved her clothes from where I'd thrown them the night before.

When she finished dressing, she bent over and kissed me on the forehead. 'I enjoyed our night; maybe we'll get together again. I go with quite an ache.'

'That'll be your heart, will it?'

'No, Craig, not my heart.' She grinned and, with that, turned and walked towards the door, hips swaying gently. She turned when she got there and waved. 'Bye.' Then she was gone.

I lay there for a while, thinking I'd had enough sex to last me for the rest of the year, but I knew I was only kidding myself.

After breakfast, I settled my bill and stood outside the hotel waiting for my taxi, reflecting that this was the first day of my new life. I looked up at the sky; dark clouds were gathering. I hoped they weren't an omen. My taxi pulled up, and I climbed in.

'6 Wolverton Mews, Swiss cottage, please.'

'Nice area, guvnor not much more than ten minutes away if the traffic's kind to us.'

The row of terraced cottages that made up Wolverton Mews looked like they might have featured in a Dickens novel. Each represented a small fortune by any standard; there wasn't a garage in sight, and I wondered what they did about their cars. I pressed the buzzer on the intercom, and Dan's tinny disembodied voice answered almost immediately.

'Who is it?'

'Have a wild guess.'

The door opened seconds later, and Dan welcomed me in.

'Dump your bag there for the moment and follow me.'

The wall of the small hall was a mass of paintings, and these continued up the staircase to the first floor. We turned right into a spacious lounge; it, too, had its fair share of paintings in addition to the various bronzes and ornaments displayed on small tables and pedestals. Dan was clearly a collector with a modernist taste if my very limited knowledge of such matters was correct. The lounge was furnished with what I knew as Scandinavian-style furniture, comfortable but formal. Everywhere was pristine; there wasn't even a casually discarded newspaper to be seen.

I whistled appreciatively. 'Nice place, Dan, I'm envious. What have you got upstairs?'

'Two bedrooms, both with a bathroom, nothing remarkable. The kitchen-diner is at the end of the hall. I'm not giving you a tour; you'll see it all later; we've got things to do. By the way, how did you find Gail?'

'Fantastic, she knows how to please a guy, doesn't she?'

'Wouldn't know.'

'Really?' I showed my surprise and waited for an answer.

'Doesn't interest me, Craig, let's change the subject.'

'Sure, no problem.'

I began to wonder about his sexuality. There had been no advances made in prison, but perhaps he had a partner tucked away somewhere. *Christ, maybe he just didn't like sex.* I made a mental note to find out another time, though really it was none of my business.

'I've got three flats you can look at. All with a single bedroom and a separate bathroom, open-plan lounge, diner, and kitchen. They're decorated and nicely furnished and all fairly near a Tube station. You can move in when you're ready. The rent will be low by London standards, and I'll be your landlord.'

It all sounded too good to be true. 'Just what I'm looking for; where are they located and bear in mind, I don't know London?'

'Willesden, Highbury, and Finsbury Park; none of them is more than a few miles from here. It's too expensive to get much closer to the centre, and the good thing is, they all readily connect by Tube to where you'll be working.'

My ears pricked up instantly, 'And where will that be?'

Dan shook his head. 'You'll see soon enough; let's get your flat sorted out before we do anything else.'

'Leave Finsbury Park to the last; I like the sound of it.'

I followed Dan through the hall and out a door into the garage, which I now realised lay behind the property.

The Morgan sat there, gleaming; a real gem. 'Not the Roller then?'

'Garage isn't really big enough.'

He triggered his remote, the garage door slowly lifted, and out the Morgan nosed out.

'You never fail to impress Dan, I'm envious.'

He just shrugged. 'Your turn will come; if you're a good boy, that is.'

I took his last remark as another warning.

Dan seemed to know London as well as any of their famed taxi drivers as he took a succession of traffic-avoiding shortcuts down lanes and back streets to the Highbury flat.

Willesden followed, and then finally, Finsbury Park. Internally they were all exactly as he described and complete with carpeting and new contemporary furnishing. I suppose I should have felt excited. It was the first place I'd ever had to myself, but somehow, renting didn't fire me up in the same way as ownership. I felt ungrateful and told myself that I was lucky to have such a good choice. I didn't dither, although any one of the three would have been acceptable.

'I'll have this one.'

Dan just shrugged, and I wondered if I'd made a wrong choice. 'It's entirely up to you.'

'I like the view over the park.' I wandered over to the window. 'I assume that that is Finsbury Park?'

He nodded, 'Yeah.'

We were on the third floor of a post-war brick-built block of flats; I was in flat 12 of 15, going by the number of mailboxes and the entry control system. A central lift and staircase served the upper floors and there was garage parking in the basement, not that I had a car. Being on the top floor appealed to me; it put maximum distance between me and the traffic noise.

'It's perfect, Dan, know anything about the neighbours?'

He shook his head, 'I expect they'll be the usual assortment; hopefully, none of them too noisy. You'll have to come up with a background as to how you came to arrive in London and that kind of thing; somebody is bound to ask you sooner or later.'

'I want to discuss that with you tonight.'

'That's settled then; move in when you want.' He handed me the keys. 'You'll need to get the telephone re-connected, sooner the better. Now let's go for a light lunch.'

Ten minutes later, following another mazy run, Dan wheeled into a small car park. The welcoming sign said 'Customers Only. Unauthorised vehicles WILL be towed away.' I said nothing; Dan could read and make his own decisions about parking violations. He must have sensed my unease and explained. 'I know the owner.'

We made the short walk to the main drag, and a few minutes later, he surprised me by walking into a small sandwich bar called 'Crazy Dave's'. I had been expecting a jazzy French bistro, judging by Dan's standards.

'This seems modest for you, Dan?'

He smiled broadly. 'You should be pleased then; you're paying for this one.'

'Cheap and cheerful suits me.'

We made our choices and sat down to wait whilst the owner, a tall, lanky guy in his sixties wearing a Sioux headdress, made up our order. Dan shook his head when he saw my look of surprise. 'Don't ask; he's a nutter, thinks he's a re-incarnated Indian chief.'

'Fill me in, Dan. What is our mission?'

He gave me a warning scowl. 'Not here, talk about football or last night's shag; keep work for the office.'

'Christ, you are a cautious bugger. I wasn't expecting a detailed run down; some shorthand would suffice. Don't forget I'm completely in the dark.'

He glared at me. 'Did you see the Arsenal game?'

I got the message, and we chatted idly for the next fifteen minutes. It wouldn't be easy, but I could see that I was going to have to get used to Dan's ways and live by his set of rules if we were to remain on good terms.

Outside again, I looked for a street name to identify where we were, and it wasn't long before I saw that we were on Camden Road. Dan led the way and surprised me again by turning into Camden Art Gallery. *Christ, didn't he have enough paintings?* I looked round the walls; every conceivable genre seemed to be on display.

A tubby, pig-tailed, flamboyantly dressed middle-aged man, presumably the owner, made his way forward.

'Mr Rawson, how nice to see you again.' He reached for Dan's hand and shook it warmly. 'And what can we do for you today?'

'Henry, let me introduce Craig Murray, a friend of mine who has an interest in art.'

Henry peered into my face. 'Pleased to meet you, Mr Murray. Might I enquire what kind of art interests you?'

'15th and 16th century bronzes and figurines; you know the kind of thing. As for paintings, I'm rather fond of the Impressionists, albeit I don't own any.'

Dan raised an eyebrow at this revelation, and Henry beamed.

'We'll have to see what we can do for you.'

'Look forward to it, Henry.'

Dan stifled a smile at my deception and tried to look serious.

'I'm looking for a good landscape, Henry, something English, I think.'

'Straight through to the next gallery, Mr Rawson, I'm sure you'll find something in there.'

Dan walked briskly over to an open door to his right, with me close behind. The gallery was just a smaller version of what we'd just left. Paintings of all sizes and descriptions covered the walls from top to bottom; others stood on the floor. I heard a noise behind me and looked round to see Henry closing the door; an audible snick suggested he'd locked us in. I was about to query this with Dan, but he beat me to it.

'It's OK, Henry's with us. Watch me.'

He drew me over to a door in the corner, 'Now watch carefully.' Reaching forward to a portrait, he pushed up a small adornment on the top of the frame and swung the painting towards him. Behind, recessed into the wall, was a small keypad into which he entered some numbers. 'Right, now you enter a four-digit code you'll remember, and don't show me.'

I chose 1066, the date of the Battle of Hastings, and stood back. Dan then entered some further numbers. 'That's it, you're now authorised. I'm the only one who can issue codes, and from now on, every time you come here, the time will be recorded, as it will when you leave. Understand?'

I was beginning to feel like an MI5 operative and starting to wonder what I'd let myself in for. 'Sure, can't wait to see what's in there.'

'Each time you come to the gallery, you'll tell Henry that you're interested in something or other, and he'll show you through. I'll show you how to get out later. Now punch your number in, and I'll introduce you to our planning set-up.'

I did as I was told, and the door swung open.

'Before you enter the room, swing the painting back into position and return the release to its position in the frame. If you don't, the door won't close. OK?'

I nodded, inwardly quite excited as we entered the room; for the first time, I felt like I was on the team. I took in the scene before me and was disappointed; it all seemed so ordinary.

The room was about twenty feet long and twelve feet wide, carpeted, no windows, a door on my left. An unremarkable boardroom table attended by ten chairs was placed centrally. There was a long worktop to my right with an in-built sink at one end and a cupboard above; I guessed this contained whatever serviced the lonely-looking electric kettle beneath. At the other end of the worktop, there was a television, a screen, a small film projector, a slide projector, an overhead projector and an electrical appliance I wasn't familiar with. Most of the remaining floor space was taken up with cupboards and plan chests. Dan stood beside me, patiently watching me appraise the layout.

'Seems to be well equipped.' I remarked amiably, knowing some comment was expected. 'I look forward to getting started.'

'A word about our house rules before we start. Anything you bring in to help the plan stays here; you never take anything out without my say-so. All your work is to be done here so that nothing can ever be found in your flat. Understood?'

I nodded agreeably; caution was clearly Dan's watchword. 'Sounds very sensible.'

'You leave the place as you find it, tidy with everything back in place, no dirty cups left lying around. The room has been soundproofed so it's safe to talk freely. If you're ready, I'll show you how everything works.'

'You can skip the kettle; I'll work that out for myself.' I replied jokingly.

Dan gave one of his weak smiles and walked over to the electrical equipment. 'I assume you have some knowledge of this gear?'

'I'm OK with television, slides and overheads, but just run through the film projector for me. I've used one before, but not this model.'

The projector demo was over. I pointed to the remaining appliance. 'You'll have to go step by step with that one; I don't even know what it is.'

Dan was clearly proud of this particular toy. 'It's the very latest. There aren't many around yet, but it's going to be big; over the next few years, everybody will have one. It's a video recorder; it plays through the television and uses cassettes instead of the reels a projector uses. In fact, we've transferred a lot of our film footage onto cassettes.' He went over to one of the storage cupboards; it was lined with shelves and housed at least a hundred cassettes. 'You should find everything you need in here; the boxes are all labelled and dated.' He took out a box at random, removed a cassette, switched on the gizmo and showed me how to insert it into the machine. 'OK? Now switch on the TV and press 'play' on the video.'

I did as I was instructed and watched as a large brick building slowly filled the screen; after a few seconds, two men could be seen approaching a door, one of them pressed a button on the wall. At that point, Dan pressed the stop button and then the rewind. 'Make sure you always rewind before putting the cassette back and keep them all in order. Now you try it again from the beginning.'

I repeated the process and completed the routine by filing away the cassette.

'Impressive, Dan, very impressive; it's much easier than running a projector. Now that I'm up to speed with the equipment, it's about time you told me what the target is.'

He went over to the planning chest and pulled out a large street map then spread it out on the table. 'This is it.' He pointed to an area outlined in red, 'PMR Ltd, Precious Metals Reclamation Limited. The payload will be around three million if we time it right. This company is one of a few of its kind in the UK; it recovers gold, silver, and platinum, mainly from jewellery, and melts it down to produce ingots. Once processed, the ingots are held on-site in a strongroom. When they've got enough, it's sold on the market. We already have the combinations to the three locks that secure the strongroom.'

'How did you manage that?'

'The usual way, good contacts, and lots of money; or, if it proves necessary, blackmail. It's not something you need to know. My client has his own connections.'

'Sorry, just curious. So, what exactly do you want me to do?'

'I want you to get us in and out without being noticed. In addition to the usual alarms connected to John Law, they have a round-the-clock link to a private security company, with a guaranteed response within five minutes, which doesn't give us enough time to load the ingots. We have film of an exercise carried out to test the system, and it worked well on the day; the response team attended in four minutes. There's an abundance of detail about the company, plant layout, construction details, security, etc in the files. Believe me, you've got a tough task ahead of you; I haven't been able to crack it so far.'

'When do I get to see the place?'

'Agree that with me first, I don't want you or anyone on the team going near there until necessary. For the moment, this is your workplace; plan it all from here and report to me as and when you need to.'

I was beginning to see how Dan wanted to handle this; I wasn't his cellmate now, not even his partner; he was my employer. He was my boss, and I was there to do what I was told. It wasn't the time to challenge his perceptions, so I gave him the answer he was looking for. 'Will do, sir, no problem. And I take it you'll introduce me to the rest of the team when you judge it to be appropriate?'

He nodded appreciatively and grinned, noting my deference.

'You're learning, Craig.'

For my part, I was learning; learning that I didn't much like being bossed around, though there was nothing I could do about it. *For now, that is.*

Dan glanced at his watch and drew the proceedings to an end.

'I'm going elsewhere now; you can make a start. Come and go as you like; you've got three weeks to come up with a workable plan.'

'And if I don't?'

His expression hardened, 'I don't even want to think about that eventuality.'

'And if I do?'

'I report back to my client, and if he likes what he hears, we'll get the go-ahead. Then you'll get to meet the team.'

'OK, got the picture.'

'And don't forget, Craig, you'll be taking part in this job if it gets the go-ahead. When you want to leave or take a break, use that door over there.

Just punch in your code; the door opens and closes automatically but check that it is secure.'

'You're not coming back for me then?'

'Nope, you've got to get used to public transport or get a car; I won't always be able to run you around and, to be honest, wouldn't want to. Here's a key to my flat; let yourself in if I'm not around. Good luck.' With that, he was off, leaving me to familiarise myself with the PMR set-up. Three weeks, Christ, I hope that's long enough.

I wanted some space and freedom to do what I wanted when I wanted; I decided that I'd only spend one more night at Dan's. After that, I would move to my own place at Finsbury Park, provided, of course, he'd let me, and there were some matters I needed to resolve with him before I got further involved.

Chapter Twelve

For the next three hours, I studied plans, trying to get a feel for PMR. It was eye-straining, repetitive work, but I didn't mind; I was excited and felt I was on the verge of something big. Towards the end of the session, however, I was beginning to realise the extent of the challenge; the place was a veritable fortress.

The site perimeter was secured by a fifteen feet high brick wall, four bricks wide to resist impact damage. The single entrance for transport and employees was under the watchful eye of the firm's security staff. Inside their cabin, there was a series of screens serving a closed-circuit television system covering the entire external perimeter. On top of that, the security man himself was the subject of a televised transmission to a rapid response security service. Any unexplained absence or action involving him would result in the Response Unit being activated.

Inside the perimeter wall, the site could be divided into four distinct sectors: office accommodation outer left, strong-room centre left, processing plant centre right and beyond that, a large boiler house serving the site and a local district heating scheme. At first sight the access point seemed the most vulnerable point in the perimeter, but it just led into a narrow yard at either end of which was a massive steel gate. These were under the control of the security guard. Only one gate could be opened at a time; in effect, it operated like a giant airlock; every worker and every vehicle would be stopped in this yard for an inspection and identity check.

The walls could be scaled easily enough, but they were under closed-circuit surveillance. A tunnelling job would be slow and fraught with risk from the twin threats of discovery and underground obstructions. Finally, there was the little matter of retrieving, loading and removing the ingots.

There was a myriad of roads leading to and from PMR, but my knowledge of London was poor, so Dan or some other member of the team would have to advise the best routes in and out. I made a note to ask Dan about just how far my responsibilities for the plan went. By the time I had absorbed what the plans had to offer, my stomach was in complaint mode. In any case, it was half past six and time to go back to Dan's; I felt I'd made a reasonable start, though I hadn't come up with any bright ideas for the robbery itself. Tomorrow, hopefully, I'd be visited by a flash of inspiration, but for now, it was time to experience London's Underground in the middle of the rush hour.

Dan was there when I got back and greeted me cheerfully. 'Welcome back, Mr Planner. A glass of wine? I hope you haven't eaten. I've ordered us a couple of pizzas; they'll arrive in,' he glanced at his watch 'fifteen minutes.'

'Sounds great to me. I'm starving; it's been a long afternoon.'

'How's it gone?'

'Alright I suppose, it's certainly not an easy one; there's no light at the end of the tunnel that I can see.'

Dan pursed his lips and offered comfort of a kind. 'It's early days, and if it had been easy, we would have rattled its cage by now. I spent ages on it and came up with zilch.'

I felt my gut tighten. 'Am I being set up to fail, Dan? Is this an impossible task?'

'No way, Craig, everything is possible; I didn't expect you to come up with an answer this early. This is a great opportunity. Crack this one, and your standing will skyrocket with my client, and better still, I'll earn lots of brownie points.'

'Great.' I put some sarcasm into my tone. 'Surely there must be easier targets around? This one is fiendish, and your client can't be short of a dosh.'

'Craig,' Dan wagged his finger and put on his schoolmaster tone, 'the job isn't always about money; my man's got more than he can ever spend.'

'Why then?'

'He just likes trying to beat the system for the sheer hell of it. The tougher the problem, the more he enjoys cracking it. Let's drop it, I might have said more than I should. Just do your job and leave the target selection to me.'

The caution and secrecy grated on me, and I let my irritation show. 'Sorree, very fucking sorree, I can't help asking questions; it's only natural.

And there will always be things I need to clarify if you want me to deliver on this ball-breaker of a job.'

Dan tried to mollify me, unsuccessfully as far as I was concerned. 'I guess so, and I'll answer where I can, but sometimes there's no room for debate; try to recognise those times.'

Before I could comment, the buzzer sounded.

'That'll be the pizzas; I'll get them, and maybe you could set up the table.'

Meal over, we settled down with a coffee, and Dan got down to business.

'Going back to earlier on, you mentioned that some 'things' require clarification?'

I nodded. 'Easy one first; I'd like to move into Finsbury Park tomorrow.'

He looked at me enquiringly, and I felt the need to offer some explanation.

'Essentially, there is no easy Tube connection between here and Camden. Travel is a nightmare, and I don't want to keep spending out on taxis.'

'Fair enough, you've got the key, you move in tomorrow. Next?'

'I want to set myself up with a bank account and be able to behave like a regular citizen. You know, rent a telephone, hire a car, etc.'

He shrugged. 'So, go ahead, what's stopping you?'

'I'll need references.'

'No problem, I can arrange that.'

'And I was thinking of something more radical.'

He looked at me warily. 'Meaning?'

'I've got a criminal record, and I've still got sixty grand that doesn't belong to me.'

'So, I can't see where you're headed; those are inescapable facts.'

'I want to stop being Craig Murray; I want to change my identity. If I open a bank account in that name, I bet it'll trigger some sort of alert.'

'They'll still have your fingerprints and mug shot on record no matter what you call yourself.'

'True, but they only cause problems if I get caught. I just want to have the kind of identification that's needed for a normal life.'

Dan went into deep thought mode and seemed to be taking ages; I could feel my patience draining away, but finally, he nodded.

'It can be done, Craig, but it'll set you back quite a lump.'

'Cost isn't an issue. How much?'

'Five grand, last time I used the service.'

I inhaled sharply; it was much more than I had anticipated. 'And for that, I'd get a birth certificate and a driving license?'

'And a passport'

'I haven't got a passport now.'

'It comes as part of the package, and you'll need one sooner or later. You'll need to pay upfront, and I'll do the rest.'

'Great, just one thing; I'm happy to have Craig as my first name; it would probably be easier.'

He shook his head. 'Sorry, can't promise that; there are constraints on what identity we can pick up on, especially with the birth certificate. I'll need to know your year of birth, though, to get a credible match. Let me have the money before you leave in the morning.'

'First of all, at five grand, I don't want to be older if I can help it, and I guess you'll need a photograph for the passport.'

To my surprise, he smiled, shaking his head. 'We've already got photographs.'

'But how?'

'That's my little secret. Now, are there any other clarifications?'

'Two more; first, how far do I go with the plan? For example, transport, acquisitions.'

'You're not involved with either of those; it's your job to tell us how to get in and out; others will do the rest.'

'That's great news, which brings me neatly to asking what prize can I expect when I produce this plan? And I don't just mean membership of the club; I'm talking about my cut.'

'I thought you would never ask. You get one-third of whatever I get.'

'Which is?'

'I get twenty per cent of the take after setting-up expenses have been deducted. Obviously, the more involved it is setting the job up, the more expenses there are and the less there is to go round. A word of warning, Craig: don't cut corners. Success brings reward; failure could be punished rather severely.'

I took his warning seriously and pressed him further. 'Have you ever failed Dan?'

'Nope, but I've seen what happens to those who do. Let's leave that side of things. Was that your last 'clarification'?

I pondered on asking how come he ended up in gaol with a one hundred per cent success rate but thought better of it and shook my head. 'I guess that's it for now.'

Next morning, after breakfast, I counted out five grand and handed it over to Dan, then gathered my gear ready for departure. Dan agreed to drop me off at Finsbury Park but said he wouldn't hang around whilst I installed my things in the flat. That suited me; it would give me the opportunity to experience the Tube when I went to Camden later that day. During the drive, I thought I'd try one more question and risk Dan's ire. 'What about you, Dan? Are you working on anything at the moment?

He didn't even take his eyes off the road. 'You're being nosy again, Craig.' He sighed just to give emphasis to his reply.

I raised my hands in mock protest, 'Sorree, sorree, naughty Craig, smack wrist.'

'By the way, you'll have to sign a rental agreement; I have a copy for both of us.'

'No problem, but I'm surprised you bother with such a formality.'

'It's the way we operate.'

'I wouldn't dream of asking why.' A thought occurred to me. 'Perhaps it should wait until we've sorted out my new ID, get the name right?'

'Fair point; it'll keep till then.'

'When should I be in touch?'

'Anytime you need to; otherwise, I look forward to hearing from you at the end of the month, when, hopefully, you will have cracked the PMR job. I'll keep the evening free in my diary.'

Determined to do what I could to maintain the level of fitness I'd built up in prison, I ignored the lift and climbed the stairs to my new home, Flat

12, Park View Mansion, Finsbury Park. *Maybe join a gym, Craig.'* As I opened the door for the first time, I had to acknowledge that it felt good to have my own place. I took a closer look at my draft rental agreement, which showed D.Rawson as my landlord. There was no mention of the owner, and I wanted to know who he was. I made a mental note to find out in the hope it might give a lead as to the identity of Mr Big. I was curious to know just who was pulling Dan's strings. There was work to be done, so I didn't hang around; I just dumped my bag and set out for the Tube Station. The morning rush was petering out, and the journey to Camden was uneventful.

The ever-enigmatic Henry greeted me as I entered the gallery and waved me through. 'There are some good impressionist-style paintings in the small gallery if you're interested, Mr Murray.'

I nodded cheerfully, 'I'll take a look later, Henry and please call me Craig.' I made a mental note that he was the only person, other than Dan, who knew me as Murray. Until I got my new name, I'd have to keep my head down back at the flat and avoid the other residents if possible.

Over the course of the next two weeks, the journey between Finsbury and Camden became indelibly etched in my mind, and Henry became a good friend. Every morning, seven days a week, I left the flat before seven and didn't return till around seven in the evening, always using the stairs to avoid awkward lift encounters. I'd seen a couple of the other residents but had managed to side-step introductions. PMR had my undivided attention every waking hour; it was with me when I went to bed and immediately in my thoughts when I woke up. I went through option after option, most of them ridiculous, but with one week to go I didn't even have the glimmer of a solution; I was beginning to think that my career as a planner of crime would be short-lived.

I watched hours and hours of film footage and reckoned I knew more about PMR's routines than any of its employees did. I studied dozens of drawings and learned all there was to know about the factory's layout and construction. I could find my way round its electrical systems and engineering services, but all this knowledge wasn't helping me to deal with the fundamental problem: how to get past the company's security arrangements. They were fundamentally simple but effective, very effective. Everyone, management, employees, and deliveries, had to enter and leave via the single entrance point to the site, the yard 'airlock' system. Each end of the yard had a huge, solid steel gate, and only one of these could be open at any moment in time. Cameras located around the perimeter wall provided continuous viewing of the exterior; everything was under the watchful eyes of the security guy, who, I had to assume, was diligent. *I'm fucking stumped; game over, Craig.*

Initially, I had concluded that the only way to get in and out without raising the alarm was to nobble the security guy, but PMR had that eventuality covered. I was coming to believe that I had been dealt an impossible hand and I entered the final week no further forward than when I started out. No wonder Dan and his mates hadn't cracked PMR; it couldn't be cracked. As I began my final week of deliberations, my enthusiasm had all but drained away and I was wearying of the routine I had fallen into. I was thoroughly fed up with the whole operation. Dan hadn't been in touch, and I hadn't contacted him; perhaps he felt he was best out of it. The excitement of planning a robbery had deserted me and left me with a hangover of frustration and a boring routine. Only five days were left to come up with some answers, or I'd be drummed out of Dan's set-up, and he'd walk away with my ideas for the second: The Great Train Robbery. Not that I had told him everything, but given time, he could fill in the gaps I'd left. *Fuck it, fuck it, I can't let that happen.*

Another day over, I let myself into the flat and popped another ready-made meal into the oven to cook whilst I had my bath. Another evening of television lay ahead; I was watching too much, but it helped to take my mind off PMR, which was fast becoming my Nemesis. By eleven, I was yawning, my eyes struggling to stay open. I was tired, but it seemed that getting into bed just served as a wake-up call, triggering my thinking processes into life again. I knew that I would lie there, going over the same old ground again and again, so I flicked through the channels, looking for something that might provide a distraction. There wasn't much of interest, but I settled on an old black and white British film, 'The Wooden Horse,' which transpired to be about a group of prisoners tunnelling out of a German POW camp. It held my attention, and when I eventually tumbled into bed, I slept soundly; soundly, that is, until four, when I was awakened by one of those inexplicable flashes of subconscious enlightenment. In that moment, I knew how to do the PMR job. Through the mystical workings of the mind the key to the PMR job had been presented to me on a plate.

I felt like phoning Dan right there and then, but caution tempered my exuberance; I needed to work out the detail and be able to answer all those difficult questions that would surely arise. Anyway, he had been quite clear that Friday was the day for unveiling my plan if I had one, so I was quite happy to let him sweat it out, wondering how I was getting on.

It was long past nine when I got to the gallery to be greeted by a worried-looking Henry. 'You're late today, Craig, everything OK? Had a heavy night?' He seemed genuinely concerned.

'Kind of Henry, the best night I've had in ages.'

'Sounds to me like you've been round the ladies, young man.'

I winked and touched my nose with a finger, humouring him. 'Say no more, Henry.'

The feeling of excitement that I'd lost returned, and I set to immediately by pulling out the PMR site plans. I needed to prove to myself that my plan really was workable, and by lunchtime, I knew I had a winner. There were still problems to be resolved, but these related to the execution of the plan, not the plan itself. Dan and his team would have to deal with those.

By the close of play on Tuesday, I had worked out every possible detail, listed every requirement and played out every scenario I could think of, but couldn't fault the concept. I wondered, though, how many designers decided their ideas were perfect only to have them demolished by those who had to turn their ideas into reality. I was confident that that wasn't going to happen to me.

I had three days to kill until Friday; it was time to become a tourist again, and I devoted the next three days to history and culture. Westminster Abbey, St Paul's Cathedral, the British Museum, the Natural History Museum, and a sight-seeing sail up the Thames to Greenwich, home of the National Maritime Museum. I wasn't a culture freak, but I enjoyed every moment of it. I also took Henry out for a five-star lunch as a sort of thank-you for his friendship and took the opportunity of telling him I was hoping to change my name. Ever the soul of discretion, a raised eyebrow was his only display of curiosity.

After lunch, I went through the plan yet again; I didn't really need to, but I wanted to be word-perfect when I reported back to Dan. His words came back to me about not taking anything to do with the robbery out of the plan room, so all the details had to be stored in my memory.

Chapter Thirteen

The red eye on my answering machine was blinking when I got back to the flat; it had to be Dan; he was the only one who had my number. I pressed playback and listened to the message; he sounded relaxed. 'Hi, Craig, meet me tonight, eight at Toni's on Endymion Road; it's a short walk from your place. It's Italian, and the dress code is smart casual. I've booked a private room; ask for me when you get there, and they'll roll out the red carpet. See you later; hope you've got good news.'

I wondered if he had decided it was best to meet on neutral territory so that if I didn't produce the goods, we could just walk away from each other, and that would be that, as they say.

I got there a few minutes early; Dan's Morgan was already in the car park. Toni's was a small Georgian mansion house on the edge of Finsbury Park, covered in ivy with all windows softly illuminated on both floors. Inside, the lighting was subdued, the walls were frescos of Tuscany's finest scenery, and the low-level background music very Italian. A waiter, dressed in black trousers, a white ruffled shirt, and red cummerbund, appeared at my side almost immediately and welcomed me to Toni's.

'I'm a guest of Mr Rawson. I believe he has a private room for this evening.'

'Certainly, sir, please follow me; Signor Rawson arrived a little earlier.'

I tagged on as he made his way past twenty or so tables, about half of them occupied. He passed through an archway and knocked gently on the first door on the left, then pushed it open and signalled me to enter.

'Your guest has arrived, Signor Rawson; I'll send Mario to attend to your requirements in a few minutes.' With that, he departed, closing the door behind him.

Dan came towards me, smiling broadly, hand extended. 'Good to see you, Craig, seems ages.'

'Nearly three weeks, I guess we've both been busy.'

I got an enquiring look, but I gave nothing away, and he went on with the hospitality. 'Might I suggest a pre-dinner drink; I have champagne on ice, a little bird told me you're partial to some fizz.'

'Hmm, I hadn't realised that Gail would be reporting back on my preferences. God knows what else she's told you about that night.'

He smiled. 'Nothing you wouldn't be proud of.'

I let it pass but made a mental note to be careful what I said to Gail should I avail myself of her services again. *Champagne,* I mused. *The perfect drink for any occasion, whether celebration or commiseration.*

I looked on as he carefully filled the crystal champagne flutes and found myself shaking slightly with nervous anticipation as I reached forward and took one from his hand. He chinked my glass and looked me straight in the eye, 'OK, Craig, let's have it, success or failure?'

I dwelt on my answer, savouring his uncertainty. 'Success.'

I don't think I'd seen him smile more readily. 'I knew you could do it; tell me about it.'

I was desperate to show him how clever I was but wanted to keep him in suspense a while longer. 'I'm starving, mate; at least let's order our meal.'

Dan pressed a buzzer, and a waiter, presumably Mario, an olive-skinned young man with black curly wavy hair responded in seconds. 'Signors, you are ready to order?' He stood there patiently whilst we perused the menu and came up with our selection. 'And some wine, perhaps?'

Dan answered at once, 'A bottle of your best Chianti.'

Mario nodded. 'The best it shall be, Signor Rawson.'

The door closed, and Dan looked at me expectantly, eager, desperate almost, to hear how PMR was to be cracked. I stalled a little longer; there was still the matter of my new identity; I had paid for it upfront.

'Dan, I know you want to get down to business, and so do I, but Mario will be back soon, and I don't want to be interrupted, so how's about we deal with my new identity.'

'Oh yes, sure.'

He reached into his inside pocket and spread the contents on the table. 'There you are: birth certificate, passport, and driving licence.' My birth certificate revealed that I was now Seamous Dorian, apparently born in

Newtownards, Northern Ireland. My father was one Charles Dorian, my mother Rhoda Coulter.

Dan sensed my disappointment. 'Sorry, we couldn't get anything with the name Craig. I know you're not Irish, but there are historic ties between Ulster and Scotland. I thought you might say that your parents moved to Scotland when you were young, and as time went on, you didn't care for the name Seamous and decided to call yourself Craig. So, you're now Craig Dorian unless, of course, you want to be a Seamous.'

'I'll stick with Craig. These all seem to be the real McCoy.'

'They're all genuine; the birth certificate relates to a child that died early on. You'll have to get to know your new birth date.'

My rebirth took place on the 7th of January 1940. 'Quite a coincidence; I'm still a Capricorn, and better still, I'm two years younger.'

'And you've got a passport valid for ten years along with a brand-new driving licence.'

'How on earth did you manage these?'

He touched his nose with his index finger. 'Friends in the right places and money, of course; money can solve any problem in my experience.'

'And the passport photograph?'

'As I told you previously, we had occasion to photograph you, Craig.'

'We?'

'My client wanted to know what you looked like. It's one of his foibles; if he doesn't like the look of someone, he won't work with them.'

'Fair enough, I can empathise with that; I'm the same. When do I get to see him?'

Dan looked at me sharply. 'You don't, Craig, you don't.'

It wasn't the time to push but I was determined to find out whom I was working for, sooner or later.

A light knock on the door interrupted our conversation, and I quickly pocketed my new documents. Mario entered, wheeling a laden food trolley and immediately began setting up the table, followed by a theatrical uncorking of the wine.

'The Signor would like to taste?'

Dan nodded and took the customary sniff at the wine, swilled the glass and took a sip.

'Excellent, Mario, you can pour and then leave us; we'll buzz when we need you.'

Our glasses filled, Mario bowed dutifully and was gone.

'Right, Craig, down to business. I don't mind if you talk with your mouth full; I can't wait to hear this plan of yours.'

Over the course of the next hour and a half, between mouthfuls of pasta and slurps of Chianti, I went through the PMR job. I began by describing the set-up in detail, the site layout, construction features, operational and security regimes. I told him how many hours of film I'd watched, and how many drawings I'd studied over and over again. He listened attentively enough, but I could see he wanted me to get through the preliminaries and onto the main event. Dan cut in at one point, 'I know how many hours you've put in, Craig; I've checked your attendance out on the gallery entry system.'

'Nice to know I'm trusted, Dan.' I countered icily.

'You haven't earned anybody's trust yet, Craig.'

I frustrated him further by going through the options I'd discarded and why: a helicopter drop-and-lift, tunnelling, taking out the security guard, somehow blocking the response team, unannounced Council visit. He wasn't impressed.

'Yeah, yeah, I considered all those, Craig; I'm looking for a flash of genius, not bread-and-butter solutions that won't work.'

'And that's exactly what I'm giving you; pure fucking genius.'

I stopped then and poured the last of the Chianti, taking my time watching his impatience grow.

'Have I missed anything you came up with?'

'You know you didn't, you bugger. You've had your fun; time to spill the beans; get on with it.'

I was enjoying myself and pushed him a bit further. 'What about a coffee and a liqueur before I get to the finale?'

He looked as though he was going to protest, but instead, he sighed and buzzed for Mario. 'This had better be good, Craig; strike that, it had better be perfect.'

'Signors, how might I be of service?'

'A large jug of coffee and a good cognac for me. What about you, Craig?'

'A Drambuie on ice and make it a double, please.'

'OK, Craig, you've milked it to the limit; it's time to impress me. I've been monitoring your hours, and I suspect you had your breakthrough on Tuesday since Wednesday was a short day at the gallery, and you haven't been back to the plan room since. You could have phoned to let me know that you had cracked it.'

'You could have phoned and enquired.'

He smiled broadly. 'Fair point, let's stop fencing; you win this round.'

Mario appeared, served up our coffee and liqueurs, bowed and departed.

'I hope everything is finally to your liking, Craig and now can you fucking get on with it.' His eyes were twinkling, and we both burst out laughing. 'Christ, I hope you're not always this difficult when you've got the upper hand.'

'You can count on it, Dan.'

The time had come, and I began explaining exactly how we were going to relieve PMR of several million in assorted bullion. I explained every step, addressed every detail, laying out every acquisition, answering Dan's questions as I went along. There were none I couldn't deal with to his satisfaction. I could almost hear the cogs of his brain whirring as he searched for flaws in the plan. When I finished, I glanced at my watch; I had taken thirty minutes.

Dan said nothing, just sat there thinking, and then poured us another coffee. He lifted his cognac and smiled. 'To PMR, may they have a bumper month.'

'Worth waiting for?'

'Perfect mate, just fucking perfect; my client will be like a dog with two tails. I take my hat off to you.'

We sat for several moments, saying nothing, each of us with his own private thoughts. Dan broke the silence.

'Fancy another?'

'Not for me. I'm already feeling a bit light-headed.'

'I'll pass as well.'

'So, what now, Dan? Where does it go from here? Assuming I'm allowed to ask, that is?' I added with barely disguised sarcasm.

'I report back to the Man, get his approval, then I set up a meeting with the rest of the team. You'll be in on that. You haven't forgotten that you'll have to take part in the raid.'

'No, I haven't forgotten, though I had hoped you might.' His reminder made a dent in my warm glow, but I didn't have an alternative. 'What time scale do you have in mind?'

'If it suits him, I'll try to see my client tomorrow; he knows I was seeing you tonight. Assuming he gives the go-ahead, I'll set up a team meeting ASAP.'

'And the job itself?'

'No idea, mate, that's down to my client; he has the contacts to find out the most profitable time to strike.'

'So how come he's able to do that?'

'He moves in the right circles, Craig, and that's all you need to know.'

The mystery surrounding Mr X was making me more determined than ever to find out who he was, and I had one or two ideas about how I might do just that.

'By the way, Craig, I know this has been your baby, but I'll do the presentation to the team; you'll join in when I ask you to. OK?'

I didn't argue; it was best to keep Dan sweet. 'No problem, I'm your assistant, pure and simple.'

'In the meantime, I want you to prepare a list of everything, every little item needed to make this job work. Make eight copies for handing out at the meeting.'

'Already done, I anticipated you would need one. I'll do the rest of the copies tomorrow.'

'I want you to check the plan one more time; make sure it's watertight.'

I shook my head. 'I've done that several times; it's tight as a drum, believe me.'

He glared at me. 'Do it again, Craig.'

I was getting fed up with being bossed, but I just shrugged; there was no need to argue; he'd never know whether I'd checked the list again or not.

We said our goodbyes outside in the car park, and I set off on the short walk back to the flat. I felt good; I had a new identity and was about to meet the team. True, there was my direct involvement in the execution of the plan, but hopefully, a totally inexperienced newcomer wouldn't be trusted with anything too arduous. It was just a matter of waiting for Dan's call.

Next morning, I opened three bank accounts, depositing £10,000 in each, claiming that my eccentric grandfather didn't believe in cheques and had given me cash to set myself up in business. I used the name Seamous Craig Dorian, and nobody challenged the fact that I'd given myself a middle name that didn't quite match up with my documentation. When I got back to the flat, the answering machine was blinking; Dan's message was brief, 'You and I meet at the gallery on Monday evening, seven-thirty; the others will join us half an hour later. Henry will be there as usual. Bye.'

Chapter Fourteen

'You're early, Craig.' Henry opened the door of the Gallery, 'Dan won't be here for another fifteen minutes.'

'I know, darling, I just couldn't put off seeing you a minute longer.'

'Yes, dear boy, and I'm in love with you too.' He camped up his reply for my benefit and stepped towards me, rolling his eyes and lowering his voice, 'I'll wait for you after the meeting.'

'But first duty calls; I have work to do. Oh, make a note, I'm now officially Craig Dorian.'

Henry shrugged, 'A rose by any other name would smell as sweet.'

'You know Henry, I do believe you're getting serious about me.'

'No thanks, dear boy, I'm more than happy with my cats; they're much more of a comfort than people.'

I let myself into the plan room and went through the job for the umpteenth time; it was still perfect, and I made no changes. There was no doubt in my mind that it would work if everybody played their part; just one thing made me uneasy: what role would I have in the operation? I wondered, too, who would make that decision? Hopefully, it would be Dan; he knew my feelings; surely Mr Big wouldn't get involved in the details. I convinced myself that all would be well, Dan would see me OK.

The door opened, and Dan came in smiling, 'Beat me to it, I see. I just want to familiarise myself with the plan and go through the list with you. I bet that's exactly what you've been up to.'

'Absolutely.' I spread out the key drawings, then switched on the projector and went through the slides, cross-referencing the drawings where necessary. Finally, we dealt with every item on the list. It was short and self-explanatory and didn't take long to deal with. He underlined a single item, 'That's the only thing to worry about.'

'Don't see why; there are plenty of them around. I've got some ideas on getting hold of one.'

'Not part of your remit, Craig; don't make any suggestions unless you're invited. These guys are professionals and take pride in their work, just like you do. Now let's go through it all again.'

I sighed, but he was right; if there were any flaws, now was the time to find them. When that was done, he leaned back in his chair, 'I can't believe how simple it's turned out, just can't believe it.'

'Your turn to be more enlightening, Dan. Who's coming tonight?'

'You'll meet the five other members of the top echelon. You won't meet many of the others lower down in the organisation; we tend to work in smallish cells so that no one person knows too much; it's better that way in case things go sour, then nobody can spill too many beans. Mind you, it's unlikely that anyone would become an informant. If **you** ever get caught, keep your mouth closed, and you'll be well looked after; say too much, and you'll be looked after in a somewhat different manner.'

'How much do the others get paid; it seems to me that some will be doing more than others?' I was keen to learn everything I could about how the organisation worked.

'Not something for you to concern yourself with; I do those negotiations, and everybody gets what's fair. You know what you're getting, and that's all you need to know.'

'OK, OK, just trying to learn from the maestro, that's all.'

Our conversation ended as the door opened, and a small, stocky guy strode in purposefully, reaching out his hand to Dan. 'Good to be working with you again, Dan. It's been a while.'

Dan smiled ruefully, 'Enforced holiday, Charlie, you know the sort of thing.'

'I did hear about it, bad luck.'

'Charlie, meet Craig Dorian. Craig, meet Charlie Booker.'

We shook hands, and Dan explained Charlie's role. 'Charlie is the logistics expert; anything we need, except bodies, is Charlie's responsibility.

'Dan tells me you've been helping him; not often he accepts assistance.'

'I had minor input, believe me, Charlie.' I lied, keeping on the right side of Dan; it was his show. Dan made no effort to correct the deception, so I'd made the right decision.

Charlie turned back to Dan, 'So what are we up to and when?'

'Later, Charlie, when everybody's here.'

'Fair enough; excuse me whilst I grab a cup of coffee.'

The door opened again, and two men moved into the room; one of them was baby-faced and looked like a gangling teenager; tall, fresh-faced with a crew cut. The other man looked like a villain; small, close-set eyes, faded scars on his face, hair greased back with a centre parting. They waved over to Charlie on their way across to Dan and me. The younger guy was dressed casually and acknowledged my presence with a smile; the older of the two completely ignored me. Dan shook hands with both of them, then made the introductions.

The younger one was Eddie Milton, whom Dan advised was a wizard with electronics and communications. The older man transpired to be one Tony Sherwood.

'Meet Craig Dorian. He's been helping me with this one.'

'Hi, Craig, I'm not really as clever as he thinks, but don't tell him.' Eddie shook my hand enthusiastically, 'Looking forward to working with you.'

Sherwood sized me up briefly, then turned back to Dan, but I didn't let him ignore me.

'And do you have a speciality, Tony?'

His head snapped back; his eyes boring into me; perhaps he thought I should know what he did. Dan spoke before he could reply, 'Tony is our armourer; he deals with weapons and explosives.'

My stomach knotted; the thought of armed robbery hadn't crossed my mind, nor had any other kind of violence. 'Guns, you use guns?' I failed to keep disapproval out of my voice.

Sherwood looked at me like I'd crawled out from under a rug. 'Clever boy, you know what an armourer does. Of course, we carry fucking guns. What do you think we do if things go wrong; fart and hope the smell sees them off?'

I clapped my hands softly; I wasn't backing off. 'Very funny, Tony. I see you specialise in comedy as well.'

'Do you see me laughing, sonny boy?' He was starting to sound angry.

'Temper, temper Tony, you'll do yourself a mischief.' I smiled at him and held his stare, clenched my fists, ready for action.

Dan intervened to cool things down, 'Leave it out, you two. We carry guns, Craig; we must have insurance if the job doesn't go to plan. Sometimes, people need to be persuaded to co-operate; the investment is too big to take chances. This far, we've never had to use them, and if the planning is good, we shouldn't have to.'

Deep down, I knew he had a point, and I didn't want to get into an argument with Dan; I had to concede, 'Fair enough.'

Sherwood nodded, 'You're learning kiddo.' With that, he wandered off to join Charlie Booker.

Eddie Milton smiled at me sympathetically. 'Don't mind him; Tony's always touchy. None of us like guns, but as Dan says, they're insurance.'

Just then, the two remaining members of the gang turned up, and shock hit me for the second time; one was a woman. Dan put his hand on my back and eased me towards the two arrivals; I suspected that he wanted to put maximum distance between Tony Sherwood and me.

'Craig, let me introduce you to Angie Goodall who has responsibility for surveillance; she finds out all there is to know about targets, their routines and whereabouts, that kind of thing.'

I put Angie in her mid-thirties with looks bordering on attractive. She wasn't doing herself any favours with her fair hair pulled back in a bun and not wearing any make-up. Her mini skirt was cut just above the knee, short enough to be fashionable but not too short to hold anybody's attention for long, which was a pity because she had nice legs. The thought struck me that she would readily blend into any situation, exactly what her role called for.

'Welcome to the team, Craig.' She flashed a teeth-perfect smile, her hand was soft and warm; I felt that she was genuine, or maybe I just favoured women.

'Pleased to meet you, Angie; I hadn't expected to find a woman on the team, a pleasant surprise, I hasten to add.' *Prat! What a sexist remark.*

'Time's moving on, Craig, some of we little women are daring to step outside the kitchen and the bedroom into the big bad world. Being a woman is an advantage in my job; people trust me, especially the blokes.' *She was right about that.*

'I stand admonished, Angie, and promise to better understand women's role in society.'

Dan and the last member of the gang had listened to the exchange with some amusement. 'And this old soldier is Ralph Mason. Ralph does all our recruitment; whosoever we need for the job, he finds them; seems to know everybody and never forgets a name or a face.'

The man in front of me looked close to sixty, on the small side and portly. Under his grey short-cut hair, he had deep-set, intelligent eyes and a ruddy complexion that suggested he enjoyed a drink or two.

'Delighted to meet you, Craig.' His handshake was firm, and he held on whilst he formed early impressions.

'Likewise, Ralph. I admire anyone who can put names and faces together; I'm hopeless at names. And you were in the army; Dan referred to you as an old soldier?'

'Not at all, old chap, I was with the Met, got to be a Chief Superintendent.'

My mouth dropped open; I couldn't image someone who had held that rank becoming one of the bad guys.

'Don't worry, Craig, all that's in the past; the pickings are much better on this side of the fence. Set myself up as a Theatrical Agent. I seem to have a bit of a gift in that direction, and it's a good cover.'

'OK, you've met everyone now, Craig. Let's get started, everybody.' Dan interrupted, keen to get down to business.

Dan moved over to the table and seated himself behind the projector. 'You'll find the usual list on the table; we'll deal with it in due course, so ignore it for now.'

Conversation died down as soon as he spoke. Nobody lingered; everyone moved over to the table. I took a seat on Dan's right and was pleased when Angie Goodall sat next to me. Tony Sherwood sat opposite me, and I could sense him appraising me; our eyes came into contact and locked. I should have looked away, but I got the feeling I was being tested in some way, so I winked at him. I saw him tense, and he started to get to his feet, but Dan looked up and realised something was going on and glared at both of us. 'Knock it off, you two; we're not here to see who can piss the furthest. Now, let's get on. First slide, our target, Precious Metals Reclamation Limited. There's probably over three million in gold, silver and platinum bullion on site even as I speak.'

Money is a sure attention grabber, and he had their interest instantly; they all watched attentively as he showed a series of slides to familiarise the group with the general layout and security.

'That's the prelims over; any questions at this stage?'

I was somewhat surprised when Tony Sherwood spoke first; he was only providing guns, and I didn't think he'd bother much about the execution of the robbery unless, of course, he was going to take a direct involvement. 'Doesn't look like this is an easy lift, Dan; security looks to be as tight as a drum.'

Eddie Milton nodded, 'I can't see that I'll be of much help; you seem to know all there is to know. I'll check the site out, though, to be sure of what the latest position is.'

Dan looked round the table, but there were no further comments. 'You're both right; it is a real toughie, but Craig and I have put a lot of work into this and come up with the answers.' It might have been a coincidence, but I thought he dwelt on Tony Sherwood when he mentioned my name, making sure that I got some credit for my efforts.

'Moving on, this is how we are going to crack PMR wide open; it's an ingenious plan, and more importantly, it's a simple plan.' He then proceeded to go through the job in meticulous detail, anticipating questions by explanation as he went along. Every detail of the plan was laid bare, and I could see that everyone was on board when he finished. It was a masterful performance, and my respect for Dan reached a new level.

'Any questions?'

Again, it was Tony Sherwood who spoke first, 'Shit hot, Dan; you make it sound like a piece of cake.'

Dan went round the table, in turn ending up with Charlie Booker who I remembered was the logistics guy; he looked worried. 'It's sweet, Dan, I'll give you that, but I can see what's coming, and I'm going to have my work cut out. I hope you've left enough time on this one.'

'As always, Charlie, it's the Man that sets the date, not me; when he says go, we go.'

He looked round the table. 'Anything else before we move onto the action lists?'

Nobody spoke up. 'Nothing; OK, we'll go through each item in turn and agree on who's doing what. And no ifs and buts about the timings involved; save that till you have the full picture. Craig, you'll keep a record of what we agree; just mark the appropriate initials against each item on the list. The rest of you mark the items you're responsible for and pass your list back to Craig when we're finished; then, we'll cross-check.'

'Craig, you'll prepare individual lists for each of us and get them to me by midday tomorrow. I'll get in touch with all of you individually with your copy of the list, and we'll agree on money at the same time; have your bid ready and don't be greedy. That ends our business, we can all go home.'

It was beginning to sound like a military operation with Dan, the Commander-in-Chief, and I suppose that's exactly what it was. People started to get up, but Sherwood stopped them in their tracks when he came up with a belated query.

'Dan, sorry, I should have asked this earlier, but it just occurred to me. Are we certain that we've got enough time on-site to load the bullion? The timetable sounds very tight?'

Dan turned to me, 'Craig,'

I nodded and addressed Tony. 'We've calculated the time we'll have on-site very accurately, but we can only guess at how much bullion there is based on previous occasions. We've used those two bits of information to calculate how many heads we need for loading. If we haven't loaded it all when our time runs out, we leave what's left behind. I reckon we can load three million in the time allocated; anything over that is a bonus. In short, the harder we work, the more we get.'

To my surprise, Tony Sherwood voiced his agreement, 'Can't see how it can be any other way really.' I caught his eye and nodded my thanks; there was no reciprocation. None of the others made any comment.

Dan spoke again, 'Talking about loading reminds me; the Boss has decided that Craig takes part in this job. As part of his initiation, he'll be helping with the loading; he did the calculations, so he'll have a chance to prove that he got them right.'

I felt physically sick and had to fight hard to keep the dismay I felt out of my expression. I just sat there with knotted guts, trying to make it look like it was another day at the office. I shifted my gaze round the table; nobody was objecting, but nobody was jumping for joy either. The Boss had spoken, and that was the end of the matter. I resolved more than ever to find out who he was and try to meet him face to face.

Angie Goodall softened the situation, 'Sounds like a good idea to me; Craig knows the plan back to front, and his hands-on experience, if you'll excuse the pun, can only be beneficial.'

Ralph Mason looked anxious, 'Obviously, we've all got to go along with what the Man says, but it does seem like Craig has been thrown in at the deep end; he'll be working under pressure. I just wonder if it wouldn't be better if he cut his teeth on a smaller operation; this is a big job, and if something goes wrong, it's always better to have somebody with experience involved.'

I rose to the bait and retorted sharply, 'Firstly, nothing is going to go wrong, and secondly, I've already been involved in a smaller operation, so I'm not entirely inexperienced.'

All eyes were on me, waiting for further explanation that I didn't want to give. Luckily, at that point, Dan closed the debate down. 'The decision has been made; I wasn't putting this up for debate. Now, I suppose you would like me to tell you when we're going to carry out this job?'

Dan grabbed everyone's attention in an instant, expectancy showing on every face. 'And the answer is......., I don't know. And I don't know because the Boss doesn't know. He's working on it, and we'll be given a date as soon as he has one; best guess is four weeks.'

Charlie Booker shook his head furiously, 'Not possible, Dan, I can't do it; I reckon I'll need eight weeks.'

'Work on four weeks, Charlie. OK, people, the meeting is closed. I'll be in touch as soon as I have something for you. In the meantime, I'm sure you've got things you can get on with. Craig, can you hang on a bit? I'd like a word.'

My new colleagues didn't hang around, but all of them acknowledged me as they took their leave; even the redoubtably Tony Sherwood nodded his farewell.

When the room cleared, I turned on Dan, 'Fucking hell Dan, I didn't want to get involved in this job to that extent.'

'There wasn't an option; it's what the Boss wants, and that's an end to it.'

'You could have at least warned me.'

'It was a test of your self-control and composure, and you passed with flying colours. You're collecting ticks in all the right boxes.'

'You might think so, but I nearly shit myself. Has Tony Sherwood got a problem with me?'

He smiled. 'Tony doesn't like anybody much. In his business, you don't develop friendships too readily.'

'Being a gun dealer doesn't mean you can't be civil, surely?'

'He sometimes does a bit more than deal in guns.' He laughed wickedly. 'You could say he was a people person.'

'Spell it out, Dan, you're confusing me; a people person he isn't.'

'He is in the sense that he deals with people who are a problem.'

'Meaning, he's a heavy or something like that?'

'All that and more; now I think I've said enough about Tony Sherwood, but I do advise you to be careful how you deal with him.'

'I can look after myself.'

Dan sighed, 'Christ, Craig, you're a fucking amateur by his standards; he doesn't operate Marquis of Queensbury rules. Go carefully, my friend.'

I nodded; he was right. I had a lot to learn. 'I liked the others at first acquaintance, some more than others. Angie was a bit of a surprise; I just didn't expect a woman.'

'Angie is great at what she does, maybe the best at what she does. She's happily married with two kids.'

'No! Does her husband know about her activities?'

'Of course, and what's more, he assists; you could describe it as a family business.'

I just shook my head in wonderment. 'Amazing.'

'Now, I assume you can get these lists to me by noon tomorrow?'

'No problem.'

'By the way, I'll be briefing Charlie Booker to liaise with you. Tell him exactly what you want, be as helpful as you can; everybody has their responsibilities, but there are no solid lines of demarcation. We operate as a team at all times.'

'Suits me; he seemed nervy about the four-week deadline.'

'Charlie would have been anxious about an eight-week deadline; that's how he is.'

'Outline the stepping stones to D-Day for me, Dan.'

'One, you bring me the lists. Two, the Boss tells me the date. Three, I meet with the team on a one-to-one, hand over the lists, tell them the date and negotiate their fees. Four, I have one more meeting; it's usually very short. Five, I activate the run-down to the raid. Happy?'

'Sounds good. I can't wait for the big day; it's the waiting I hate.'

'Waiting is all part of it: waiting for the plan, waiting for information, waiting for the go-ahead, waiting on the day, waiting afterwards, waiting for the next job. Get used to it. That's how it is.'

'I suppose so.' The thought of all that waiting around took the shine off the high I'd experienced earlier.

'Right, if there's nothing else, I'm off. See you tomorrow.'

'I'll just say goodnight to Henry.'

'Henry went long ago; he usually leaves when the last guy arrives.'

As I journeyed back to Finsbury Park, I felt elated yet somehow deflated, too. The plan had been seen as a success, but one thing was gnawing away at me; despite all the promises I had made to myself, I was going to be up to my neck in a crime. *Shit! Worst of all, a crime that involves guns, I've fucked up big time.*

Chapter Fifteen

Dan had done his stuff; things were happening, though I knew nothing of them at the time. I never really got to know the ins and outs of setting up the job, other than what I gleaned from the odd conversation after the event and, of course, whatever Dan deigned to tell me. My fellow conspirators were closed-mouthed before, during and after the event, and in truth, I suppose that was no bad thing; many villains had been brought to book because of careless talk. I got the lists to Dan on time, but from that minute on, I was put on hold and told I would be contacted when necessary.

The Man duly came up with a date; the raid would take place on the 13th of November give or take a day either way. That gave us five weeks to put everything in place; hopefully, Charlie Booker would cope.

'Why is the date not specific, Dan?

'He'll let us know the exact date as soon as he has it. PMR's holdings will be at a maximum around that time. I guess he'll be trying to find out when the bullion is due to be shipped out, and we'll grab it the day before.'

Peter McCann cleared his plate of the last vestige of food and licked his lips. He was a regular visitor to the driver's section of the Hungry Trucker, a greasy spoon of an eating hole just off the M1. He checked the time and decided he could take another ten minutes to finish his mug of tea, read the sports pages of his newspaper and contemplate what he would do that evening. The likelihood was he'd do what he almost always did after work: go home to his flat in Tower Hamlets and watch television. McCann was forty-five and a bachelor; women just didn't find him attractive, and he'd long since given up looking for, or even hoping for, a mate he could share his humdrum life with. His life was dull to the point of boredom, and today would be no different. An only child whose parents had long since left this world, he'd learned to live with his solitude. Angie Goodall had chosen him well; he was a creature of habit and one who wouldn't be missed to any great extent when he dropped out of life's scenery.

His lunch finished, he folded his newspaper, yawned, rose lethargically to his feet and made his way out of the Hungry Trucker. Outside, he crossed the concourse and strolled along the row of cars towards the commercial parking area. As he neared his vehicle, he fished in his pocket for his keys, found them, and was reaching for the cab door when he heard a voice.

'It's Peter, isn't it? Peter McCann?'

He swung round with a mixture of surprise and pleasure that he'd been recognised by someone who knew him. The voice belonged to a man, a man much his age and dressed like any other lorry driver. The guy was smiling, looking friendly, but Peter was sure he didn't know him.

'I'm sorry, do I know you?'

'No, Peter, you don't know me from Adam. I'm afraid we're going to have to interrupt your routine for a few days. Give me the keys to your van, please.

McCann wasn't a brave man, and fear was already creeping into his body; he looked around anxiously, but nobody was nearby.

'Wh..wh..why would I give you, my k..k..keys?' His stammer always surfaced when he was nervous or ill at ease.

The man smiled, 'Because I'm asking you for them, and besides, I've got this.'

McCann followed the man's glance downwards, his eyes widening with terror when he saw the gun.

'Oh God, please don't shoot. You can have the keys; I don't care. Here, take them; I'll say nothing, I promise. Please don't hurt me.' He thrust the keys forward at arm's length, his hand shaking violently.

'Thank you, Peter; that's very sensible of you. Now don't be afraid, but I've got some more bad news for you. I want you to get into that blue van over there. I promise you that you won't come to any harm. We're going to borrow yours for a few days.'

The unfortunate McCann gulped, 'There's nothing in there; it's empty; I've finished my deliveries.'

The man smiled again. 'I know that; now be a good chap and get in the van. Don't force me to do something nasty.'

McCann was terrified; he looked around for some escape from his nightmare.

'Last time of asking, Peter; please don't make me kill you; I will if I have to.'

Tears welled up in his eyes. He was afraid to get into the van but even more afraid of not doing what the man asked; he was sure the man meant what he said. There was nothing he could do; he turned and began to walk slowly towards the van, all the time praying for some sort of divine intervention. None came, and he reached the van, conscious of the man's presence behind him.

'Open the door and get in, Peter. I promise you won't come to any harm if you behave yourself.'

He did as he was told, and the waiting driver gave him a friendly smile. 'Hi, Peter, make yourself comfortable; we're going for a little ride.'

McCann slid into the passenger seat, noting that the driver didn't appear to have a gun. His thoughts raced. *I'll make a move when we're in a busy area; I'll pull the wheel over and crash the car like they do in the pictures.*

The fantasy died as quickly as it arrived when the first man reached across and put a restraining harness across his chest and around the seat, pinning his arms to his side. Another followed around his knees, then a third around his ankles. Any movement was now out of the question; he was well and truly trapped. The man still wasn't finished with him; he was putting a blindfold over his eyes. There were sunglasses attached to the outside of the blindfold to mislead the casual onlooker. The sun visor was pulled down to partially shield the unfortunate victim from outside view.

'Comfortable, Peter?' The driver was speaking to him.

He nodded his head, his mouth dry, unwilling to form words.

The van door slammed closed, making him jump, and without another word, the driver pulled away.

Charlie Booker had completed the first stage of his mission just four days before his target date of 12th of November. The police would mount some sort of operation to find the vehicle and its driver, but it was unlikely to be given high priority. McCann had been safely locked away and would be treated well if he behaved himself. Release would come when the job was over.

With less than a week to go, nobody had been in touch, and I was in danger of dying from a cocktail of boredom and frustration. I'd done London's tourist scene to death, taken in a few shows, and even availed myself of the services of an escort agency, but time was still dragging. I'd phoned Dan a couple of times, but all he would say was that everything was on course and to be patient, I'd be invited to get involved when the need arose.

I did put some of my time to good use by trying to find out who the mysterious boss man was. On the assumption that he might well own Finsbury Park Mansions, I went to the Land Registry and carried out a search. The property was in the ownership of a company called Horizon Developments. I checked out the other properties Dan had taken me to and found that these were also owned by the Horizon Developments. Just out of curiosity, I looked up Dan's pad, and there it was again: Horizon Developments.

My next stop was Companies House to find out what I could about Horizon Developments. A helpful assistant turned up the records I wanted and ushered me to a desk where I studied the last three years' accounts. The company had been set up to own and develop property and had a portfolio valued at £100 million. The Board comprised Lord and Lady Averton, General D.F. Carew, and a Mr H.M. Harburton. Ruling out Lady Averton, since the boss was always referred to as a man, I felt that I had narrowed Mr Big down to one of three people. It was a big step forward. My money was on Lord Averton, but I couldn't immediately think of a way to prove it. There was also a full listing of the properties making up the portfolio, and I made a note of them.

On the 7th of November, I was making ready for bed when the phone rang.

'Craig? Charlie Booker here. Sorry to ring so late. I could do with your input; your instructions are clear enough, but just to be sure we get it right, I'd like to have you around tomorrow to talk me through.'

'No problem, Charlie, I'd welcome the chance of having something useful to do; I'm bored out of my mind. Just tell me when you want me and where. By the way, I don't have a car.'

'I'll pick you up at eight-thirty if that suits you; Finsbury Park Mansions, I believe.'

'That's fine; I'll see you outside.'

The intercom buzzed at eight-thirty prompt the next morning.

'Your chariot awaits you, young man.'

'I'll be right down.'

Charlie Booker's shiny black Humber Sceptre sat outside. It matched his persona: solid, dependable, and built for comfort. We chatted about nothing in particular as Charlie wove his way steadily and patiently through the morning rush hour. He didn't reveal where we were headed; my patience ran out, and I decided to ask.

'Where are we headed?'

'To an area of North London's industrial wasteland; I doubt if the address would mean much to you, Craig.'

I tried asking him about his background and how he'd got involved with the gang but got nowhere.

'A word to the wise: don't go asking personal questions; it's just not done in this set-up. I'm sure Dan has warned you; he certainly told me when I was recruited.'

'Sorry, no more questions, I promise; it's just not natural, and I keep forgetting.'

'Best you don't forget, Craig, or you'll upset someone, and there's no saying what might happen.'

We had been on the road for about forty minutes when Charlie turned into what had once been an industrial area. The weathered, fading sign at the entrance advised that we had entered Thameside North Industrial Estate. I vaguely remembered that it was included in Horizon Developments' property portfolio and made a mental note to check. It didn't take too much imagination to see how property sales and acquisitions could be used to move large sums of money around.

Just as Charlie had described it, it was indeed a wasteland of derelict warehouses and factories, relics of days gone by. Charlie drove to the end of a service road that seemed to bisect the estate, then turned right, coming to a halt in front of one of the better-looking buildings. He sounded the car horn three times, a door opened, and a man dressed in blue overalls stepped out, waved, then disappeared back inside. Presumably, he pressed a button to activate the large door that gave access to the building, and it began to rise.

Although I had no way of knowing, what had been Peter McCann's vehicle slowly came into view.

'Only picked it up yesterday; I don't dare carry out this kind of steal too far in advance; gives John Law too much time to investigate and for the activity round here to be noticed.' Charlie explained.

'Looks good, Charlie; you know you'll have to change the livery.'

'Do me a favour, Craig.' He retorted. 'The paint job and the number plates get done at the end of the conversion. Follow me. I'll introduce you to Pete, my mechanic, and you can go through your requirements with him. While you're doing that, I'll say hello to Pete's mate, name's Jimmy.'

He called Pete over and made the introductions, then left us together for me to describe in detail exactly what was needed. Pete was a young bloke, I reckoned about twenty, and I wondered whether he had the experience to do what I wanted. I anticipated protestations, technical or practical or both, but Pete didn't even blink.

'Gotcha, guv, exactly as the job sheet says in fact, I can't see any difficulty. I guess it will take about two days to do that lot; then you can come back and give it the once-over. After that, we'll do the paint job, change the plates and age it a little.'

'Age it?'

'Yes, guv, don't want it looking too new, tends to attract more attention. Now, if that's all the chat, I'll get on with the work?' Without waiting for my reply, he turned away and began getting an oxy-acetylene set-up ready for use. I suppose my input had been useful, but I wasn't sure in what way; the guy was on top of the job.

Charlie rejoined me, 'Pete happy?'

'Seems to know what he's doing, didn't really need me.'

'Pete's a clever boy; some say he's the best in the business. Thanks for coming; I find it's best to put the designer and artisan together on these jobs; avoids any misunderstandings. If you're happy, I'll take you back now.'

'I'm happy to hang around; I've got nothing else to do.'

'Thanks, but no thanks; best we leave them to it. Don't want them thinking we don't trust them.'

I nodded. 'I can understand that. Drop me at the nearest Tube station, and I'll find my own way back; it's all part of getting to know London.'

I went back again on the morning of the third day, cadging a lift from Charlie again. Pete and his mate stood watching as I carried out my inspection.

'I've really got to hand it to you guys; a perfect job, Pete. You and Jimmy have done a great job.'

Pete grinned like a Cheshire cat. 'That's what I'm paid for, guv. Just got the paint job and plates to do; come eight tonight, it'll be finished, and we'll be off. Maybe we'll meet up another time. I hope so; you're very clear on what you want, and that makes it easy for us.'

Dora Hagen was in the kitchen clearing up after tea, as she still called her evening meal when the doorbell rang.

'I'll get it, Alf,' she called out to her husband, who was relaxing in front of the television as he always did after his evening meal. Dora was approaching sixty, a rotund, cheery-faced lady who didn't enjoy the best of health. A degenerative heart disease had prematurely aged her and continued to take its toll. Even walking was difficult, but she was determined not to become an invalid and did all she could to pull her weight around the house. She was devoted to her husband and wasn't going to let some unexpected caller disturb his evening cuppa, especially when he was going off to work shortly.

Shuffling slowly down the hallway, she reached the front door just as the bell rang again. 'People, they're so impatient nowadays', she muttered.

'You all right, love?' The second ring had alerted Alf.

'Yes, Alf, I'm there now.'

She pulled the door open and looked a little anxiously at the man standing in front of her. She didn't know him; he was dressed in a suit, carried a briefcase, and looked very official, just like a man from the Council.

'Good evening, Mrs Hagen. I assume it is Mrs Hagen?'

'That's right, I'm Dora Hagen. Who are you?

The man reached into his waistcoat pocket and retrieved a business card, which he handed over. Dora Hagen squinted at it, her eyes struggling with the small print.

'I'm David Ross from the Co-operative Insurance.'

'Insurance?' Dora echoed nervously; she didn't know anything about insurance, 'There's nothing wrong, is there?'

The man smiled and shook his head, 'No, no, not at all, Mrs Hagen; everything is fine.' His voice was soft and reassuring, putting her at ease. 'I'm here with regard to your enquiry.'

'Enquiry, what enquiry? We don't need any insurance.'

The man looked puzzled. 'Perhaps you've forgotten; you wrote asking about life insurance.'

'What's wrong, Dora?' Alf Hagen appeared behind his wife, concerned about what was taking her so long. He was a well-built man with a craggy face below a mass of curly white hair, just two years short of retirement.

Alf made his way forward. 'Well, I haven't written, Dora, did you?'

'This gentleman says we've written about insurance.'

'No, dear, you know I'd never do anything like that.'

'I thought as much.' He fixed his gaze on the man. 'Looks like you've had a wasted journey, mate. We're not interested in insurance; can't afford it.'

Ross smiled again, 'Mistakes do get made. Would you mind if I took a quick look at the letter? I'm sure it's got your name on it?'

The Hagens looked on as Ross opened his briefcase and reached in; they were certain he wouldn't find a letter with their name on it.

'What the hell?' Alf's mouth gaped open as he watched the man draw a gun from the briefcase and point it at them. Dora went into shock and

200

trembled violently; she'd never seen a real gun before. She was sure they were going to die, right there and then, on the doorstep. Her eyes were fixed open, locked onto the gun; she wanted to turn and run.

The man was speaking to them, his voice soft, unhurried. 'I don't want to harm you, and I won't harm you if you do exactly what you're told. Do you understand me?'

Neither Alf nor Dora Hagen made any reply; neither moved as though frozen in position.

Ross pushed the gun forward, 'Now I want you both to turn around and go back into the lounge.'

Alf hesitated briefly; he'd been a Commando during the war, but time had moved on, and Dora was between him and his adversary. He put his arm round his wife's waist, 'Come on, Dora, we'll do what he says.' He eased her round and gently guided her towards the lounge, anger mounting in him when he felt the tension in her body and the little tremors of fear. 'It'll be alright, dear; we'll do what he wants, then he'll leave us in peace.'

Alf heard the front door close as he led his wife away; the man followed closely behind them. In the lounge, they turned to face their unwelcome visitor; the gun was still pointed at them, and Alf noticed that it was fitted with a silencer.

'Mrs Hagen, I'd like you to sit in that chair over there.' Ross waved the gun towards an armchair facing the television. 'Mr Hagen, I want you to put on the wall lights and draw the curtains, please, and perhaps you could turn off the television for the moment.'

Alf bit on his tongue; he resented being bossed about in his own home, but he did what he was told; the gun was a great persuader. 'If you're after money or valuables, you're wasting your time; we're not rich. We're just ordinary people.'

Ross continued to speak softly; his voice free of menace. 'I'm not here to steal anything, Mr Hagen; all I want is your co-operation.'

'What do you mean by co-operation? Why the hell should we co-operate with you?' Alf 's anger was rising; a stranger giving him orders in his own home.

The man waggled his gun. 'You'll co-operate because of this, Alf and because you don't want Dora to come to any harm.'

The commando in Alf surfaced. 'I'm not afraid of guns; I saw hundreds, thousands during the war.'

The smile on David Ross' face vanished, and suddenly, his voice held menace. 'Then I suggest you try to remember the damage they can do and think of your wife.'

'Oh Alf, please do what he says, dear. I couldn't bear it if you got hurt.' Dora pleaded with her husband, tears forming in her eyes.

Alf gave his wife a cuddle. 'So exactly what is it you want?'

Ross nodded. 'That's better, Alf. All you have to do, is follow your usual routine, nothing more, nothing less.'

'Meaning what exactly?'

'Meaning that you are due to leave for work shortly and I want you to do that at your usual time. You'll drive to your depot, pick up your vehicle and take it to an address I'll give you. Someone will meet you there and give you further instructions. We know that you are due to make a delivery to PMR tonight; that is correct, isn't it?'

'How do you know that?'

'We know quite a lot about you, Alf, your military service, for instance; I understand you were a commando. We know that your wife has a serious heart condition, and we should try not to alarm her any more than is necessary.'

'Bastard, as if you care.' Alf spat out his words, his face twisted with rage.

'That's not fair, Alf, I really do care, so please co-operate.'

'Please, Alf.' Dora wailed; she was near to a breakdown. 'Please do what he says.'

'Thank you, Dora,' Ross said, smiling again. 'I'm sure Alf will have your best interests at heart.'

The gun moved back to Alf. 'Time you got ready for work, isn't it?'

'My gear's in the bedroom.'

Ross nodded. 'I'll come with you just in case there's a telephone up there; I wouldn't want you to do anything silly.'

'There's only one telephone, and it's in the kitchen.'

'I'm sure that's the case, Alf, but I'll check anyway. Lead the way.'

Alf had told the truth, and satisfied, the pseudo-insurance man returned to the lounge. Alf, now dressed for work, rejoined his wife in the lounge.

'Now what?'

'As I told you, Alf; you drive to work, pick up your vehicle and head for West Elton Street. Halfway along on the left, you'll be met by a motorcyclist; he'll wave you down.'

'I don't know West Elton Street.' Alf was lying, 'So I can't help.'

'I'm really sorry to hear that, Alf. I had hoped to avoid any unpleasantness.' Ross swung his gun round and pulled the trigger.

Dora screamed as the gun went off with a loud plop, her hands clasping at her chest in horror at the sight of her cat flying backwards as the bullet tore into its skull. She buried her head in her hands, sobbing, moaning. Alf took a threatening step forward, then stopped as the gun swung back, pointing at his head. Dora struggled to get to her feet, 'You horrible, horrible man, you've killed Poppy, my poor Poppy. How could you kill a harmless creature?'

'Please stay in the chair, Mrs Hagen; it's best if you do. I'm sorry about the cat, but it could have been avoided if Alf hadn't tried to play games with me. Now think hard, Alf. Can I help you to remember where West Elton Street is? We both know that you drive along it regularly. Please co-operate; don't make me kill both of you; we do have alternative arrangements in place just in case you refuse to help us.'

Alf gulped; he had to do what he was told, and he knew it. 'OK, I'll do what you want, but I promise you, if you harm Dora, I'll kill you.'

'Off you go, Alf; no harm will come to Dora if you do exactly what I've told you. You'll be followed by a motorcyclist, so don't get any ideas.'

Alf moved over to his wife and knelt, reaching forward to put his arms round her. 'It'll be all right, Dora, I promise you. We'll be back together before bedtime.' He looked over his shoulder, mouthing, please, for Ross to confirm.

'Absolutely.' Ross caught Dora's eye and smiled at her. She didn't feel reassured. This man was a killer, and a smile didn't change that. Alf kissed his wife, gave her one more comforting hug, and then stood to face the man that had violated their home. 'You had better look after her, just like you've promised.' Ross nodded and watched as Alf made his way out.

Outside in his car, Alf Hagen's thoughts were racing. *Double back and catch the man by surprise; he could slip in by the back door? Phone the police? Tell his boss at the depot what was happening?* He dismissed them all; he couldn't put Dora's life at risk. He'd drive to the depot, collect his vehicle, go to West Elton Street and do whatever they wanted. *Fuck them; just what the hell did they want?*

Chapter Sixteen

Alf Hagen glanced at the rear-view mirror, and sure enough, a motorcyclist was tailing him at a discreet distance. The ever-cautious Ralph Mason, the pseudo-insurance representative, had made sure that Alf carried out his instructions. The black-helmeted rider continued down the road as Alf's car turned into the depot. Reassured, the rider doubled back to where he could wait for Alf's tanker to set out from the depot.

Inside the depot, Alf parked his Morris Minor in his usual place and made his way over to the timeclock to sign on for duty. His supervisor came towards him with a cheery smile. 'Hi Alf, how goes the day?'

'All right, I guess; I'd rather be at home with my feet up.'

Alf's supervisor was mildly surprised. 'That's not like you, Alf. You wouldn't be getting paid if you weren't here.'

Alf grimaced and felt guilty and wanted to tell his boss what had happened but knew he daren't. Instead, he forced a lame smile. 'True enough, Ted, so what have you got for me?'

'Your usual run, Alf; first call PMR, then back here to load up again.'

Ted Bryant handed over a sheaf of papers. 'That's all the delivery notes; it'll be a steady night for you.'

'Steady night? It'll be the worst night of my life. If only you knew, Ted. 'OK, I'll get on my way.'

'There's time for a cuppa if you want one; I've just made a pot.'

'No thanks, Ted, I'd best be going.'

Bryant raised his eyebrows; drivers rarely missed an opportunity for a cup of tea and a natter on the firm's time. 'You all right, Alf? You seem a bit down tonight.'

'I'm fine, Ted, just feel like getting started, that's all.'

The motorcyclist watched as Alf's tanker nosed out of the depot and turned left. He kicked his engine into life and accelerated away, overtaking his target before it had travelled a hundred yards. The motorcyclist raised a hand to signal the unfortunate Alf to follow. The journey was short, and it took only a few minutes to reach West Elton Street.

Alf felt his tummy knot when he saw the motorcyclist pull into the side of the road and wave him down. Whatever was going to happen was starting. He came to a halt behind the bike, clenching his fists to stop his hands from shaking, then sat waiting for his instructions, fearful of what was about to take place. The motorcyclist made no move to get off his bike, and he began to wonder if something had gone wrong. He didn't see the approach of the man who came from behind his vehicle and pulled open his cab door.

'Here, what are you up to?' Alf reacted angrily, startled by the intrusion.

The intruder was young and looked tough, his instructions to the point. 'Move over, Alf and keep your mouth shut from here on.'

Alf slid over to the passenger seat and watched as the man fumbled in his pocket.

'Here, put this on.' A thick black blindfold landed on his lap.

Alf did as he was told and sat back in trepidation, his body bathed in sweat.

The tanker moved forward jerkily as the driver got used to the gears and clutch, but it soon gathered speed and was on its way. Alf tried to memorise the number of left and right turns, but he wasn't good at that kind of thing and gave up after a few minutes. He guessed about ten minutes had passed when he felt his vehicle slow and turn sharply, stopping briefly then lurching forward again before coming to a halt.

'Keep your blindfold on, Alf, or you might just get yourself shot. I'm going to come round and help you out.'

Alf listened as his captor got out, fear of the unknown gripping him. He turned sightless towards the noise of the cab door opening, inhaling deeply as a welcome rush of cool evening air flowed into the cab. A hand grabbed hold of his arm. 'Get out, Alf, I'll steady you.'

What now? He eased himself awkwardly onto the ground, completely disorientated, still trying to cope with his unaccustomed world of darkness.

'Come with me.' Alf allowed himself to be led forward, one arm extended in front, like a blind man. Suddenly, the man halted; he could hear a cab door being opened. *Christ, what was happening?* He could hear scuffling sounds he didn't understand.

The man was speaking to him again. 'Reach up and climb in Alf.'

Alf reached forward, his hands searching for something familiar, something secure, eventually grasping metalwork; he thought he recognised the feel of another tanker. There were three steel steps leading upwards, and it certainly felt somehow familiar. *Surely, he wasn't back in his own vehicle? What the Hell was going on?* He wanted to pull off his blindfold but feared the consequences; the stakes were too high. Gingerly, his hands searching for grip, his feet feeling for the steps, he climbed in and settled into the seat. He was conscious of the man climbing in beside him, then the roar of the engine as it started up; it sounded just like his own vehicle. It had to be his. But why make him get out, only to have him get back in? It didn't make sense.

They had driven a fair distance when he felt the vehicle slow and come to a halt, the sound of the handbrake ratchet. The engine kept running. *What now?*

'You can take your blindfold off now.'

Alf complied eagerly, anxious to know where he was, peering around as his eyes adjusted; the area was vaguely familiar.

'This is as far as I go; you'll take the vehicle on to PMR alone and follow your usual routine. You know what will happen to Dora if you don't. My friend and I will be following behind on the motorcycle just to make sure you don't get lost.' The man glanced at his watch.

'You're a little bit behind schedule, so if anybody asks questions about that, put it down to roadworks or an accident. When you've made your delivery, you will return to West Elton Street, where I'll be waiting for you. Do you understand all that?'

Alf nodded. He knew something big was going down, but what? *A robbery at PMR? If it was, they were wasting their time; the place was tight as a drum.*

'Answer me properly, Alf. Think of Dora. Are you clear on your instructions?'

'Yes, I fucking am.'

'Don't get stroppy, Alf; both you and Dora are…shall we say, vulnerable. Catch you later.'

Alf watched the man walk back to the waiting motorcycle, climb on to the pillion and pull on a helmet. The man waved at him. Alf gave him the V-sign; he felt braver now that he was alone in the minor fortress of his cab. It was a futile act of defiance; he had no intention of not doing exactly what they wanted.

Alf had no way of knowing he wasn't alone in his vehicle; he had five passengers. If he had been able to witness events at the changeover, he would have seen the men, all wearing dark blue boiler suits and face-covering headgear, climb into the rear of the tanker. The cab was fitted with two concealed miniature microphones. Anything said in the cab or nearby would be overheard.

PMR, here I come. Alf pushed the gear lever forward and immediately realised that this wasn't his vehicle; it looked, felt, and sounded the same, but it wasn't. They had been clever, all his bits and pieces were in the cab, including his latest delivery notes, but they had missed the knob on the gear change. His was stubbier, its leather softer, well used. *So that was why I had to get out… to change vehicles.* This minor discovery caused him to smile; somehow, it represented a victory over his captors. *What further discoveries lay ahead? What else was different about this vehicle?*

I had been the last of the five passengers to be picked up; the other four guys were already in the grey Dormobile that conveyed us to the yard where the tanker changeover had taken place. Each of us had been provided with a boiler suit and black nylon ski-masks; just pulling on the latter had made me feel like a real villain. I recognised only one of my four companions, Tony Sherwood, who gave me a thin smile; the others had nodded or flicked their heads. It was noisy and uncomfortable inside the body of the tanker; without seating, we were jolted and swung around like puppets.

Thankfully, it was only a short journey to the PMR site. I began to feel anxious; although I had complete faith in my plan, an element of fear pervaded my thoughts as I contemplated what lay ahead. I could feel the adrenaline rush and my heartbeat quickening as we got ever nearer to the crime scene. There was no lighting inside the vehicle, and we all sat in silence in the pitch-black; Tony was in charge and had instructed us not to talk unless there was an emergency. Suddenly, there was a noise; the man on my left started to emit a low moan, then muttered indistinctly.

'Ssssssshhh.' Knowing Tony's short fuse, I tried to quieten the guy.

'I can't stand it, it's claustrophobic, I can't stand it.'

'What the fuck's the matter? Who is that?' Tony hissed.

'I can't stand it. Let me out.' The guy was starting to rave.

'If you don't shut your fucking mouth, I'll put a slug in you.' Sherwood snarled out the ultimate warning, the kind you didn't want to receive from a professional hitman.

'Let me out, let me out.' The guy was either deaf or had a death wish. I could hear him trying to get to his feet.

Suddenly, there was a light; Sherwood was shining a torch past me to the man on my left. 'Shut up, you bastard, I won't tell you again.'

'Please, Tony, let me out. I can't stand it, I can't. It's fucking killing me.'

Sherwood raised his gun, its silencer in place. 'Don't say I didn't warn you.'

I looked on in horror as the man's face contorted, 'Please, Tony, I can't help it, I just can't help it.'

I had to act and act quickly; there was no way I was going to witness one of Sherwood's executions. I reached up and grabbed the man, pulling him down. 'What's wrong with you?'

The man sensed salvation, and a moment of calm replaced his panic. 'I can't stand confined spaces, I'm claustrophobic, I must get out.' He started to get up again, and I saw Tony swing the gun up again.

There was only one thing to be done to save him from a bullet, and I didn't hesitate; I hit the guy full on the chin with a vicious uppercut. He slumped forward, pole-axed; those Westmoor punch-bag sessions had paid off, though without gloves, my knuckles felt painful.

I turned round to face Tony. 'A bad choice for this job; he can't help himself.'

'He never said nothing about claustrophobia to me, bastard wanker.'

'It's a condition, Tony, and there's nothing he can do about it. He'll be out for a while; don't worry about him.'

'He's the one who should be worrying; I'll deal with him later.' He switched off his torch, and the excitement over the journey proceeded in silence.

Alf pulled up outside PMR and dismounted from his cab; as usual, he left the engine running. He knew something was about to happen, and he would be part of it; there was no escape now. As he'd done many times before, he approached the intercom and pressed the buzzer.

'Yes.' The disembodied voice was one he recognised as belonging to Ken Shields.

'It's me, Ken, Alf Hagen.'

'Look straight at the camera, Alf; you know the drill.'

He looked up at the camera, making sure his expression didn't reveal the turmoil he was going through.

'You're looking grumpy, Alf. Don't tell me the missus has cut off your supply again?'

'Ha, ha, fucking hilarious. Doris isn't too well as it happens.'

'Oh, I'm sorry to hear that. Nothing serious, I hope? I'll open the outside gate. Drive in, stop before the inner gate and switch off your engine.' Shields knew that Alf didn't require instructions, but he had to follow procedures to the letter, or he'd be in hot water.

Inside the vehicle, the men listened in on the conversation; it was all going to plan, and they knew what would happen next. The engine revved up, and the vehicle rolled forward the short distance into the enclosure, coming to a halt between the two massive gates that protected the PMR site. Alf braked and shut down his engine, wondering yet again just what part he and his vehicle would play in whatever events lay ahead. *Shit why can't this all be nothing more than a bad dream.* Behind him, the outer gate was rolling closed.

He followed his routine, climbed down from his vehicle and pulled a dipstick from its storage tube, doing what he had done many times in the past. He stood then, awaiting further instructions from Shields. The security guard appeared at the armoured glass window and spoke into a microphone. 'OK, Alf, show me a nice dry dipstick.'

Hagen moved forward to the window and ran a clean, dry duster down the length of the dipstick. That done, he spread the duster in front of Ken Shields showing it to be unstained.

Shields nodded. 'You've passed your first test, Alf, now dip the tank.'

Alf was running on automatic, carrying out a routine he'd done dozens of times for PMR; they were the only company who made this check nowadays. But his thoughts were still with Dora; she was all that mattered. *Where are they? When are they going to make their move?*

He climbed up onto the roof of the tanker and started to undo the lid to the dip slot, and that's when the thought struck him. *The bastards were inside the tank. No wonder the tanker had responded to the acceleration and braking more readily than it would have done with a full load. Oh my God, they were going to be caught when the dipstick came up dry. Dora would be hurt, and it wasn't his fault. What could he do?*

Inside the tanker, the gang listened to Alf climbing up onto the roof and heard him shout to the security guard, 'I can't undo the lid, Ken.' He lied.

Tony Sherwood uttered an oath. 'Fuck it, what's gone wrong.'

Shields was a stickler for procedure. 'Try again, get a spanner or something. If you can't open it, I won't let you in, you'll have to reverse out.'

Alf was enveloped in despair; no matter what he did, it didn't bode well for Dora. He'd have to take a chance and hope that the gang had allowed for the situation. *Oh God, please help me; please don't let Dora come to any harm.* He made a show of wrestling open the lid and slowly lowered the dipstick into the slot, holding his breath as it disappeared out of view, dreading what would happen when it came out dry.

The moment he'd feared melted away; there was a film of oil running the full length of the dipstick he was now in the process of withdrawing. *How had they managed that?*

In record time, he'd closed the lid and clambered down to stand in front of the security window, holding the glistening rod in front of Shields for inspection, cleaning it, and waving the oil-stained rag at the vigilant guard.

'All clear, Alf, in you go.'

In the darkness, I smiled smugly, congratulating myself; my idea had worked. The one-inch diameter sealed steel tube I had asked to be installed from the floor of the tanker to its roof immediately under the dipstick slot had been a stroke of genius. The tube had been filled with fuel oil just to cover the eventuality of the tank being dipped. The test completed I opened a valve to allow its contents to drain into a similarly sized tube lying on the floor of the tanker. In the unlikely eventuality of the tanker being dipped on the way out, the dipstick would come out dry.

Alf waited until the inner gate rolled open and eased the tanker, slowly moving forward into the PMR site. He didn't understand what had happened. Maybe he was wrong; maybe they weren't inside the tanker after all. He was still afraid for Dora, but in a strange way, he enjoyed the situation and was intrigued as to what would happen next. *When are they going to make their move?* He'd done his bit, but what would happen when the fuel-gauge didn't show any oil going into the storage tank? *That's when the shit will hit the fan, and the bastards will be caught red-handed. Please, God, don't let them harm Dora.* He felt his stomach churn, but there was nothing he could do except worry. He steered the tanker round the site to the three massive oil storage tanks, glancing at his paperwork to determine which he was loading. Number three. He stopped the tanker at the oil fill point and shut down his engine. *Now what? Follow routine and fill the tank. That's what would be expected.* He jumped down out of his cab, landing lightly on his feet given his age, and, wasting no time, went straight to the end of the tanker. As he'd done hundreds of times, he reached forward for the fill hose. 'What the fuck?' He heard a scuffling noise and stood back, amazed, as the end of the tanker swung open.

'Christ.' His jaw dropped open and stayed open as he watched four men clamber out of the tanker's innards. One of the men was speaking to him, telling him to do something.

'Leave that, Alf. Go and sit in your cab and stay there until I tell you otherwise.'

The cold night air was acting on his bladder. 'I need a leak.'

'Go find yourself a corner and make it quick.'

Alf wandered over behind the Number Two tank, taking up a position where he could observe what was happening. He was fascinated. *They were well organised; he had to give them that, and they seemed to know their way round the site. Two wheelbarrows, what the fuck were they for?*

As he urinated and watched, one of the men pulled a length of heavy hose out of the tanker and began connecting it to a fire hydrant. *Whatever was he up to?* The man completed his task and began to climb up the fixed steel maintenance ladder to the top of the Number Three tank. *Christ, they were going to fill it with water.* He reacted without thinking, barely finishing his pee, hauling his zip up and ran towards the man as he climbed back down the ladder.

'Don't do that. The boiler will stop working, and the alarm will go off.'

The man just stared at him and said nothing. He felt a hand grab his shoulder from behind, pulling him round roughly.

'You've had your piss, now get back in your fucking cab and stay there. We know Number Three tank isn't in service.' Sherwood shouted angrily, pushing him away roughly in the direction of his cab. Alf stumbled and regained his balance; he wanted to turn back and give the guy a smack like he would have in the old days. *Who was he kidding; he was too old for that kind of thing nowadays.* He climbed back into his cab, closing the door to keep out the cold; all he could do now was sit and wait.

I remembered the guy in the back of the tanker; he should have been conscious by now. 'What about our other guy, Tony?'

'He won't be no trouble; I gave him another tap.'

'We could have done with his help loading.'

'I know but I couldn't risk any hassle when it comes to getting back into the tanker. We'll all have to work harder, that's all.'

I nodded in agreement. 'You're probably right.'

'How long have we got, Craig?'

'I'm just about to turn on the hydrant; when I've done that, we've got about twenty minutes, but we must stop when the water starts pouring out of that tank. The security guy will be watching progress on the tank contents gauge in his office, and he'll know when the tank's full.'

Tony didn't argue; thankfully, he understood the point I was making and nodded readily. 'OK, do the necessary; let's get this show on the road and start loading all that lovely bullion.'

Inside his office, Shields glanced up at No 3 Tank's remote fuel gauge, saw the needle flicker and, knowing the fill would take twenty minutes or so, settled down to read his book. PMR was so confident about its outer security measures that it had never seen the need to install surveillance on the inner site; that mistaken view would change after tonight's work.

The bullion shed stood about twenty metres away; a solitary brick-built building secured by a pair of steel doors just wide enough for a forklift truck to gain access for pallet loading. The doors were secured by three combination deadlocks, just as we knew they would be, but there was no alarm system. It was laughable, really, all that bullion with so little protection. I couldn't understand PMR's thinking; an alarm system would have cost pennies; such was the faith they had in their outer site security. Tony moved forward and dialled each of the three combinations in turn, pushing down a lever handle each time; then, the sequence completed, he pulled the door open. We were in. To my surprise, Tony stepped back and motioned me forward.

'I think you should have the honour of loading the first barrow, seeing as this is your baby. But get a move on, time is money.' He laughed heartily.

I hesitated just long enough to take a deep breath, then shone my torch around the shed; my heart gathered pace as the beam picked out the piles of ingots, gold, silver and the slightly duller platinum piles. I wheeled my barrow into the nearest stack of gold bars and began loading; Tony wheeled past me to the next one and set to. The ingots were heavier than I expected. 'Christ, these are heavy, Tony. Don't overload the barrow. We can't risk it collapsing. And now, with only three of us, I think one should stay at the tanker and stack the bars away. The other guy should be watched anyway, just in case he wakes up and does something silly."

'Good point. Do as he says, Harry; if the sleeping beauty wakes up, give him a clout.'

The man I now knew as Harry ran back to the tanker and climbed in, ready to receive the bars. I wasn't long behind him; my arms were straining, but I ran; time was precious and was first back to the tanker. Maybe I had taken fewer ingots than Tony. We were in the process of unloading when he turned up.

'Get a move on, you fuckers, time is money.' He laughed again.

Thankfully, good old Charlie Booker had got us wheelbarrows of industrial quality, and they stood up to the ever-heavier loads we put in them. As we got tired, we stopped running back and forth, and eventually, we were reduced to a slow walk.

'How much is left, Tony.' I puffed; I was nearly knackered.

'Hard to say, maybe two more loads.'

As he spoke, I heard the splash of water; the tank was full.

'That's it, Tony; we go as soon as we get this last load in the tanker, and we've got to do that in double time.'

He protested, reluctant to abandon a small fortune.

'Another couple of loads won't make much difference, let's go for it.'

I didn't give way. 'We go now, Tony, I mean it; anything out of the ordinary could jeopardise the whole operation.'

He stared at me for what seemed like an eternity, then shrugged. 'Fuck it, you're right; a bird in the hand and all that shite.'

Whilst Tony unloaded his last barrowful, I turned the hydrant off and went to alert Hagen that we would soon be off. The cab light was on, and he was sitting deathly still, just staring straight ahead. I guessed the poor guy was worrying about his wife and what would happen to him in the aftermath of the robbery. I knocked on the cab door, and he rolled down his window; he said nothing, just looked at me enquiringly.

'We'll be going shortly; you can start up your engine and be ready for our signal.' As an afterthought, I added. 'Your wife will be fine, I promise you.'

'Easy for you to say; she's got a bad heart, and God knows what this lot will do to her.'

'I'm sorry to hear that, honestly, I really am; I hope she's OK. Take her on a long holiday when this is over.'

'I would if I had your kind of money.'

'Just remember this, Alf, you're going to be famous tomorrow; the Press will pay a fortune for your story.' I saw his expression change as he recognised what I was suggesting, but before he could say anything, Tony appeared.

'What the fuck are you two gassing about? It's time we were gone.'

'I was just reminding Alf to follow instructions.' I winked at the driver, and he nodded.

Tony wanted to be gone and snarled. 'Well, don't just sit there, Alf; start your fucking engine. I'll flash my torch when I'm ready; after that, count to ten, then move out. That gives me time to get on board and close the door. When you leave here, go straight to West Elton Street and stop when you're waved down. Understood?'

Hagen nodded compliantly, sensing, for the first time since his nightmare began, that everything was going to work out. 'Understood.'

There was no rigmarole involved in departure other than the gate sequencing security, and then we were soon on our way.

'You know something, Tony?'

'What's that then?'

I patted the ingots. 'This must be the most expensive, most uncomfortable seat I've ever sat on.'

I think Tony was warming up to me; he let out a huge laugh.

Alf Hagen drove back to the changeover spot and stopped as instructed; he knew what was expected of him and slid over onto the passenger seat. The same man who had accompanied him earlier climbed in and handed him the blindfold. 'You know the drill, Alf.'

He complied meekly; his ordeal would soon be over; he would do exactly as he was told.

Back at the gang's warehouse, Alf was helped down out of the cab, led still blindfolded to his own vehicle and driven back to West Elton Street.

As the journey progressed, Alf felt increasingly relaxed and started thinking about the stories he was going to tell the Press. The guy was right; there was money to be made, and he'd try to spice up the events best he could; that way, the newspapers might just pay a bit more. Maybe an exclusive would be the best deal; they paid well for exclusives.

The tanker braked suddenly, interrupting his thoughts. 'It's over, Alf; you can drive back to your depot and tell them what's happened. A phone call has already been made to our man, and you'll find that Dora is at home waiting for you, none the worse for wear.'

Alf watched as the man climbed onto the back of the motorcycle and was driven away. Momentarily he thought about phoning 999 but chose instead to play safe, no point in upsetting the gang at this late stage. He set off for the depot, practising his spiel for the Press interview.

Back at the warehouse, the tanker was driven away, heading for a remote barn where the bullion would be removed and placed in crates labelled 'MACHINE PARTS'. From there, it would be transported to its destination. The tanker itself would be driven to a large commercial parking area and be abandoned. These two final elements of the whole operation would be accomplished within the next four hours, long before the police had gotten their game plan together.

The original tanker driver, the hapless Peter McCann, was released somewhere in the countryside, none the worse for his experience, but with a real tale to tell for the rest of his life. Like Alf Hagen, the Press would pay well for his story.

Along with the others, I was transported to our various drop-off points by the same van that had kicked the job off just a few hours earlier. Being rich felt good, but I suppose my best feeling came when Tony Sherwood made a point of shaking my hand. 'The sweetest job I've ever pulled, Craig, you did well; I hope we work together again.'

'That goes for me too, Tony. You're a real professional, a vicious bastard as well, of course.'

He laughed heartily and poked me in the chest. 'And don't you forget it, kiddo.'

'Tony, I know it's not my business, but don't be too hard on the lad with the claustrophobia; he really can't help his condition.'

He shot me a warning look, and his tone was cool. 'You're right mate, it's none of your business; it's down to me and Ralph Mason.'

I never did get to know what became of the guy.

Chapter Seventeen

Dan had ordered that there be no contact between gang members for three weeks to let police and media interest cool down; I was very firmly instructed to keep away from the Camden planning centre. He would be in touch when he thought it appropriate and did not want to be contacted unless some emergency arose. For my part, even as I had made my way back to Finsbury after the robbery, I was already thinking about the future. With nothing much to do, the weeks ahead looked increasingly boring.

I was coming to realise that the life I was getting into was destined to be a lonely one if I persisted with my policy of avoiding any relationships. Just the thought of love brought memories of my time with Sam flooding back. In my quiet moments, I had told myself that I'd pursue crime planning for five years or so and then opt out, but judging by my recent experience, five years seemed like a lifetime. There would be high spots, of course, but there would be lots of low ones as well, and realistically, how many big jobs could be pulled off in five years? The more I thought about it, the more I came to accept that there couldn't be that many.

I needed another interest, something that involved a bit of brainpower and, ideally, one that would provide a source of regular income. Sooner or later, I would be asked to explain how I was supporting myself, especially if I did find a partner. On impulse, I decided to dabble in the Stock Market and made a note to order the Financial Times for delivery with my daily Guardian. I was also missing female companionship. It wasn't just sex; I could always pay for sex. It was those feelings of closeness that only living with a woman could bring. Pictures of Sam flashed before me again, and I thought of getting in touch, telling her that Crewe was a terrible mistake that would never be repeated. It was a ridiculous idea; I wasn't ready to give up crime, and I couldn't expect her to share the life it involved. In my more thoughtful moments, I liked to delude myself that somewhere down the way, if she was still around, maybe we could put the pieces back together. It was crazy thinking, someone like Sam wouldn't be on her own for long. End of story.

My best bet was probably to check out the female residents of Finsbury Park Mansions; I reckoned there were at least four on the go. They might all be spoken for, but I had to start somewhere. Where better than the girl next door? Next time I bumped into one I'd make an effort, or maybe just walk along the corridor, knock on a door and ask to borrow the traditional cup of sugar. Whatever came to pass, I needed some sort of cover story. The Stock Exchange involved risk, and risk was in my blood; I decided to set myself up as an Investment Advisor. I needed a few props and made a note to get some letterheads and business cards printed in the coming week. With that done, I would go to a financial advisor and make an investment of £10,000 just to give me an insight into the process; in any case, I had to do something with the cash lying around from the Crewe job.

I slept fitfully when I finally went to bed; there was still too much adrenaline flowing through my veins, and I kept reliving the raid, time and time again. I wanted to hear the morning news, read the newspapers, see how the robbery was reported. I even made up my own headlines.

Police Baffled by Bullion Raid

Gold Standard Robbery

The Trojan Tanker Heist.

I tossed and turned for ages but eventually slipped into a deep sleep and didn't open my eyes till gone eight. I rose quickly and went straight to the radio. Eventually, they 'took us over' to the PMR site, where there were interviews with police and management describing the raid. The Company was offering a £10,000 reward for information leading to the capture of the robbers; not generous considering how much we'd lifted. My ego sated to some degree; I showered, dressed and wandered down to my post box to retrieve my newspaper, eagerly unfolding it to see the headlines. The editor hadn't been too imaginative; it simply said £3MILLION GOLD BULLION THEFT.

'Shocking, isn't it?' The voice came from behind me; I turned to find an attractive young woman looking over my shoulder at the headline. She was wearing a smart light-grey business suit and carrying a briefcase, obviously on her way to work.

'Yes, I guess so,' I answered feebly, 'but it seems to be quite a clever robbery.'

She gave me a disapproving smile. 'It's still stealing no matter how you dress it up.?'

Christ, why were some people always so fucking righteous? But I played along.

'It is indeed. I hope they all get their just desserts.' I tried to sound convincing.

She nodded her agreement. 'Me too, well must go, bye.' With that, she was off before I could engage her further

'Bye. I'll see you around.' I called after her. She raised a hand in acknowledgement but didn't look back.

Damn it, Craig, you missed an opportunity there; you didn't even ask her name.

Back in the flat, I read the complete report, and my heart missed a beat when I read that *'the police were following up some strong leads.'* Hopefully, it was something they always said just to put on the frighteners.

The story hung around for a few days, then faded away. My conscience got a lift when I read the interview given by Alf Hagen, smiling at how he garnished his experience; happily, it seemed that his wife was none the worse for her experience. They both said some bitter things about how the cat was killed, the first I'd heard about it; not that it bothered me much. The happy couple were going off on holiday to Spain to recover from their ordeal.

Ten days had passed since the robbery, and time was dragging. Stocks and shares weren't really holding my interest, and I resorted to looking at holiday brochures with a view to going away to somewhere sunny for a week. I ended up with Tuscany, Crete, and Monte Carlo on my short list, but kept going round in circles when it came to making a final choice, so I gave up. Monday arrived. It was late morning, and I was still dithering where to go when, out of the blue, Dan rang.

'Hi Craig, it's me.'

'Dan! I hadn't expected to hear from you for another week or so. Nothing wrong is there?' I asked with just a trace of nervousness.

'Not a thing. I've got some news that will please you. Can you come round to my place tonight, say seven-thirty?'

My curiosity was aroused, but I asked no questions. 'Can do.'

'Good. I'll get in some eats for us.'

'See you then, bye.'

News that would please me; now, what could that be about? I decided it must be about money, though it seemed a bit quick to be paying out.

Dan greeted me like a long-lost brother, even down to a hug; he looked and sounded like he was on a high. 'Good to see you, mate. Thanks for coming at such short notice; I trust it doesn't interfere with any social engagements?'

'Alas, not. In fact, I'm beginning to feel like a monk.'

'You should be able to sort that out, a man of your means. Anyway, first we eat, then we talk.'

As we dined, we talked, Dan asking questions and me answering them. Mainly, he wanted my perspective on the job. What was good? What was bad? Any changes?

Christ, is this the only reason you wanted to see me? I had hoped for more exciting conversation, but it was his show, and anyway, I had nothing better to do. 'Just about everything went to plan, witness the fact that we rode off into the night with the bullion. How much did we get anyway?'

'I'll come to that later. Did anything not go to plan?'

I told him about the guy's bout of claustrophobia and the obvious risks it presented at the time.'

'Yeah, Tony briefed me on that. Nobody's fault, as far as I can see; just bad luck.'

'Hmm, I guess so, but it could have been disastrous; it's the sort of bad luck we should try to eliminate. What happened about the guy, by the way?'

'We won't be using him again.'

'Meaning?'

'Change the subject, Craig.' Dan answered obtusely for the second time, clearly warning me off.

I knew better than to press for a fuller answer. 'But other than that, the job went really well; good crew, good logistics, good organisation.'

Dan nodded 'Tony said the same, more or less; same sentiment, different words. You really impressed him, Craig; I reckon you might just have made an important ally.'

'Not sure about that, but I can reciprocate. Tony played his part well.'

'In retrospect, is there anything you would change?'

'Two things.'

Dan looked at me sharply; I think my reply surprised him. 'Go on.'

'Firstly, Tony was the only one with the combinations to the strong room locks; if anything had happened to him, the operation would have failed.'

'But it didn't though, did it?'

'No, but that was good luck. Claustrophobia was bad luck. What if Tony had fallen off the tanker and ended up unconscious or worse? We should do all we can to reduce risk to a minimum.'

Dan pondered for a moment, then nodded. 'You're right; we'll cover anything like that in the future if the need arises. And the second change?'

I smiled broadly. 'Simpler, but it might not be as easy to solve.' I paused as Dan looked at me expectantly. 'It all went so well I thought I'd ask for a pay rise when the next job comes along.'

To my relief, he burst out laughing. 'Knowing you, I'm not surprised. We'll discuss remuneration when the time comes. We might squeeze another one or two per cent out of the kitty for you; I'll think about it.'

'I'll hold you to that. And what did his majesty think of the job?'

'That's partly why I asked you to come tonight; the Man wanted me to pass on his congratulations. He's over the moon with the result.'

'Pleased to hear it; mind you, I'd be delirious with the kind of money he's pulled in.'

'I've already told you money isn't what he gets off on. Sure, the bigger the job, the better, but only because it brings bigger headlines, which is more reflected glory for him. And the more baffled the police are, the better he likes it.

'When it comes to the job, he knows he's a sleeping partner but likes to think of himself as a master criminal holding the strings of a successful organisation. He's got more money than he'll ever be able to spend.'

'To each his own, I suppose. I like to count my thrills in hard cash, which leads me nicely to my next question. Exactly how much did we take?'

'That I can tell you; that's where the Man excels; recycling the spoils is his forte. That side of the business is all tied up before the job takes place, thanks to the network he's built up. For example, the bullion crossed the Channel before noon the following day, and what's more, he has the contacts to have it all dealt with as legitimately as it makes no difference.'

My respect for the Man doubled; I was still carrying around most of the sixty grand from the Crewe job and was afraid to even put it in a bank in case it attracted unwelcome attention.

'OK, Dan, I'm suitably impressed; the Man knows his business just like we know ours. So, impress me some more by telling me how much we're going to get out of this.'

Dan drew breath, and I was sure his eyes lit up; the thought of it was making him excited. 'Listen up; the bullion fetched three million, eight hundred and fifty-six thousand. Less the set-up charges, we have a cool three million for the pot.'

'Over eight hundred grand to set up?' I voiced my surprise and scepticism.

Dan nodded. 'It is a lot, I'll grant you, but don't forget it's not just the expenditure before the raid; it's getting the loot away and absorbed into the system. There are transaction fees and commissions involved and, most importantly, knowing the right people to deal with. Believe me, these things are expensive and need to be executed with infinite care. Anyway, it's not open to challenge; the Man determines that figure, and that's an end to it.'

There was no point in having a debate; nothing would change, and I was going to be rich. 'So, what was your cut?'

'As I told you before the job, I get twenty per cent, which is six hundred thou, and that means you get two hundred.'

I let out a long whistling exhalation. 'Two hundred grand, two hundred grand, I can't believe it. I never dreamt I'd have so much money in my wildest dreams. 'And when do I get my hands on it?'

He looked over his shoulder. 'It's in a bag under the bed.'

'No!' I gasped. 'I don't believe it.' I shook my head, but I found myself looking beyond him to the bedroom, nevertheless.

'Of course, it isn't there, you dickhead; you could never handle that much loot in one hit, Craig.'

'Still, it would be nice to have in my pocket figuring out what to do with it; that way, I'm in the driving seat.'

'Relax, it's already in your pocket, in a manner of speaking.'

Dan passed me a card. 'That's your new bank, Zweichardt Freres, Zurich, Switzerland.'

'It's a helluva way to travel for a withdrawal.'

Dan ignored the quip. 'I've written your account number on the back of the card, and your password is GLASGOW. I thought you would like that, given your origins.'

I flicked the card over and studied the ten-digit account number.'

'Not easy to remember, is it? And how do I access these funds?'

'Either in person or by telephone, just quote your account number and password and tell them what you want.'

'OK,' I hesitated, choosing my words carefully, anxious not to offend. 'There's just one little problem.'

Dan raised an eyebrow. 'Yeah?'

'Well, much as I trust you, Dan, I don't like the idea of you, and God knows who else, knowing my account details.'

'Is that all? Well, you can stop worrying; both the account number and password are temporary just to get the money into your name. You now go over to Switzerland, present yourself at the bank, and they'll set up a permanent account for you; only with that done will you have the details. You'll need to do it within the next fourteen days. An open flight has been reserved for you with British European Airways, along with two nights at the Hotel Eden au Lac in Zurich. And before you start moaning about cost, it's all at Zweichardt Freres' expense, provided you leave your money with them. Like all Swiss banks, their reputation is built on absolute discretion; your details will never be imparted to anyone else and that includes the legal fraternity. I have my pile salted away over there gathering tax-free interest.'

'Sounds good. I might go over this week; I'm at a loose end now the job's done. I've even taken to dabbling with Stocks and Shares. Which reminds me to ask if you know a reliable dealer who won't ask too many questions if I wanted to make a cash investment of around ten thousand?'

'Cromer and Kilroy, they're in the telephone directory; ask for Nick Adams, mention my name, and you'll be OK.'

'I knew I could rely on you, thanks Dan.'

He sat back with a look of a contented Cheshire cat. 'And now I have some really good news for you; it might just help to fill in some of that time you have on your hands.'

I looked at him expectantly. Surely, there wasn't another job coming up already.

'The Man wants to go ahead with a repeat of the Great Train Robbery just as soon as everything can be set up. More than that, you're trusted now and needn't take part in the job unless, of course, you liked the excitement.'

I was bowled over at this unexpected turn of events. 'Great fucking news, Dan, I really want this one, and a big **no**, I don't want to take part; at the end of the day, it's a risk I can live without.'

'I thought it would please you; the dividend on this one will make the PMR job look like chicken feed.'

'A happy thought, but we've got to pull it off first. When do we start?'

'Anytime you're ready, you'll be leading on this again.'

My enthusiasm had run away with me. There were two issues I wanted dealt with before I got involved with my new commission.

'There are two matters we need to sort out before we go any further.'

He looked at me long and hard; I guess there was something in my tone that signalled I was going to come up with something difficult.

He sighed resignedly. 'I guess that money will be one of them. No problem; I was thinking that you were worth forty per cent of my take on this one.'

'I appreciate the offer, and you'll always be the senior partner, but I think that fifty-fifty would be a fairer split on this job, seeing as how it's my idea.'

He shook his head. 'No can-do, Craig; I've largely set up this organisation, and how it works, fifty-fifty is out of the question. You would get nowhere with a job this size without my contacts. I'll give you forty-five per cent on this job, but only because it's your baby, it's not a precedent. That's my final offer: take it or walk away; the choice is yours.'

I'd anticipated more resistance and would have gone ahead with forty per cent, but business was business. I had screwed as much as I could out of him this time round; I extended my hand, and we shook on the deal.

'And the other matter?'

I took a deep breath. 'You won't like it.'

'Knowing you, it won't go away because I don't like it. Try me.'

'You're right about that, Dan. I won't let this one go. I want to meet the Top Brass, the Big Cheese himself; I'll deliver on the Train Robbery, but I want to meet him face to face just like you have.'

I saw fear in Dan's eyes for the first time since I'd known him; the idea horrified him.

'I can't do that, Craig; I just can't do that. You don't know him; it would be more than my life's worth to reveal his identity, yours too, for that matter.'

It had really rankled me when the Man had insisted that I took part in the PMR job, something I'd told myself I'd never do after the Crewe fiasco. I wanted to hit back, and I could see no other way of doing it.

I was batting on a sticky wicket; all I could do was walk away, and I didn't want to do that just yet. And Dan was the only link to the Man. If anything happened to him, where would that leave me? But I had an instinctive dislike of generals who never put their heads above the parapet, and I went into stubborn mode, ready to bite the hand that was feeding me. 'It's not negotiable, Dan, and it's not your fault that I'm insisting on it. He can always say no, and you'll survive; he needs you even if he doesn't need me.'

'You're crazy, Craig, think about it. Are you sure you know what you're doing? What difference can it possibly make knowing who the top dog is?'

I shook my head; I was well and truly dug in. 'My mind's made up. If he doesn't want to meet me, fair enough; I'll go paddle my canoe elsewhere.'

'You're putting me in a very difficult position, Craig; I don't know how he'll react.'

'I'm sorry, Dan, I've made my mind up.' *Christ, why was I being so stubborn? I was already richer than I ever dreamt possible, yet here I was risking everything.* A touch of insanity had entered me and wouldn't let go.

Dan shook his head in resignation, his face racked with anxiety, but he knew there was nothing he could say to change my mind.

I didn't hang around for long after that; our conversation became stilted and backward-looking. Dan did offer me a lift back to Finsbury, but I made out that I fancied a walk in the night air. He tried to dissuade me right to the last moment, calling after me as I walked away.

'I won't be seeing my client till Friday morning. Call me if you change your mind. I urge you to think it over, Craig. Please.'

I refused to leave the door open, even a crack. 'No way, I really have made my mind up, mate, sorry.'

Despite my bravado, I did chew over my demand as I journeyed home but failed to persuade myself to budge from my decision; the die was well and truly cast, as they say. If the worst came to the worst, I would just call it quits and walk away with two hundred thousand pounds. I reckoned I could get by on that for the foreseeable future. The subject wasn't even on my mind when I climbed into bed; at least, I thought it wasn't.

Chapter Eighteen

I hadn't gone to sleep dwelling on my encounter with Dan, but the cranial cogs must have kept running through my slumbers, and I awoke with a start shortly after seven, a nasty thought filling my head.

Christ, my two hundred grand; the Man will have it stopped as soon as Dan tells him I'm being difficult. Fuck it. Why had I been so damn stupid?

My mental turmoil abated when I recalled that Dan wasn't going to see him until Friday. It was only Tuesday; I could put things right if I acted quickly.

I did my morning ablutions, had breakfast, and looked up the telephone number I required.

'British European Airways, how can I help you?'

'My name's Dorian. I believe that you're holding an open flight for me to Zurich. It was reserved by Zweichardt Freres on my behalf.'

'Please hold whilst I check.'

I drummed on the table anxiously, relieved when the agent came back to me promptly.

'Yes, I can confirm that a return flight is being held in your name. When would you like to travel?'

'Today, if possible?'

'Returning when?'

'Thursday morning would be ideal.'

'Please hold whilst I check availability.'

A few minutes later, the agent was back with me.

'I can offer the ten past one flight today from Heathrow, returning on the eleven forty-six on Thursday morning.'

'Wonderful! Thank you very much for your help.'

'Your flight tickets will be available for you at the BEA desk in Terminal One, Heathrow.'

My next call was to International Enquiries to get a number for the Hotel Eden au Lac in Zurich. To my relief, the guy on the hotel desk spoke perfect English and was familiar with Zweichardt Freres's practice of reserving rooms. He confirmed that there were two nights available in my name and booked me in for that evening, leaving on Thursday morning. Next on my call list was the Bank itself; I explained the purpose of my call and was put through to a Monsieur Lefevre.

'How can I help you, Monsieur Dorian?'

I explained my requirements and, gave him my account number, and waited for him to ask for my password, but he didn't.

'I see that this is a temporary account. To change it, you will have to visit the bank and present your passport, your account number and, of course, your password.'

'I'll be arriving in Zurich this afternoon and leaving on Thursday; an appointment on Wednesday would be ideal.'

'Certainly, shall we say ten-thirty?'

'That will be fine. Thank you for seeing me at such short notice.'

'I look forward to meeting you, Monsieur Dorian. I trust that you have taken up our offer of accommodation at the Eden au Lac.'

'Yes, I have, thanks, and I can confirm that the Hotel and BEA were very efficient.

The journey to Heathrow and onwards to Zurich was uneventful, but as I walked towards Immigration Control, my heart beat a little faster when I remembered that this was the first test for my new passport. Tension continued when he looked at me, then my photo, then at me again before leafing through the pages.

'A new passport Monsieur Dorian?'

I smiled cheerfully. 'Yes, it's brand new; this is my first trip abroad.'

He nodded happily, 'Well, in that case, thank you for making Switzerland your first visit. Are you here on business or pleasure?'

'A bit of both, I hope.'

He handed back my passport, and I made my way to the arrival concourse, where it suddenly dawned on me that I had no Swiss francs, so my first port of call was a Bureau de Change. I had about £100 in my wallet and decided to change half of it into francs, which I thought would meet my needs over the next two days, given that the Bank was picking up my main costs. I saw respect in the taxi driver's eyes when I told him my destination was the Eden au Lac; it didn't return when I settled up, adding what he clearly considered to be an inadequate tip to his fare. The hotel was truly impressive, and I felt self-conscious as I walked up the wide stone stairs and had the door held open for me by a tall, uniformed doorman. My unease continued as I made my way across the luxuriously appointed lounge to Reception and introduced myself to the chic young woman seated behind the desk.

'Welcome, Monsieur Dorian, you will be in Room 14 on the first floor. Will you dine in the hotel this evening?' She sensed my hesitation, 'Our cuisine is excellent, and as a guest of Zweichardt Freres, you will be well looked after.'

I flashed a smile. 'On your recommendation, I will, of course, dine here. Seven-thirty, if that's all right?'

'Certainly. If you wait a moment, I will call for someone to take you up to your room.'

'I'll make my own way if that's alright; I only have hand luggage.'

She shrugged. 'As you wish, monsieur here is your key. You can use the lift or stairs behind you, turn left, and your room is along the corridor. Enjoy your stay.'

The Eden was the swankiest hotel I'd ever been in by a big, big margin; opulence announced itself wherever you chose to look. In truth, I felt like the beggar at the feast place, but with my newly gotten affluence, I was going to have to learn to deal with the better things in life. I pushed open the door of my room and stood there gaping. I felt like a houseguest in Buckingham Palace; it was palatial and sumptuously furnished. The marbled bathroom looked like something out of a Hollywood epic, and it had the fluffiest towels I had ever seen; I now knew what luxury was. The view from my window was breathtaking, looking as it did across Lake Zurich to the Alps beyond; Zweichardt Freres had done me proud. I had to remind myself they were really acting for the Man; Craig Dorian was just one of his foot soldiers.

I asked at reception for directions to the lake, and it didn't take long for the image I had of Zurich as a staid financial centre to be dispelled. My route took me to the edge of the old town, the Allstadt, where I made a turn towards the river Limmot to cross one of its old bridges. On the other side, I followed the Limmatquai path to Lake Zurich. *This is beautiful; no wonder rich people come here. I'll bet that's why they brought their money here in the first place.* I spent some time wandering along the lake's shoreline, and by the time I'd had enough, it was getting dusky as I made my return to the hotel; lights were starting to come on in the old town, adding to its attraction and making me wish that I'd elected to eat there.

Back at the hotel, I bathed, changed, and made my way down to the dining room; on the way, I glanced over to Reception, but my attractive introduction to the Eden au Lac wasn't on duty. Entering the elegant chandeliered dining room and seeing couples chatting at their tables, I found myself wishing I had a woman on my arm to share the evening with. *Was I always going to be asking for more than I had?*

I was shown to my table and offered a drink. I said the first thing that came into my head. 'A glass of champagne please.'

The waiter nodded and handed me a leather-bound menu, thankfully an English version. The choices, to my uneducated eye, were incredible. I took the easy way out and elected to have the six-course Menu Gastronomique. It was very expensive, but that was Zweichardt Frere's problem, not mine. Another waiter attended to take my order but bade me wait when I mentioned my choice. The chef or one of his assistants appeared and went through each course with me, explaining each in great detail. I was offered alternatives and had difficulty making choices; everything sounded so good. He was very patient, and with his judicious prompting, I got there in the end. The sommelier, who had witnessed our discussion, came forward with the wine list when the chef left.

I'd made enough choices for one evening. 'Please, could you recommend a half bottle of white and a half bottle of red to accompany my meal; good quality but not too expensive.' I didn't want to rip the bank off unreasonably, and in any case, I doubted if I had the palate to appreciate a fine wine.

He smiled, and I wasn't sure whether it was because I was asking his advice or because he recognised my ineptitude. He pointed the wines out to me, and expensive though they were, they were mid-range in Eden au Lac terms; I nodded my acceptance.

It was undoubtedly the tastiest, most mouth-watering meal I'd ever had, and when I fell into bed at the end of a long evening, I felt a king; la dolce vita was a new experience, and I loved it.

Next morning, still replete from my dining experience the previous evening, I limited myself to tea and toast, though the delightful aromas wafting in from the kitchen nearly broke down my resolve. Breakfast over, I headed for Reception to get directions to the bank and was pleased to see a head of black curls bent over the desk.

'Good morning.'

She looked up, smiled and pleased me by remembering my name. 'Monsieur Dorian, good morning; I hope you slept well.'

'Extremely well. I need directions to Zweichardt Freres, and I'm afraid I have to cancel my dinner reservation for tonight.'

She looked quite troubled. 'You did not enjoy your dinner last night?'

'Quite the reverse, it was by far the best meal I've ever had. It's just that I couldn't manage such a sumptuous dinner two nights running; I'm not used to it, I'm afraid.'

She smiled sympathetically. 'I understand.' She gave me directions to the bank. 'It's not far, about ten minutes.'

I thanked her and turned away. *Another opportunity lost Craig.* I turned back.

'I'm going to dine in the old town tonight; I wonder if you could recommend somewhere. I'd like it to be cosy with traditional local cooking. You know what I mean by cosy?'

She laughed. 'I think so. You mean warm, friendly, intimate, that kind of thing.'

'That's exactly it. And if you can think of somewhere, just to make it a perfect evening, I wonder if you would like to join me?'

'I'm sorry; it's against hotel policy.' Her expression suggested disappointment, and I persisted.

'Please, I go home tomorrow. There are no strings attached, I promise. I'd just like some company; choose your favourite restaurant. Please, no one will ever know.'

Our eyes locked for a moment, and my small prayer was answered. 'I'll meet you tonight in front of St Peterschirke in the Allstadt at seven-thirty. I shouldn't be doing this, not a word to anyone in the hotel and remember,' She smiled, a twinkle in her eye, 'no strings.'

'I promise I shall be the perfect gentleman.'

An even wider smile lit up her face. 'Then I shall have nothing to worry about.'

'I don't even know your name.'

'Collette.'

'Mine's Craig, I'll see you this evening.'

Zweichardt Freres wasn't like any bank I'd encountered. It stood in a terrace of stately sandstone buildings, which looked remarkably Georgian. There was no grand sign to announce the bank to the world, and I had to look closely at the traditional brass plaques mounted to the side of each door to identify it. The large glossy black panelled door was impressive to some degree, but it all seemed so understated. The door was locked, and I had to gain entry via the intercom.

'Bon jour.'

'Monsieur Dorian for his appointment with Monsieur Lefevre.'

I heard a buzz, the door opened, and I stepped forward into a large vestibule. The door closed behind me, and a security guard standing in the corner gave me the once-over. I seemed to pass his test, and he opened the door to a plush reception lounge, motioning me through without a word spoken.

I raised a finger to my lips as I passed him. 'Shsssss.' There was no reaction, and I guessed he wasn't amused.

A tall, distinguished grey-haired man came towards me, hand extended. 'Monsieur Dorian, I'm Pierre Lefevre. Welcome to Zweichardt Freres. Please come with me.' He led me along a short corridor with half a dozen doors leading off on either side; the second door on the left stood open, and he invited me to enter. Time had stood still; Dickens wouldn't have felt out of place. He settled in behind a huge partner's desk, indicating that I should sit opposite.

'I hope you are enjoying your visit to Zurich?'

'The city is beautiful, and I hope to explore it further later today.'

'And your room at the hotel is satisfactory?'

'It's magnificent. Thank you for placing me there.'

He spread his hands; his expression dismissive. 'Our pleasure. Your time is short, so let us turn to business. Your account number and Passport, please.'

I handed over my Passport and rattled off my account number. He glanced briefly at my photograph and handed it back. And your password?'

'Glasgow.'

He looked down at a ledger on the desk and nodded approvingly. 'And will you be opening a permanent account with us?'

I nodded. 'Yes, please, I've been very impressed by all that you've done for me so far.'

He nodded his appreciation. 'Thank you, monsieur. And you will transfer all funds across to this new account?'

'Yes, please, except I wonder if you could let me have two hundred francs; I'm rather short of local currency?'

'Certainly.' He buzzed on his intercom and issued instructions to the other party. 'That is arranged. Now could you complete this card, please? You will see that it has your name, your current address, and your passport number. Your new account number is shown at the top right-hand corner. Please make a note of it at this point. It will never be given out or shown to any other party under any circumstances.'

'What if I lose it or forget it?'

He shook his head. 'You must avoid that happening. Henceforth you or anyone who has your account number and password can access your account without any challenge by the bank.'

I frowned; it seemed a very inflexible arrangement. 'No one forgets or loses their details intentionally.'

'It is one of our rules, Monsieur Dorian and that of most Swiss banks.'

I wrote the first six numbers in reverse on a date at the front of my diary and the last four in reverse on Christmas Day. I wasn't sure why I was employing this subterfuge, but it couldn't do any harm to be cautious.

Monsieur Lefevre referred to the ledger again. 'Let me see, two hundred thousand pounds sterling at today's exchange rate plus interest to date. He punched the figures into his calculator and showed me the resultant sum in Swiss Francs. I wasn't in any position to challenge the figures and nodded in acquiescence.

'I will now enter this sum on your card as your opening balance. It will be modified every time you make a transaction. Your account will be available for your inspection at any time, on production of your account number and password.'

At that moment, there was a tap on the door, and a young man entered with a small sheaf of banknotes. Monsieur Lefevre initialled his authorisation, and the young man departed.

'Your money, Monsieur Dorian, and now all you have to do is write your password on the card in the bottom left corner, sign opposite, and our business is complete.'

I took the offered pen, wrote down WESTMOOR as my password, signed, and handed back the card.

He glanced at it and looked up. 'I know Glasgow, of course; is Westmoor also in Scotland?'

'No, it's a small village in Cumbria; I have connections there.'

'I see.' He stood then and offered his hand. 'I hope you enjoy the rest of your stay in Zurich and have a good journey home.'

I felt uneasy; I was leaving behind a small fortune. 'I'm sorry, I'm new to this, but do I get a record of our transaction.'

He smiled, shaking his head. 'No, Monsieur Dorian, we operate entirely on a basis of trust. You can access your account at any time, in person or by telephone. We will carry out your instructions or those of anyone acting on your behalf, although I would advise against the latter except in extreme emergencies.'

Monsieur Lefevre led me back along the corridor and left it to the ever-cheerful security guard to show me from the premises.

I spent the rest of the day touring the old town area of Zurich, starting with the Grossmunster, an 11th-century cathedral with magnificent views from the top of one of its twin towers. I wandered aimlessly along the cobbled twisting streets, following my nose, and found myself at the town's most important cathedral, the Fraumünster, another impressive religious edifice.

Hunger was setting in, so I made my way into a small inn for a light lunch. I wasn't a culture freak by any means, but felt I had to take the opportunity to apply some of the knowledge I'd acquired from Henry over the last few months and see more of the city. I set out to visit the local art scene. Top of my list was the Cursthaus art museum, followed by the Schweizerisches Landesmuseum; the latter was housed in a fantastic old castle. Time flew by, but by the end of the afternoon, wonderful though it all was, I started to get culture fatigue and made my way back to the Eden au Lac.

The moment I'd been looking forward to all day finally arrived, and I felt on top of the world as I set out to meet Collette; it struck me that I felt happier than I had all day. I went directly to the St Peterskirche and got there ten minutes early; Collette turned up just five minutes later. As she walked towards me, I thought again how pretty she was. Her smile was a winner, and as she drew near, I thought her large brown doe-like eyes held a sparkle. She was dressed casually but smartly: pale green slacks below a rich burgundy top and an olive-green leather jacket. A silk scarf swept round her neck added a touch of femininity.

I wasn't sure how to greet her, but she made it easy, reaching forward to kiss me on the cheek. 'Hi, Craig.'

'Good to see you, Collette; thanks for coming. You look gorgeous.'

She giggled and linked her arm to mine like we'd known each other for years, and we were on our way. We chatted about my day as we wandered through the Allstadt towards the river, passing a plethora of restaurants on the way.

'My goodness, you do like art.'

'I have to confess I know very little about art and don't think I've ever visited a gallery in the UK, but I have a very knowledgeable friend I hope to impress.'

She laughed. 'I see. Here we are; I hope you like it?'

'Looks good to me.'

The Hausmunster looked like a Swiss chalet; it was decorated with fairy lights and an abundance of small brass bells which tinkled unobtrusively when the wind caught them. The interior was softly lit, with seating taking the form of small, intimate alcoves.

'This is perfect, Collette.'

'It really is my favourite restaurant, simple, warm, and unpretentious.'

We enjoyed an inexpensive meal, which I persuaded Collette to choose for both of us. I felt very relaxed and really enjoyed listening to her as she told me about herself, her family and her ambitions; there was no mention of a boyfriend. I gave her an unashamedly glamorised account of me and what I wanted out of life.

Afterwards, we wandered around, and she pointed out the town's nightclubs; I persuaded her to have a nightcap in the Bar Odeon, where no less a person than Lenin had enjoyed a tipple whilst he spouted his communist ideals. All too soon, the evening was over, and we stood opposite each other, somewhere in the old town, saying our goodbyes.

'I must go now, Craig. Thank you for a lovely evening; I hope we meet again sometime.'

A thought struck me, and I gave her one of my phoney business cards. 'If you're ever in London, please call me, even if you're with a friend; I'd love to see you again.'

'I promise, and you must do the same when you return to Zurich.'

She looked at me, seemingly waiting; I bent forward and kissed her full on the lips. I stood back immediately; for such a short acquaintance, I felt inexplicably sad that I wouldn't be seeing her again.

'Goodnight, Collette.' I spread my hands, 'You see, no strings as promised.'

Maybe I imagined it, but she sounded wistful. 'Ah yes, of course, no strings. Maybe another time, Craig.'

She flashed another of her smiles, then walked away, turning once to wave goodbye as I stood there watching.

Alas, Collette wasn't on duty the next morning when I checked out.

The flight back to London was on time and unremarkable, though I experienced another gut-wrenching episode when I presented my phoney passport for inspection. It was duly stamped, and I resolved not to worry about it in future. The taxi driver was waiting for me in Arrivals, and the journey home gave me plenty of time to think about what lay ahead.

There were three messages from Dan on the answering machine, all requesting that I give him a call. I wasn't in the mood for an argument, but

I rang anyway and was pleased that he wasn't available. I left a brief message.

'Hi Dan, it's Craig; sorry not to get back to you before now, but I've been away for a couple of days. I can guess why you're calling, but I haven't changed my mind. I'm around this evening if I've got it wrong and you've got something else on your mind. Bye.'

You've done it now, Craig; there's no going back.

I watched television until near midnight, but Dan didn't come back to me; I really had burned that final bridge.

Chapter Nineteen

Dan Rawson steeled himself as he pressed the intercom buzzer to the penthouse flat of 4 Belgravia Circus; he wasn't looking forward to what lay ahead.

'Yes?'

'It's Dan Rawson.'

'Come right up, Mr Rawson, he's expecting you.' Miss Black's voice was, as ever, impersonal, neither cold nor welcoming, devoid of emotion; he'd known her for eight years, but she had never used his first name, nor he hers. He listened for the electronic click, heard it, and made his way in; the lift doors opposite stood open; the penthouse had its own lift, which rose smoothly and noiselessly, its doors opening when it reached its destination. Miss Black, middle-aged, her hair pulled back in a bun, stood waiting, dressed in her usual smart dark-grey business suit.

'Good morning, Miss Black. New suit?'

'No, Mr Rawson, it's not.' Miss Black was not one for compliments or the niceties of social contact and smiling seemed to be out of bounds for her. 'He's ready for you.'

The man seated behind the desk was small and thickset, his tanned face lined, and ruggedly handsome, black hair slicked back. He rose immediately and came out from behind his desk, hand extended, a smile breaking out on his face.

'Dan, good to see you, thanks for coming.' He turned back to the attendant, Miss Black. 'Coffee, Jean, please.' then as an afterthought 'Or you can have tea if you prefer, Dan?'

'Coffee will be fine.'

Miss Black gave a small nod and departed, closing the door behind her.

Rawson was first to speak. 'I suppose you're busy as always?'

'Business is ever-present, but that's how I like it. Keep dabbling in this and that; some wins, some losses.'

'Knowing you, sir, I'm sure the former will predominate.'

The man opposite was susceptible to praise, and a touch of smugness crept into his voice. 'Oh yes, that's very true; I'm usually ahead of the game.'

A soft knock on the door heralded the return of Miss Black, complete with a tray laid out with silver service and fine china. 'Shall I pour, sir?'

'No, that's all for the moment, Jean.'

With her customary nod of compliance, Miss Black took her leave.

The man opposite wasn't the complete host. 'Be a good chap and do the necessary, Dan, then tell me where we're up to with our next venture. Some good news will be welcome; I've hit a bit of a problem with one of my properties, a very expensive property.'

Rawson raised an eyebrow, seeking enlightenment, which didn't come. 'Sorry to hear that, sir. I don't suppose it's anything I could help with?'

'Not unless you want to pick up a million pounds worth of remedial work for me. I'm meeting a friend for lunch who might just be able to help. Anyway, enough of that, let's hear what you've got to report.'

The moment Rawson had been dreading had arrived, but first, some good news to soften the unavoidable anger that lay ahead. 'The clear-up after the last job will be completed today, and our Scotland Yard source tells us that CID doesn't have any leads left to follow up. It won't be too long till they consign this one to the unsolved pile.'

'Excellent, excellent, I do like to leave them baffled. And the meeting with our latest recruit; how did that go? I hope you passed on my congratulations.'

Rawson hesitated for only a split second, but it was long enough for the man opposite to detect that all wasn't well. 'I detect a touch of unease, Dan. Don't tell me your friend is having second thoughts. Perhaps you're not paying him enough.'

The plummy upper-class accent had taken on a harder edge, as it always did when the man scented things weren't entirely going his way.

'No, no, it's not money; he wants more after the recent success, but I can handle that.'

'What then?' The man's irritation was slowly building as he sensed his lieutenant's reluctance to explain the nature of the problem. 'I pay you to sort out problems; if you can't, I'll start looking for someone who can.'

You arrogant bastard. 'I can't sort this one out; it's not under my control. I'm sorry.'

'Spit it out, stop the damn waffling, Dan.' The man's steely grey eyes narrowed and hardened, boring into Rawson, seeking an explanation.

'Dorian says he won't do the job unless he gets to meet you.'

The man's fist slammed down on his desk as he sprang to his feet. 'Who does that little shit think he is, demanding to meet me? Does he know what he's messing with? Why the hell haven't you sorted him out?'

'I've told him, I've threatened him, I've begged him; I've done all I can. He says it's up to you; he gets to meet you, or he walks away.'

The man's fist thumped down again. 'Does he now? I'll sort the little sod.' He grabbed the telephone, scanned his diary, and punched in a number. The call was answered almost immediately; Rawson watched and listened as the man conversed in fluent French with the other party. The conversation was short, and the anger in the man's expression showed it had not gone to his liking. His eyes were blazing when he gave Dan Rawson his attention. 'Your friend is too clever for his own good; he's already transferred his payout into a new account. The little bastard is a step ahead of us.'

261

'I'm sorry, sir; what would you like me to do?'

'Answer me one question and think carefully before you reply. Can we pull off the train job without him? No ifs and buts, I want a plain yes or no.'

Rawson was cornered; he wanted to say yes, but he couldn't be certain. If he tried and failed, his future would be on the line. 'He's keeping his cards close to his chest, and I have the impression that he knows something about security that might not show up when we check it out.'

The man sighed wearily. 'Give me a straight answer, Dan. Yes, or no?'

Rawson was in deep water; if he said yes and the job went sour, what then? If he said no, the Man was left with the decision, but his standing would be severely dented, and anyway, he wanted to keep Craig on board; his friend had flair.

'No, I'm sorry, sir; I can't give you a guarantee. We need him for this job.'

'I'm very disappointed, Dan, you've let me down rather badly. If you can't control your people, I'll have to reconsider our relationship. Damn it, I can't understand his motive for wanting to meet me, but I want this job, so I'll agree to the meeting.' He leafed through his diary. 'I'll see him tomorrow at three. Where have we got that's free? He can't come here, that goes without saying.'

'We can use our Highbury flat.'

'Make sure you get him there first; I'll arrive shortly after. And Dan, tell him nothing whatsoever about me, absolutely nothing. He'll meet me, but no introductions. Got that?'

Rawson nodded. 'I assure you he's learned absolutely nothing about you from me, nor will he.' He felt sick inside; his standing had been seriously undermined.

'And two more things; he plays an active part in the next job, or the deal's off. It's not negotiable.'

'Understood.' Rawson nodded, wondering what was coming next.

'And I don't care how good he is, we don't use him again irrespective of what bright idea he comes up with. Have I made myself clear?'

'Perfectly.' Rawson was unhappy at Craig's potential exclusion, but he'd managed successfully before he came along, and he'd do so again. And maybe, just maybe, the Man might change his mind.

'Good. Meeting over; I'm going on now to my next appointment. You have let me down badly, Dan; don't ever let that happen again.'

'I won't sir, I promise.' The words nearly stuck in his mouth, and he felt like a sycophant. *I hope the day comes when I can tell you to go and fuck yourself.*

Rawson's stomach was churning as he made his way home; his relationship with the Man had been damaged and might never be restored

263

to what it had been. *Christ, why am I so concerned? Smug bastard needs me as much as I need him. Maybe it's time to start thinking of getting out.*

'Craig, it's Dan. I've had my meeting. You've really fucked me up, but he's agreed to meet you. I'll pick you up at two thirty tomorrow.'

I could hear the scarcely concealed anger in Dan's voice and wondered if our friendship remained intact.

'Great, I'm glad it's worked out.'

'Listen to me, Craig and listen good, I'm only saying this once.'

'I'm listening.'

'There are two conditions. You take part in the next job, and second, you don't get to work with us again. Got it?'

'No problem, as long as I get fucking paid.'

'I won't welsh on a deal, Craig.'

'I know you won't, Dan; it's not you I have in mind.'

'I'm fucking annoyed at this whole situation; you've damaged me, Craig, damaged me badly. I hope neither of us lives to regret it.'

'It'll all work out in the end when he starts counting the money and reading those banner headlines. He needs us, Dan and he knows it. Otherwise, he wouldn't be seeing me,'

'I hope so for both our sakes; we're way out of our league. See you tomorrow.'

I had to clear the air. 'Dan, are we still mates?'

To my relief, he didn't hesitate. 'Only fucking just, you bastard. See you tomorrow.'

It was all arranged; I was getting to meet the Man, but I knew I'd have to watch my back.

The Man was rattled as never before; he was used to getting his own way, but he'd deal with the situation another day. First, he had a meeting to attend. He buzzed the redoubtable Miss Black on the intercom. 'Jean, have the car brought round. I'm off to my lunch appointment. I shan't be back; I'll be going straight home. Sarah is entertaining some of the local worthies this evening.'

Two men sat opposite each other in the plush armchairs of the members' lounge at Whites. They had asked for a quiet corner where they could converse in private and had given instructions that they were not to be disturbed. They'd enjoyed a satisfying meal and were now dallying over coffee and the expensive decanter of brandy that stood on the small walnut table in front of them. Over lunch they had exchanged all the usual pleasantries and shared anecdotes about events past and present, but now was the time for matters in hand.

They were much the same age, both extremely successful in their respective fields, both rich, one of them, the Man, **very** rich. They came from very different backgrounds but shared one great weakness: they were both very greedy.

The Man watched as his companion rolled a generous brandy round the goblet cupped in both hands, gently warming the amber liquid. The ritual completed, the goblet was raised to welcoming lips, and the vintage Napoleon cognac sipped appreciatively.

'I trust it meets with your approval?'

Sir Peter Leaney ran his tongue over his lips, savouring the taste. 'That it does, David, that it does. I'd venture to say it's the match of the best Jamesons.' His accent was soft and lilting, as an Irish accent should be. He was a son of Ulster, though his forebears straddled both sides of the border, and he favoured a United Ireland. His donations to Sinn Fein were generous, though they reached the Party by an indirect route.

'Now, tis always a pleasure to be meeting your good self, especially over a splendid lunch that you're paying for, but I'm wondering all the same if there's something I can be doing for you?'

His host smiled. *Trust Peter Leaney to come unerringly to the point.* 'How are things in the building world, Peter?'

Sir Peter Leaney was Chairman, Managing Director and main shareholder of Leaney's, a company he had founded and built into a blue-chip company. He had been knighted for his services to the building industry, plus, of course, his donations to charities and whichever mainland political party best suited his business interests. Neither Her Majesty and her Establishment or Her Government, had any knowledge of his links to Sinn Fein.

The Irishman eyed his friend knowingly. 'We're up to our eyes with work, David, but if you've got something in mind, I'm sure we could accommodate you.'

'Well, I do have a property in the City which has proved something of a disappointment and badly needs some care and attention. It came to me to pay off a debt, but it needs a lot more doing than I was led to believe.'

Sir Peter Leaney smiled and poured another brandy. 'No problem, I'll have my surveyors take a look at it and let you have a price. You'll go to the top of the list.'

'Thank you, Peter. I knew I could rely on you. Thing is, it's a big job, and a prohibitively expensive one; asbestos, dodgy steelwork, tired electrics, all that kind of thing. I was wondering if you could do business with it, the same kind of arrangement we've had in the past? It's been a while since we went down that path; should be safe enough.'

The Irishman's ears pricked up. 'Divine intervention, so to speak?'

'You were always perceptive, Peter. It's in the City, so maybe some of your countrymen would be interested in a commission; they've been quiet lately. A bit of publicity might help negotiations move in their direction.'

It was Peter Leaney's turn to smile; the thought of killing two birds with one stone always pleased him. 'Leave it with me, David; I'll see what I can do.'

The Man pursed his lips and stroked his chin. 'The thing is, Peter, I'm up against a bit of a deadline; I need to make decisions rather quickly.'

Leaney took his cue. 'Pour me another brandy whilst I make a phone call. The City, you say?'

Ten minutes later, Leaney returned, smiling as he relaxed into his chair and reached for his brandy.

'I've spoken with a friend, and tis likely we'll be able to help you in the very near future. It seems that he's been looking at the City for some time now, it being an Establishment enclave and all that sort of thing.'

'I wouldn't want there to be any casualties, Peter.'

'And neither would I, David, neither would I.' Both men knew there could be no guarantees and didn't really care one way or the other; money ruled.

Leaney had his price. 'You know, I was just thinking about that place of yours down in Provence; a beautiful area if ever there was one and, of course, the weather to match. You still have it, don't you?'

The man opposite smiled, recognising that his friend was looking for his personal reward.

'Of course, though it's been a while since I've been there, I prefer Tuscany nowadays. You can use it any time you wish.'

Leaney beamed, 'That's generous of you, David, though I was thinking of something more permanent, like a long-term exclusive lease. Do you think you could manage that for an old friend?'

The Man smiled; the deal was all but done. 'That won't be a problem; I'll have the papers drawn up.'

'Sure now, tis a pleasure doing business with you, David; we'll all be getting something out of it, except, of course, the Insurers, and who cares about them. Let's have another brandy just to seal the deal.'

I was watching from the window when Dan's sports car drew up outside at two-thirty precisely and was pulling on my jacket as the intercom sounded. 'I'm on my way.'

Dan confined himself to a nod as I climbed in and said very little as we drove along. He seemed preoccupied with the time, glancing at his watch every few minutes.

'Where are we going?'

'You'll see when we get there and be careful how you conduct yourself; this guy is lethal.'

'I note your watch getting a lot of attention.'

'I don't want to be late or too early.'

As he drove into the parking area, I knew exactly where we were: the flat I'd been offered in Highbury.

'This is one of the flats you showed me. Surely, he hasn't moved in?'

'Don't be stupid; he wouldn't let his dog live here. He's agreed to meet you, not invite you round for afternoon tea. Don't expect him to roll out the welcome mat.'

'OK, OK, keep your hair on. I've got the picture.'

We let ourselves into the empty flat, and I sat down on the sofa under the window. That way, my face would be in the shadow, and the man would be facing me when he came in.

'He'll be here shortly.' Dan paced around the room and lapsed into silence; his whole demeanour showed he was struggling to deal with the situation. Thankfully, we didn't have long to wait. Just five minutes later, the intercom buzzer sounded, and he virtually raced over to deal with it.

'Yes, Sir, we're both here.'

Minutes later, the doorbell chimed, and Dan, who had hung around near the door opened it immediately; I'd never seen him so nervy. He ushered the immaculately dressed man forward with an air of deference. I rose to my feet respectfully and stepped forward, hand outstretched, taking in every detail of the Man's appearance.

'I'm Craig Dorian. It's a plea....'

He cut me off mid-sentence, ignoring my hand. 'I know who you are, and I can't say I'm terribly interested, Mr Dorian or Murray, whatever you're calling yourself nowadays. This is the first and last time we'll meet; I've kept my part of the bargain. Make sure you deliver yours.'

What a haughty, supercilious bastard you are. I bit back an angry retort and looked at Dan.

'Aren't you going to introduce me to your employer, Dan?'

The man answered. 'He most certainly isn't. I agreed to meet you, Mr Dorian and I've done that; I didn't undertake to be introduced. Our meeting is over, and I'm taking my leave; I've got better things to do than converse with one of the hired hands.'

He smirked and turned on his heel, satisfaction written all over his face.

You smarmy piece of shit. I wanted to run after him and loosen up some of his well-cared-for teeth. The red mist came down; I wasn't going to let him walk away just like that.

'I always thought manners were a thin veneer where the upper classes were concerned, but introductions aren't necessary; I know who you are, **Lord Averton.'**

The man spun round like he'd been caught in a tornado, his fists clenched, his eyes blazing, his face beginning to redden. He snarled at Dan. 'I told you to keep your mouth shut.'

Dan stood there, gulping for air, head shaking, words struggling to get out.

I hadn't meant to drop Dan in the shit and sought to rectify the situation. 'Dan didn't tell me anything. He's been as tight as a drum regarding your identity all the time I've known him. You're just not as clever as you think you are.'

I had his full attention; curiosity seemed to have restored his calm. His voice was soft, enquiring, refined again. 'Then how?'

'Horizon Holdings.'

'What about Horizon?'

'A visit to the Land Registry revealed that it owns this place, my place, Dan's place, as well as many other imposing properties. With that knowledge, a visit to Companies House showed that Horizon Holdings has a small Board comprising Lord and Lady Averton, a General Carew, and a Mr Harburton. The major shareholders are yourself and Lady Averton, and I didn't think that she would be involved in the kind of business you like to conduct.'

'And now that you have this information, what will you do with it?' Lord Averton, plain David Averton, before he was honoured for his generous gifts to various charities and judicious political donations, displayed no sign of concern. If anything, I thought I detected a touch of respect, as sometimes happens when being outmanoeuvred by an opponent.

'Nothing, nothing at all. For me, it's a matter of principle; if I were to continue working for you, I wanted to know who was pulling my strings. It will go no further; you have my word.'

Averton studied me, gathering his thoughts. Then, his mind made up, his face relaxed into a smile, and he surprised me further by extending his hand.

'Your word is accepted, and I hope we can both put this unfortunate interlude behind us. Though I should be careful with those principles of yours, old chap; best not let them take over. Well, that's done with, I'll be off now.'

I watched thoughtfully as Dan followed him to the door. *Was he genuine? Did he really forgive so readily? I doubt it. You'll have to watch your back, my boy.*

Dan came back, shaking his head, slowly and deliberately from side to side. 'You've been lucky, Craig, very lucky, believe me. We've got to deliver big time on this next job, believe me.'

'That's exactly what we're going to do, Dan. So, when do we start?'

'Meet me at Camden tomorrow morning at ten. The sooner he's got a job to focus his mind on, the better his mood is likely to be. You had better watch out for yourself, mate. I doubt if he's buried the hatchet that easily, my friend.'

'I really am still your friend then?'

'By a cat's fucking whisker; but I promise you that will change if you step out of line again.'

Dan dropped me back at the flat, declining my invite to come in for a coffee. Our conversation on the way back had been affable but not matey; he was still shaken, and it would take time to repair the damage. He reminded me to be at Camden in the morning at ten and drove away.

All that evening, I worked on the details of how the train robbery was going to be carried out, determined to impress Dan when we got together next morning. I wrote it all out on a timeline basis, with zero hour being when we brought the train to a halt.

By the time I finished, the table was covered with sheets of notes and the floor strewn with crumpled papers bearing discarded ideas. Finally, I had it to my liking; all the pieces seemed to fit with just one major gap, and that would be down to His Lordship to sort out. I knew I was breaking Dan's rule by working on a job in the flat, one that I agreed with, but it suited my purpose, and who was going to tell him? I felt weary as I gathered up all the scrap and tore each sheet into small pieces for disposal the next day.

The clock was showing two when I climbed into bed, mentally exhausted but satisfied; it had been a good day. For once, I set the alarm, determined not to oversleep; I planned to get to Camden long before Dan.

THE BIG ONE

Chapter Twenty

I was waiting outside Camden Gallery next morning when Henry turned up, resplendent in an emerald green velvet jacket, pink shirt, and crimson cravat; it was shortly before nine.

'How nice to see you, dear boy. Pray tell what brings you to Camden so early?'

'Couldn't stay away from you any longer, Henry.'

'Yes, yes, sweet child, do pull the other one.'

'We've got a rush job on, and I've got some preparation to do.

'Perhaps we could have lunch.'

'I'd like that, Henry, I really would, but it'll depend on what Dan has in mind. Keep it free though, and we can chat about my visit to the Zurich Art Galleries.'

I let myself into the plan room and set to work transferring my hand-written timeline to several flip charts, then pinned them to the wall in time-line order. I checked the sequence thoroughly as I went along, making sure it all made sense. It seemed perfect, and I gave myself a mental pat on the head for a job well done. On the last flip chart, I listed the manpower requirements and the acquisitions.

There were two outstanding matters to be dealt with, and they weren't my responsibility. I finished it all with ten minutes to spare and was sipping coffee when Dan joined me.

'Hi Dan, how are you this fine day?'

'You're sounding pleased with yourself; Henry tells me you've been here since nine.'

'Must confess that I'm excited by this one. It's been on my agenda since my Crewe days; I've been setting out my thoughts, and I think we're just about there.'

'Really?' He raised his eyebrows and sounded slightly incredulous. 'You haven't been working on this outside the plan room, I hope?'

I had my explanation ready. 'Only in my head, Dan; don't forget I've lived with this one for over three years. It didn't all come to me this morning.'

'OK, let's see what you've got; the devil's usually in the detail.'

'If there's a flaw, you'll sniff it out; that's why we make a good team. I thought if I did the donkeywork, I might just ingratiate myself with you and repair some of yesterday's damage. Hopefully, it will impress the Man if we come up with a good proposal this quickly.'

'Don't count on it; he's a mean, unforgiving bastard under that posh veneer. Anyway, let's try to forget yesterday and go through your presentation.'

Thirty minutes later, I was finished; a twenty-million-pound robbery reduced to four flip charts and a half-hour chat.

Dan sat down, stoking his chin, impressed but worried too. 'I need some time to digest this, Craig; I can't fault it, and that worries me; every chain has its weak link.'

I nodded. 'Agreed. Mull it over, and I'll get us a caffeine shot.'

Dan sat there silently, studying the charts, sipping coffee, and coming up with nothing. I understood his unease; sometimes, it was nice to find something wrong, and then you could put it right and decide everything was perfect.

'How many men do you reckon?' Dan broke the silence.

'Fifteen, including me, of course, to keep the Man happy.'

'By the way, I see that you've got over your aversion to using guns.'

'I still don't like them, but there's no other way. That reminds me; if Tony can be persuaded, I'd like him to lead Team One.'

'Can't promise that; it's his decision. I'll tell him it's your request; he'll see the irony in that.'

His reluctance puzzled me. 'But you're in charge of the operation. Surely, at the end of the day, you can insist.'

He smiled wryly. 'Where Tony Sherwood is concerned, I try to avoid insisting.'

We went over the timeline step by step for another hour, but in the end made no changes. Then we dealt with manpower, and he had one valid query.

'How do we ensure the railway guys do precisely what they're expected to?'

'We have to assume they'll be in fear of their lives when they see the guns. Otherwise, Team One should have a railway signalling expert on board.'

Dan shook his head. 'It's a very specialised area; I'm not sure we can arrange that.'

'Best if we could; we've got time to work on it.'

Next up, we went through the acquisitions, and Dan raised one concern.

'Where do we get this gear from? I can't see that they'll be sitting around on a shelf?'

'No idea, that's Charlie Booker's problem; possibly the same source as British Railways.'

Dan shook his head. 'They would be too easily traced.'

'There are railways all over Europe; I can't see that it's much of a problem.'

I sat back and watched as Dan walked back and forth, stopping from time to time to study a flip chart. After ten minutes, he seemed to be satisfied, though his brow was still furrowed with anxiety.

'Scares the shit out of me, Craig.'

'Why? You won't be involved in the action.'

'It's not that, there's millions involved, and you've made it seem as easy as shoplifting. I can't believe how easily you've come up with an answer to the loading problem; that was always the bugbear with this job.'

I tapped my forehead. 'Put it down to sheer genius.' I said boastfully.

'Genius, my arse, it's the product of a criminal mind.'

'Just one big fly in the ointment, Dan.'

His mouth dropped open. 'What's that? Hit me with it; I thought there would be a catch somewhere along the line.'

'We don't have a fucking clue when these special trains run; I'll bet there's only three or four a year at most.'

Dan shrugged. 'We've done our bit, finding that out will be down to the Man. Someone somewhere knows when these trains run and that someone will be high up in the banking world. That's where his Lordship comes in; he mixes in these circles, it's his problem.'

'And of course, getting rid of twenty million in used notes won't be a picnic, especially when the newspapers are full of headlines. How will he do that?'

'I haven't a clue, Craig, and I don't much care; that's his area of expertise. That's why this organisation is so successful, first-class people from head to toe.'

'I've just had a very pleasant thought, Dan. Say we clear twenty million, you get four million, and my share of that will be £1.8Million. That means that little old me will be a fucking millionaire.'

'Don't count on that much, Craig. I fancy legitimising that much loot will be expensive.'

'I know, mate, but I can dream, can't I? Whatever happens, it'll be the biggest pay day ever.'

He nodded ruefully. 'At this rate, it won't be long till you'll find yourself getting like Averton; power and the kudos are what matter; the money stops being important. Anyway, I think I've heard enough at this stage. All I can say is a big, well done; you've excelled yourself.'

'So, what now, Dan?'

'Same as last time. I see his Lordship and get the nod, then I call a meeting of the gang. Don't call me, I'll call you.'

Henry was still around, and we had a light lunch in a bistro overlooking Camden Lock. If he knew anything about what went on in the plan room, he never mentioned it, and I kept my mouth closed on the subject just in case there was feedback to Dan. Our conversation focussed on art, particularly my visit to the Zurich galleries. Thankfully, I had a retentive memory because Henry had been there in recent years and quizzed me on what I had seen. It was like master and pupil, and I was glad when the subject changed to the generalities of life.

'You're looking a bit peaky, dear boy; you seem to have lost a few pounds since I last saw you. You need a good woman in your life. He paused, then, with a twinkle in his eye, added. 'Or a good man, for that matter.'

'One thing for sure, Henry, I won't need a mother whilst you're around. Anyway, I have a commission for you. I'm in the market for two or three paintings, nothing too expensive, say five hundred to a grand each. You know the kind of thing I like watercolours; Impressionist preferred.'

'And I expect you'll pay cash for these?' He had a knowing look on his face.

'Of course, what else would one do?'

I had two other matters to attend to when I got back to the flat early afternoon; both related to the remainder of the cash from the Crewe job, which was still kicking around in my holdall. I had started out with sixty-one grand, spent five on a passport and opened three bank accounts with ten in each. That left me with twenty-six thousand to play with.

I phoned Cromer and Kilroy, the stockbrokers recommended by Dan, and asked for Nick Adams and was put through.

'Nick Adams speaking, how can I help?'

'My name's Craig Dorian; you were recommended by Dan Rawson.'

'That's good of him.'

'I have ten thousand pounds I'd like to invest, ten thousand in cash; I'll deal with commission separately.'

'Not a problem for a friend of Dan's. Do you have any preferences for investment?'

'No, I'm a rank novice; I'll take your advice.'

'Good, come in, and we'll talk about it. I'm free tomorrow morning if that's convenient for you.'

'I can get there for nine-thirty.'

'Perfect, see you then.'

That left me with sixteen grand; I settled on six for working capital and living expenses, which left a further ten grand, which I'd decided to send to Harry Connor. I'd always felt guilty about how the Crewe job had unravelled and reckoned he deserved something out of the Fairweather robbery, though I suspected Anne wouldn't be too happy about it. I still had his address and telephone number and confirmed he was still in residence through Directory Enquiries. I stuffed the money into an envelope and addressed it, then put it inside another sturdier envelope and addressed that as well. That was as much security as I was going to use; I didn't want to do anything that might be traced back to me. There was no need to enclose a note; he would know who it came from.

My meeting with Nick Adams went smoothly, with no awkward questions about the source of the money; Dan had trained him well. He blinded me with jargon and waffle, told me how clever he was and what good stockbrokers Cromer and Kilroy were. I went along with his recommendations, making notes on his spiel for future reference; it would be useful to Craig Dorian, Investment Advisor. The chit-chat finished; he accepted the cash, promised to send me the paperwork and the deal was done.

When I left Cromer and Kilroy, I headed straight to Paddington and caught the first available train to Oxford. I'd always wanted to visit the city of spires, but more importantly, I was going to post Harry's letter from there. I was probably being unnecessarily cautious, but better safe than sorry, as they say. Posting the money to Harry salved a raw layer of my conscience and finally brought closure to the Fairweather robbery as far as I was concerned. Inevitably, the train journey brought back memories of Sam and our first meeting and all that followed; how I missed those days.

It didn't take long to find a Post Office and despatch Harry's letter. That done, I devoted the rest of the day to sightseeing and Oxford didn't disappoint. Walking around the town on a bright, sunny day proved to be a sheer joy. I'd always had a love of old buildings, and largely thanks to the University, they were there in abundance. As I viewed the buildings and witnessed the students happily engaged in each other's company, for the first time in my life, I got the feeling that I might have enjoyed University life. On the other hand, I was rich, and those poor sods had yet to make their way in life.

Harry Connor was still living in Nantwich and now eking out a living felling and logging trees; a skill he'd learned as a young boy working on his father's smallholding. It was hard work and involved long hours, but self-employment had been the only avenue open to him after the robbery.

He couldn't afford the right equipment or transport to take on the bigger, more lucrative jobs and had to get by with the family car, a small trailer, and a second-hand chainsaw.

'Who do you know in Oxford, Harry?' Anne Connor called out to her husband from the kitchen, where she was preparing their evening meal.

'Nobody; what makes you ask?'

'I forgot to say when you came in; there's a letter here for you with an Oxford postmark, a big envelope.'

'Let's have it then.'

'You come in here and open it where I can see what you're up to.'

Harry screwed up his face. 'Wish I was up to something; life would be more interesting.' He studied the package and shook his head. 'I don't recognise the writing; I wonder who it's from?' He studied the writing again and hefted the envelope in his hand a few times. 'Quite heavy, I wonder what's inside? Can't think who would be sending me a letter? I'm not expecting anything.'

Anne was losing patience. 'Darling, why don't you just open it instead of all this wondering?'

Harry took a knife, sliced the envelope open and tilted it to release the contents, puzzled as another envelope revealed itself.

'Another envelope; how strange.' He stood looking at it for a few seconds.

His wife stamped her foot. 'For goodness' sake Frank, get a move on; my curiosity is killing me.'

The knife did its work again, and he peered inside, turning to face his wife, his mouth wide open in astonishment.

'It's money, love; a lot of money.'

He tipped the contents out onto the kitchen worktop and counted the little bundles of fifty-pound notes.

'My God, there's ten thousand pounds here, ten thousand pounds. It's a dream come true, Anne.'

'But who would send you ten thousand pounds, Harry?' She knew before her husband whispered the answer to her question.

'It can only be Craig.'

She threw up her hands in horror, agitated by the link to the past. 'We're not keeping it; you'll have to send it back.'

'Send it back to who exactly? Craig? We don't know where he is. Fairweather? That old bugger will have collected the insurance money long ago and a bit more besides, if his reputation is anything to go by. The Insurers, whoever they are? No chance, they don't need it. No, Anne, we're keeping it whether you like it or not. It's little enough compensation for what we've been through, and we'll be able to do so much more for our kids.'

Anne Connor began to weaken; the money would set them up for life if they were careful, and maybe her husband wouldn't have to work such long hours.

'It's against my better judgement, but you win, Harry; it will give the kids a better life. But nothing's changed; I won't let Craig Murray step through the door or even speak to him.'

'No love, nothing's changed in that regard. We won't see him again, I promise you that, but you must admit, it was kind of Craig to send the money, nevertheless. He didn't need to think of us, did he?'

His wife shook her head vehemently. 'More likely his conscience giving him trouble for what he did to you.'

Harry shook his head in disagreement, but he wasn't going to argue. 'Have it your way.'

Dan Rawson had tried to contact his boss on several occasions following his session with Craig, but the stony Miss Black had denied him access. 'His Lordship is not available, and I've been told not to make any appointments until he tells me otherwise. Try again in a few days' time; the situation might have changed.'

You're enjoying this, aren't you? Well fuck you and your Boss

He knew that Averton was just showing him who was in charge, and he didn't press her. But he persisted, and after several attempts, she made an appointment for him to see his Lordship.

Lord Averton was studying some papers when Rawson was shown into his office; he didn't acknowledge his visitor for several minutes or make any effort to excuse himself.

Here I stand like a fucking schoolboy in front of the Head, waiting for my punishment to be handed down, fuck you, Averton.

Eventually, Averton looked up, his face set, no welcoming smile, no invitation to sit down.

'What can I do for you, Dan? I hope it won't take long; I'm rather busy.'

Bastard. 'It's about the train job; I can come back another time if you're busy.' For once, Rawson's voice lacked its usual deferential tone; he was tiring of the man's superior attitude.

'What about the train job?' Interest flickered in the man's eyes; he was hooked.

Got you now, you old bastard. 'Do you mind if I sit down?'

Averton spread his hands, still unwilling to display any semblance of courtesy.

'Craig has come up with a way to do the job, and I'm a hundred per cent sure it'll work.'

'Run through it for me.'

Twenty minutes later Averton leaned back in his chair, smiling, nodding. 'I don't much care for our friend Dorian, but I've got to hand it to him, it's masterful. How much do we reckon this job could pull in?'

'It's difficult to find out, but the last rumour we caught indicated that it would be around twenty million.'

'Twenty million? A tidy sum, if we can pull it off.'

Dan Rawson's confidence was growing again. 'Of course, at the end of the day, it all hangs on being able to find out the train schedule. We're reliant on you for that information.'

The Man pursed his lips. 'It's a difficult one, Dan; I know the Governor, of course, but I doubt if he gets involved, and I can hardly ask him a direct question.'

Well, use your fucking head; work it out. 'I appreciate that, but perhaps an idle question about what happens to old notes might give you a starting point.'

A smile formed on Averton's face. 'Hmm, good point. I'll have a think about it. I'm not even sure how often he gets into the Club. Leave that one with me. I'll come back to you when I've got something. I might have the germ of an idea; Lady Averton might just be our solution. Now, our friend Murray, or Dorian as he calls himself, it seems to me that we don't have further need of him now that he's put all his cards on the table.'

'What do you mean, sir?'

'I mean, we cut him out of this entirely.'

Rawson grimaced, but he'd half expected this to arise. 'No can do; he has a key part in the job.'

'What can he do that someone else can't do?'

'For a starter, he knows how the Railway operates, signalling, rules, layout, and the rest of the team would be very unsettled if Craig wasn't involved. The whole team was very impressed with the PMR job, and they've got faith in his planning skills, and he's developed a close friendship with Tony Sherwood.'

Averton frowned, *Sherwood,* thought for a moment, and then gave way. 'Hmm, put that way, perhaps you have a point. But after the job, he would be dispensable, would he not?'

Dan drew breath, but he knew better than to challenge the Man's assertion, and anyway, he was right. *What have you got in mind you duplicitous bastard?*

'You made it clear we wouldn't use him again, and he knows that.'

'Exactly, and you wouldn't need to pay him.'

Rawson had principles and dug in. 'I'm sorry to disagree, but a deal is a deal; I think we should all be bound by our word. Things can get nasty when thieves fall out; the organisation would be damaged if news leaked out. Craig would make sure everybody knew what had happened, especially his newly acquired mate, Tony Sherwood.'

Averton gulped and sought cover. 'You're right, of course, Dan, forget I ever mentioned it. In any case, it's your money, and it's for you to decide. Thanks for the rundown, and well done. You can set the wheels in motion. Now, I must get on. I've got a meeting shortly.'

Before he set out for his next meeting, Averton made a telephone call. The idea of another Great Train Robbery had been on his wish list since the headline-grabbing original, and he wanted to get things moving.

'Hello, Sarah darling. I've got a little job I'd like you to do for me.'

'Another one of your schemes, dear? Who do you want to get into a corner this time?' Lady Averton knew nothing of her husband's nefarious pursuits, but she had arranged numerous lunches and dinners to facilitate his business interests.'

'I was thinking of a Sunday lunch, say eight of us, with some croquet thrown in.'

'And who do we want to see on this occasion?'

'I'd like Sir John Crowson and his wife to be there, but you can choose the others.'

'I can't stand Sybil Crowson.'

'I know, dear, and nor can I, but just this once for your darling husband…. please.'

Sarah Averton didn't hide her sigh of resignation. 'This is going to cost you, David; I saw a necklace to my liking the other day.'

'Of course, my darling; whatever you want.'

'And no doubt you want this to happen soon?'

'Anytime within the next few weeks will do. Start with your friend Sybil; check out which dates suit the Crowsons, and don't forget to mention the croquet. Bye darling, see you tonight.'

'What an asset you are, Sarah; you'll find a way, I know. I hope my recollection is right about John Crowson being a croquet enthusiast. Not many croquet lawns around nowadays but ours is in good shape. Still, I'll get one of the lads to look it over; I want it at its best.'

Chapter Twenty-One

Christmas and New Year had passed by the time Dan gathered the gang together. There hadn't been too much for me to celebrate over the festive season, though I had managed to get an invite to a New Year's Eve party in one of the flats. The woman I'd encountered the morning after the bullion job was there, and that gave me the opportunity to get to know her. Her name was Sally Thomas, age 27, to my eyes, very attractive, and currently unattached. She was by no means boastful, but, reading between the lines, she was a high-flier with Marsh Edwards, a recruitment agency in the city; I tried to look impressed when she mentioned the name, but it meant nothing to me. For whatever reason, we generated some reasonable chemistry, and after a few drinks and smoochy dances, we'd got into a few clinches after midnight, but she declined my offer to come back to the flat for a coffee, probably judging the invitation to be a pre-cursor to what I had in mind. It was a disappointing start to the New Year, but she did promise that we'd go out for a meal as soon as she completed her current commission.

Dan and I met up late morning before the others arrived and went through the plan in depth one last time, just as we'd done for the PMR job. I fully expected him to take the lead again, but to my surprise, he passed the whole show over to me. 'It's your baby, go for it.'

Henry closed the Gallery for the afternoon and put a sign on the door advising customers that there was a 'Private Viewing in Progress'. Dan must have been expecting a long session; nibbles and beverages were laid on, but his rule of no alcohol still applied. Tony Sherwood was first to arrive, and I was pleased when he came straight over to me, 'Hi Craig, how's it going?'

'Not getting enough, mate.'

'Enough what?' He was genuinely puzzled.

I give him a cheesy grin. 'I'll give you one guess.'

'Oh, shagging.' He shrugged. 'Loses its priority when you get older.'

'Christ, you must be older than I thought, Tony; I hope I never find out.'

'You will; wait and see. Now, what's on today's menu? I'm sure you're in the know?'

I grimaced, wanting to tell him, keen to strengthen our budding friendship, but resisted the temptation.

'I do know, but best it waits till Dan gets things started. It's big stuff though, I can tell you that, very big. It'll make the PMR deal look like pocket money.'

His eyes glinted, 'Sounds like my kind of game.'

'It's right up your street, Tony, and I hope you'll be a player; my name is on the team sheet again.'

He shook his head. 'I never commit until I know the whole game plan, but I reckon if you're in, I'll be in.'

The others arrived, one by one: Charlie Booker, Eddie Milton, Ralph Mason and last of all, Angie Goodall. This time, she was wearing make-up and looked like she had just stepped out of a hairdressing salon; she could be a good-looking woman when she wanted to be.

I made with the compliments. 'You look great, Angie. I'm guessing that you're going somewhere special tonight?'

'Rich is taking me out to dinner; birthday celebration.'

'Happy birthday; he's a very lucky man to have such a gorgeous wife.'

'We're both lucky, Craig.'

Dan waited till all the social greetings had come and gone, then called us to order; everyone moved over to the table immediately. As usual, he sat at the head; I sat mid-way with Angie on my left, Tony on my right and the others opposite. He grabbed our attention instantly. 'Good news first; this job could bring in twenty million. There's no way of knowing exactly how much, but it will be big.'

There were whistles and gasps all around the table.

'Not the Bank of England, old chap?' Charlie Booker chirped up, grinning.

'Not quite, Charlie, but you're closer than you think.'

'Intriguing, pray tell us more.'

Dan nodded, 'All will be revealed, but first, some bad news. We haven't got a clue when this one might run, but the Man wants us to go ahead with recruitment and acquisitions. He's trying to get a fix on the date, and we must be ready to move when he gives the go-ahead. Understood?'

There were nods all around the table, though Tony Sherwood sounded a note of caution. 'That'll make recruitment a bit awkward, Dan; we can't keep good people hanging around indefinitely. They'll move on to where there's a pay cheque.'

Ralph Mason nodded vigorously, 'Took the words right out of my mouth, Tony.'

Dan shrugged, 'I can see the problem, and you'll have to deal with it; that's why you're here. Let's take a raincheck on that and come back to problems when we've run through the plan. Now, I'm going to ask Craig to take us through this one; it's one hundred per cent his plan.'

I walked over to the wall with my roll of flip charts and pinned up the first one. It was intended to make an impact, and it did.

GREAT TRAIN ROBBERY NUMBER TWO

£20 MILLION RAID

There were murmurs all around the table; I heard Tony draw breath, but Charlie Booker was the only one to voice his thoughts, a touch of frustration showing through.

'But Dan, we've looked at this job before and agreed it wasn't workable.'

Dan said nothing, just pointed him back to me.

'Bear with me, Charlie.' I carried on pinning up my charts; that done, I took them through the plan, slowly and deliberately, explaining the key stages in detail. I had allowed thirty minutes, but so determined was I to allay their scepticism that I overran and took forty-five. When I did finish there was absolute silence.

'Come on then.' Dan filled the hiatus. 'Cat got your tongues? Let's have comments and questions; you're not usually stuck for words.'

Tony spoke up first. 'Can't fault it; it's clever yet so simple, provided we can handle the logistics, that is.'

Charlie responded confidently. 'Can't see any problem getting the gear.'

It sounded too good to be true, and I posed the question to make sure he was absolutely committed. 'You're confident about the heavy gear, Charlie? It's key to this venture.'

'Can't see why not; it'll probably come from Holland or Germany; I'll check with my sources. It's a damn sight easier than what you've taken on if I might say so; you get your bit wrong, and the whole job unravels.'

'I won't get it wrong, Charlie, believe me.'

There were laughs round the table; I didn't join in, knowing just how risky it was.

'I see you've come to terms with the need for firepower, Craig.' Tony alluded to my previous reticence, smiling though there was no malice in his voice.

'I'm a late convert, Tony; guns are essential for this job; the end justifies the means. I hope we can work together on this one?' I maintained eye contact and breathed a sigh of relief when he gave me an enthusiastic thumbs-up.

'You can count me in; I wouldn't miss this caper for anything. We'll be as famous as Ronnie Biggs if we can pull it off.'

Ralph spoke up. 'I've got a fair idea of the people I would want for this job; they're expensive, but they're good. Timing will be the key, though; they won't sit twiddling their thumbs for too long. The guys I have in mind are always in demand.'

'Money isn't an issue, Ralph, unless their demands are unreasonable; if they're as good as you say, we might consider a retainer.' Dan offered his assurance. 'We'll hit the jackpot if everybody does their job right.'

Ralph smiled and shrugged. 'I'll remind you of that when I'm putting forward my costs.'

'Can't see that there's anything in this one for me,' Angie added, pouting 'more the pity.'

'Don't be too sure of that, Angie.' Dan offered some hope. 'It'll depend on what the Man comes up with; we don't know what will be needed at this stage.'

'Can't see anything in it for me either.' Eddie looked downcast. 'A real shame, I'd like to have some sort of role in this job; it'll go down in the history books, I reckon.'

I had an idea I wanted to explore with him. 'Can we talk after the meeting, Eddie? I've got an idea on how you could be very useful.'

He nodded eagerly. 'Sounds good, Craig.'

Dan looked round the table, but questions seemed to have dried up. 'If there's nothing else, I'll close the meeting and let you lot get busy. Help yourself to what's left of the food.'

I had started to retrieve the charts when I felt a hand on my shoulder; it was Tony. 'Good job, kiddo. I look forward to working with you again.'

'The feeling's mutual, Tony. I'm sorry we got off on the wrong foot at the first meeting; put it down to inexperience. Guns were never my thing, still aren't really.'

He shrugged. 'All water under the bridge as far as I'm concerned; you're cool under pressure and act like a pro; that's what matters in this business. Catch you later.'

Eddie signalled me from the other side of the room, and I made my way over.

'What you said earlier, Craig, what have you got in mind?'

'I was wondering if you would be the expert with Team One? It would be great if you could; it's all electrical and electronic stuff.'

His eyes widened, and he shook his head. 'I don't go on jobs, Craig; I haven't got the bottle. More to the point, I don't know fuck all about that kind of stuff.'

'You could pick it up with a bit of research. Look at it as an adventure. Think about it; we've got time. It'll be the biggest pay-day you've ever known.'

'I'd hate to let anybody down.'

I persisted. 'I reckon you're up to it; don't decide now; give it some thought. Please?'

He nodded reluctantly. 'OK, Craig, but no promises.'

I collared Dan just as he was leaving. 'Two things, Dan; I'm trying to persuade Eddie to be the expert with Team One.'

He looked dubious. 'What does he say?'

'He's nervous but said he'll think about it.'

'Understandable, he hasn't been on a job before. And the second thing?'

'These charts, do you reckon it's OK to leave them here?'

'Not really, but it's not safe to walk about with them under your arm either. Stick them at the bottom of a drawer in one of the plan chests for now, but the sooner you type out the requirements, the better and then destroy the charts.'

'I'll make a start when everyone has gone, might just finish it before I go. If I do, I'll destroy these; a pity really, they'll be worth a fortune someday if we pull it off.'

I got my head down and managed to finish all the paperwork just after nine that night. I reflected on my own words regarding the value of the flipcharts in the fullness of time and wondered if I should hide them away somewhere as a future nest egg. I pictured myself on TV, aged 80, revealing all. *Idiot.* Common sense prevailed, and I tore them into little pieces and put a match to them in the wastepaper bin; if it all went to plan, I wouldn't have need of a nest egg.

Dan called me a week after the meeting to say that there would be no progress regarding the date for at least another month. He confided that Averton was arranging a social gathering with the right kind of people, and this was taking time to bring about. There were things I could have done to sort out some important details of the robbery, essentially exactly where to make the hit, but instead.

In the meantime I decided to make more effort with Sally Thomas and knocked on her door one evening to remind her of our dinner date; it must have been a good moment because she didn't hesitate. She didn't ask me in for coffee either, so I guessed I was still in a no-go zone. Over the course of the next four weeks, we saw more of each other: all the usual things like meals, pictures, and some of those organised London Walks, but nothing came of my efforts with Sally other than a kiss and a cuddle.

Time passed and we did get it together eventually, though she wasn't what you would call the most eager of lovers. She was very intelligent, though and had a good sense of humour; I really did enjoy her company. I found myself wondering whether our relationship would blossom if we spent more time together.

Lady Sarah Averton, it transpired, had distant links to the monarchy and was a renowned socialite in the upper echelons; people wanted to be associated with her; that meant when she extended an invitation to any kind of event, she rarely received a refusal. And so it was that that Sir John and Sybil Crowson, along with two other worthy couples, gathered at Averton Manor, a large Elizabethan house set in sixty beautifully landscaped acres in Surrey.

Her Ladyship had decided that the croquet session requested by her husband would take place in the afternoon and be followed by cocktails on the lawn, after which guests would retire and change for dinner. Sir John, unlike the other guests who were enthusiastic beginners, was an accomplished croquet player. He gave no quarter and demolished everyone except Averton, who described himself as competent. Both men had won all their games fairly easily and hadn't played each other due to David Averton's manoeuvring. But the inevitable outcome arrived, and they faced each other for what was the final game of the afternoon.

'Tell you what, Sir John; I'll play you best of three for a magnum of Moet. What say you?'

'Never been known to resist a challenge, especially from a peer of the realm.' The Banker readily accepted, having no doubts that he was going to win.

Averton would have let his guest win if needs be, believing as he did that Sir John would chat more readily if he was in good humour. But truth to tell, he was able to play his best and still prove no match for Sir John, who won the challenge by taking a two to nil lead.

'Well played, old chap; the champers will be there for you when you leave tonight. You're much too good for me.'

'Luck of the day, David; I expect you'll turn the tables when you come to my place.'

'I doubt that very much. Let's tuck into the cocktails, though; see who can drink the most.'

After dinner, Averton engaged Sir John in conversation and made his opening gambit in the quest to find out more about the trains that transported used banknotes to London for destruction.

'You know, John, I believe you're the only fella I know with money to burn.'

'Not at all, David,' Sir John Crowson protested, waving his hands about in agitation. 'I'm not short of a bob or two, but I'm not in your league, I assure you.'

'You misunderstood me; I was alluding to all those used banknotes that go up in smoke.'

Crowson laughed heartily. 'Oh, that stuff, wish it was mine, I'd make it last a year or two longer.'

'Just how much does go up in smoke each year?'

The Governor pursed his lips, 'Can't say off the top of my head, a hundred and fifty million at least, maybe as much as two hundred.'

'Does it still go by rail? You had that little difficulty a few years back.'

'Yes, the train is still the safest form of transport for that particular task, and we've tightened up security a great deal since that disastrous episode. To tell the truth, I don't know much about the details. That side of things is handled by the Bank's Director of Security.'

Averton nodded his understanding. 'Who would that be? I don't think our paths have ever crossed, though I've been along to a few of your functions.'

Sir John grunted. 'Not surprised, Morgan Evans doesn't socialise much; keeps himself to himself most of the time. I get the feeling he likes to keep his wife out of harm's way; she's bloody gorgeous and half his age. Can't for the life of me think how he managed to get her into his fold. Given half a chance, I wouldn't mind getting between the sheets with her. Old Morgan's coming up for retirement in a year or so; I can't say he'll be missed, though he does have a tight rein on security.'

Averton leered at his guest. 'You know, John, I do believe there's more than a hint of jealousy in your voice.'

'You're right, old chap; expect you would feel the same if you saw her. Oh, oh, looks like I must go; Sybil is giving me one of her looks.'

Next morning the Man telephoned Dan Rawson. 'Dan, it's me; finally able to come back to you regarding that party you're planning. A good chap to invite would be Morgan Evans; works in the city and runs the Bank's security set-up. Can't tell you more than that, except that his wife is gorgeous, and the Governor would like to have his way with her. Not much more I can add; don't know the chap myself. Come back to me when you know more.'

'Thanks; it's not much, but at least we have a starting point.' *Thanks for what? A fucking name; I'd hoped you could come up with more than that. Looks like you've got a job on Angie.*

'Angie Goodall.'

'Hi, Angie, it's Dan. I wonder if you could do something for me. I'm trying to trace an old friend, Morgan Evans. We lost touch along the way; he used to be in bank security when I knew him; might be with the Old Lady herself nowadays. I'm organising a reunion later this year and would like him to be involved. Any chance you can help? You're good at this kind of thing.'

'I'll give it my best shot, Dan, but might take a week or so. You haven't given me much to go on.'

'I know, but it's all we've got; just do your best and be in touch when you've got something.'

Angie was pleased to be involved, though she had no way of knowing just how important it was to get a lead on Morgan Evans. Where to begin, that was the question. She didn't know where he lived, didn't even know what he looked like, so the starting point had to be where he worked.

'Bank of England.' The operator sounded as well-bred as the Bank itself.

'Could I speak to Morgan Evans, please? I believe he is Head of Security?'

'Mr Evans is Director of Security.' The voice gently corrected her. 'I'll put you through to his secretary.'

Angie had decided on a direct approach; it wouldn't be without risk, but the stakes were high.

'Mr Morgan's secretary, who's calling please?'

'Tessa Cartwright, I'm an independent journalist.'

'Does he know you, Miss Cartwright?'

'No, I'm afraid not.'

'Can I ask why you want to speak to him? I should say that he rarely grants interviews to journalists.'

'I can understand that; he must be very busy. I'm doing a series of articles on Men in the City, particularly those operating at Board level.'

'Please hold, Miss Cartwright, whilst I speak to him.'

Men in the City was a catchy title, and Morgan Evans was not without vanity. It wouldn't hurt to enquire further about what was involved.

'Miss Cartwright, Morgan Evans speaking, tell me more about these articles of yours.' Though his name suggested otherwise, there wasn't a trace of Welsh in his very English public school accent.

'Thank you for speaking to me, Mr Evans. I know how busy someone in your position must be.' Angie smiled to herself; flattery rarely went amiss.

'I'm a freelance journalist hoping to produce a series of articles for sale to an appropriate publishing house. You would, of course, be consulted before the article was released, and you would have editorial rights. The articles would focus on eminent individuals occupying key positions at Board level, like your good self.

Evans mentally preened himself; he did indeed have an important job which never got into the public eye, except when things went wrong.

'And who else would be included in this series of articles?'

'I have in mind about ten articles covering banking, commerce, private enterprise, and public service. People like Bart Zeigler, Spencer Thompson, Richard Ferguson; all top of their respective fields.'

Angie had done her homework well; Evans was duly impressed.

'An impressive list, Miss Cartwright, have they all agreed to be interviewed?'

'I have to confess that I haven't approached them yet.' Angie Goodall applied another ladle of flattery. 'Frankly, I wanted your agreement first; I feel that with you on board, the others will probably follow. A Bank of England director is a prestigious post.'

Evans puffed out his chest; he was flattered, and he was weakening. 'And how much of my time would you require, Miss Cartwright?'

'I would reckon about an hour, not much more than that. It would entirely depend on how much you wanted to tell me.'

Evans wanted to say yes; he'd never been asked to be the subject of an article before, not even when the Bank appointed him. But he was cautious and wanted time to think about what was being proposed.

'Give me your telephone number, Miss Cartwright, and I'll have my secretary call you back one way or the other.'

On the other end of the phone, Angie Goodall smiled and gave over a contact number. 'That's fine, Mr Evans, thank you for your time.'

Evans leaned back in his chair; hands clasped behind his head in a reflective pose. Retirement was looming; there hadn't been many highlights in his fairly dull career, and now somebody wanted to interview him because he was important. It would be impressive to see his name in print, provided the article said the right things, and he would ensure that it did.

'Liz, I think I will grant Miss Cartwright an interview; I'll put her telephone number in your in-tray. But before you make an appointment, please check with the Press Bureau to ensure that Tessa Cartwright is an accredited journalist.'

He was right to be cautious, but Angie Goodall had anticipated that Morgan Evans would be likely to check out her pseudo credential; he was, after all, a security specialist. Tessa Cartwright was a respected journalist of similar age and general appearance to Angie Goodall; that was why her identity had been chosen. All that was needed was the right documentation of the type an accredited journalist would have, something that the ever-resourceful Dan Rawson had been able to arrange for a previous scam. There had been a risk that Evans might have known the real Tessa Cartwright, but out of sight, and at the end of a telephone, Angie could have been dealt with that eventuality easily enough.

Late next morning, she got the telephone call she was hoping for; she had been granted an interview with Morgan Evans.

Chapter Twenty-Two

Tessa Cartwright, posing as Angie Goodall, presented herself at the Old Lady of Threadneedle Street ten minutes before her ten o'clock appointment. The security guard eyed her up and down and scrutinised her Press credentials.

'Miss Cartwright.' He was tall and broad-shouldered, in his late fifties and looked like he might have served in the military.

Angie looked at him enquiringly; she had never understood why, in such circumstances, it was necessary to state the name, having just read it. *Checking for pronunciation, perhaps, asking for confirmation, showing an ability to read and speak English, or, maybe, they just liked the sound of their own voice.*

'Who are you visiting, Miss Cartwright?'

'Morgan Evans, Director of Security, I'm due to see him at ten o'clock.' She smiled at him sweetly. 'He's probably your boss, is he not?'

The guard frowned. 'That's correct, though I don't report to him directly; he's much too high up in the command structure.'

Definitely a military man. Tessa smothered a smile and looked on whilst the day's list of expected visitors was perused.

'Ah yes, here we are. Can I ask you to sign, please and record the time; I make it nine fifty-three. Do you agree?'

'I'm sure you're right.' She signed and stood back expectantly.

The guard handed her a neck-chain Visitor Pass. 'You must wear this security pass at all times and hand it back to me before you leave. You'll be required to sign yourself out.' Having exercised his authority, he pointed across the entrance hall towards a marble staircase. 'Go to the first floor, turn left along the corridor, and you'll find Mr Morgan's secretary halfway along on the right. I shall phone and let her know you're on your way.'

Tessa smiled. *No chance of wandering off then.* 'Thank you; you've been very helpful.' She strode purposefully across to the stairs; she had rehearsed her role for a week and felt confident about the task that lay ahead.

Morgan Evans was sixty-four, small and rotund, clearly built for comfort rather than action. He had a full head of black hair that had somehow evaded the greying of age; a chubby face housed a slightly ridiculous Adolf Hitler moustache. His most striking feature, however, was his eyes, which were dark, piercing, and set too close, somehow adding menace to an otherwise benign countenance. Angie felt them bore into her as they shook hands. She had dressed carefully that morning: a business suit, skirt short but not too short, sheer stockings to show her long legs to advantage. Her jacket was unbuttoned, affording a good view of her low-cut blouse.

'Do sit down, Miss Cartwright.' He motioned to a pair of soft leather armchairs. She sat down, making no effort to adjust her skirt as it rode up, just as she knew it would. She saw his eyes drop, pause briefly, then return to her face.

'I've been calling you Miss, but I see you're wearing a wedding ring.'

Well spotted, Mr Evans. 'It is Miss; I was married once but not now. The ring helps me to deflect unwelcome approaches. And what about you, Mr Evans, are you married?'

'Yes, I'm happily married; very happily, in fact.'

Angie looked over the banker's shoulder to the photographs sitting on his desk. 'Is that your wife?'

He followed her pointing finger. 'Yes, it is.'

'Do you mind?' Without waiting for a reply, she rose and moved over to the desk.' My word, she's stunning I'd give my right arm for looks like that.'

Evans beamed. 'Yes, she is, isn't she? I'm a very lucky man.'

'What's her name?'

He hesitated briefly, unsure as to why he was being asked his wife's name. 'Karen.'

Angie returned to her seat, watching as his eyes sought out her skirt again, dwelling for longer than last time.

'Been married long? This is all useful background.'

'Five years. I ….' He stumbled over the words. 'I met her when she was 18 during one of my trips to Wales.'

'Any children?'

For a brief moment, he looked slightly embarrassed by the question. 'No. I'm a bit long in the tooth for that kind of thing; too old to want babies now.' Evans regained his composure and changed the subject. 'Could we move on to my responsibilities as Director of Security, which is why you're here?'

'Yes, please. Can you begin by giving me your career details, a potted version of your CV, really?'

If Evans was pressed for time, it wasn't reflected in his attention to detail; he took fully fifteen boring minutes to describe his working life.

Angie gazed into Morgan Evans' eyes, her expression one of pseudo-admiration. 'That was fascinating, Mr Evans; you were certainly a highflyer, destined for the top ranks from an early age. Would I be right in saying that you are more interested in operational matters than strategy and that you enjoy solving problems? You're probably more at home working behind the scenes rather than in the shop window?'

Evans pursed his lips. 'I suppose so, though that's a simplified analysis, and I'd like to see how you portray those conclusions in the article before it went to print.'

Angie nodded. 'But, of course, you will always have editorial control. Let's start by telling me about a typical day.'

He shook his head. 'No such thing in this job.'

'Perhaps you could tell me about what you'll be doing this week, how often you report to the Board, what makes a good day, what makes a bad day and so on.'

Evans droned on for the next hour, happily answering questions; there was no doubt that his favourite subject was Morgan Evans.

Angie glanced at her watch. 'Oh, my goodness, I've taken an hour and a half of your time; I could listen to you all day. It'll make a great article.'

Evans didn't want to be let off the hook; he was enjoying his moment. 'I've enjoyed it, and I've still got some time until my next meeting if there's anything else you'd like to know.'

'Well, perhaps just one more question, and I can guess at the answer; what has been your worst day as Director.'

He grimaced and puffed his cheeks. 'Obviously, the Great Train Robbery; it was a nightmare. I'd just taken over and was thrust into the spotlight, though I'd had nothing to do with the security arrangements in force at that time. An absolute nightmare, believe me.'

'You poor thing, what a dreadful baptism.' Angie almost cooed her sympathy.

The banker nodded. 'I assure you it could never happen again, not with the security I've put in place. Quite apart from my innovations, the Railways brought in a new rule that comes in to play when a train stops unexpectedly. There are other precautions that I can't tell you about for obvious reasons.'

'Of course not, and I wouldn't expect you to. We can't have a repeat of that unfortunate incident, can we?'

She rose to her feet. 'I think I've outstayed my welcome, and I've got enough for an excellent article. I'll prepare a draft and let you have it for comment. Not sure when it will be ready though, I've just been given an assignment in the Middle East for the BBC.'

'Really?' It was Morgan Evans's turn to be impressed; his eyes widened.

'Yes, can't talk about it, though; I've signed a confidentiality clause. You'll understand, I'm sure? Could take two months, but don't worry, yours will be the first article to run.'

'I look forward to hearing from you.'

Angie snapped her fingers as though recalling something.

'I almost forgot; you've obviously left Wales, but where is home now?' It was an important question but deliberately asked in a casual manner.

'London, not far from Chiswick Bridge.'

'Don't tell me that you're on the river; I'd die for a place on the Thames.' Angie feigned envy.

Morgan smiled proudly. 'My rear garden goes right down to the Thames. I have a dock and a small boat, though I don't use it much; Karen's not keen on boating.'

'What a shame; any other interests?'

'I play golf; got a twelve handicap as a matter of fact.'

'Does Karen play?'

Evans laughed out loud. 'Excuse me laughing; she doesn't, but she's a happy golf widow. We have an arrangement where we go away to a hotel or a Country Club every weekend; I go on the fairway whilst Karen goes to the health spa or whatever.'

'Sounds idyllic; you're so well matched.' She glanced at the photographs on the desk again. 'Is that your place?'

He moved over quickly, proud to show off the aerial view of his home with the Thames in the foreground.

'It's beautiful, Mr Morgan; you're a very lucky man, but then again, you've worked hard for it. Well, I really will go this time. Thank you very much for seeing me.'

Angie Goodall was pleased with the outcome of her efforts; she was starting to build a picture of Morgan Evans and his interests. Next day, she would head for the Town Hall at Chiswick and examine the Electoral Roll to ascertain the Morgan's address.

Karen Morgan rose with her husband, as she always did, and got dressed. Well, hardly dressed; she wore only a bra and pants under her silk dressing gown. The gown wasn't tied closed. Morgan liked it open so that he could catch glimpses of her scantily clad body. He never seemed to tire of seeing her that way, never seemed to tire of the caresses he would give her when the fancy took him. But his lust never went further than touching; the poor guy was permanently impotent. He had done the honourable thing and told her about his problem before he'd asked her to marry him. For her part, at eighteen, she hadn't been a virgin and had made this known to him.

He had made it crystal clear that he would never be able to consummate the marriage and that there would never be a place for children in his life, adopted, fostered, or otherwise. She had convinced herself that sex didn't matter all that much and had happily married him for his wealth and, more importantly, to get away from her parent's remote farm in Wales. She enjoyed a lifestyle she could only have dreamt of and found him to be kind and companionable, though there were times when she longed for sex and the firm body of a young man. His futile manual attempts to please her were little more than an embarrassment, not that she ever complained; it was important that he believed he satisfied her.

He had retained one safeguard, an important practical safeguard; he had promised that when he died, she would inherit everything, but if she were ever unfaithful, she would get nothing. He had recorded their agreement in a Memorandum of Understanding, which they had both signed in the presence of a Solicitor. In their five years of marriage, she had learned to cope with her circumstances and had remained faithful.

She kissed him goodbye and endured his final fumbles before he set off for the office, then made her way to their bedroom. She selected one of her vibrators, stretched out in bed and began to pleasure herself. Morgan knew about her sex toys, and occasionally, he would ask to use them on her, but she preferred to be alone and indulge her fantasies. *Poor Morgan, all your money can't buy you an erection and poor old me, all I can do, is fuck myself.* Karen took comfort from their thirty-plus years age difference; sooner or later, she would be very rich with plenty of time left to enjoy life. And maybe, as time went on, Morgan would be less possessive and less watchful; an affair would be fun, but in the meantime, she wasn't going to risk her future for some short-lived pleasuring. The vibrator buzzed on till her moment came and passed, barely satisfying her needs.

'Dan, its Angie. We need to meet. I've got something for you.'

'Sure, here or Camden?'

'Either suits me. I was wondering if Craig could join us? We need to put our thinking caps on.'

'No problem let's meet here at eleven tomorrow morning, assuming I can get hold of him. I'll come back to you if I can't.'

Next morning, the trio gathered over coffee, and Angie reported on her meeting with Morgan Evans.

'He's very confident that there can't be a repeat of the Great Train Robbery, lays great store on the rule changes British Railways have made.'

Dan glanced at me.

I nodded. 'Rule 55: essentially, drivers must contact the signal box within a few minutes of the train coming to a halt. I told you about that.'

Angie shrugged. 'As long as there's nothing else, we don't know about.'

Dan offered some encouragement. 'You've done well in a short time, Angie, but we are still a long way from finding out the date.'

'Any ideas as to how we can move forward?'

Angie responded. 'There's a diary on his desk, and he might have one at home or carry one with him, but he's a cautious type, and I wouldn't be surprised if he didn't write the date down.'

Dan pursed his lips. 'We can't break into the Bank of England and go through his desk diary, and if we mug him and take his diary, he'll get suspicious. And, as you say, Angie, it might not be recorded in it anyway.'

Angie nodded. 'So that leaves his home, or we look at the Railway end for the information.'

An idea flashed through my head, and I mulled it over. Dan spotted me drifting off immediately.

'You've got that thoughtful look on your face, Craig; out with it. What have you got?'

'I think the gorgeous Mrs Evans might hold the key. Angie says she can't see what Karen Evans sees in her husband. I reckon it's obvious: money, clothes, nice house, social standing. Need I go on? Evans, on the other hand, has a beautiful wife of whom he's very proud. Like most men, he's likely to be possessive, and he's bound to know why she married him. He might even take her with him when he goes off to Glasgow to see the next train on its way.'

Dan wondered where this was leading. 'So, what are you saying, Craig? That we get Karen Evans to phone us up and tell us my husband is off to Glasgow on one of those top-secret trips.' His voice was heavy with sarcasm.

I nodded my head, smiling. 'That's exactly it, Dan, and this is how we do it.' I spelt out my idea, and ten minutes later Dan was persuaded.

'A long shot, but I reckon it's worth a go. I'll set the wheels in motion. Are you game, Angie?'

She shrugged. 'Sounds like I've got to be, but it'll cost you.'

One morning, two weeks later, Angie and Eddie Milton sat in the latter's beige Morris Minor outside the Evans' property, waiting for Karen Evans to make her exit on the way to her exclusive Health Club in Chiswick. Her husband had long since departed for the city.

'You had better make a start, Eddie. She's due out any minute now.' Angie warned. She had spent the last two weeks observing the habits of the Evans duo.

Eddie nodded, got out and went to the boot, where he removed a jack and wheel spanner. He was in the process of removing the near-side rear wheel when Karen's red convertible Porche approached the pair of high ornamental ironwork gates that guarded the entrance to the driveway. The gates swung open slowly, and the Porche drove forward cautiously, making sure the road was clear. She noticed the man changing the wheel on the Minor but didn't give him a second glance. The road clear, she pulled out and accelerated sharply away.

The iron gates began to swing back, but before they could close fully, Milton had squeezed between them and began to walk up the drive to the house. He was dressed in what would pass for gardening clothes just in case he was unexpectedly observed, not that it was likely, given the distance to the neighbouring properties. As he neared the house, his eyes scanned the exterior for alarms and for the easiest point of access. He smiled when he saw the Georgian glazed windows in the front elevation. *Fingers crossed, they're the same at the rear; leaded lights were very pretty but very vulnerable.*

At the rear of the property, he looked through windows, noting the function of each room: dining room, kitchen, rear door, utility area and finally, the lounge on the corner with large picture windows on two walls.

Dining room looks like the best bet. He hurried back to the dining room window and used a tool he had designed and made to make a diagonal slice through the lead in each corner of the small pane nearest to the casement handle. That done, he carefully eased back the lead all round the glass and gently levered out the pane. Another of his patent tools released the window lock, and within seconds, he was able to open the window and climb in.

He headed immediately to the kitchen, scanning the room for the inevitable calendar. The kitchen, which was also a breakfast room, was generally the centre of family activity, and he was confident there would be a calendar. He looked round the room, his heart sinking when he didn't see one. *'Shit; must be in the study.'*

He turned back, face breaking into a smile; there was the calendar hanging on the wall, hidden from view behind the door he had just opened. The information he was seeking was written up on the calendar, the Evans' weekend destinations and arrangements for the next six weekends. It was all there: the hotel, tee-off time, and health club booking. Karen Evans had conveniently written in the hotel telephone number in each instance.

Milton recorded the information he wanted in his notebook and, within minutes, was climbing back through the dining room window. His final task was to press the gate release on the keypad Angie would be keeping lookout and would wedge it open in readiness for his return. He closed and secured the window, then set about replacing the pane of glass, carefully smoothing down the lead and then smearing the cuts he'd made with dirt. Close inspection would reveal that the pane had been removed, but only the window cleaner was likely to see it, and the odds were he'd take no notice. His task complete, he strolled nonchalantly back to the gate and slipped through the gap, breathing a sigh of relief that the job was done. The block of wood retrieved, he watched the gate swing and clunk shut, then climbed into the passenger seat of the waiting car. He leaned back, smiling as Angie drove away.

'A piece of cake, Angie, a piece of cake. Here, I hope you managed to tighten up the wheel, you being a woman and all that?'

Angie gasped and put her hand to her mouth. 'Christ, I knew I had forgotten to do something.'

'What?' Eddie relaxed when he saw Angie grin.'

The following Saturday, Karen and Morgan Evans set off promptly at nine for Eastbury Manor Country Club, a luxury venue not far from junction 14 on the M4. He would be teeing off at eleven on the splendid eighteen-hole golf course; she would head for the health spa for all the usual pampering. They arrived at ten-thirty and, being regular guests, were checked in with minimum formalities. As part of its service, the Hotel had arranged the foursome that he would play in, as far as possible, ensuring that the golfers were of similar standard. Morgan Evans had a respectable handicap of twelve.

'Got time for a coffee, darling?' Karen asked her husband.

'No, dear, best not; coffee gets the old bladder going these days. I'll head for the clubhouse and maybe get a few swings in before we start.'

Karen pouted dutifully, not that she really minded, but she knew it pleased him. They wandered back down to reception, where Evans took his leave and set out for the Clubhouse.

'Enjoy yourself, darling; I'll see you later.'

Even in her tee shirt and leisure shorts, Karen Evans attracted admiring glances as she made her way to the coffee lounge overlooking the golf course, not that she was interested in golf, but it provided an attractive outlook. She took a seat near the panoramic windows, and a watchful waiter hurried over to take her order.

'A jug of filter coffee, please.'

'Will that be all madam?'

'Yes, thank you, charge to room twenty-one.'

She felt totally relaxed as she sat pondering on what she should have done to herself; there were so many possibilities. She would have a massage, of course, and would try to ensure that she got the masseur that she wanted: a fair-haired, bronzed Australian called Ross. There would be nothing improper, of course, but these sessions represented her only opportunity for physical contact with a male; it was nothing more than a cheap sexual thrill but an enjoyable one, nevertheless. She was still lost in her thoughts and was scarcely aware when the waiter returned to set out her table; Eastbury Manor was horrendously expensive, but it did everything with style: silver service, fine china and a waiter who wore white cotton gloves.

'It looks like we're both golf widows. Mind if I join you?' The accent was transatlantic; the woman older than herself but very attractive; she, too, was dressed casually. Before Karen could respond, the woman rose and moved over, coffee jug and cup in hand.

'I get fed up sitting around, don't you? It's all right for the guys, hitting a little ball around for three hours.'

'Sure, no problem, but I'll be heading for the salon shortly, and I'll be having everything that's on offer.' Karen giggled.

'That's the way, babe, though, with your looks, I can't see that you need beauty treatment. I'm Judy Waistcott a Yank, in case you hadn't noticed. With that soft lilting accent, you must be Welsh, am I right?'

'Got me in one.'

'Let me get you a coffee.' Judy began to pour.

'Thank you, but you should have used my pot.'

'I promise to have another cup from yours, OK?'

Karen took a long sip from her cup. 'Hmm, lovely; I've been gasping for this. I do need my morning caffeine.'

'Me too, babe.' Waistcott then began to appraise Karen of her ancestral connections with the UK and her lineage back to the Norman Conquest.

'Fascinating, you Americans are so good at researching your family origins.'

'Can you blame us? Our origins don't go back too far on the other side of the pond. Tell me about yourself, about Wales. Do you know I haven't been there?'

Karen was finding it hard to focus; the woman's face was blurred, her head beginning to swim. She put down her near-empty coffee cup and put her hands up to her brow.

The woman's hand was on her shoulder. 'Say, are you OK?' She was asking a question, her voice distant and echoing.

'Yes, I'm…' She stopped. *Christ, what's wrong with me?* 'Please excuse me, I feel a little strange. I can't think what's come over me. I think I'll go back to my room and lie down for a while.' She started to get to her feet, wobbling as she did so.

Angie Goodall knew she had about ten minutes before Karen Evans passed out completely. 'Here let me help you back to your room and let your husband know. What's your room number?'

'Twenty-one. Please don't trouble Morgan, I'll be OK.'

'We'll see about that.'

Angiel took Karen firmly by the arm and led her towards the lift. Mario Gizzi, her accomplice, had been observing what was happening and had called the lift; it stood ready, doors open.

'Hold that lift, please.' Angie called out her instruction. 'In you go, Karen. How are you feeling now?'

'I feel woozy, can't understand it. It all happened so suddenly.'

The lift came to a halt, and the two women got out. Angie held on to the hapless Karen as she felt her stumble. Mario Gizzi followed behind at a safe distance.

'Nearly there, dear. Have you got your room key?'

Karen handed over her bag, saying nothing; she was no longer capable of speech; she just wanted to collapse. *Christ, what's happened to me? Oh God, I hope I'm not having a stroke.*

'Here we are, in you go.'

Karen slumped and would have fallen had Mario Gizzi not caught her from behind.

'Get her onto the bed, Mario. I'll alert Snap; then I'm out of here.'

Angie walked along the landing to room sixteen and tapped lightly on the door; it was opened almost immediately by a small, nondescript man.

'Mario is waiting for you in room twenty-one.'

Hating the situation, she had brought about, she didn't wait for his reply, wanting to get away as quickly as possible.

Tony Pearson, sometimes known as Snap, gathered up his equipment and made his way to room twenty-one minutes later. He knocked twice, and within seconds, Mario Gizzi's head appeared around the door. 'Come in, she's ready for us.'

Karen Evans lay naked on the bed, her clothes scattered on the floor. She looked peaceful, her eyes closed, her lips slightly parted.

'Christ, what a looker.' Pearson gaped at her. 'You lucky bastard, I wish it was me.'

Gizzi laughed. 'Let's face it, Tony, you ain't got my looks, and you ain't got a dick like this either.' The Italian was also naked, ready for what lay ahead.

Pearson looked enviously at his accomplice. 'Maybe not, but mine's genuine English beef, not pasta like yours, and God knows where it's been.'

The two men knew each other well, having worked together in the porn business for many years.

'Let's get on with it and remember what Angie said, Mario, minimum penetration, just what's necessary.'

Gizzi smirked. 'Yeah, sure, but the photos have got to look good; Angie ain't gonna know, and nor is this one. So, what's first? Let's do a back shot.'

He pulled Karen round and turned her over to face down on the bed, her feet resting on the floor. You ready, here goes.' He entered her from behind, his face taking on an image of ecstasy, head thrown back, hands clutching her hips.

Deep in her subconscious, Karen Evans knew something was happening; she was dreaming, fantasising.

'OK, that'll do it, Mario. Missionary shots next.'

Gizzi eased Karen Evans into position and climbed on top of her.

'Hold a sec; I've got some adjustments to make.'

Gizzi grinned. 'So, who's in a hurry? It definitely ain't me; I can work at this all day.'

Pearson was pushing a piece of foam padding into Karen Morgan's mouth; he wanted it open as though gasping in passion. Next, he used some theatrical gum to hold her eyes open and stood back to admire his work.

'OK, make it good.' Pearson went to work with his camera. He didn't need to direct; there wasn't anything Mario needed to be told about making a porn shot look good.

'That'll do it, Mario; get her on top now.'

The Italian rolled over and supported Karen whilst Pearson placed her legs astride her pseudo-lover. Gizzi reached up and held her by the shoulders, his mouth on her breast, his back arching up and down as the camera clicked.

'OK, relax, lover boy. Time to change the bed sheet and the pillowcases.

They wanted two separate backgrounds in the photo just in case Karen was able to explain what had happened to her and claim that she was nothing more than a drugged victim. One session might be explainable, but two would be impossible. Gizzi put on a gold necklace and a flashy watch to add to the effect of different time, different occasion. Pearson gathered Karen's hair in a bunch at the back, a small change but one that would be readily noticed. The second photo session was much the same as the first, just subtle changes here and there; the two men were good at what they did.

'OK, Mario, that's it; I reckon I've taken fifty pictures or more.' Pearson began to put away his props and equipment. Gizzi stood looking at his victim; Karen occasionally mumbled in her sleep but didn't waken.

'OK, Snap, get outta here. I'll get her dressed.'

'I'll give you a hand.'

'Fuck off, you pervert; I don't need you; now get going.'

Pearson eyed his accomplice suspiciously. 'What are you up to? I don't trust you; you've got that look about you. Just remember what Angie said.'

'I know what she said, but she ain't here, is she? Now fuck off.'

Pearson shrugged. 'You're a bad bastard, Mario.' But his protest was over; he gathered up his equipment and made his way back to room sixteen.

Gizzi studied Karen, admiring the contours of her body, wishing that she was conscious and able to respond to what he was about to do.

'Get ready, sweetheart; the grand finale is about to begin.' Five minutes later, his lust satisfied, he dressed. 'It's a shame I can't be here when you wake up, Honey. I bet we could make sweet music, but I gotta go.' He gathered up Karen's clothes and dressed her, leaning over to kiss her when he'd finished. 'Thanks, Babe, you were.... very receptive, shall we say.' At the door a thought struck him, and he turned back to the bed, took her right hand and pushed it down under her shorts and inside her knickers.

'Naughty girl, Karen.'

His work finished, he left and joined up with Pearson in their room.

'Well? Done your Italian manly bit, have you?'

Mario gave him the thumbs up. 'Has the call come?'

'Reception wants us to call them.' He pointed to the red light blinking on the bedside phone.'

'Best do it; then we're out of here.'

They had known there would be a call to Reception summoning them back to London; it was all part of the plan.

Karen Evans felt a sensation surfacing, some part of her reaching for a feeling she'd almost forgotten, but the dream faded away and was gone. The drug had done its work; the effects began to wear off, and she began to awaken. Her head ached, and her eyes were still unwilling to focus, but slowly, normality was coming back. She blinked herself awake; she was in a strange bed, in unfamiliar surroundings; memories came flooding back.

She was in a hotel and had had a dizzy spell; a helpful American woman had brought her back to her room. She tried to push herself up, but something was wrong; one arm wasn't responding; it was there but caught somehow. She tugged then realised that it was trapped under her tracksuit, inside her knickers. She smiled weakly at the thought she'd been pleasuring herself in her sleep. She could vaguely recall a dream and tried to remember more, but nothing came. Gradually, she began to feel better and caught sight of the note on her bedside cabinet.

Karen,

Hope that you're feeling better. I'm afraid I've been called back to London on an urgent matter. I haven't said anything to Morgan, just as you asked. Enjoy the rest of your stay. Bye

Judy Waistcott.

Thank God you were around, Judy; I would have felt such a fool if I'd passed out in the Coffee Lounge. Christ, I hope this headache doesn't hang around. I feel like I need a shower, and if I can get rid of this headache, I'll have a gentle massage. Now, do I tell Morgan or not? No, he'll only fuss and want me to see a doctor; best to say nothing. She felt good down there; hmmm, I wish I could remember more of that dream.

Chapter Twenty-Three

The weekend over, Karen Morgan was back home and had just settled down to her elevenses when the intercom buzzed. *Shit.* The clock was showing 10.45, the postman had been and gone, and she wasn't expecting any visitors. She rose reluctantly; there were times when she hated being disturbed, and morning coffee was one of them. The intercom buzzed again.

'Yes?' She almost snapped into the intercom.

'Special delivery for Mrs Karen Morgan.' The voice sounded young and cheerful.

'Put it in the post box; I'll collect it later.'

'Sorry, Mrs Morgan, it requires a signature.'

Her pretty face broke into a frown. 'Hold on, I'll be right with you.'

Unenthusiastically, she pulled on her tracksuit bottoms and trainers and set off down the drive. She could see the young man standing at the entrance gates, a large brown envelope in his hands.

'Good morning, Mrs Morgan, sorry to disturb you. I've been asked to give you this.' He passed the envelope through the railings, smiling as he did so.

Karen took the envelope, looking for a clue as to the sender, then back to the young man who had watched the puzzlement grow on her face.

'I don't understand; this isn't addressed to anyone.'

'I did say it was a special delivery, Mrs Morgan.'

'I know that, but who's it from?'

'Can't say, I'm afraid. You'll get a telephone call about its contents at eleven thirty.'

Karen's annoyance surfaced. 'Look here, whoever you are, I want to know who sent this envelope, and you said you required a signature.'

The young man's smile left his face, and his voice sharpened. 'Just be near your phone at eleven thirty.' Before she could respond, he turned on his heel and jogged away. He hadn't far to go; his motorcycle was parked nearby, out of sight of the gates.

Back in her kitchen, Karen Morgan slammed the heavy envelope onto the table and poured herself a fresh cup of coffee. *Who did he think he was, telling her what to do? Eleven thirty indeed, for all he knew, she might have been going out.* She was wrong about that; her movements were well known. Annoyed but intrigued, there was no point venting her umbrage on a package; she would do that when she answered the phone. She reached forward for the envelope, tore it open and spilt its contents onto the table. *Pornographic photos. Who the hell was sending her those?* Mild revulsion pulsed through her, but it didn't stop her from wanting to look at them. The photograph she was looking at showed the rear view of a man lying across a woman, her legs draped over his shoulders. *Nice work if you can get it, girl.* She put it aside and took the next one, her titillation turning to horror when she realised, she was looking at herself. Sickness welled in her stomach as she slumped back in the chair. *How can it be? It's some kind of trick, with a double. It can't be me.* Her horror grew as she spread the photos over the table. Tears filled her eyes. *Oh my God.* Photos with her eyes open, her mouth parted; she was enjoying it. *Oh God, oh God.* Then she noticed the blue sheet and matching pillowcases and the man with and without a gold neck chain. It had happened on more than one occasion. *How? When? Where? Oh my God, what would Morgan think?* Suddenly, she needed to vomit and rushed to the toilet; she had never been so afraid in her life. *It was all a set-up, but what would Morgan think? It would finish her marriage.*

Karen visited the toilet three times, her insides rebelling against the fear she felt. There was nothing she could do but wait. She sat trembling, staring at the phone, not knowing whether she wanted it to ring or not, trying to regain her composure; they were going to blackmail her, whoever they were. Whoever it was had her at their mercy; she couldn't tell Morgan. He would never believe her; the photos were too explicit, and he would see that it had happened on more than one occasion. *But how? Was she going mad?* She couldn't claim that she had been a victim, and yet she must have been. *That was it; she must have been drugged, but where? How? Who by?*

She would give them whatever they wanted; except she had nothing to give. Morgan dealt with all money matters, and whilst she had a generous allowance, she had no savings. *Morgan will never believe her; he's too jealous. He'll think that I've had an affair. Oh God.* She could give them jewellery, not that there was much; she didn't like jewellery, and anyway, how could she explain its loss to Morgan? That left her Porsche, and they could have that; she'd tell Morgan it had been stolen.

The telephone rang, breaking abruptly into her thoughts; it sounded shrill, insistent.

'Yes?' Her mouth was dry, her voice hollow and full of foreboding.

'Mrs Morgan?'

'Yes.'

'You've looked at the photographs?'

'Yes, but it's not me, there's some mistake. I couldn't have....'

'Mrs Morgan,' the caller interrupted her, 'let's not get off on the wrong foot. I know it's you, and you know it's you. What you must ask yourself, is this: what would your husband believe if he saw the photographs?'

Karen wretched at the thought, but there was nothing left in her.

'I haven't got any money or any worthwhile jewellery; you're wasting your time if you're thinking of blackmailing me.' She tried to sound resolute, defiant even. 'You can have my car. It's a Porsche; I'll make it easy for you to steal it.'

'Mrs Morgan, we don't want any of your possessions. We just want your help with a little problem we have.'

'What kind of problem?'

'We need some information that you can get for us. If you do that, we won't have to send the photos to your husband and his friends at the Bank.'

Oh my God, Morgan's friends as well. 'Tell me what it is you want.' She knew she was beaten, but there seemed to be a lifeline on offer.

'That's better, Mrs Morgan. Your husband goes to Glasgow quite regularly, doesn't he?'

'Yes, he does, every two months or so. What about it?'

'Please don't ask me questions, just tell me what I want to know. Understand?'

Karen wanted to tell him to go fuck himself but replied meekly. 'Yes.'

'When did he last go to Glasgow?'

'Quite recently, last Wednesday, in fact.'

'Good. What I want you to do is find out when he's going again.'

'He doesn't give me much notice.'

'Do what we want, Mrs Morgan; having seen the photos with what you've got on offer, I'm sure he'd be delighted to take you with him. If I were you, I'd insist that you go with him on his next trip; it would be in everybody's best interest. You understand what I'm saying?'

'Yes.'

'One more thing, we know that he'll want to do some business when he's in Glasgow.'

'Obviously, or he wouldn't be going there, would he?'

'Don't get smart, Karen. Whilst he's engaged in that business, I anticipate that he'll leave you on your own. As soon as he leaves, you let us know. Understand?'

'Yes.'

'Good, now I want you to note down a telephone number; call it as soon as you have a date for me. Use the same number when you're in Glasgow. You're the only one who has this number. Have you got pencil and paper?'

'Yes.' Karen did as she was told, starting to feel relief now that there seemed to be a way out of her predicament.

'Read the number back to me; we mustn't get this wrong?'

Her voice wavered as she read the number back, fear irrationally creeping in at the thought of what might happen if she lost it.

'Good; now, one last thing: if we don't hear from you within eight weeks, we'll distribute the photos. And make sure you destroy your copies; we don't want Morgan coming across them, do we?'

Angie Goodall's husband ended the call and turned to his wife. 'All done, I'm sure she'll comply.'

Karen slumped into her chair, drained, her thoughts in turmoil. *Why on earth did they want to know when Morgan was going to Glasgow? They were up to no good, but why? I'll try to find out, but Morgan is so secretive about his work; he's never told me why he goes to Glasgow. But my whole future is on the line. I'll do what the bastards want, whatever they're up to*

Out of the blue, I got a call from Dan telling me that we were on the starting blocks; things were on the move at last. 'We've got a maximum of two months. If we're not ready in time, we'll have to wait for at least another two.'

'Not a problem. I can do what I have to do over the next few days.'

'Go to it, Craig. Give me a ring when you're ready, and I'll set up a meet with our friends.'

Following Dan's call, I went straight to Millet's and equipped myself with outdoor walking gear, a rucksack, a compass, and a pair of binoculars. I also arranged a car hire and thought again about buying one but couldn't convince myself that I really needed a car in London. A long drive lay ahead, up the M1, then onto the M6 as far as Junction 37 near Kendall on the edge of the Lake District. Once there, I'd leave the motorway and follow the road system, keeping as near to the railway as possible till I found what I was looking for. The decisions I would be making were key to the success of the robbery.

I set off very early to avoid the morning traffic congestion, aiming to get to Kendall in time for lunch. The drive North proved to be uneventful and undemanding, and the sky blue when I started out, but the clouds thickened and darkened, eventually blotting out the sun as I passed through the Birmingham sprawl. The turn-off for Crewe and Nantwich brought

339

memories of Sam flooding back, and for an irrational second, I let my thoughts dwell again on making contact, but the moment passed. The weather continued to worsen, and by the time I got to Cumbria, it was raining heavily; still, I made it by lunchtime. I pulled off into a motorway service area for sustenance and a desperate comfort break, pausing briefly on my way to look at the local forecast on display near the entrance. I was heartened to see that the weather was expected to improve later that afternoon.

My creature needs satisfied, I set off again, taking the next first turning off the motorway. Thereafter, I continued north, keeping the railway in sight as best I could, occasionally pulling off the road to view the terrain through my binoculars. Using Ordnance Survey maps of the area, I had identified a possible location, one with good road access running close to a level stretch of railway track and with no dwellings nearby. Nearing the end of my journey, I turned onto the B6260 to Orton, passing through the village to the B6261. Just half a mile ahead, I knew that there were two unclassified roads coming off to the left, both ending up in the village of Greenholme, effectively forming a loop. The first turning was the more direct of these roads and passed under the M6; it was this one that interested me. The railway also crossed over this road, which meant that the track would be on an embankment, and that suited my plan.

I took the second turning and parked a little way along; it was time to become a birdwatcher. My knowledge of birds was minimal, but if anyone were to ask, I'd tell them I was on the lookout for Harriers or Buzzards. The road was narrow but well-made, with an open landscape on either side, just as I'd hoped. The bridge was about half a mile further on, and when it came into view, I felt my pulse quicken; it was exactly what I was looking for. There were no farms or cottages in the immediate vicinity, reducing the chance of encountering a local resident at an inopportune moment.

The embankment was steeper than I would have wished, but that had its pros and cons. I scrambled up the bank and looked around; there was good visibility for about two miles in both directions and more importantly, the track was level. Over to the East, about a mile away, I could hear the rumble of traffic on the motorway. It was closer than I would have liked, but it would be dark, and we were unlikely to be seen. I spent an hour walking the track in both directions, by which time I had gathered all the information I required. There were a few train hoots from passing drivers, but I just returned a friendly wave, confident that they would assume I was just another technical type carrying out an inspection. My track hike completed, I headed back to the car, by which time it was nearing six, and I felt quite tired when I climbed into the car; it had been a long day but a successful one. I'd successfully completed my objective.

My next task was to look for somewhere to bed down for the night, and I headed for Tebay, having made up my mind to take the first B & B I came across. I fantasised that by happenstance, I might find myself with an attractive landlady on the lookout for a dalliance with a passing traveller. It wasn't to be; Miss Millway turned out to be a spinster of mature years, welcoming enough but more matronly than motherly.

341

My day's travail ensured that I slept soundly, and next morning, after a hearty breakfast, I set out for Carnforth Station to fill in another piece of the jigsaw. Two boring hours were spent at a suitable vantage spot observing the comings and goings through my binoculars. To the casual observer, I probably had the appearance of a trainspotter; nobody appeared to be interested. Job done, I pocketed my notes and travelled South again, to Tring some two hundred miles to the South. My visit there didn't last long, and I was on my way within twenty minutes.

Back at the flat, I phoned Dan to tell him that I was ready to brief the others. He, in turn, told me where they were up to with Karen Evans and put me on standby; we'd make a move as soon as he had the date. I thought about Karen and what we had done to her; I was increasingly coming to realise that crime was an ugly business and wondered if I would have been able to violate her in that way. I didn't like the answer I came up with; in my heart, I knew that I would always find a way to do what was necessary to get what I wanted. *Where were **my** limits? Did I have any? Probably not. No limits. It was a sobering thought.*

A week had gone by since her ordeal, and Karen Morgan had come to terms with her emotional turmoil and wanted desperately to bring closure to her horrible experience. She knew she could only achieve that by getting the information her blackmailers wanted. To do that, she had to get Morgan into the right frame of mind and had prepared the occasion thoughtfully. There were lighted candles on the table; she had dressed seductively and, opened a bottle of his favourite red wine and cooked a rich lasagne, one of his favourite meals.

'Hmm, that was delicious, darling; there wouldn't be any left by chance?' Normally, she would have chided him about his waistline, but not this time.

'For you, my darling, of course, there is.' Her mother had always insisted that a way to a man's heart was through his belly, but she wasn't sure; the men she had known had been more interested in her anatomy than her culinary skills. She poured him another glass of Merlot, his third of the evening, leaning over him so he could admire her cleavage. 'Had a good day, darling?'

He pulled his eyes away from her breasts. 'Not bad, I suppose, quite uneventful, really.'

'I shall be glad when you retire, Morgan. I don't see enough of you; I felt lonely today. In fact, I missed you lots, darling.'

Evans smiled; he liked the idea of being missed.'

'Only today, darling?' He said teasingly, his hand straying to her bottom.

'Of course not,' She protested. 'I miss you every day, but today more than most.'

The banker sipped his wine reflectively. 'I get like that sometimes.'

'Morgan.' Karen decided to make her move.

'I was listening to a programme about Glasgow today, and it sounded quite interesting.'

'Really?' Morgan Evans was surprised; he didn't like the city. 'In what way?'

'Well, everything really; the shopping and restaurants seem to be first class. It just got me thinking it would make a change to go somewhere completely different, maybe go to Edinburgh at the same time. You go to Glasgow, don't you?'

'I do, but I confess that I don't know too much about it. As soon as my business is completed, I like to get home to you.'

Karen took the plunge. 'Well, maybe I could come with you on your next trip to Glasgow, maybe take in Edinburgh too?'

Evans thought for a moment, then nodded. 'That's a good idea; we'll do just that. I'll do what business I must do, then we'll have a couple of days looking round.'

'Thank you, darling, I'm very spoiled. I hope it won't be too long?' She looked at her husband expectantly and squeezed the hand that was still fondling her bottom.

'Hold on, let me think. It'll be the twenty-eighth of next month.'

'Don't you want to check your diary, Morgan? I'll want to book an appointment to get my hair done; I must look my best for you when we go away. What day is it, I'll check the date?'

He shook his head. 'I don't know what day it is; it doesn't work like that. Believe me, it's the twenty-eighth this time.'

'I'll just go and check what day that is; you have some more wine, then we'll cuddle up in front of the television.' She returned promptly, smiling broadly. 'It's a Thursday, darling. Does that mean we could stay until the Sunday?'

The fourth glass of Merlot was taking its toll; Evans was feeling decidedly mellow. 'If that's what you want, darling, that's what we'll do.'

His wife nuzzled at his cheek. 'Oh, I just had a dreadful thought. You won't go off to some stuffy old business meeting and leave me on my own, will you?'

'I must do **some** work, poppet. Otherwise, I can't charge my trip to the bank.'

'What exactly do you do up there anyway, darling?'

Her husband smiled smugly. 'Sorry darling, I'm not allowed to tell you, security and all that. Best you don't know.'

Karen pouted, 'Well, I hope you won't leave me on my own for long?'

'Not very long, darling, I promise. I will have to go out for an hour after breakfast on the Thursday, then again around nine in the evening for about half an hour. It's all a bit of a bore, but we'll have an early meal that night; if I know you, you'll be tired after I've taken you shopping and bought you some nice clothes.'

'Oh, Morgan darling, you're always spoiling me.'

Next morning, as soon as her husband went to work, she dialled the telephone number she had been given, hesitating when a woman answered.

'It's Karen Morgan.'

'I know who it is; you're the only one who has this number. Do you have the information?' Angie Goodall felt a pang of guilt and wanted the call to be as brief as possible.

'Yes, it's the twenty-eighth of next month, the last Thursday. Morgan says he'll go out after breakfast on the Thursday, then again at nine in the evening.'

'You've done well, Mrs Morgan. Keep note of this telephone number and call us if there's any change to the date. When you get to Glasgow, keep us informed about your husband's business commitments, and phone us the minute he leaves in the morning. Understood?'

'Yes. Will you destroy the photos now?'

'Not until the information proves to be correct.'

Karen sighed when she put down the phone; her agony was going to continue for a while longer.

Dan wasted no time in gathering us all together in Camden, and I briefed everybody on the job that lay ahead. I went into every detail and prompted some protests when I insisted on going through it all again. I answered the usual sprinkling of questions and finished by reminding them that the stakes were thirty million and this was probably a once-in-a-lifetime opportunity. 'Let's get it right, guys.'

Dan told them to liaise with me as and when necessary. He'd decide nearer the time whether we needed to meet again. During the weeks that followed, I worked closely with everybody and must have done my job well because Dan decided it wasn't necessary to meet again.

As the day approached, my only concern was whether Eddie Milton was up to the job or not. To his credit, he had researched the technical side of his role and impressed me with his knowledge. He just seemed to lack the hard edge that might prove necessary; I consoled myself that Tony Sherwood would more than make up for any shortcomings Eddie might have.

Chapter Twenty-Four

We had our plan and our date; I was enjoying the adrenaline-fuelled emotions that came with the approach of a job, like an actor, during last week rehearsals. I insisted on allocating the various responsibilities, and Tony Sherwood had supported me despite the mutterings round the table.

I divided the troops into teams, each one with a leader. Team A, two men, they would do the business around Tring. Team B, six men including myself, would be at Greenholme Bridge. Team C, two men both armed, would tackle the train. Team D, two men, both armed, with responsibility for site security, on the lookout for unwanted visitors, police included. Finally, there was Team E, responsible for Operational Control, three armed men, including Tony Sherwood and Eddie Milton. In all, there were fifteen of us, and I had five weeks to teach them all they needed to know about railway working and their precise role in the robbery.

As it happened, Ralph Mason had taken on board my initial briefing, and I was happy with everybody he recruited, particularly those in Team B, where I had emphasised the need for strength and stamina along with the ability to work at pace, and, equally importantly, as a team. With all this involvement, the days flew past, and as the big day drew near, I became increasingly confident that we had a competent crew. There were no dimwits and no loose cannons; everybody appreciated the need to follow instructions to the letter. My respect for Ralph and the organisation, in general, continued to grow; I could see why it had been successful.

Charlie Booker came up trumps with the equipment; it had been stolen from a railway depot in the south of Germany and would be very difficult to trace to any source on this side of the Channel. Given that the intention was to abandon the gear on site, this was particularly important. I tried to quiz him on how he went about the theft but got nowhere; he just tapped the side of his nose with his forefinger.

In between times, I went out with Sally, and she surprised me with her perception. 'You've seemed a bit distant lately, Craig; you're not going off me, are you?'

'Not at all, Sal, it's not intentional, honestly. I've got a big investment proposal going through, and I guess my thoughts keep drifting. I'm sorry, sweetheart, but you know how it is when you've got a big deal on the go. You get wrapped up in it; thoughts keep intruding. It'll be all done and dusted by the end of the month, I promise.'

'You're sure? I'd rather know where I stand.'

'I'm one hundred per cent sure. In fact, I was wondering if you would like to come to Tuscany with me at the end of the month. Two weeks of leisure and pleasure would do us both good.'

Her eyes lit up. 'Are you serious? You're not doing this on the spur of the moment in response to my doubts? I know Tuscany is beautiful, but it's very upmarket and expensive.'

'I'm serious, believe me; I've been thinking about it for some time. Can you come or not? I want to go somewhere special to celebrate the success of this deal I'm involved in.' My reassurances were genuine, and they worked.

'Well, I am due some leave; I'll see what I can do, though the boss might not want me to take two weeks at such short notice.'

I pulled her to me and kissed her gently. 'Do your best; I'll take a chance and get a Travel Agent on the case tomorrow.'

'It's a bit of a risk, Craig, I can't promise, and what if this deal of yours doesn't work out?'

'We just have to keep our fingers crossed.'

Karen Morgan was quizzing her husband again about his business in Glasgow. 'I hope you won't leave me on my own for long, Morgan?'

'I won't be long, darling, I promise; the Bank has everything ready for my signature.'

'What is it you'll be doing, Morgan?'

The Evans duo were having breakfast in Glasgow's Central Station Hotel, and Karen was doing all she could to get to know about her husband's plans. She was determined to get the blackmailers off her back and get back to normality; besides, she was genuinely curious as to why her husband's trips were of such interest to these people. What on earth did they want?

For his part, Morgan Evans enjoyed secrecy and wasn't giving anything away.

'Nothing too exciting darling, just some papers that require my signature. I'll be back as quickly as I can, then I'll whisk you away on that shopping trip I promised.' Evans didn't really need to be in Glasgow in person, but he enjoyed his trips away at the Bank's expense and signing for such a vast sum of money made him feel important. Breakfast over, he took his leave and Karen wasted no time in making her telephone call. It was answered almost immediately.

'Hello.' Angie Goodall had stationed herself at the phone since seven that morning.

'My husband has just gone to his appointment.'

'Thank you, Mrs Morgan. Just one more call, and you'll be free of us. You will phone this evening, won't you?'

'Of course.'

The telephone died, leaving her still puzzled as to what was going on.

Morgan Evans stepped out of the hotel into a cloudy, damp Glasgow morning and set out for the Royal Bank of Scotland; he wasn't aware of the small, nondescript man who followed him all the way to his destination. The gang knew where Evans would head for but wanted to be certain; changes did happen, and if they did, Dan Rawson needed to know sharpish.

The phone call from Karen was little more than re-assurance that things were on track.

'Good morning, Morgan; how nice to see you again.' Charles Fraser, Evans' opposite number at the Royal Bank of Scotland, made his guest welcome though truth to tell, the two men had little in common.

The Scot was a well-travelled, well-read extrovert who spent much of his free time socialising and found his present company to be a bore of the first order.

'Would you care for coffee before we get down to business?'

'Thank you, but not this time, Charles. I have my wife with me on this trip, and she's keen to go shopping, so I won't hang about. I hope that's all right with you?'

Fraser smiled, nodding sympathetically and enquired hopefully. 'Not at all, I quite understand, and does this mean I won't have the pleasure of your company for lunch either?'

'Afraid not, old chap, sorry to disappoint you. We'll make up for it next time.'

Fraser breathed an inward sigh of relief; Evans was a decent sort but best encountered in small doses; added to that, he had expensive tastes when it came to food and wine.

'Shame. Well, let's not delay. I'll take you straight down to the holding vault.'

The pair made their way to the vault, and the Scot pushed his passkey into the lock, turned it, and pushed the three-inch-thick steel door open.

'There we are; ready for your inspection; here's the manifest.' Fraser handed his guest four copies, 'Will you be checking off each box?'

Evans glanced at the neatly stacked rows of sealed green wooden boxes and shook his head.

'Not on this occasion, Charles; if the Bank of England can't trust the Royal Bank of Scotland, what would the world be coming to.' He was conveniently forgetting that it was he who had, up to then, insisted on checking the unique number on each box against those on the manifest.

'Let's see, five boxes deep, three wide, four high, sixty boxes in total and that ties up with the manifest total. 'My God!'

Fraser heard the surprise in Evan's voice. 'Problem?'

'The manifest says thirty million; that's quite a bit more than usual. As a matter of fact, I can't recall a consignment this large.'

'It is more than normal, but that's not a problem, is it? The economy is growing, and so are we.'

Morgan shook his head. 'No, no, not at all; the population are becoming increasingly affluent, and I suppose it follows that there are more notes in circulation.' He signed the four copies of the manifest and handed three to his host.

'Now Charles, what are the arrangements for tonight?'

'I need you back here at nine-thirty, Morgan; the train goes at ten past ten. We're using the usual carrier.'

'That'll be Safehaul if my memory serves me correctly.'

Fraser nodded. 'It serves you well, Morgan, as always. Shall I reserve us a table for dinner before we witness despatch and loading? Perhaps Mrs Morgan might care to join us?'

Evans thought briefly and declined. 'Thanks for the offer, but I'm sure Karen will have plans for the evening. I'll see you at the rear entrance at nine-thirty prompt.'

'As you wish, Morgan.'

'I think we should be getting back to the hotel, darling; I'd like to relax and enjoy the luxury of a bath before dinner; besides, I don't think I can carry anything else.' Karen Evans had had a very successful shopping trip. Morgan had given her a budget, one she regarded as generous given his usual prudence, and after three hours trailing round Glasgow's leading fashion stores, she had spent every penny.

Evans had watched the budget decrease steadily with mixed feelings; Karen had several wardrobes full of clothes, and he couldn't understand why she needed more, but, on the other hand, as soon as the money was gone, they could head back to the comfort of the hotel room. His feet swelling, his back aching and the last pound spent, Evans indicated that he was going to hail a taxi. To his dismay, his wife declined.

'Not yet, darling; I've got some money of my own to spend, and I need a couple of pairs of shoes to match what you've just bought me. You don't mind, do you darling, it's so much fun shopping together?'

Her husband sighed wearily but managed a weak smile. 'No dear, do carry on.'

Back in the hotel, nearly two hours later, the banker sank into a hot bath, memories of the shopping trip disappearing by the second, only his tired body reminding him otherwise.

'What time for dinner, darling?'

He looked round to see his wife standing in the doorway, naked. 'I've booked for seven and I can't be too late; I must be back at the bank for nine-thirty.'

'Shall I come into the bath with you?' Karen put a sexy coyness into her voice. 'I think Morgan deserves a little reward for being so good to me.'

Evans licked his lips. 'Oh yes, please, darling, it's been a while since we did that.'

At a quarter after nine, Evans rose wearily from the dinner table. 'Must go, darling. I'll be as quick as I can; definitely before ten. Perhaps we could have an early night and carry on where we left off in the bath.'

His dutiful wife feigned a mild shock. 'Goodness Morgan, you're never satisfied.'

She accompanied her husband to Reception, kissed him goodbye, watched him disappear through the revolving doors and immediately made her way to the hotel telephone kiosk. She hoped that she was about to make her final telephone call to her blackmailers.

'Hello, it's Karen Morgan.'

'Go ahead, Mrs Morgan.'

'My husband has just left the hotel. He's due at the bank at nine-thirty and will be back here for ten.'

'Thank you, Mrs Morgan.'

'What about the photographs?'

'We'll keep to our side of the bargain if your information proves to be accurate.'

Karen nodded glumly. *I'll just have to trust them.*

Evans arrived at the rear entrance to the Royal Bank of Scotland a minute before his nine-thirty appointment and pressed the intercom to announce his presence.

The door opened almost immediately, and Charles Fraser extended his hand.

'Punctual as always, Morgan; I hope you and Mrs Evans had a good day in the city?'

'Almost too good, Charles; I don't think I can afford to bring Karen with me too often. Why do women need so many clothes?'

'To look their best for us, old chap; one wouldn't want it otherwise. Safehaul are waiting for us and, of course, the usual escort team.'

The pair made their way to the holding vault where two security guards stood on duty; a third had stationed himself at the door at the end of the corridor leading to the transit yard.

Fraser duly opened the vault door and looked at Evans. 'We await your instructions, my lord.'

Evans ran his eye over the green boxes and satisfied himself that they seemed unchanged from his previous visit; then keen to get back to his wife, readily gave his assent. 'Seems to be the same as we left it this morning; you can begin loading. I'll check every tenth box number against the manifest.'

The loading process commenced, with the senior of the guards checking every box number against the manifest; he would be signing the manifest on behalf of his company. Every box was sealed, and the contents of each were only listed on Evans' and Fraser's copies. The boxes were loaded onto a trolley and wheeled out to the transit yard, where they were transferred to the waiting van. It took five trolley journeys to complete the transfer, after which all parties signed the appropriate manifest copies.

Loading complete, Fraser opened the huge steel external entrance gate to the transit yard, and the two bankers watched as the van drove away with its four security guards.

'That's it then, Charles; it's all down to British Railways and Safehaul now; we've done our bit. Thanks as always. I'll see you in a couple of months or whenever.'

'I look forward to it, Morgan, and maybe I'll get to meet your wife next time.'

Evans nodded affably, but he wasn't sure he wanted his wife to meet the charming Charles Fraser.

Outside the transit yard, a taxi pulled away from the roadside and took up position a safe distance behind the van. The driver saw the vehicle but wasn't concerned; taxis were common in the city centre at that time of night. But he remained on alert and was aware that it continued to follow him on his journey to the station; he wasn't unduly concerned. Many taxis went to the station.

His eyes narrowed when the taxi followed down the lane to the rear of the station; caution kicked in, and he alerted his colleagues. 'There's been a taxi with us since we left the yard, probably nothing, but be prepared.' Reaching his destination, the driver signalled right and stopped the van in front of the large railing gates that secured the access to the Goods platform. He watched the taxi continue on its journey and informed his mates, 'False alarm, he's gone.'

The Station Manager in person was expecting the important delivery, and there was no delay in opening the gate and signalling the van to enter. The van then proceeded directly ahead onto the platform.

The taxi drove round the block and parked in front of the station in the taxi rank; its passenger, Willie Miller, got out and made his way inside the station. He knew where he was going and crossed the concourse to where he could observe the contents of the van being transferred to a closed Good's van halfway along the train. The loading operation completed at two minutes to ten. He moved away and checked the Train Information Board; the display indicated that the night sleeper to London would depart from Platform One at ten o'clock and was on time. Miller lingered, watching the overnight travellers board their allocated coaches, noting too that it left on time. It was all going to plan.

He returned to observe the Goods platform where the Safehaul guards stood talking; they were keen to get home, pleased that their shift was nearly over; they had no idea how much money they were responsible for at that moment. At eight minutes past ten, the railway guard and the engine driver held a short conversation, and the former made his way to his van at the rear of the train, where he climbed on board. Miller heard the guard's whistle and saw him wave a green flag; it was ten past ten precisely when the train pulled away to become part of history.

The tiny Glaswegian made his way back across the concourse to a public telephone to perform his final task. 'Hello, it's Willie Miller reporting in.

The sleeper left on time, and our train left at ten past ten; the packages are in the fourth van back from the engine; I reckon that there are at least fifty packages.'

'Thanks, Willie, we'll be in touch.'

'Sooner the better, hen, my piggy bank is empty.'

Angie Goodall smiled contentedly. So far, so good; she too, had a phone call to make.

'Craig speaking.'

'It's Angie; our train left at ten minutes after ten. The night sleeper left at ten as per the timetable. Our goods are four vans back from the engine; there are at least fifty packages.'

'The more packages there are, the richer we'll be, Angie. Thanks, and good night.'

'Good luck, Craig.'

I put down the telephone and left the public phone box, a tremor of excitement flowing through me; it really was happening. One of my dreams was coming true. I crossed the road to the waiting box van; all done out in British Railway colours, another Ralph Mason production. As I climbed into the van, my nerves tingling with excitement, the game had begun.

'OK, Bert, head for Greenholme Bridge.'

The rest of the team sat huddled together uncomfortably on the floor in the rear of the vehicle; there was no conversation. Tension ruled. My best guess was that the night sleeper would get to the bridge sometime between eleven fifty-five and five past twelve; Team C would have to be in place by eleven forty-five at the latest. I worked out that we would get to the bridge shortly after eleven, allowing for two tasks on the way. Bert turned off the B6261 and pulled up opposite a Police car parked at the side of the road; we weren't worried by its presence. It was another Ralph Mason ringer.

Sandy, a tall, rangy Yorkshireman with a ginger moustache, eased out of the car and ambled across. The fake police uniform looked convincing, and I wondered if it was real or dress hire.

'We ready?' he asked gruffly.

I nodded. 'Close the road at eleven forty-five. We'll see you when the job's done.'

'Right.' A man of few words, he turned on his heel and settled back into the car, immediately lighting up a cigarette. The roadblock was in good hands; Sandy had a reputation, and he was armed.

'On your way, Bert.' The van edged forward and gathered speed, heading towards the bridge, though we weren't stopping there this time round; we passed under, driving towards Greenholme village and our next roadblock. The second fake patrol car was in place; Sid Elton, a cheerful little man, strode purposefully over.

'All right, boss?' I liked being called boss; it meant people knew I was running the show.

'No problems, Sid, everything is hot. Set up the Accident Diversion sign at eleven forty-five.'

'Take it as done, boss. No one gets in or out after eleven forty-five.'

'Anything happening on the police frequency?'

'Dead as the proverbial dodo; I reckon this is a crime-free zone. Good luck, catch you later.'

We were now secure or would be when the no-entry signs went up. My nerves were settling down, and my confidence growing as each piece of the plan fell into place. There was some risk, of course; a late-night traveller wouldn't be a problem, but an authentic passing police car might get nosy and ask some awkward questions. I wasn't too concerned; the boys were armed and would deal with that eventuality.

We drove on into Greenholme and strode across to its lone public telephone box, where I had one last call to make.

'Hi Angie, final contact; we'll be going in around midnight. Tell the Tring boys in place for three; when you've done that, you can go to bed.'

'Will do, Craig. Good luck.'

'Thanks.'

I climbed back into the van feeling good; we were on our marks and ready to go. 'OK, Bert, head for the bridge, its curtains up.'

The guys were relieved to get out of the van, stretch their legs, have a pee, light fags, whatever. I let them do their own thing for a few minutes; I wanted them relaxed. The weather was being kind to us. We couldn't have picked a better night; it was mild, and there wasn't a cloud to be seen in a clear starry sky. It was time for a final briefing. 'OK, guys, listen up. The road barriers will go up at eleven forty-five, so we won't be disturbed after that. Until then, we are just railwaymen carrying out some maintenance work should any passer-by come along and show an interest.

'Team B, start getting the gear out of the van and into position on top of the embankment. And a word of warning: listen out for trains. I don't want any of you guys mowed down, at least not till after we've done the job.'

Tony Sherwood added. 'After that, we don't give a fuck, it'll be a bigger share-out for the rest of us.'

There were a few titters, but deep down, they knew Tony wasn't really kidding.

'Carl, Ronnie,' I spoke to the two gunmen that formed Team C, 'get into position for the train and don't get distracted or offer to help Team B with the gear. Carl, you're at the signal; Ronnie, best guess is for you to be two hundred paces north. When the train stops, you know what to do. I'm not going through it again.'

Carl nodded, 'No need to, Craig, it's a piece of cake.'

I liked his confidence. 'Sure is, and you guys really look the part.'

They were both wearing the dark blue serge suits and the long dark trench coats often worn by railway Operating Inspectors. At the last possible minute, they would pull down ski masks to conceal their faces. The rest of us had donned dark blue boiler suits and gloves; we were ready to roll.

'Tony, Eddie, Mike, back to the van for you. Bert knows exactly where to drop you. Good luck; you guys are key to the whole operation. Tony, I would go in at eleven forty-five, probably a bit early, but you won't have to hang around for long.'

Tony grinned broadly. 'Leave it to us, Craig; this will be like taking milk from a baby.'

I glanced at Eddie Milton; he looked pale and tense, much as I anticipated.

'You OK, Eddie?'

'Sure, n..n..no problem.'

I wished he hadn't stammered; he would have sounded more convincing. He was undoubtedly the weakest link in the chain; thankfully, he was alongside Tony.

'It'll be fine, Eddie. You're in good company. How about you, Mike?'

'Can't wait to get started.' Mike, the third member of the team, was an old pro, and nothing much phased him by all accounts.

'That's it then; go to it.'

I watched them get into the van and drive away. There was nothing I could do now except hope that everybody did what they had been trained to do.

Chapter Twenty-Five

GREENHOLME BRIDGE: 11.15 pm.

I gathered the five members of Team B around me to issue my final instructions. Bert and four well-built young men; they would need good muscle for what lay ahead.

'OK, we're nearly there. Bert, you will stay in the van ready to go at any time; you don't wander off, you don't help the guys, and if you need a piss, do it on the front wheel below the cab.'

Bert, who had a few years under his belt and looked more like a grandfather than a robber, saluted sharply. 'OK, chief.'

'Rich, Dave, Paul, Grant, get the gear up onto the embankment and in between the tracks. Tell me when you're ready and I'll check the final positioning. Go to it, and a final warning: listen out for trains; I don't want any dead men lying around. Keep your gloves on, no matter what; if we hear of any prints being found by the coppers after the job, Tony Sherwood will pay you a visit.'

I looked on as they laboured to haul the equipment up the steep slope; they needed to be strong. It really was a difficult task; I found my feet slipping on the grassy bank as I clawed my way up to the tracks, reminding me just how difficult a job they had in hand. Up top, I paced out exactly where I wanted the equipment placed and marked the locations with a small pile of track ballast on the appropriate sleepers.

Meanwhile, the boys completed their task, and I let them have a well-earned rest before directing them to manhandle the equipment into its final position. Away in the distance to the South, I heard a train; the others didn't seem to hear it; maybe with my railway background, my ears were more attuned to the distinctive sound.

'Train coming, clear the track; lie down flat on the embankment.'

The guys scampered onto the embankment, and minutes later, a passenger train clattered past at high speed.

'OK, it's clear, back to work. Let's get this job finished in the next ten minutes.'

Further down the track to the North, I occasionally caught a glimpse of Carl and Ronnie lingering near the signal but mostly my thoughts were with the Control team. I wondered how Eddie Milton was standing up under pressure. Thank God for Tony Sherwood; he would be, as ever, ice-cool and as safe as the Bank of England. Given what we were up to, that last thought made me smile.

TEBAY SIGNAL BOX: 11.45 pm.

Tony, Eddie, and Mike climbed out of the rear of the van, closed the door and rattled the bodywork; Bert waved and headed back to the bridge.

367

'OK, mask up, gloves on, and we're straight in. And remember, Eddie, no names in there.' Tony Sherwood gave his instructions and pulled on his own black nylon ski mask and gloves. They were all wearing dark blue overalls, and only height distinguished one from the other.

'Great, your own fucking mothers wouldn't recognise you. Now get your gun in your hand and follow me.'

'Do I have to, Tony? I've never fired a gun?' Eddie Milton asked nervously.

'Fucking right you do; I don't want any of those bastards seeing you as a weak link.'

The electronics wizard sighed but obeyed. *A weak link was exactly what he felt he was.*

'Right, follow me. Mike, once we're inside, you take the door and deal with any unexpected guests. You know the drill: be safe, but only use the shooter if you must. Eddie, stay close to me and keep calm.'

The three men climbed the flight of external stairs to the signal box, and, without hesitating, Tony Sherwood pushed the door open, and the three men bundled inside. Two very startled signalmen swung around in their wheeled chairs. The younger of the two was first to react and stood to face the intruders, 'What the....'

Tony Sherwood cut him off. 'Shut up and sit down. From now on, speak only when you're spoken to. Got it?'

The younger was slow to comply, but he did what he was told; the older man uttered a soft, uncertain 'Yes.'

'Good, we understand each other. Now, listen carefully. I'm only going to say this once. There's a train on its way from Glasgow, and it's got something on it we want. Something we want so badly we'll kill for it if we must that's why we've got these.' He waved his gun in the air. 'We just want you to carry on as normal; do the job you always do, and that way nobody gets hurt. If you don't, you'll be very badly injured; killed if you really annoy me.' Sherwood moved forward to the younger man, who he judged to be most likely to cause trouble. 'This isn't a fucking toy. Would you like me to test it on you?' He jabbed the gun into the young man's kneecap. To his credit, the young man didn't panic; he just shook his head and responded in a quiet voice. 'No need for that. We'll do what you want; the Railway doesn't pay us enough to die for them.'

Tony lifted the gun to the young man's eye level. 'I can see we're going to get on well. And just in case you think about getting clever; my friend here knows all about railway signalling.'

He motioned at Eddie. 'Keep him happy, and you'll go home at the end of your shift. Otherwise….'

Sherwood took a half turn and squeezed the trigger firing into the door just three feet from where Mike was standing. Mike just stood there; he didn't flinch or even blink; it was an act he and Tony had worked on previously. The bang shocked the two signalmen, as well as Eddie Milton, who jumped back startled. The bullet tore through the door, sending splinters flying in all directions.

'Told you it wasn't a toy.'

He thrust his gun under the older man's nose, 'Imagine what it would do to your fucking head.'

Beads of sweat broke out on Jack Brown's brow, his hands trembled, mouth silently sucking in air.

'Now, my friend here is going to give you some instructions.' He glanced round at Eddie Milton who was as still shaken by the turn of events. This was a key moment; Sherwood locked his gaze on his accomplice, willing him to do what was expected of him.

The moment he had dreaded had come; Eddie drew a deep breath and addressed the signalmen.

'Who's handling the Down Line?'

The young man, Pete Wilcox, raised a hand. 'Me.'

'OK, you carry on as normal until I tell you otherwise.'

Eddie turned to the older man, emulating Tony, pointing his gun at him for emphasis. 'So, you're on the Up Line?'

The signalman nodded, his tongue endlessly licking his lips.

'I've got plans for you. Where's the train operating schedule for today?'

Eddie was warming to his role; he followed Jack Brown's gaze to a desk behind him and walked across to where the schedule lay conveniently opened at the page he needed. He studied the train timings and glanced up at the clock; it showed midnight. 'I make it that the next train is the ten o'clock sleeper from Glasgow, right?'

The older man nodded, white-faced, eyes blinking nervously, anxious to please.

Sherwood barked out. 'Answer the man. You're not fucking dumb, are you?'

'No, sorry, yes, it's the Glasgow to London sleeper.'

Eddie's confidence was rising; he spoke with newly found authority. 'OK. That one passes through just like it always does.'

He swung round to Pete Wilcox. 'You; there's nothing due on the Down Line for an hour, right?'

'Next one is a postal to Carlisle, but they can always add an unscheduled train if they want to.' He answered sullenly, still seething with anger.

'We'll deal with that if it happens.'

Eddie looked up to the Signalling Control Board; it showed the track layout and signalling installation for thirty or forty miles around Tebay. Without warning, a sharp bell-like clang emanated from the board. The older man spoke up instantly, anxious to please his captors.

'It's on its way, the Sleeper.' He looked at Eddie and waited for his instructions.

'Well, get on with it. Accept it and pass it through.'

Brown did as he was told and watched the tracks illuminate on the Control Board as the train progressed. Minutes later, the train sped past the Signal Box and carried on South.

'It's about to leave our control now.'

Eddie nodded. 'I can see that. Don't hang about: bell him through to the next Signal Box.'

The knowledge he had acquired over the last few weeks was serving him well; the older man reached forward and complied.

'Thank you…. what's your name?'

'Jack Brown.' The signalman was regaining some of his composure; everything would be fine as long as he co-operated.

'Thank you, Jack. The next train is the one we're interested in. Listen carefully to what I want you to do; you'll accept the train under your control, then put signal TB69 to red. Got me?'

The older man hesitated; it was against his natural instincts to stop a train. It'll stop the train.'

Tony Sherwood had been waiting for this crucial moment to show some muscle again. He thrust his gun into Jack brown's face and snarled, 'Of course, it'll stop the fucking train, that's why we're fucking here.'

He turned and fired another bullet into the door. 'If I have to fire this again, it'll be into your thick fucking skull; now do what the man says.'

Terror showed on the signalman's face. 'Yes, yes, I'm sorry; I was only trying to help.' His hand shook badly as he reached forward to the Control Board to put TB69 to red. 'Done it.'

Sherwood smiled approvingly. 'There you are. That wasn't difficult, Jack, was it?'

SIGNAL TB69: 12.05 am.

Carl Smith saw the signal turn red. 'That's it, Ronnie, get into position. It won't be long now.'

The two men checked their guns and gave each other the thumbs up; Ronnie Mathers then made his way down the track to where he had been told the rear of the train would come to a halt.

On board the 10.10 Special, Reg Harvey sat musing in his cab, his thoughts drifting hither and thither, settling on nothing in particular. But like all drivers, he was alert to the needs of his train, the sound of the engine, the beat of the wheels on the track, and the signals, above all the signals.

'Well now, what's happening here?' He voiced his thoughts; far ahead, he had seen TB69 turn to red. He reacted instinctively and gently eased off

373

the power, keeping his eye on the signal as the train began to slow. *No need for brakes, Reg, it'll change back; there's never a hold-up around here.*

The train passed a double yellow; the next signal would be a single yellow. Up ahead in the distance, he could still see a red signal. He eased the power off completely, allowing the train to coast under its own momentum.

The signal far ahead remained on red, and he would soon be passing the single yellow; it was time to apply the brakes. The train lost speed quickly and drew to a halt at signal TB69.

Harvey was curious; it was unusual to be stopped at this time of night. He opened his cab door and had made ready to descend backwards down the two steps when he heard the voice.

'No need to get out, driver, get back into the cab.'

Harvey nearly jumped out of his skin but instinctively obeyed the instruction, then turned round to see its origin. He gasped when he saw the tall, dark, masked figure holding the gun.

'What do you want?' He was scared but determined not to show his fear.

Carl Smith spoke softly, but his voice was laced with menace. 'Step right back to the other side of the cab. I'm coming up.'

The driver backed away warily as his captor climbed up the steps. He wondered how his Guard was getting on at the rear of the train. The tall man with the gun seemed to read his thoughts. 'Don't worry about your mate, by the way; my colleague is looking after his welfare. Listen to me carefully and do as I tell you; speak when you're spoken to, and you'll go home safe and sound. And please, please, don't make me prove that this isn't a toy.' He raised the gun for effect. 'Now, get into the driving seat and wait for instructions.'

Harvey complied; he had no wish to be a hero or die in some retaliatory action.

'See the green lamp?'

The driver looked through the front cab window to a point beyond signal TB69; he could see the lamp being swung from side to side. Somebody knew their stuff; in railway terms, he was being invited to move the train forward. 'I can see it.' He replied gruffly.

'Pull forward slowly and stop when you reach it.'

Back in the rearmost van, the Guard, Stevie Gillespie, balefully eyed his captor. *Bastard, if you didn't have that gun, I'd kick the shit out of you.*

Gillespie was a hard man, but he wasn't stupid. The man had a gun. *Best to wait your chance, Stevie, old son. I wonder how poor old Reg is getting on.*

Ronnie Mathers was experienced and sensed that the Guard might be ambitious; the guy had an aggressive look about him. He was alert to any potential attack, but prevention was best; he didn't want to put a bullet in the man if he could avoid it.

'We're about to pull forward, Guard, and we're going to be with each other for some time, so a bit of advice: listen carefully. You might have some idea of overpowering me; if you even try, I'll kill you. We don't need a Guard, or a driver for that matter: my mate up front can drive this train if he has to. Think about that, think about dying young and missing out on a lifetime's fun.'

Gillespie said nothing; he'd wait his chance.

GREENHOLME BRIDGE: 12.10 am.

I watched the train come to a halt at TB69, but it was too dark to see Carl and Ronnie, so I had to assume they had boarded. I switched on my signalling lamp and exposed the green lens, then swung it back and forth across my body. The train started to pull forward, and I felt my heart pounding; it was happening. Great Train Robbery II was about to begin. The train crawled toward and drew level with me. I switched the lamp to red, halting it exactly where I'd planned. From now on, everything had to be done at speed, and the next manoeuvre was critical. 'Driver.'

Reg Harvey heard me shout and told the driver to open his window.

The driver stuck his head out. 'Yes?' I could hear the fear in his voice.

'We're going to uncouple the fourth van along. When I give the signal, I want you to set back slowly; you know the procedure.' I shouted back to two of the boys. 'Get ready with the wheel chocks.'

I heard the chocks being hammered into place, then two calls. **'Ready right'** followed immediately by **'Ready left.'**

'OK, driver, set back gently for me to uncouple. Stop when I tell you.'

I made my way along the track, grateful for the moonlight. I flashed the green light, and Reg Harvey did as he was told, gently easing back till he felt resistance, then braking and holding the train in place.

I ducked under the buffers and carried out the uncoupling; the money van was now separated from the rear section of the train. It then had to be pulled forward a few feet, the chocks replaced behind its rear wheels and the backing up procedure repeated. My last task would be to uncouple it from the front section of the train so that the van stood free. It was a task that I'd learned about during my time with the Railways. The driver co-operated fully, and the whole process was completed in just a few minutes.

The others had watched the process, eager to get started and raced into it when I gave them the go-ahead. 'That's it, get going.'

Time was of the essence. Success or failure was in the boys' hands.

Reg Harvey was puzzled. *What the Hell are they up to?* The train was listed as a 'special', but he had no idea what its cargo was; he'd asked the Safehaul supervisor back in Glasgow, but all he got was a smile. He was tempted to ask his captor but thought better of it.

Meanwhile the other members of my team were heaving the two stolen heavy-duty jacks of Dutch manufacture into position. We had mocked up the underside of a van, and they knew exactly where to locate the jacks under the main supporting steelwork. They knew too, that it was essential to raise the jacks in unison.

I could hear the grunts and groans, the scraping of steel on steel and then a voice asking, 'Ready?'

'Yip.'

'OK. On the count of three, get set, one, two, three, go.'

I could hear the sound of the jack levers going up and down and the occasional shouts. 'Steady. Take it easy. Keep in time.'

Then, finally, the words I wanted to hear rang out.

'It's going, it's going.' There was a rush of air, a loud sustained creak, and then the dark mass that was the money van tumbled over and thumped, rattled, and slid its way down the embankment. Its roof stopped right on the edge of the road, just where we'd hoped it would. I listened to the yells of excitement and the scrambling of feet, then a buzz of conversation as the guys descended onto the van. Every vestige of tiredness evaporated as they levered open the van door and set about the unloading of those precious green boxes.

TEBAY SIGNAL BOX: 12.21 am.

The phone rang, and Jack Brown looked anxiously at Tony Sherwood.

'I'll have to answer that. The next Box will be wondering where the 10.10 is; we're ten minutes overdue.'

Eddie reassuringly looked at Tony. 'I've been expecting it. Answer and tell them the driver is dealing with a sheep on the line. Tell them it'll only be another couple of minutes.'

The signalman nodded and picked up the phone. 'Yes, sorry, I was on the blower to the driver when you rang.'……. 'No, it's in hand, just a sheep on the line, the Driver's seen it off. He'll be on his way shortly.'…… 'No worries, I'll stop it if I need to.'

The signalman turned back to Eddie. 'He's worried about the next Down train; I told him I'd stop it if needs be.'

Eddie managed a smile. 'Well done, Jack. We'll soon be out of your hair.'

GREENHOLME BRIDGE: 12.22 am.

'Driver.' I shouted up to Reg Harvey.

'Yeah, what now?'

'I'm going to couple up again. Set back slowly.' The driver took the brakes off and gently reversed, slowing the instant he felt the train make contact with the rear section. I flashed the red lamp and shouted back to him. 'OK, driver, hold it there.' I ducked under the buffers again and wrestled the brake hose and the coupling into place; nervous tension must have drained my strength because I struggled to make the two connections. My brow flooded with sweat, and I was relieved when I finally got them to snap into place, making the train secure for its onward journey.

'Driver.'

'Yes?'

'You can resume your journey.'

Reg Harvey protested. 'I'll need to tell the signalman, and what about him?' He looked over to Carl Smith, who stood nearby, gun in hand, ever menacing.

'He's going with you all the way to Tring. When you get to Tring Station, you stop, and he gets off. Just do whatever he tells you; drive normally and try to make up some of the time you've lost. There's no need to contact the signalman; our people are in control of the Box. Just get going.'

'But....' The driver started to object, stopping when he felt Carl's gun push painfully into his ribs.

'Get fucking going, Reg.'

Harvey's heart sank; he'd hoped his ordeal was over, but he did what he was told, and the train pulled away on its journey south. *Christ, what a story I'll have to tell the boys.* He recalled that the last time a train was robbed, the driver had been seriously injured, and that wasn't going to happen to him; he would do exactly what they told him.

Back in the rear van, Stevie Gillespie, the guard, felt the train lurch, then pull away, gathering speed by the second. He rose to his feet. 'What the fuck's happening?' He took half a step towards the masked man.

'Get back on your arse and stay there till we reach Tring.'

'Fuck you. Are you no getting aff.'

'Naw, I'm no getting aff.' His captor mocked Gillespie's Glaswegian accent. 'I'm gaun wi you a' the way to Tring. Now, you sit there and behave yourself, and you might just get to go home in the morning. Just remember, we don't need a Guard; personally, I don't care whether you get to Tring alive or dead.'

I watched as the train sped away and then scrambled down the embankment to join the rest of my team; the last few boxes were about to be loaded. Less than a minute later, the guys climbed into the van; it was very cramped in the van with all those boxes, and they must have been very uncomfortable not that you could tell from their huge grins.

'Well done, boys. Bert, we're on our way to the rendezvous; don't spare the horses.

TEBAY SIGNAL BOX: 12.22 am.

Eddie Milton was the first to see the change on the Signalling Control Board as the 10.10 resumed its journey. 'It's on the move.'

Four pairs of eyes joined his, watching the progress of the delayed train.

Tony Sherwood took the floor again. 'Now listen up, you two. We're going to be staying with you till the train gets to Tring. Understood?'

The two signalmen nodded glumly, both working out that they would continue to be prisoners for another couple of hours at least.

'Good. As of now, you work as normal; any funny business will be severely punished.' He waved the gun for emphasis.

Eddie looked up from the timetable. 'Looks like it's due at Tring at five past four, depending on how much time the driver makes up. Now, how about a cup of tea? I'm sure our friends don't mind sharing. The electronics wizard felt elated; he'd been tried and tested and had passed with flying colours.

TRING STATION: 4.09 am.

Carl Smith congratulated the driver as the train pulled into the deserted station.

'Well done, Reg, only four minutes down. You might just get the Driver of the Year award. I'm about to get off, and so is my mate in the rear van. When we've done that, I want you to pull away and carry on with your journey. Got me? I know you'll be desperate to get to a phone, and that's OK, just do it well away from here. Reg Harvey nodded sullenly; he'd have to drive on, but he knew exactly what he was going to do at his first opportunity. In the rear van, Ronnie Cole was issuing similar directions to Stevie Gillespie; the Glaswegian was still toying with the idea of tackling the masked man, gun or no gun.

'If I ever catch up wi you anither time, I'll kick yer fucking heid in.'

'Is that right, you thick Scotch bastard? Keep your eyes open for me; I'll be the one wearing a black ski mask.'

Gillespie snapped and lunged forward. Ronnie Cole anticipated his actions and took a step to the side, lashing out a heavy blow to the guard's head.

'Silly bastard; all you'll get for that is a painful bump on your noggin. He stepped over the prostrate man and made his way to the front of the train to join Carl Smith. The two robbers stood side by side on the platform and waved as the train pulled away. Their job done, they climbed over a small side gate and made their way out of the station onto the road and a waiting car. The car engine was running; the driver had heard the train pull in and was ready to go. Both men climbed into the back seat and sat there smiling the smile of success.

'Everything go to plan?' The driver, Josh Timmins, didn't know the full extent of the plan; he was a very minor cog but felt he had to enquire.

'Smooth as silk, Josh. London, here we come.'

The car had been stolen earlier that day, and its number plates changed. It was now headed to a scrap yard in London, owned by Horizon Holdings and leased to an ex-con who had, to all intents and purposes, gone straight; nowadays, he only transgressed the law when the organisation required him to. At the scrap yard, it would be put through a compactor; the clothes used in the robbery would be incinerated. The guns would be concealed and collected by Tony Sherwood in due course. The gang would then drive out of the yard in a legitimate but identical car to the one compacted, just in case their arrival had been witnessed by a casual passerby on the way to work.

SOUTH of TRING STATION: 4.10 am

Reg Harvey braked the train violently to a halt at the first signal south of Tring Station and hurriedly climbed down the engine steps. He was about to raise the alarm, except he couldn't; the phone lay on the ground, ripped from its socket. 'Bastards.' He crossed the track to the opposite signal, dismay filling him when he saw the handset lying uselessly at the foot of the signal. 'Fuck it.'

Stevie Gillespie arrived at his side, blood staining his forehead, cursing when he saw Reg Harvey kick the useless instrument.

'Christ, what happened to you, Stevie?'

'Tried it on and came aff worse. Tell ye aboot it later. Get back on the engine. We'll have to run to the next signal.'

Both men climbed up into the driver's cab, and Reg Harvey set off again. The two men found the same situation at the next signal and the one after that, by which time they began to despair. Josh Timmins had done his job well; it was just about the easiest earner he'd ever had.

'Fuck it, Stevie, the clever bastards anticipated our every move. I wish I'd knocked up the nearest house; they'll be miles away by now. Fuck it.'

Reg Harvey was livid. He didn't get to raise the alarm until he reached Berkhamsted.

TEBAY SIGNAL BOX: 4.10 am.

Tony Sherwood had been watching the clock tick round, all too slowly from his point of view, but there was no alternative other than to sit it out and let time pass.

'Right,' He rose to his feet. 'Ten past four, we're out of here.'

The two signalmen glanced at each other, relieved that their captors were finally leaving, relieved too that they hadn't been physically hurt.

'Got the tape. Mike?'

Mike Crowley nodded and made his way forward, pulling two rolls of industrial duct tape from his pocket.

'What the fuck?' Pete Wilcox reacted as Sherwood wheeled his chair over to his colleague's.

'Shut up. You didn't think we were going to leave you to raise the alarm, did you?'

He turned Jack Brown's chair around so that the two signalmen were back-to-back. 'Tape them up, Mike.'

The two signalmen endured helplessly whilst they were bound with circle after circle of tape.

'Want them gagged?'

Sherwood shook his head. 'No need, nobody is going to hear them out here.'

The three robbers made their way outside and down the stairs to the area of wasteland next to the signal box. There were three cars there. Two belonged to the signalmen. The third had been brought there earlier by Sid Elton, who sat ready to drive away, his police uniform now in the boot of the car. He watched in his rear mirror as his three companions pulled off their blue overalls, masks, and gloves, willing them to get a move on; he wanted to be on his way. It had been a long, boring night, and it seemed that the job had gone like clockwork, but he was never one to press his luck and wanted to make his escape. The trio dumped their discarded clothes into the boot for later disposal but retained their guns just in case some unexpected trouble lay ahead.

Tony Sherwood climbed into the front seat. 'Good to see you, Sid. How did it go?'

'Perfect at our end, Tony, didn't see a soul. And you.'

'Poetry Sid, pure poetry. Come on then, don't hang about; head for the rendezvous.'

COOPER'S FARM

The rendezvous was a farm near Newtown, fifteen miles west of Newcastle. The drive took about an hour and a half; I had been comfortable up front with Bert, but the poor jokers in the back must have had a rough ride. It was a few minutes after two when we arrived at Cooper's Farm and drove straight into the huge barn where the end game was about to be carried out. I checked later, and as I suspected, Coopers Farm was owned by

Horizon Holdings. Yet again, I had to respect Lord Averton's organisation, the man certainly had foresight when he put together his property empire. What I didn't know was that it was leased to another ex-villain who had 'gone straight'.

I literally gaped when I found Charlie Booker waiting for us. 'Christ Charlie, what are you doing out of bed at this time of the morning?'

'Slumming, dear boy and making sure everything goes smoothly. Get your boys to unload sharpish, Craig; we've got a ferry to catch.'

'What ferry would that be, Charlie?'

'Still asking questions, Craig? North Shield to Amsterdam, if you must know. After that, I don't know; I've asked, and the driver doesn't know either. He hands over the van to some other worthy outside the ferry port. You'll have to ask Dan if you really need to know.'

'No, Charlie, my job's done. Just idle curiosity, that's all.'

The guys worked fast; they were keen to get home, and it took them less than fifteen minutes to transfer the boxes to a large, closed lorry. There was one more job to be done before the lorry could leave; the two men screwed a false back panel into position to conceal the loot. They then did their own bit of loading and filled the remaining space with cardboard boxes. Judging by their ease of handling, they weren't very heavy.

'What's in the boxes, Charlie?'

'Don't you ever relax, Craig? You're far too curious for your own good. It's an assortment of clothing and linens, nothing too exciting. Satisfied now?'

Loading complete, the two men set off for the North Shields Ferry Terminal.

I couldn't help but smile; the police would be searching the British Isles from head to toe in the morning whilst the cash was being salted away across the Channel. I was confident that it would end up in a Swiss bank.

Mission completed, we didn't hang around for Tony and the others; there were no plans to meet up.

My team bid me farewell, climbed into two cars and headed off; they would take separate routes back to London and have their alibis ready if they were stopped at some roadblock for questioning.

Charlie kindly offered me a lift back, and I was pleased to climb into his ultra-comfortable Rolls Royce; nobody was going to stop a vehicle like that. Feeling safe and cradled in its warm, silent opulence I soon fell asleep, not wakening until we reached the outskirts of London. It had all gone as planned, but I could hardly credit that we were home clean with nothing to link us to the robbery. The van would be dismantled and destroyed, and the clothing incinerated. It really had been a sweet operation.

Charlie dropped me outside my flat; I was home safe. It was hard to accept that only six hours ago, I had been involved in the UK's, and probably, the World's biggest robbery. But once indoors, my thoughts weren't with the huge sum we'd stolen; creature comforts kicked in, and all I could think about were the joys of a hot bath and cooked breakfast.

'Thanks, Charlie, I owe you.'

'Not at all, old boy, you're making me a very rich man; keep up the good work.'

That last throwaway remark set me wondering about what I would do with my pay-off and my time once the dust settled.

I could never have imagined what life had in store for me.

DARK CLOUDS
GATHERING

Chapter Twenty-Six

Morgan Evans slipped stealthily out of bed, taking great care not to disturb his wife. He was due on the golf course at eight-thirty, earlier than he would have wished, but he loved golf and always seemed to get on well with whoever made up a foursome. By eight-fifteen they had all gathered in the clubhouse, making their preparations, making ready to set out for the practice green when Tommy Cleghorn grabbed their attention with an item from the morning news.

'Did you chaps catch the news?' There was a distinct trace of excitement in his voice, so much so that they all stopped what they were doing to hear his announcement.

'It seems there's been another Great Train Robbery, and they've made off with thirty million quid. Not a trace of them, apparently. They're bloody villains, but you've got to hand it to them; apparently, it's the biggest haul in history by a huge margin.'

Evans almost went into giddy mode, his stomach urging him to throw up; he knew instantly what had happened. He couldn't see that the colour had drained from his face or that his mouth hung open like a fish gasping for air.

'What's wrong with you, old boy? You look like you've seen a ghost.'

The banker shook his head. 'Nothing Tommy, it's nothing, I'm OK. This robbery, it's not a hoax, is it?' It was a question born of desperation, and he knew it.

Cleghorn shook his head. 'No way, the BBC doesn't go in for hoaxes. It's a heist for sure, somewhere in the Lake District, it seems. Thirty million, what about that for a haul? And it's all used notes. I can't begin to imagine what that much money looks like. Can you? Morgan, where are you going?'

The banker waved his hand weakly over his shoulder but didn't stop. 'Sorry, can't play, I've come over funny.' Evans headed to the nearest toilet to be violently sick. *Oh God, why is this happening to me?*

He tried to look normal as he entered the hotel's reception area, acknowledging the 'good mornings' afforded him by friendly staff. He pulled a newspaper out of the rack and scanned the headlines, relieved when he saw no mention of a train robbery. He didn't allow for the fact that they had been printed and despatched whilst the robbery was still in progress. *Oh God, please let it be a hoax after all.*

Back in his bedroom, he switched on the television, his heart sinking as the picture formed to show a reporter standing near a railway van lying on its side at the bottom of an embankment.

'Oh my God, it's true, I'm done for.' The poor man sank into a chair, desperately trying to come to terms with what he was seeing and hearing.

'Morgan, do we have to have the television on at this time in the morning and so loud? I was in such a lovely sleep.' His wife shouted plaintively from the bedroom.

'I'll have to resign, Karen. I won't be able to go on; I'm finished.' He shouted to his wife, though she had no idea what he was talking about.

'Resign, finished, whatever are you on about Morgan? Come back to bed. I'll make it all better for you.'

'Damn it, Karen, this is fucking serious. There's been a massive train robbery. Thirty million pounds has been stolen, and I'm to blame.'

Karen wasn't used to being rebuked so sharply by her husband and protested as she made her way through to the lounge. 'How can it possibly be your fault? You weren't to know they were going to rob the train.' Then she bit on her lip; the horrible truth of the situation was beginning to dawn on her; that's why she had been blackmailed. *Please, God, don't let Morgan find out its all my fault.* Evans didn't notice the expression of despair on his wife's face, or if he did, he took no notice.

'Of course, I'm to fucking blame, I'm Head of Security; it's my job to stop fucking robberies from happening. What a way to end my career.'

Karen burst into tears. 'Oh, Morgan, you're swearing at me; you've never done that. It's only money, a job's only a job; we'll still have each other.'

Evans immediately rushed over to put his arms round his wife. 'Forgive me, darling. I'm sorry, but things are going to get very bad for me.' He buried his head into her shoulder and sobbed silently.

'There, there darling, it'll all be OK. I'll look after you.' Karen tried to soothe her husband, patting his back gently. *Poor Morgan, what have I done to you?*

The media had a field day, glamourising the robbers, criticising the police, ridiculing security and, worst of all, they barely hid their admiration of the way the raid had been carried out. Evans didn't wait to be pushed; he made a brief statement announcing his resignation with immediate effect.

I was eager to see the headlines, see the effect of my robbery, the world's biggest ever, and was probably the shop's first customer that day. I edged slowly along the newspaper rack, taking in the headlines. There was only one topic filling the front pages that day, I wouldn't be named but I had made history.

Great Train Robbery II Thirty Million Vanishes

Biggest Robbery in History: Thirty Million Stolen

'As safe as the Bank of England? Ho Ho Ho.'

Lake District Heist Thirty Million Disappears

I gathered up four newspapers and headed back to the flat, looking forward to feeding my vanity and reading how clever I was. It was beginning to dawn on me that we'd got away with thirty million, not the twenty we had anticipated; I was going to be rich, very rich. It wasn't just the thought of the money that was giving me a high; it was the headlines and the stories that were stirring my adrenaline. Maybe I wasn't all that different from His Lordship in that respect.

Two news items did trouble me; it seemed that Scotland Yard was considering that there may be a link between this robbery and the PMR job; they were creating a new Serious Crimes Squad to investigate. One newspaper carried a photograph of the man in charge, a rising star by the name of Commander Mark Hanley. I remembered him as Inspector Hanley, the officer who arrested me in Crewe. The unease that this coincidence generated stayed with me for the rest of the day as I toyed with the thought that he might just be my nemesis. Perhaps it was as well that there were no other jobs in prospect; it was time to lie low.

A Police Press Statement outlined how the robbery had taken place and gave details of times and places, ending with a request that members of the public report any unusual sightings. The robbers were armed and dangerous, shots had been fired, and it was fortunate that nobody had been injured; I knew that would have been Tony putting the frighteners on. Equipment had been abandoned at the scene, and detectives were confident of tracing the source and from there, establish a link back to the robbers.

The Bank of England was offering a reward of £100,000 for information leading to the arrest of the ringleaders. The Royal Bank of Scotland distanced itself from the robbery, pointing out it wasn't responsible for transportation or security.

A taxi picked Sally and I up at nine on Saturday morning and took us to Heathrow.

'So, when are you going to tell me exactly where we are going?'

'We're on our way to Tuscany, sweetheart.'

'Fab, where exactly in Tuscany?'

'We are on our way to……. Florence. I know that you're not keen on beach holidays, so I thought some culture would do us both good.' I was genuine; my long chats with Henry had given birth to a growing interest in Architecture and Art. She gave me a hug and a kiss. 'Perfect, Craig, I'm so excited.'

'I've booked us into the Hotel Continental; it's directly opposite the Ponte Vecchio.'

'Gosh, it sounds expensive, Craig; something more modest would have been fine.'

'No problem. I made a goodly sum on that investment I told you about; anyway, only the best for you, my darling. There's just one problem: I could only get us a double bed, so I hope you don't snore.'

'Cheeky devil. I just hope my clothes are up to the standard of the Continental's clientele.'

'You always look stunning, Sally, so don't give it a second thought. I meant to tell you how pleased I am that you managed to get two weeks' leave; that gives us lots of time to see Tuscany.

We really did have a superb holiday, wall-to-wall sunshine, unlimited culture, golden beaches, delicious food, and sex on demand. It was a dream come true for me. The hotel arranged a limousine and driver, and we did everything in style. I never did add up what it all cost; I was rich and had to start spending; otherwise, what was the point of it all. There was just one thing lacking: love. Passion was never far away, but the vital spark I had hoped for didn't put in an appearance. Our relationship was great, but it wasn't leading anywhere; we shared some memorable times but love just wasn't an ingredient. I think that below the surface, we both felt the same. Sally never once got possessive or talked about the future; maybe that was her way of showing me that she had no plans for the long term. When we got back home, she thanked me profusely for her most wonderful holiday ever. I'd just said, *'Same for me'* and tried not to read too much into the fact that neither of us asked when we would next see each other. Her last words were, *'See you around'.*

There were no fewer than eight messages on the answering machine, the first seven of them from Dan ranging from 'where the hell are you?' to the more conciliatory 'I guess you've gone away; phone when you get back.' It was the last message that raised my curiosity, and I called back the number straight away; surprisingly, I had recognised the voice immediately, though I hadn't heard it for ages.

'Hello.'

'Craig Murray, returning your call, Earl; I'm obviously surprised to hear from you. How can I be of help?' I used my old name because that was how Earl Cousins would remember me.

'You remember me then.'

'Of course, I do, Peter Earl Cousins, chess king of Her Majesty's Prison, Westmoor.'

He laughed heartily. 'Champion my arse; I would have been a chess loser without your intervention.'

'What can I do for you, Earl? I take it you want something or wouldn't be calling a minnow like me.'

'I don't want anything, Craig; it's what I can do for you this time. And just in case I forget, this is a one-off conversation; never call me on this number again. Forget it even exists.'

I was even more intrigued. 'I've got the message; go ahead, I'm listening.'

What he had to tell me left me reeling. I thought about it for a while and decided that my starting point had to be Dan. *Christ, I bet that's why he's been trying to get me.*

'Hi Dan, sorry I haven't been in touch, just got back; I've been on holiday with Sally.'

He responded perfectly normally, and I began to think he wasn't in the picture. 'Where did you go?'

'Tuscany, mostly Florence but we took in Sienna, Livorno etc, etc.'

'Lucky guy; I love Florence; in fact, I love just about anywhere in Italy.'

Sally didn't get a mention; there was none of the ribald humour that usually flowed between blokes in such circumstances.

'Haven't seen you since the big night out and thought we might meet up and reminisce.'

'I'd like that, Dan, and to tell the truth, I've got a touch of the post-holiday blues, so what about tonight?'

'You're on. I'll pick you up around seven thirty, and we'll go to Toni's; I'm sure he'll find us some private space if I ask him nicely.'

The buzzer sounded at seven twenty-five.

Your chariot awaits you.' Dan sounded quite breezy.

'I'll be right down.'

My head was still in a spin following the Earl Cousins's revelation, and my conversation in the car was disjointed, so much so that Dan commented.

'Are you OK, Craig? You don't seem your usual self.'

'I'm fine; just wondering about my relationship with Sally and what I'm going to do with myself over the next few months.'

'Can't comment on Sally; and anyway, I don't give advice on relationships. But if it's about future work, don't worry; I'm sure the Man will relent and have you back on the team given a bit of time. I'll be putting a good word in for you wherever possible, I promise. Your head's big enough, but you're a talent we can't afford to lose.'

'Thanks, Dan, I hope you mean it.'

Mario apologised for the small room he gave us, 'The best I could do at such short notice, Signor Dan.'

'It's fine, Mario; just serve us your recommendations tonight, accompanied by a fine wine, on the house, of course, and all will be forgiven.'

The Italian laughed. 'OK, Signors; leave it all to Mario.'

It wasn't long till we were tucking into our meal and talking freely.

'The job went perfectly, Craig, as far as I can tell. Anything you would do differently?'

'Not a thing, Dan, not one iota. The only worry for me is all that gear we abandoned and whether any of it is traceable or not.'

'It isn't Craig; it's tight as a drum; we can trust Charlie, believe me.'

I smiled. 'Or as safe as the Bank of England perhaps; we mustn't get complacent. Mind you, why should I care; I'm not part of the set-up now. Does His Lordship know you're seeing me? I'm sure he wouldn't like it.'

'I respect him, Craig, fear him too, but he doesn't choose my friends.' He was usually deferent to the Man, too deferent in my view, but I believed him.

'I see that Scotland Yard have set up a Serious Crime Squad under Commander Mark Hanley; he's the copper who sent me down.'

Dan shook his head. 'Sent Craig Murray down, not Craig Dorian; our inside source tells us that the Yard is baffled and going nowhere, so relax.'

'I'm just being ultra-cautious, Dan; we had a lot of guys involved this time, and there's a reward of £100,000 available.'

'They're all good men, all tried and tested; not a grass amongst them. And they all know that Tony Sherwood is the gang's enforcer.'

I could see the point he was making. 'He's a good man to have around in these circumstances, I'll give you that. What did the Man think of the job, by the way?'

'Never seen him so animated; his desk was covered with newspaper cuttings; he absolutely revelled in the headlines. He told me to pass on his congratulations.'

'Really? I guess the thirty million take was a shock to him, given that we only planned on twenty.'

'He's delighted, though as I told you, he gets his kicks from the reflected glory; the money is secondary. He did say that the extra ten million had proved difficult to launder. Getting the best exchange rate must be problematic in those circumstances; thank God he has the right connections.'

'What sort of end sum are we talking about?'

'He reckons eighteen million.'

'What? He's creamed off twelve million, I don't believe it.'

'Hold on, Craig, currency deals usually exchange for less than 50%; try to think of the process involved. It's got to go from stolen to legitimate, and the huge sums involved can only be laundered by a crooked private banker who's got his Treasurer and his Accountant on board. It must be a nightmare dealing with an exceptionally large sum of cash; God knows how they feed it into the system. Think about it.'

I grudgingly acknowledged the logic. 'I suppose so, but twelve million should buy a lot of goodwill. Let's drop it; we don't have any other option. It's not as if he's going to open up his books to us, is he? When does he reckon to settle up with us?'

'I've already been paid, Craig.'

'Christ, that's quick; lucky old you.'

'What's wrong with you tonight? You're a miserable bastard, yet you should be on top of the world. You're rich beyond your wildest dreams, brighten up.'

'What? You mean you've been paid already?'

'Yes! And you've been paid. I get paid; you get paid. That's why I've been trying to contact you. One million, six hundred and twenty thousand pounds has been paid into your old account number, and the bank has moved it across into your new account. You can check if you don't believe me.'

I felt really guilty about how fragile trust was in our business. 'I trust you implicitly, Dan, whatever comes along.' I squeezed his shoulder. 'Believe me.'

He gave me a long, hard look. 'OK, Craig, out with it; what the hell is troubling you?'

The moment had come to face Dan with what I'd been told. 'There was a call from Earl Cousins waiting for me when I got back, asking me to get in touch.'

Dan looked astonished. 'Earl Cousins? Really! Why did he get in touch with you? I didn't think you were known outside our group?'

I stared Dan right in the eye, ready to scrutinise his reaction to what I was about to say.

'Because Lord Fucking Averton has placed a contract on me with Earl's hitman.'

My announcement floored him; he jerked back involuntarily, eyes wide, mouth agape.

'The bastard, the lousy bastard; I swear I knew nothing about this. I've got nothing to do with it whatsoever. Christ, that's bad news, very bad news.'

'I believe you, Dan; he probably thought you would tip me off, and I'd do a runner. Earl's repaying a debt as he sees it; he's put the brakes on. His boy won't make a move for two weeks. But that's as much time as he can give me. As he says, it's business, and if his man doesn't do the job, someone else will. At least this way, I've got two weeks, though I guess if I run, they'll come after me, and I'll spend the rest of my life looking over my shoulder. So, what do I do, Dan? What do I fucking do? Am I just a walking dead man for the rest of my life?'

Dan shook his head. 'I'm not sure, mate; I know that I can't influence Averton. Anyway, it's best that he doesn't know that you know. Off the cuff, I can only think of two options.'

'And they are?'

'You either kill him or persuade him to call off the contract, and I don't think you have a hope in hell of achieving the latter, which means you have to kill him before he gets to you.'

Neither option appealed to me; I shook my head. 'I can't see me personally getting hold of a gun and shooting the bastard, much as I'd like to. That leaves me having to find my own hitman, and I don't expect Tony would be prepared to bite the hand that feeds him. Maybe he could give me a name, though. But I've got to be very careful, Dan; if push comes to shove, Tony might well be inclined to protect his own interests.'

Dan nodded in agreement. 'You're right, Craig, and there's just a chance that Averton approached Tony first, and Tony declined the job; he likes you a lot.'

'I guess that means I've got to go on the run.'

'Last resort, mate; they'll come after you and almost certainly track you down.'

'Which leaves me with a very long shot indeed.'

Dan squinted at me, puzzled.

'I can't persuade him to drop this, nor can you. So, I have to find someone who can. I must find a heavyweight who could use my services and, in return, would intervene on my behalf. Just one snag: I haven't the faintest idea as to who that might be.'

Dan shook his head. 'It won't work, Craig. You're not known outside our circles. You can hardly go up to somebody and say, 'Hi, I'm Craig Dorian, I've just pulled off the latest Great Train Robbery, and I'd like you to get Lord Averton out of my hair. It's fraught with risk; they could turn you in and walk off with £100,000 reward money. Forget it, and don't think you would be safe in prison; you wouldn't be. We've got to come up with something else.'

'I'm desperate, Dan, I've got two weeks.'

'Let me think about this for a few minutes. I might just have the glimmering of an idea.'

I sipped my wine slowly, almost resigned to running away overseas somewhere. That got me thinking about where I'd go. Europe was too close and America too strict on immigration; the undeveloped world didn't appeal to me, so broadly speaking, that left the Antipodes. I started to debate with myself as to whether Australia or New Zealand would be the best bet. All the time I was watching Dan and could see that he was grappling with an idea. Finally, he shrugged his shoulders as though he had reached some kind of conclusion.

'You've thought of something, haven't you?' I looked hard at him, willing him to have an answer to my problem.

'It's a long shot, Craig, if it gets out, I'm a dead man, we'd both be dead men; I'm trusting you, big time.' He pulled a diary out of his inner pocket and wrote something down. He tore the page out and handed it to me, doubt still lining his face.

'Contact this man and offer him your services in return for his assistance. This guy has a set-up that fears nobody, but you'll have to come up with something he wants, and God knows what that might be.'

I glanced down at the piece of paper; it had a name and telephone number written on it. 'Sean O'Connell; sounds Irish, who is he?'

Dan sucked in some air; his voice unsteady. 'He's as Irish as you can get; he's the Commander of the local Provisional IRA Service Unit.'

I pushed the note back to him. 'IRA! Are you fucking crazy, Dan? I'm not helping those bastards commit carnage; I'd rather take my chances.'

'It's your call, Craig; I'm offering you a lifeline, a slender one, but a lifeline, nevertheless. I wasn't suggesting that you help with their bombing campaign. These people need resources to operate; you could help them sort out a big heist.'

'It's still blood money, plain and simple. I couldn't, Dan, I couldn't; from what I know, they have no finesse. They're little more than smash-and-grab raiders.'

'Suit yourself, Craig, that's all I have to offer. Think about it; see if your conscience will let you die.'

Suddenly, a thought struck me. 'How come you know the name and telephone number of a Provisional IRA Commander? It's not exactly public knowledge?'

He looked really shifty and took evasive action. 'I...I just know that's all.'

He was hiding something; he had to be. I took a shot in the dark.

'Out with it, Dan; there's a link somewhere between the IRA and Averton. There must be, or you wouldn't have suggested them. Tell me, mate, I swear it will go no further.'

He stared at me, and I could see that he was agonising over whether or not to tell what he knew. 'This is conjecture on my part; I don't know for sure, but over the years, it makes sense. I think there's an unholy triangle: Lord Averton of Horizon Holdings, Sir Peter Leaney, Chairman of Leaneys, the major builders, and the London Active Service Unit of the Provisional IRA.'

'I don't get it, Dan.'

'I overheard a conversation sometime back between Averton and Leaney whilst I was waiting in his outer office; for once, I wasn't under the watchful eye of the dreaded Miss Black. The intercom had been left on open, and I heard him telling Leaney that there was a contract available for him if one of Horizon's London properties could come to grief. Averton would claim insurance, Leaney would get the reconstruction contract, and presumably, the IRA would get some sort of pay-off. Horizon Holdings would effectively get its building refurbished at no cost. I heard Leaney say he'd have a word with Sean O'Connell, and he phoned him right there and then.

All this happened in my early days when I wasn't well-established and not sure if I could trust Averton. I still don't completely trust him; he's ruthless, and your situation confirms that. Anyway, I did some digging, looking for some insurance if Averton ever double-crossed me. I found out that Sir Peter Leaney is a strong advocate for a United Ireland and directs substantial funds to the IRA via an American outfit he owns. So, if you can come up with something attractive for Sean O'Connell, he might be willing to persuade Leaney to influence the Noble Lord.'

I was stunned. I just didn't realise how dirty business could be. 'What a despicable bastard; Averton is a Lord of the realm, supposedly loyal to Queen and country. What an arsehole, what a fucking greedy unprincipled arsehole.'

'You're in no position to moralise, Craig; in our game, there's a bit of the undesirable in all of us. There isn't much we wouldn't do to get what we want. It's down to you now to come up with something that might appeal to the IRA and capture Sir Peter Leaney's imagination.'

'Something that's got to be within my limits of acceptability, something I can't think of right this minute. I don't like the idea of even talking to the IRA; perhaps I should go straight to Sir Peter Leaney.'

'Sleep on it, Craig, you're not thinking straight. Sir Peter would go straight to Averton or, worse still, tell the IRA to take you out immediately.'

'You're right, Dan, thanks. I mean it, mate; whatever happens here on in, you've been a great help. Who knows, you might even be a lifesaver.' I needed time on my own to think matters through. 'I'd like to go home now; I've got a lot of thinking to do; it's going to be a sleepless night.

Dan gave me one last warning when he dropped me off at the Mansions. 'Craig, be very, very careful. I mean it; don't treat these IRA guys as fools; they're clever, and they're unscrupulous; watch yourself.'

I lay awake for hours that night, willing my brain to come up with an idea, exploring options, then dismissing them, searching endlessly for new inspiration. A hundred times, I asked myself, *what could I do that might interest the IRA?* I couldn't give them a plan for their avowed goal of a

United Ireland; God knows that had been beyond successive Governments. Maybe I could help plan a gaol break and get some of their operatives out of prison but that hardly seemed a big enough prize. Hours passed, and I was beginning to contemplate flight to the Southern Hemisphere when suddenly it came to me. It would be a massive challenge and one that I would enjoy, but could I pull it off? In any event, I had to clear my first hurdle, Sean O'Connell, London's IRA Commander.

Chapter Twenty-Seven

'Hello.' The voice answering my call had a soft Irish brogue.

'Is that Mr O'Connell, Sean O'Connell?'

'Who am I speaking to?'

'My name's Dorian, Craig Dorian.'

'Craig Dorian….. Craig Dorian can't say that I recall the name. How would I be knowing you, Mr Dorian?'

'We have a mutual friend.'

'I'm sure we both have many friends, but tell me more, Mr Dorian; Dorian is a good Irish name, but you sound Scots to me.'

'My parents moved from Northern Ireland to Scotland when I was young.'

'Indeed now. And what did you say your friend's name was?'

'I didn't say, and I'd rather not.'

'Well now, I think our conversation is over, Mr Dorian.'

'I know your connection to Peter Leaney.'

There was a long pause as my shot hit the target. 'I don't know anyone of that name, you're mistaken, Mr Dorian. I'll bid you goodbye.' But he didn't put the phone down; he wanted to know more.

'I'm not mistaken, Mr O'Connell. You and he share common interests: buildings and a United Ireland, I believe.'

The pause was even longer this time. 'You **are** mistaken, but I'm curious; tell me what you want, Mr Dorian.'

'I'd like to meet you; I have a proposition I'd like to put to you.'

'Is that right? Well, I don't know Peter Leaney, and I can't think of a proposition you might come up with that would be of interest to me, but I'm a curious sod by nature. Tell me more about this proposition of yours.'

'I think I can be of assistance to you and your Cause.'

'I don't know anything about a Cause as you call it. It would be helpful if you could explain yourself.'

'I can't explain over the telephone; it's too sensitive.'

Another long pause followed by a soft sigh; a decision had been made.

'I think you're a crank, Mr Dorian, but as I say, you've aroused my curiosity. I'll be in the Pig and Fiddle in Kilburn this evening around nine; you can buy me a drink and tell me your story. Just ask for me, and please, bring your Passport.'

O'Connell didn't wait for my reply, and I was left with a dialling tone.

My mouth was dry; I had taken the first step along a dangerous road, and I knew full well that I was playing with fire. If I didn't gain O'Connell's trust, I would probably end up dead. The more I thought about it, the more attractive running away became. *And why did he want me to bring my passport? Probably to check that I was who I said I was, but any undercover threat would be equipped with a fake passport. It didn't really make sense.*

As the day progressed, my nerves gathered strength, and I marshalled my confidence as I set out for Kilburn. I didn't know where the pub was, but a fellow passenger leaving the Tube station gave me directions.

'Sure, turn left, and it's two or three minutes along the road on this side.'

The Pig and Fiddle had a small frontage, dark green paintwork, and there were shamrock patterns etched onto the window on each side of the entrance. It looked dowdy, the kind of pub that only the most dedicated drinkers would visit. Inside, it went back a fair way and was bigger than it looked from the outside.

The floor wasn't covered with sawdust, but other than that small blessing, first impressions weren't good. The furnishings were stained and tired, the lighting dull, and a pall of smoke hung in the air. Perhaps if I was fired up with whisky and there was a ceilidh in full swing, it might have taken on an altogether different atmosphere. As it was, I hoped my business wouldn't take long. Maybe I was being fussy; there were about twenty drinkers in there, all men, not bad for a Thursday night.

Heads turned to give me the once-over as I walked towards the bar; the barman's gaze didn't leave me from the minute I walked in the door. With his black curly hair, ruddy cheeks, and green eyes, he looked Irish, and his accent confirmed it.

'What can I be getting you, sir?'

'Two Jamesons, please.' Jamesons was the only brand of Irish whiskey I was familiar with.

'Two?'

'Yes, the other's for Mr O'Connell. Is he around?'

He looked away from me to his right and nodded. 'I'll pour the Jamesons; Sean will be over in a jiffy.'

Sean O'Connell didn't look like the IRA terrorist I'd pictured in my mind's eye; he was in his late fifties with a mass of wavy hair, grey was taking over from the black. He was slightly smaller than I was at 5'9' or 10', with a build I'd describe as comfortable, verging on portly. In his green tweed jacket, denims, and a pale green roll-neck sweater, he looked more like a gentleman farmer than a city dweller. He had a handsome, unlined face, but it was his striking pale blue eyes that ensured he'd draw second glances. His smile seemed welcoming and genuine, and his hand delivered a firm handshake.

'Good of you to come, Mr Dorian. Do you mind if I call you Craig? I'm Sean to everyone, though God knows what they call me behind my back.' He chuckled at his own humour.

I returned his smile and pushed a Jamesons towards him, lifting and raising mine as he reached for his.

'Slainte', I gave the Scots Irish toast.

'Slainte.' He drank it down and waved his hand at the barman. 'Another, Seamous.'

The barman refilled our empty glasses; measures didn't seem to be used in the Pig and Whistle.

'I'll get these.' I offered.

'They'll go on my account; after all, you've come all this way to see me. Maybe you could begin by telling me about this proposition, and while you're at it, I'm still curious as to who gave you my name and telephone number.'

I made a point of scanning the room, looking for a quiet corner, and O'Connell took my meaning.

'Ah, you're looking for some privacy. Seamous, I'll be using the back room for a while; make sure we're not disturbed. Follow me, Craig.'

He set off to his right, crossing to a corridor with a sign above it that said 'Toilets'. He stopped just inside the corridor and opened a door on his left, waving me past him into the room. I stepped forward and found myself facing two unfriendly faces that stopped me in my tracks. A firm push from O'Connell propelled me forward, causing me to stumble into a table in the centre of the room. I sensed movement behind me, felt a blow to the head, and watched the floor coming up to meet me as I passed out.

I don't know how long I was unconscious, but when I started to come to, my head felt like it was being squeezed in a vice. My vision was blurred and disinclined to focus; I felt better with my eyes closed. I tried to raise my right hand to the epicentre of the pain in my head but got nowhere; it wouldn't respond. My left wouldn't move either; then my brain finally figured out I was strapped into a chair.

I wrestled with my eyes, telling them to open, and eventually, the scene in front of me began to materialise. I was in some kind of industrial building, long since emptied of its machinery or whatever had given it purpose in the past. The lighting was poor with only an occasional flickering fluorescent illuminating the gloom. Three men sat in front of me; O'Connell and the two heavies I'd encountered in the back room of the Pig and Whistle. I could see O'Connell's lips moving and thought I heard water mentioned. One of the men got to his feet and moved off; I licked my dry lips, eagerly anticipating a drink of cold water. The man returned out of the darkness carrying something I couldn't make out, and before I could figure out what was happening, a bucketful of cold water hit me full in the face. It had the desired effect; I took a massive stride into consciousness and enjoyed catching the odd rivulet of water as it ran down my face.

'Welcome back, Mr Dorian. Sorry we had to drag you away from the Pig and Fiddle, but you did want some privacy. Hopefully, you're not too uncomfortable?' O'Connell mocked me in that gentle Irish accent of his. 'Not that I mind much one way or the other.

'I'm fine, fuck you.' I was angry at the way in which O'Connell had abused my trust and determined not to show any weakness.

'Did you hear that, Davie? He's fine; give him a clout to teach him some manners.'

Davie strolled over to me, smirking, and smashed his right fist into my ribcage. He wasn't finished with me; he delivered a heavy punch to my solar plexus, leaving me gasping for breath.

'Bastard.'

O'Connell shook his head. 'You disappoint me, Craig.' He gave Davie the nod, and two more punches rattled me hard on both sides of my ribcage. I raised my head and smiled, but I kept my mouth shut this time.

O'Connell shook his head again. 'You're being very difficult, Craig; I don't think you understand your position. Quite apart from the fact that Davie here could pound away at you all night, look over my shoulder and tell me what you can see.' I squinted into the fluorescent light, and fear gripped me when I saw what he was alluding to: a hangman's noose suspended from one of the girders over a small table. My stomach convulsed, and I nearly vomited; the distance between death and me was disappearing rapidly.

'It's for you, Craig, unless by some chance in a million, you can persuade me otherwise. Now, how did you get my name?'

'If I tell you, my source will die and me along with him. I promised I wouldn't tell.'

O'Connell shook his head. 'Not good enough, Craig. Davie, Clancy, get him up on the table.' The two men closed in on me.

'Please, listen to me. Let me at least tell you why I wanted to see you.'

The two men stopped and looked back to O'Connell for instructions, relaxing when he raised a hand.

The Irishman wagged his finger at me. 'Last chance, boyo; I think maybe you're wasting my time, but I'm in a generous mood, though I warn you, it won't last for long.'

I took a deep breath to settle myself and began my pitch. 'I work for a London-based organisation planning major crimes, and I've got on the wrong side of the head man. He's taken out a contract on me, and I'm dead unless I do something about it.'

The Irishman shrugged. 'I can't see what it has to do with me, but how did you find out about this contract? In my experience, only the buyer and the contractor know.'

'A tip-off from a gang-land boss who owed me a favour.'

'And he would be?'

'I can't say; it would be more than my life's worth.'

'As we speak your life isn't worth a penny candle. But go on, where do I come into this?'

'The man who's taken a contract out on me is Lord Averton of Horizon Holdings; you've blown up some of his buildings at the request of Sir Peter Leaney. I'm sure you've heard of him; he's a generous supporter of your Cause.'

O'Connell tried to conceal his surprise, but his eyes widened. 'You're well informed, my friend; I'll give you that, but even if what you say is true, your little problem is none of my business. In fact, I could string you up here and now and claim the contract fee from Averton. I just can't see where I come into this equation.'

'I want you to ask Leaney to persuade Averton to call off the contract. I've got a week or so left before I'm taken out.'

O'Connell laughed. 'The way you're going on, Craig, you've got minutes left; the rope's waiting for you unless you can give me a reason for helping you. I assume you've got something to trade?'

'If you can get the contract called off, I'll give you, the IRA, the Cause something beyond its wildest dreams.'

The Irishman smiled broadly; I could see that he didn't believe me, but I still had his attention.

'And what might that be? Go on, Craig, amaze me.'

The moment had arrived. I was in Last Chance saloon. I gulped, knowing that my revelation was all that stood between death and me. 'The

Crown Jewels; I know a way of stealing the Crown Jewels.' I heard desperation sound in my voice.

I watched O'Connell's expression turn to disbelief and saw his lips part in a sneer. 'The Crown Jewels,' he shook his head, 'you'll have me believing in Leprechauns and crocks of gold at the end of rainbows. I was hoping you would come up with something more realistic.' He turned to his two henchmen. 'String him up.'

'No, please believe me, give me a chance; it can be done, I promise.'

O'Connell strode forward and thrust his face into mine. 'You're insulting my intelligence; the Crown Jewels indeed. It can't be done; we've looked at it over the years, and I tell you, it can't be done.'

He turned to his men again and flicked his head in the direction of the noose. My life hung by a thread; I had one last avenue of appeal.

'I can do it; that's what I'm good at. I pulled off the Great Train Robbery a few weeks ago and the PMR job before that.'

O'Connell nodded patronisingly. 'Of course, you did, and I'm Paddy McGinty's goat.'

'I swear on my life.'

'You won't have a life for much longer.'

'Can't you see what a coup it would be for the IRA; the publicity, the leverage it would give you? Listen to me, and I'll tell you how it can be done.' I held my breath, my heart in overdrive; life or death was staring me in the face.

'Alright, Craig; tis your lucky day; you've got five minutes to convince me.'

He gave me fifteen, and I knew that I had won this round. O'Connell was impressed but cautious.

'You've convinced me for the moment, Craig, but only just. Davie, cut him loose.'

I rubbed my wrists to get the circulation going; my head still thumped, and I felt that my ribs were cracked on both sides.

'OK, sonny boy, you've earned yourself a reprieve. I'll give you two weeks to pull this scheme of yours together.'

'Can't be done, Sean. I need six at least.'

'Four, and that's my best offer.'

I dug in and praying to God that wouldn't upset him. 'Six. You'll only get one shot at the Jewels; I've got to get it right first time.'

His pale blue eyes bored into me, his voice soft and deliberate. 'You're a brave man to talk to me like that, Craig Dorian, particularly in the fix you're in; there's not many make demands on Sean O'Connell. Six it is. Now it's time we were going; we'll take you back to your place.'

I didn't want them to know where I lived. 'There's no need, I can make my own way back.'

'There's every need, Craig. I want to know where you bed down so we can keep a friendly eye on you. On your feet, let's get going.'

They drove me back to Finsbury Park; Davie stayed in the car whilst O'Connell accompanied me up to the flat. He looked round, taking in the layout. 'Nice enough place, Craig, though I don't care much for flats and could never live this high above the ground. I won't hang around. I'm sure you'll be looking to attend to those bruises of yours.'

He smiled wickedly. 'Just mind you report to me in the Pig and Fiddle every second Thursday at eight, and by the time six weeks are up, you had better have all the answers. And don't try to run away; we'll find you wherever you go, sooner or later. By the way, I relieved you of this whilst you were unconscious.' He held up my passport. 'It's just a little added insurance.'

'Fair enough. And in the meantime, you'll talk to Sir Peter Leaney?'

'I don't know, Sir Peter Leaney.'

'I'm no use to you dead.'

O'Connell nodded. 'Don't be too sure of that, Craig, you know more than you should. Enough chat, I'll bid you goodnight. I don't want any phone-calls, forget you ever had my number.'

As soon as O'Connell had gone, I ran a bath, pain wracking my body as I climbed in, but the warm foaming water brought some relief. My ribs objected to every breath, and my head still felt like it had run full steam into a wall. But I didn't let my mind dwell on the pain. I had other things to think about. I'd had a close brush with death, and my reprieve would last only as long as I continued to convince them that I could deliver the Crown Jewels. I wasn't proud of myself; I had saved my own skin, but I had thrown any principles I may have had out of the window. I was about to show the IRA how to steal one of the Nation's greatest treasures; effectively, I was betraying my country. Nobody would get hurt if my plan worked, I would insist on that; the IRA would have to do whatever Craig Dorian told it to do. I was fooling myself, and I knew it.

In one way it was good that the IRA were involved; it held a unique key without which the plan would be much more difficult to pull off. I ran over the operation in my head. It was so simple I wondered why nobody had tried to steal the Jewels before now, other than Captain Blood's failed attempt many years ago. There would be no cash prize for me this time round, but the newspaper headlines would be one in the eye for Averton. I thought enviously of his organisation and its resources. I was on my own now and needed help. Dan was my only hope, my starting point; he would be my first call in the morning.

Suddenly, I felt weary; the near-death experience had left me mentally drained; sleep was what I needed most. My body complained bitterly as I hauled myself out of the bath; my rib cage was beginning to display all the colours of the rainbow, and the bump on my head seemed to be growing. Bed felt like a sanctuary as I gingerly eased myself onto it and stretched to find a comfortable position. Finally, I settled, sighing contentedly as I pulled the duvet around me, praying that the Paracetamol tablets would dull my pains.

Chapter Twenty-Eight

When I woke next morning, it didn't take long to recognise that my head and ribs hadn't forgiven me for the previous evening's activity. I climbed out of bed slowly, carefully slipped on my dressing gown and headed for the kitchen, pleased that hunger was vying with discomfort for attention. I made myself a cooked breakfast and savoured every mouthful of it; with the threat that was hanging over me, even the simple things in life were becoming important.

I called Dan to report on my encounter with the IRA and could sense his relief that I'd got in touch. 'Thank God, you survived.' *How often do we thank God or pray to him when we're in trouble, then happily deny his existence when no longer required?*

'You're not out of the woods by a long chalk, Craig; the IRA are unpredictable, everything is subservient to their Cause, I doubt if you can trust them.'

'I'm damned sure that I can't trust them, Dan, but what alternative do I have? I could get bumped off any time, any place, and I wouldn't know if it was the Man or the IRA. At least the IRA might be able to get him off my back.'

'I guess so.' Dan sounded sympathetic, but then he asked the question I had been dreading. 'What kind of a job have you got in mind for them?'

'Sorry, Dan, I can't tell you, and you don't really want to know; O'Connell has told me to keep my mouth shut. But think national treasure and the Tower of London.'

'Fucking Hell, Craig, I can't imagine that even you could pull that one off.' He went quiet for a moment, then asked hesitantly, 'Craig, with the IRA involved, nobody is going to get hurt, I hope?'

'No reason why that should happen, and I certainly wouldn't be party to anything like that.'

'This is different, Craig, and you know it. These people have a track record of being indiscriminate.'

He was right, but I wasn't going to concede the point. 'Is it really different, Dan? For me, it's just another heist, though the stakes are higher, I guess. Anyway, have you got a job in prospect?'

'Not a thing; we're fresh out of ideas at the moment, and maybe a break is no bad thing.'

'If I get any ideas, I'll get back to you, and I'll always give you a view on any jobs you come up with, regardless of Averton.'

'I know that Craig, you're a mate and I'll reciprocate if ever you need me.'

'As a matter of fact, I do need a favour, a big one; I need to engage Angie's services. How do you feel about that?'

'She doesn't do tricks, mate.' He quipped, but I was in no mood for lads' humour.

'I'm serious, Dan.'

Understandably, he went quiet, chewing over the implications. 'It's OK with me, but there are conditions to this favour. She must keep it to herself; she can be trusted not to pass anything on if you ask her to keep mum. And no matter what, she mustn't know about the IRA connection. Lastly, you've got to tell her that the Man has booted you out so she can decide whether or not she wants to co-operate. I'll leave you to think up a cover story.'

'Thanks, Dan, you're a pal. Look, I must go; got things to do.'

'Good luck, mate. I'll be thinking about you.'

I called Angie Goodall as soon as Dan rang off. 'Angie, it's Craig; how are you?'

She didn't hide her surprise. 'I'm fine and can't say I've been ill, Craig. To what do I owe this honour?

'I need your help. It's a personal matter.'

'Is that all you're going to tell me?'

'I'd rather not talk on the phone; it's personal, it's confidential, and it's urgent. I was wondering if we could talk over lunch.'

'Well, you certainly know how to get a girl's attention. How about we meet in Covent Garden, there's plenty of eating places around there?'

'I wouldn't want to be overheard. How about you come here, we talk and then I take you to the Dorchester.'

'Hmm, it must be very important. So where do you hang out?'

'Finsbury Park Mansions, buzz me on the entry intercom when you get here. Can you make it for noon?'

'It's that urgent, is it?'

I glanced at my watch: half past ten. 'Sorry Angie, I didn't realise it was so late.'

'Forget it. I'll be there for noon, but the lunch had better be good.'

'That, I can promise.'

I made myself a coffee and reflected on what I was going to tell her; pondered, too, on how O'Connell was getting on with Sir Peter Leaney. *Christ, what would happen if Leaney refused to play ball?* Just how much influence did O'Connell have?

In a quiet corner of Averton's club, Leaney and his Lordship were sitting opposite each other at that very moment. Averton was fuming inwardly; he wasn't accustomed to being summoned, but Leaney had leaned hard, and he needed to keep the Irishman on board, so he exuded his customary amiability.

'You're looking as affluent as ever, Peter. Business must be good.'

'That it is, David, as much due to your good self as the market.'

'Been down to Provence lately?'

'Spent a couple of weeks there not long ago, had a wonderful time. You must miss it.'

Averton smiled. 'Now and again, Peter, but as long as you're enjoying it, what more could I ask?'

He could feel impatience rising within him and fought it back. *Why wasn't Leaney getting to the point?* 'You wanted to see me urgently, Peter; there isn't a problem, is there? Something I can help with?'

The Irishman's soft brogue held no sense of urgency or the importance of the matter he was about to raise.

'Of course, forgive me; you must be wondering what this is all about. I can understand that; I need a favour, David, a big favour, and you're the only one who can help with this little problem.'

'Only me? My, my, suddenly I feel very important.'

'Sure now, you're always important, David.'

Leaney took a sip of his coffee and locked his gaze on the man opposite. 'As you know, there are business interests we share, and there are other activities where our paths necessarily go in separate directions.'

Averton nodded agreeably. *God, why doesn't he come to the point?*

'Well, the fact is our paths have crossed somewhat unexpectedly by way of a mutual acquaintance, a young man by the name of Craig Dorian.'

His Lordship tensed instantly. *How the hell does he know about Dorian? What else does he know about my set-up?* His expression didn't betray the turmoil in his head; he thought for a second or so, then shook his head. 'Dorian, you say, Dorian?' He shook his head again. 'Sorry Peter, never heard of him.'

Leaney's smile disappeared, leaving his face stony, his eyes staring into the man opposite. 'Don't play fucking games with me, David. You know Mr Dorian only too well; you share an interest in trains and bullion, not that it's any of my business, and I'll keep it that way. But you fucking know him, so don't muck me about.'

Averton was shocked by the extent of Leaney's knowledge and by the anger in his voice. He sought to keep calm amidst his racing thoughts. 'Peter, Peter, let's not fall out; we all have our business secrets. Tell me about your interest in Dorian.'

The smile returned to Leaney's face, and he took another sip of coffee. 'Well, truth to tell, I have no personal interest in Mr Dorian.'

Averton raised an eyebrow. 'Then why…'

Leaney cut in. 'I'm acting for some associates of mine from across the water. You understand? They want to avail themselves of his services and are worried lest any harm befalls him.'

Alarm bells began to ring in Averton's head. 'Meaning?'

The Irishman sighed and leaned back. 'You're playing games with me again, David. I see I'll have to spell it out for you. If anything were to happen to Mr Dorian, my associates would be very unhappy, and I fear they would vent their unhappiness on you or your lovely wife. Take my advice David, as a friend; do what they want, cancel any arrangements you've made in respect of Mr Dorian.'

'I don't like people interfering in my business, Peter; it sets a bad precedent if they get away with it.'

'We're not talking about **ordinary** people, David. We're talking about people who would blow you away at the drop of a hat. You would be very foolish not to co-operate; this could be our last meeting if I can't give them the assurances they want. They're waiting for a phone call from me even as we speak. All they want to do is borrow him for a while; after that, who can tell what might happen to Mr Dorian?! My advice is to go with the flow and postpone your arrangement to another day.'

Averton nodded knowingly, extended his hand across the table, and the two men shook on their agreement.

Leaney beamed. 'I knew we could reach an accommodation, David. I must ask you to act promptly on this; Mr Dorian mustn't come to any harm until I give the word. Now, maybe we could both make our phone calls and put this matter behind us.'

Angie arrived at noon, and I let out a whistle of approval; she looked stunning in a pale-yellow cashmere sweater, elegantly flared fawn trousers and a matching short jacket. Her makeup was effective but understated, showing off her eyes and cheekbone structure to perfection; she was a very attractive woman when she wanted to be.

'Come on in; you look like a million dollars, Angie.'

She inclined her head gently. 'Why, thank you, kind sir.'

'Fancy a coffee?'

She shook her head, 'No thanks, I've had my ration of caffeine this morning. Anyway, you've clearly got something important on your mind, so let's save the social chit-chat till lunch and cut to the chase.'

I couldn't help but smile at her directness. I watched as she sat down, admiring her figure, thinking that she really was the complete package. I had rehearsed my piece and knew exactly what I was going to say. 'OK, here goes. First off, Dan knows that I'm asking for your help and has no objections. I want to engage your services in the same way Dan would.'

She raised her eyebrows, clearly confused at what was going on. 'Why doesn't Dan approach me in the usual way?'

'Simply because this isn't for the team, the Man has booted me out. He doesn't know anything about my latest scheme.'

'How come he gave you the bullet, Craig? I'm not keen to go against the Man; I'm independent, but he's given me a very comfortable lifestyle.'

'He showed me the door because I got too big for my boots. I demanded to meet him and made it a condition of the Train job. To tell you the truth,

I got curious and had a concern about how it would be if anything happened to Dan.'

She pursed her lips and shook her head. 'I'm not sure that I buy that one, Craig; he could have got in touch with you direct if Dan wasn't around for some reason or another.'

'I realise that now, but it didn't occur to me at the time; I fouled up, and now I want to get back into his good books. I want to come up with a scheme he won't be able to resist. Dan wants me back, which is why he agreed I could approach you.'

She leaned back, weighing up what I'd told her. 'OK, I'll check out your story with Dan, but for now, tell me what you want, and I'll help if I can.'

'No problem, but at this stage, it stays with you, Dan and me; it goes no further. Agreed?'

'Absolutely.'

I breathed a sigh of relief; without her involvement, I couldn't move off square one. 'Thanks, Angie. In case I forget to ask, what's the price tag on your services?'

'Forget it; this one is on the house. Look on it as a thank you for the money I made from your last scheme.'

I shook my head. 'Thanks, but no thanks, this is strictly business; I tell you what I want, you tell me what it costs. If I can show my plan can work, I'm sure I'll be invited back onto the team.'

'Have it your way, Craig. Let's say five grand a day for the first five days, then a grand a day thereafter till the jobs done. OK?'

'Sounds fair.'

Angie smiled, 'And of course, if the job comes off, I'll get my usual percentage through Dan. Lucky me, in a way, I'll get paid twice. Now tell me what it is you want me to do and make it quick. I'm getting hungry.'

Over the next ten minutes, I could see her expression change from one of interest to one of sheer disbelief. 'If you're up to what I think you are, Craig, you're completely off your trolley. Forget it, it's just not possible.'

'Dan said that about the train robbery. I think it is possible; I think I can succeed where Captain Blood failed all those years ago. We can be the first people in history to lift the Crown Jewels.'

She looked at me, shaking her head, smiling, almost laughing at the idea of it. 'The Crown Jewels! You're mad, but I'll play along with you. I just can't believe that it can be done and that you only need a profile for **two** people to pull it off; it just can't be that bloody simple, but I'll give it a go. Now, let's leave this fantasy world of yours and go to lunch. Where are we going, by the way?'

'The Dorchester as promised; ideal for a classy lady like you.'

She kissed me on the cheek. 'Sheer flattery, Craig, but I don't mind compliments even if they are strongly laced with a touch of blarney. I'll drive by the way; I'm occupying someone's parking space.'

We ate a great lunch and talked and laughed a lot. She was a bit older than me, but a very fanciable woman. There were times when I wished that I didn't have a rule never to mix business and pleasure. Not that I would have got anywhere; Angie was committed to Will one hundred per cent. I learned that he had been in the Guards, and I thought his background might just prove useful given the identity of one of the targets.

Angie dropped me off at the flat, and I felt guilty as she drove away; I'd lied blatantly to her about the job, and I knew she'd find out in due course. But what else could I do? My life was on the line, and I'd use her or anyone else who could help me.

Chapter Twenty-Nine

The idea of stealing the Crown jewels wasn't entirely new to me. In my fanciful moments, I'd often mused about what would be the greatest robbery, the Bank of England gold vault or the Crown Jewels. For me, the ultimate had to be the theft of Her Majesty's coronation jewellery; how to do it had always been one of my dreams. It was hard to believe that my life depended on turning fantasy into reality.

I had visited the Tower of London as a tourist on several occasions during recent months and had toyed with several ideas but never gone on to develop them; now I had to make one work. I felt traitorous. I was conspiring with the IRA, an enemy of the State, but what was the alternative? I wasn't going to let myself be executed just to salve the noble side of my conscience.

I studied the site plan of the Tower in my tourist guide, noting that the Jewels were held in Waterloo Block and were protected by state-of-the-art security. The building was protected every minute of the day, internally and externally, by closed-circuit television surveillance. Added to this was the admiring attention of hundreds of tourists. There would be security guards around and, of course, the ceremonial guards. It was going to be a high-risk venture; thankfully, I wouldn't be participating in the actual robbery. *Christ!* The thought struck me that maybe the IRA would insist I took part, even bump me off at the Tower when my services were no longer required. I tried to dismiss that eventuality; I'd cross that bridge when I came to it.

The second Thursday approached, and another meeting with O'Connell loomed; I reviewed my plan for the hundredth time, searching as ever for the flaws and weak points. I was disappointed not to have heard from Angie, but I knew these surveillance jobs could be slow and resisted the urge to phone her. She would call me when she had something to say. I revisited the Tower one last time; spending most of my time in Waterloo Block, imagining that I was executing the robbery, and by the end of my visit, I was confident I had a winner. There were, however, two problems that only O'Connell could solve.

Come Thursday, on the stroke of eight, I walked into the Pig and Fiddle, immediately catching sight of the man himself at the bar. He looked up as the door swung closed behind me, smiled broadly and walked towards me, hand extended like he was meeting a long-lost friend. I guessed that he was putting his mark on me, warning onlookers that Craig Dorian was to be treated with respect.

'Nice to see you again, my friend.' Hollow words, I knew, but he said them in a loud voice that everyone in the bar could hear. 'What will you be having?'

I shook the proffered hand warmly. 'I've been told Powers is a good whiskey, if that's OK with you?'

'That it is, young man; you're becoming a bit of a connoisseur.'

'Put it down to the company I keep Sean.'

He placed the order and turned back to me. 'You're looking better than you did last time we met. How are those ribs of yours?'

'Coming along, fortunately, there were no fractures.'

'Good, rugby can be a dangerous game. I must tell Davie his punching power needs improvement.' He winked at me. 'Now let's retire to the back room where we can have a little privacy.'

'Just the two of us, Sean; some things are for your ears only.'

He nodded knowingly. 'To be sure, Davie and Clancy are off on other business tonight.'

My stomach tightened as my thoughts travelled to what IRA *business* might be, but I made no comment. O'Connell sat opposite me, sipping at his whiskey, licking his lips and pronouncing it to be 'the finest amber nectar in the world.' That done, he wasted no time with idle chit-chat. 'OK, now let's be hearing what you have for me.'

I told him where I was up to, glossing over the fact that two vital pieces of information were missing. When I finished, he sat looking at me for what seemed like an eternity. He didn't look pleased, and it sounded in his voice. 'You disappoint me, Craig, and I'm not the kind of man you want to disappoint too often, believe me. You don't seem to have moved much further forward; your plan is much as it was last time. Though, to be fair, you've painted in some detail. But, and it's a big but, we need two names and two addresses if this is to work, and you don't have them.'

My eyes locked with his; I didn't intend to be apologetic. 'I told you that I needed six weeks to tie this up, and there's still four to go. You'll get the names; just bear with me.'

'Right.' He pursed his lips. 'Just remember that your life depends on it.'

'I'm hardly likely to forget it, and there's no need to keep threatening me; it doesn't fucking help.' I snapped back angrily.

He raised his hands in a placatory manner. 'Fair enough, fair enough, calm down, boy. Do you have anything else for me?'

'Two questions: have you thought about which of the Crown Jewels you're going to lift? You won't be able to take them all.'

His eyes glinted. 'We'll take whatever we like. That's IRA business.'

'I know that, but you still won't be able to take them all; they're way too bulky.'

He sat and thought for a minute, then nodded his agreement. 'You're probably right; leave it with me, and I'll give it some thought. We'll probably just go for what she wore at the Coronation, the Crown, and the two fancy sticks she held. And maybe another Crown, I'll see.'

'Just remember, Sean, the plan is perfect; it's the detail and execution that matters now.'

'All right, Craig, I've got the message. What's your next question?'

I thought that my second question might prove trickier, but I told him of my concern and steeled myself for his response. To my surprise, he just shook his head.

'Not a problem, I've already sorted that one; you're not the only one who can plan.'

'So, would you mind telling me? I'm supposed to be planning this venture.'

'I do mind; I've told you it's sorted, so drop it.'

I shrugged. 'Suit yourself, but it's best if I know all the facts; I don't want you to encounter any flaws on the day. It's your interests I'm looking after.'

His eyes flashed, 'The IRA have been playing hide and seek with the British security forces for years; we know how to take care of ourselves.'

I couldn't resist a sniping shot. 'I'd just remind you that you didn't think this job could be done till I came along. I don't want to see it all going wrong because **you** made some bad choices.'

The Irishman laughed. 'You've got spirit, Craig, I'll give you that, but don't be getting too big for those boots of yours; remember who you're talking to. It's a trait that has already got you into a difficulty; best you learn from your mistakes.'

He was right, and I acknowledged it ruefully. 'Touche, Sean.'

'Well now, Craig, if that's it, I'll say goodnight to you. We'll meet again in two weeks.'

I nodded and drained the last drop of Powers from my glass, rose to leave and made to follow O'Connell over to the door, where he stopped unexpectedly, turning to face me. 'Craig, make sure you have those names for me next time, or I might start thinking you're stringing me along.'

'I'll do my best, but a deal's a deal. You gave me six weeks.'

O'Connell's lips tightened, and I braced myself for another threat, but he was fair. 'That I did, Craig; that I did.'

I checked the time as I left the pub. I'd been there for less than half an hour; it had seemed much longer.

Week three passed with no news from Angie, and it was getting harder to refrain from phoning her, but I resisted the urge; she would call me if there was anything to report. Wednesday of the fourth week arrived with still nothing from Angie. I was getting nervy and fanciful; she could be in hospital or even dead, and I wouldn't know. I resolved to phone her on Thursday morning if I hadn't heard from her. In the meantime, all I could do was keep my fingers crossed and disturb God with the occasional prayer. Fearful of missing her call, I hung endlessly about the flat reading, lazing, exercising and trying to make sense of movements in the shares market.

My prayers were answered when Angie finally made contact. *Thank you, God. Come off it, Craig, you don't seriously think God is helping you to steal the Crown Jewels.*

'Hi, Craig, it's Angie. Got some news for you. Sorry I haven't been in touch, but I had to make sure there was a pattern of some kind; I'd really like longer, but I know you're in a hurry. The name I've got is Charlie Anson; I'm not sure exactly what he does, but he's on the site first thing every morning until lunchtime, then moves on to the next job. Works for a company called Topflight Maintenance. Security checks him in and out, but it isn't what you would call a thorough search; he's obviously well-known and trusted.'

'And his routine includes Waterloo Block?'

'He goes to most buildings on the site, carries a toolbox around with him; regularly spends an hour or so in Waterloo and up to couple of hours in other buildings.'

'And his home address?'

'8 Marsden Avenue, SE6. He's about forty-five, married, three kids: two girls between seven and ten and a boy of fourteen at a guess.'

'What time does he get to the Tower?'

'Nine or very shortly after.'

I was absolutely over the moon; I had all I needed for that element of the job. 'Great stuff, Angie, you're a star. Anything on the other target?'

'Will's working on it. It's proving difficult, but he might know something before the week is out. It's a tough one, Craig, believe me.'

'I've got every confidence you'll crack it given time. It would be a life saver if you could come up with the goods before next Thursday.'

'Next Thursday?' I could detect the puzzlement in her voice; this was supposed to be an exercise, not a real event.

'Why next Thursday? I hope you're not serious about this being a lifesaver?'

'Of course not,' I reassured her. 'I'm just anxious to get back into the fold, and Dan sometimes sees the Man at weekends.'

'Hmm.' I could hear that she wasn't convinced. 'I'll do my best, but no promises; you'll hear from me when I have something.'

A load lifted from my mind, I felt relieved when I put the phone down; at least I had something for O'Connell.

Come Thursday, O'Connell seemed satisfied when I fed the latest information back to him. He noted down the details, nodding his head enthusiastically.

'Good, well done, Craig. No problem there, married with three kids; plenty to lose if he doesn't co-operate.'

The tone of his voice set alarm bells ringing, and I protested immediately. 'Hold on, Sean. There's no chance of kids or anyone else getting hurt, is there?'

'Calm down, Craig, you're jumping to conclusions. The IRA isn't a gang of savages. You have my word on it; nobody will come to any harm if they co-operate.'

I breathed a sigh of relief, though I barely trusted him. Tony Sherwood came into my thoughts; he would have said something similar. All too readily, I buried my unease and let myself be comforted by the word of a Commander of the most feared terrorist organisation in Britain.

'Thank God for that, Sean; I hate to think of kids getting hurt. I couldn't go through with the job if that eventuality was on the cards.'

He stared at me intently, 'Think of what you're saying, Craig; if you don't go through with it, you're a dead man. Believe me, boy; retribution is enshrined in the IRA code.'

He was right, and I felt slightly sick as I wondered if there were no depths to which I wouldn't sink in the interests of self-preservation.

O'Connell swilled the last of his whiskey around his glass, then drained it down.'

'That's enough of Anson; what about the other man?'

I knew he wouldn't be happy with my reply and made my voice as casual. 'Sorry, details aren't available yet. We're working on it and getting close.'

I could feel those pale blue eyes piercing into me. 'You've got two more weeks to put your hand on his shoulder; two weeks.'

'It's no good rushing these things, Sean; they take time. We've got to get it right. What would it matter if we ran over a bit? The Jewels aren't going anywhere.'

He slammed his fist onto the table. 'It matters because I say it matters; two weeks is all you've got.'

I started to protest. 'Sean, be reasonable, it's…..'

I didn't finish what I wanted to say; his hand slapped down on the table again.

'Two fucking weeks Craig; the meeting is closed. I'll bid you goodnight.'

He stood, not giving me a second glance, and we didn't speak to each other as we made our way out to the bar. He didn't bid me farewell either. *You don't know how much I'm relying on you, Angie.*

My stomach juices churned all the way back to Finsbury. I was walking a tightrope and beginning to feel like an inmate on Death Row. *Christ, Angie, don't let me down.*

Fear was nagging me to phone her, but what good would it do; if she had the information, she would phone me. And I couldn't tell her that I was working for the IRA; she would drop out then and there. Alcohol seemed the only means of escape, and I downed a bottle of St Emilion before staggering off to bed. I did sleep but woke the next morning with a head full of aggravation and still panicking; the only difference was that I now had a thumping headache to accompany my upset guts. All in all, it wasn't a very good start to the day.

Somehow, I survived the week without developing an ulcer or having a nervous breakdown, but it felt like either could happen at any moment. My hand was trembling when I picked up the phone on Tuesday evening.

'Hi Craig, I've got the information you want.'

Before I could stop myself, I conveyed my state of agitation. 'Thank God, Angie, the squeeze is really on at this end.'

'Christ, Craig, you sound desperate. Just who's putting the squeeze on and why? This isn't a real job, so why the deadline? I'm beginning to smell something fishy.'

Christ, Angie, don't get difficult now. 'This is how I get when I've lived with uncertainty for too long; can't help myself. There's a kind of a mental deadline I feel I have to meet; it's just how I am. Now tell me what you've got.'

There was a pause; she wasn't happy, and I could hear it in her reply. 'Hmm, OK; I'll go along with you, but I'm becoming increasingly concerned. The man you're interested in is Captain Reginald Anstruther, early thirties, I'd say, based at Wandsworth Depot. He's on call a lot due to the nature of his responsibilities and has a pad on the base. He's married to a good-looking woman; don't know her name, same age more or less. They have twin girls who go to a private school, Mainwaring's; it's quite near where they live.'

'Boarding school?'

'No, she takes them in each day, Monday to Friday, some weekend days as well. Leaves the house at eight sharp every morning, gets to the school by eight thirty.'

'Sounds like they've got a house somewhere.'

'6 Belton Crescent, SW12. I think it's his family home; there's an elderly lady who lives there as well. Don't know anything about her, most likely the grandmother. That's all I have; you'll need to give me more time if you want more.'

'Thanks, Angie, you're a saviour; I owe you a dozen lunches.'

'Saviour? You keep saying these things, Craig. There's something going on you're not telling me about. I've been thinking about it, and it doesn't hang together. You're not being straight with me.'

'What do you mean?'

'Well, you said that this was a dummy scheme just to convince the Man.'

'True.'

'Well, it seems to me that you don't really need to know the target details just to do that. All this information could be out of date by the time the job gets the go-ahead.'

She was right, of course, and I had to come up with an excuse at the double.

'Thing is, I want to convince the Man that not only do I have a scheme, but I could go ahead without him if necessary.'

'I don't like the sound of that, Craig; you didn't tell me you were trying to twist the man's tale. I'm going to check it out with Dan.'

Damn, I had gone too far. 'I'd rather you didn't do that; it'll weaken my position. Please give me a chance to do this my way; bear with me.'

She went quiet but gave me the benefit of the doubt. 'OK, Craig, but I'm certain you're not telling me everything; you're up to something. I can feel it.'

My heart started to slow down. 'Bless you, Angie. How much do I owe you, cash, I mean?'

'Call it fifty grand.'

'How do you want it?'

'Bank draft; you can hand it over when we meet for lunch.'

'You're an angel; I owe you big time. I'll be in touch when I've got your loot.'

For the first time in nearly six weeks, I felt in control; all I had to do now was brief O'Connell, and the rest was up to him. In a couple of days, I would be free of the IRA, assuming that O'Connell was a man of his word. *What's the odds on that, Craig?*

Thursday came, and I was clearly expected at the Pig and Whistle; the ruddy-faced giant behind the bar said nothing, just pointed me in the direction of the back room. I knocked on the door and heard a muffled voice invite me to 'come in.' I pushed the door open, and my spirits sank. O'Connell was sitting at the table; his two henchmen, Davie and Clancy, leaned back on the wall behind him.

O'Connell motioned me to sit down; his expression didn't give anything away, but the atmosphere in the room was threatening. The other two stood impassively, like two vultures waiting their turn at a piece of dead meat.

'Answer me one question, Craig. Have you, or have you not, got the information we require?'

I nodded, and a smile broke out on his face. He waved a hand at the bottle of Powers on the table. 'Good man; help yourself.' I poured a generous measure and sat there waiting, saying nothing, for no particular reason other than to annoy him.

Eventually, he spoke. 'I get the impression you're playing some kind of a game with me, Craig. It's not a game I like very much, and I think you should remember the position you're in. If I had a mind to, I could hand you back to the Noble Lord Averton, or I could give you an IRA farewell. Now I suggest you tell me what I want to know.'

'Thing is, Sean, it occurs to me that once I tell you what you need to know, you could get rid of me anyway.'

O'Connell smiled broadly and chuckled. 'Sure, that's the truth of it, but look at it this way. If you don't tell me, you're a dead man; if you do, there's a chance I might keep my word. So be a good boy and tell me what I need to know.'

I was beaten, and he knew it. 'OK, but could I ask you something first?'

'Fire away.'

'It's cost me fifty grand to get this information. Is there any chance the IRA could make a contribution?'

'Not the slightest chance. Fifty grand seems cheap for your life, don't you think?'

I shrugged. 'It was worth a try.' I looked over to the others. 'Do you want them to hear what I'm about to tell you?'

He glanced over his shoulder. 'Be off you two, I'll see you later.' Without a word, his two henchmen wandered away; I thought they looked disappointed, but they made no protest.

When they'd gone, I went through every detail with O'Connell. He took notes again, asking questions, verifying what I had told him previously, and nodding with satisfaction every now and again. He put me through the wringer, but after half an hour or so, he was satisfied.

'Alright, my friend, you can go; I know where to find you if I need you.'

My mouth dropped open; could it really be that simple? I felt free, but I felt cheated, too; I was being cut out of a game I wanted to play, even if only from afar.

'Just like that?'

It was his turn to look surprised. 'What did you expect, a drum-roll or something? You've done your job; I've got no further need of you.'

'I just thought you might like me to go over the final plan, make sure it's OK.'

O'Connell shook his head. 'We've got our own planning expertise; contrary to what you might think, we're not all thick drunken Paddies.'

'I know that, Sean, but I'm good at what I do, and I want this to work; believe me, I'll help if I can. What harm can it do?'

He sat back in his chair, lips pursed, his brain working overtime with the pros and cons of my further involvement. 'I'll be honest with you, Craig, I'm not sure; I'll give it some thought. Tell you what, meet me here Monday night, usual time, and we'll see where we go.'

Back at the flat, I had my best night's sleep for six weeks.

Chapter Thirty

The Pig and Fiddle was beginning to feel like my second home when I walked in on Monday evening; the barman nodded his recognition, and there was even the vestige of a smile; I guess my seal of approval had finally arrived. Even one of the regulars raised a hand in recognition; Sean O'Connell had well and truly blessed me. The man himself was holding up the bar and greeted me with his usual smile and welcoming handshake.

'Come away through to the back room, Craig.'

Davie and Clancy were there, still unsmiling, but at least they nodded; our friendship was on an upward path. I didn't let this blossoming relationship go unrecognised. 'Hi guys.' I offered but held back on the usual social enquiries as to how their day had been. The table was adorned with the now familiar bottle of whiskey and two glasses; O'Connell clearly didn't want his henchmen joining in. What took my attention, however, was the large brown envelope.

'Make yourself comfortable and pour yourself a dram if you're so minded. As promised, I gave the matter some thought, and I can't see that it'll do any harm for you to give the final product the once-over; take a look at this.' He pulled three sheets of paper from the envelope and passed them across. 'I think you'll find it's all there: times, sequences, locations and, of course, the players. I've referred to the boys as A, B, and C; we don't want you knowing too much. Anson and Anstruther are named unknowns just as X.'

The sheets were typewritten, the layout professional, and I had to remind myself again not to underestimate the IRA. I read it through and could feel O'Connell watching for any changes in my expression. I found nothing amiss, but just to be certain, I went over it again. I still couldn't fault it.

'I've wasted your time, Sean; it's perfect, no changes necessary.'

He leaned back and smiled. 'Sure, it's your plan, Craig, my boy. If you're as good as you make yourself out to be, it would be perfect, wouldn't it now?'

'I don't suppose you're going to tell me when you're going to carry out this job?'

The Irishman sat back in his chair and gave me a cagey look. 'Yes and no; I'm not going to tell you right this moment, but if you're around tomorrow morning, I might have some news for you.'

'You mean around here?'

'No, not here, at your place.'

'I've got no plans to go out.'

'Then be there, Craig, and I'll be in touch.'

'And my passport?'

'It'll be returned after the job. You know the old circus saying, 'never give the elephant a bun till it's done its trick.' He smirked and raised an eyebrow. 'Have another drop before you go.' I was being dismissed. I declined the whiskey, and we shook hands; the stage was set; the butterflies of expectation were working flat out in my tummy. *You've done it, Craig, the Crown Jewels.* As I turned to leave, I noticed that Davie and Clancy were smiling, and I wondered if it was because of the approaching job or if, perhaps, my head was destined for their chopping block.

My new state of relative security ensured that I enjoyed another good night's sleep, and I felt fresh and lively after my shower next morning. As I dawdled over breakfast, I recalled a game I used to play, whereby I'd tried to imagine what someone close to me was doing at that same moment. Last time I'd played, I had been thinking of Sam getting ready to meet me, but all I could wonder about now was what Sean O'Connell was up to. Top of my list this morning were Anson and Anstruther; little did I know they were already on a path to fame.

Charlie Anson of Topflight Maintenance, that particular Tuesday morning, was finishing his breakfast and watching his children, Oliver, Alison, and Terry, preparing to set out on the short walks to their respective schools. He stood beside his wife at the front door and waved them goodbye, then followed her into the kitchen. 'They're good kids we have, Linda; never any trouble getting them off to school.'

She laughed. 'At least not when you're around; you don't know the half of it.'

He slipped his arm round her waist, then under her dressing gown and up to her breast, all the time nuzzling her neck. She turned round and pressed herself against her husband. 'Hmm, I don't suppose you could go into work a bit later this morning, Charlie?'

Before he could reply, there was a rat-tat-tat at the front door.

They separated and looked at each other, puzzled at the early caller. 'Who's that then? Here,' He looked at her teasingly. 'it's not your boyfriend, is it?'

She shook her head. 'Far too early for him or the postman. You go, dear; it's probably next door on the borrow again; she had two eggs out of me last week.'

Anson made his way down the hall and pulled open the door, shrinking back when he found himself facing a man in a black ski-mask. The man swung his right arm upwards, pointing a gun into his face; in his left hand, he held a large tool-bag.

'Get back inside, Charlie, and don't panic, that lovely wife of yours.' The man's accent was Irish; soft, and pleasant, completely at odds with the gun he was wielding.

Taken by surprise, Charlie Anson took an involuntary step back, then stood his ground. 'What do you want? How do you know my name?'

The man thrust the gun forward. 'Get fucking inside before I blow your head away.'

'Who is it?' Linda Anson called out from the kitchen.

Her husband half turned, gasping with pain when the gun was viciously thrust behind his ear. 'Move.'

'Oh my God, what's happening? What's going on, Charlie?' Linda stood at the kitchen door, terror showing on her face; she almost screamed the words.

'Shut up, both of you sit down.' The gunman barked out his instructions.

The couple sat down at the kitchen table, side by side, holding hands, watching their captor anxiously. The man leaned against the doorjamb, appraising the Ansons. 'That's better. Now listen carefully, very carefully. I'm only going to say this once.' The gun pointed at Charlie Anson. 'You are going to work as usual; she stays with me. I'll give you instructions; you follow them, and she lives; don't follow them, and she dies. Got it?' The couple nodded in unison, fear holding them rigid.

'Good. Charlie, you'll be heading off very shortly to the Tower; do what you do every Tuesday morning and keep to your routine. There's just one change: pay attention, and I'll tell you what you're going to do when you get there. And remember Charlie, get it wrong, and she dies. Her life depends on you following your instructions; she means nothing to us.'

The instructions were brief and simple; the maintenance man knew that he would be carrying them out. He had no idea what the man was up to, and he didn't much care; his wife was all that mattered.

'Right then, Charlie,' the intruder made a sweeping ushering motion with his hand. 'Off you go. We don't want you being late and having your pay docked, do we now?'

Linda Anson squeezed her husband's hand and kissed him. 'Don't worry about me, darling, I'll be alright, I promise.' She wanted to be brave for him, wanted to appear to be in control. Anson put on his jacket and took hold of the tool-bag the man had brought; it was very similar to his own. *Co-incidence, or had they known?* He took a last anxious glance at his wife, fought back tears of concern and reluctantly made his way out to his van.

Davie Doyle didn't remove his mask or lower his gun; this wasn't a day to take any chances. He studied the woman opposite him. 'You're an attractive lady, Linda. Charlie's a lucky man and no mistake. Make me a cup of tea, me darling. And please, cover up those legs of yours, or you'll be giving me ideas. Linda's eyes darted downwards with embarrassment, pulling her dressing gown together where it had fallen open. She rose quickly and crossed to the sink to fill the kettle; turning when she got there and stilling the tremor in her voice, asked quietly. 'Milk and sugar?'

'I like my tea on the dark side with two sugars, please?'

'How long will you be here?'

Doyle shrugged. 'As long as it takes, my darling; should be out of here by early afternoon.'

I suddenly remembered that O'Connell had promised to be in touch, or had he just been stringing me along? My thoughts drifted away, and I wondered if the IRA would really go through with it; it was a big call even for them. Little did I know that the job was already underway and that the first stage, the Anson component, had been completed.

Rebecca Anstruther closed her front door behind her and followed her two blonde angels, as she called her daughters, to the Range Rover parked on the drive. She turned back to face the lounge window and waved to Martha, her husband's elderly mother.

'Girls, give Gran a wave, please.'

Imogen and Kaye turned and blew kisses to their doting grandparent, then scrambled excitedly into the back seat of the vehicle; school was fun, and they enjoyed going. Rebecca gave a final wave, settled behind the steering wheel and turned the key in the ignition. The engine throbbed into life, and she pulled forward around the bend in the drive to where she could get a clear view of the road.

'You'll be turning right this morning, Mrs Anstruther.'

The voice startled the mother and children; three faces turned in unison to its source. The shock caused her foot to slide off the clutch pedal, causing the engine to stall. She gasped when she found herself face to face with a man crouched behind the rear seat; the black ski mask was scary enough, but it was the gun pointed at her two terrified cowering daughters that caused her most concern.

Kaye burst into tears; Imogen, braver by nature, put a comforting arm round her sister, seeking to comfort her and looked at her mummy anxiously, 'This is a bad man, isn't it, mummy?'

'Yes, darling, but I'm sure he won't harm us if we do what he says. Just sit there and behave, and the man will tell us what he wants. Kaye, don't cry darling, everything will be alright, mummy promises.'

Behind the mask, the man was smiling. 'Mummy's right me pretty ones; I won't harm a hair on your pretty heads as long as you do what you're told.'

Kaye tried to dry her tears. 'What about school, mummy? We've got sports today.'

'I'm sorry, darling, I think we'll have to miss sports today. We'll have to pretend it's a school holiday.'

Imogen, ever practical, shook her head. 'It isn't a holiday, mummy, and that man can't make it one. He's very bad. And why does he have a gun?'

The man wanted to be on his way and spoke sharply. 'The gun is to shoot mummies and little girls who don't do what they're told. We've wasted enough time; let's get going, Mrs Anstruther.'

Tears welled up in the little girls' eyes, and Kaye started sobbing again. Rebecca recognised the Irish accent and guessed immediately that the man was from the IRA. The thought chilled her; she was afraid for her children, but she knew better than to show her fear, knew too that she had to co-operate.

'Don't cry, darlings, it'll be all right; I promise.' She addressed the man in the ski mask. 'What do you want me to do?'

'Turn right out of the drive and follow my directions till we reach our destination.'

The journey took just over thirty minutes, during which Imogen gamely sought to keep her twin sister distracted.

'Turn into the entrance coming up on the left, where that old warehouse is, and drive round to the rear. Drive far enough in so we can't be seen from the road.'

Rebecca parked the Range Rover then turned round to face the man. 'What now?'

'You get out, move round to the back and open the tailgate so I can get out.' He waved his gun at the girls. 'They stay here.'

The operation completed, the two girls got out and ran across to cling on to their mother. The man nodded approvingly. 'That's what I like to see, happy families. Make your way over to that door and go in; it's your home for the day. I'll be right behind you.'

Rebecca put an arm round each of her daughters' shoulders and tried to make light of their plight.

'Come with mummy, girls and don't be afraid; this is just a big adventure.'

Imogen took up her mum's reassuring efforts. 'Goody, come on, Kaye, let's see what's inside.' She grabbed her sister's hand and led her purposefully towards the door.

The IRA man nodded approvingly. 'You've got a good one there, Mrs Anstruther. Now, give me the car keys; we wouldn't want you to go walkabouts when I wasn't watching.'

There was little chance of that happening, but it was best to reduce the risk. Without a word she handed over the keys; she knew there was a spare hidden in the glove compartment if the opportunity to escape arose. Somehow, the very thought of escape made her feel better.

The two girls opened the door but didn't go inside. 'It's dark in there, mummy, the room hasn't got any windows. I don't like it.' Imogen looked at her mother, unsure what to do.

Clancy McIlroy listened to the exchange. 'That's right, no windows and only one way out. Go ahead, Mrs Anstruther, and put the light on; the switch is on the right where you would expect it to be.'

Rebecca did as instructed, relieved to see that the room wasn't as bad as she feared. There were four cushioned chairs spaced around a table, and it was warm and clean. Colouring books, pencils, crayons, comics, and an assortment of drinks, sweets and biscuits were spread out on the table.

The IRA man observed Rebecca's relieved expression. 'Not too bad, is it? Plenty to keep the children amused. The toilet is over there in the corner; it wouldn't do for the Savoy, but we've cleaned it up best we could. I've locked the outside door behind me, so there's no escape unless you deal with me and this.' He waved the gun.

'What do you want of us? How long do you intend to keep us here?' Rebecca was calm; as an officer's wife, she knew how to control her feelings; like all mothers, she would do anything to protect her children.

'When I give the word, you're going to telephone your husband and tell him that you're being held by the IRA. After that, you'll give the phone to me and listen to what I tell him; then you'll know what this is all about. The three of you will stay here until we've done what we've set out to do; with luck, you'll be released mid-afternoon.' He checked his watch. 'It's time for you to phone your husband.'

'I don't know if I'll be able to contact him; he's at his work.'

McIlroy patted the palm of his left hand with the gun. 'It's imperative you speak to him, Mrs Anstruther; you haven't been chosen by chance; we know that he is Captain Reginald Anstruther, Bomb Disposal Unit based at Woolwich Barracks. Now phone him; let's avoid any unpleasantness.'

There was no option but to comply. 'OK. Where's the phone?'

The man pointed. 'Over there on the floor behind the chair.'

'Good morning, Woolwich Barracks. How can I help you?'

'I'd like to speak to Captain Anstruther, please.'

The voice on the other end sounded doubtful. 'I'm not sure that I can disturb Captain Anstruther. Could you tell me who you are, please?

'Rebecca Anstruther, his wife; it's rather urgent.'

Instantly, the voice became more co-operative. 'Of course, Mrs Anstruther; hold on, and I'll put you through.'

She relayed the position to her captor. Clancy McIlroy nodded approvingly. 'Well done, I can see we're going to get along just fine.'

'Becky darling, what a lovely surprise; everything's alright, I hope?'

'The girls are with me, Reggie, but I'm afraid there is a problem. There's a man with us from the IRA; he has a gun.' She heard her husband's sharp intake of breath. 'Try not to worry darling, we're being treated well.

'Christ! Put him on.'

She handed the phone to Clancy McIlroy. 'He wants to speak to you.'

McIlroy took the phone. 'Sorry about this, Captain, but we need your help.'

'Who are you? What do you want? If you harm a hair on their head, I'll kill you.'

'Stop right there, Captain; cut the bluster, you're in no position to do anything. Do exactly as I tell you, and your family will come to no harm; I'm holding them at gunpoint as part of an IRA operation.'

'IRA operation.' Reggie Anstruther felt his blood chill.

'You heard correctly, Captain. Now, listen very carefully to what I'm about to say; I'm only going to say it once. Shortly after ten, you'll receive the first of three telephone calls from Scotland Yard; you will deal with them all in the usual way. You will handle the third call personally, and this is what you'll do.'

Rebecca Anstruther listened incredulously to what her husband was told. *Please Reggie, do what you're told. This isn't the time to put duty first; think of the girls.* She glanced round at them; they were playing happily at the table, totally oblivious to what was going on.

'And that's all there is to it, Captain. Please don't be a hero, or you won't see your family alive again, any of them.' The man didn't wait for a response; he rang off and immediately dialled another number. When his call was answered, his message was brief. 'Everything secure, Anstruther has been briefed.'

Reggie Anstruther slumped into his chair, his heart pounding. *What the hell am I going to do? Fuck the IRA; terrorist bastards. His duty lay with the Queen and his Country, but his heart and his life belonged to his wife and girls. There was only one course for him; he would do what they wanted and resign from the Regiment when it was all over. People could brand him a coward if they wished.* He pulled a bottle of whisky from his desk drawer, took a long swig, and settled down to wait for Scotland Yard to make contact. Anger mounted within, but all he could do was wait.

Whilst Anstruther and Anson were being recruited, I was relaxing in Finsbury Mansions studying the Financial Times, as ever, trying to make sense of what was happening in the Stock Exchange. I was no more knowledgeable now than when I first took an interest; I doubted if I would ever become an expert in the market.

I checked my share portfolio; some up, some down, and a loss overall. Crime was a much easier source of profit it seemed to me. My door intercom buzzed, dragging me away from the world of finance.

'Yes?'

'O'Connell, let me in.'

I hadn't expected him to come to the flat, but maybe he didn't trust telephones. I pressed the door release and told him to come up; the clock showed that it was just leaving ten. I felt a surge of anticipation. What was I going to be told?

'Come in Sean, good to see you. Coffee?'

'Sure now, why not; a touch of caffeine never did any harm.'

'You've got some news for me?'

He smiled. 'Would you mind turning on the radio?'

I stared at him, but he offered no explanation. 'Why? Any particular programme?'

He shook his head and listened as the sound of a light orchestra filled the room. I studied his expression; there was something different; the smile seemed a little forced, and his brow was furrowed.

'Happy with this?' I motioned to the radio.

He nodded. 'I'm like a dog with two tails, Craig; it's all happening even as we speak. The operation has begun, and I'm here to share the moment with you and, of course, make sure you behave yourself.'

I shook my head. 'Today? No, I don't believe it.' It was all so sudden; it couldn't be happening this soon. 'Christ, you've acted quickly. I just can't believe it.'

O'Connell was grinning at my incredulity. I reflected on his words. *'Why wouldn't I behave myself?'* I didn't understand what he was alluding to. He ignored my question, offering no explanation. I was about to pursue it with him when an announcement by the BBC stopped me in my tracks.

We interrupt this broadcast to announce that Scotland Yard has received a warning of an IRA bombing campaign in London. The call is believed to be from a genuine source. The public is asked to be on the alert and to report any suspicious objects. No further details are currently.

I turned open-mouthed to face O'Connell, horrified by what I had just heard. 'A bombing campaign? That can't be right. It's just to cause confusion, isn't it? Tell me it's just to cause confusion; there aren't really any bombs.'

O'Connell was grim-faced. 'We have planted a number of explosive devices. Insurance, Craig, we must have insurance. Surely you understand?'

'You bastard, you said nothing about bombs; innocent people will get hurt. There was no need for violence.'

'Be realistic, Craig. When you did your jobs, you didn't go armed with replica guns, did you? And, of course, there was no chance of any innocent person getting hurt.' He was sneering at me. 'Don't come the high and mighty with me, boyo. We'll be giving out the usual warnings, then it's up to the authorities. We're doing what I think is necessary to pull this job off.'

I felt sick, but he was right. We had carried loaded guns and had been prepared to use them, but this was different. *How's it different, Craig?*

'Nobody had better get hurt, that's all I say.' It was an empty threat, and O'Connell knew it.

He raised an eyebrow. 'Threatening me, are you? I'd better be careful then; just as well I brought this.' He pulled a small automatic pistol from his jacket pocket and rested it on his lap.

'Don't do anything foolish, Craig; I wouldn't want bloodstains on this expensive carpet of yours.'

Chapter Thirty-One

Reggie Anstruther sat gazing at his phone, trance-like, willing it to ring. This dreadful nightmare couldn't end until it got started; only then would his family be safe.

Christ, I hope I can trust the IRA. I never thought I would countenance the possibility of doing a deal with them or any other terrorists. Bastards! Oh God, why is this happening to me? Please let it all work out. When they have what they want, what then? His family were witnesses; could possibly identify their captors. Oh God, please watch over them.

The shrill ring of the phone, though expected, still jolted him, and he knocked it off its cradle in his eagerness to grab hold of it.

'Captain Anstruther.'

It was the Duty Sergeant. 'Call for you, Captain, Commander Clayton, Scotland Yard.'

'Thank you, Sergeant, put him through.' He spoke calmly; it was business as usual as far as his men were concerned.

'Reggie, the balloon's gone up big time; we're in need of your services. The IRA has reared its ugly head again.'

The two men knew each other well. Will Clayton headed up the Counter Terrorist Unit at Scotland Yard. 'Looks like there's a bombing campaign under way; the caller used the agreed code word, so we believe it's genuine, though you can never be sure with these people. It seems we are to receive three warnings today; you'll have to deploy your resources with that in mind. The first alarm relates to Harvey Nicholls; apparently, a number of explosive devices have been planted in the store. The caller wouldn't say how many. I've ordered an evacuation and started a search; we'll need your boys to deal with anything we find. I've told the media, and the public will be informed shortly. Three callouts, can you handle that?' The Commander kept to the bare facts; he wanted to get off the phone and be ready to deal with whatever happened next.

Anstruther responded in the professional manner expected of him.

'We can deal with three from here, Will; I'll set the wheels in motion for backup. I'll send a team out now to Harvey Nichols and another two teams on standby. I'll go out with the third team; hopefully, backup will be in place by then. Any time scale given?'

'Afraid not; look, I must go. Good luck. Message ends at 10.04.'

Anstruther made his way into the outer office, his adrenaline glands working at full production. 'Sergeant, IRA bomb alert, get three teams ready. Ask Lieutenants Boyd and Merton to report to me immediately. In view of the situation, we'll go with three men only in each bomb disposal vehicle. Lieutenant Boyd will take the first team, Lieutenant Merton team two, and I'll lead team three. Whilst you're doing that, I'll call another depot and arrange some backup.'

Lieutenant Alec Boyd was duly dispatched to Harvey Nicholls at 10.10 precisely.

I sat listening to the music, barely responding to O'Connell's attempts to engage me in conversation. In the end, he gave up and just sat there smiling, fingering the gun from time to time. The programme was interrupted for a second time at 10.15 to announce that there had been an explosion at Harvey Nicholls. It wasn't known whether anyone had been killed or injured; evacuation had been in progress when the device had gone off. A Bomb Disposal Unit was at the scene.

O'Connell sought to pre-empt my anger. 'They were given notice; there was plenty of time to clear the store. I doubt if anyone will have been injured.'

I was furious; my worst fears were being realised. 'And you don't fucking care one way or the other, do you? You know those bomb timers aren't accurate. Just how many have you planted?'

He looked at me dispassionately and shrugged. 'Three.'

I felt sick. By association, I was as guilty as he was. 'You are rotten duplicitous bastard; I knew I couldn't trust the IRA.'

O'Connell's eyes narrowed, and he gave me a warning scowl. 'Your life depends on trusting me; keep that in the front of your mind.'

Anstruther dispatched his second team to Harrods at 10.23, with Lieutenant Simon Merton in command.

A BBC reporter at Harvey Nicholls advised that there had been two further explosions and there were reports of casualties. Fire had broken out, and all Emergency Services were at the scene. Listeners heard two explosions in the middle of the report from Harrods. The store was being cleared when these occurred. The Police ordered that all London stores were to be evacuated and remain closed until further notice.

I was near to being physically sick; I wished I was dead, but there was nothing I could do now but sit it out and hope that nobody would get killed. I wondered if I could have, should have, done anything different. O'Connell had taken my plan for a bold theft and turned it into a nightmare for London. Another announcement advised that eight shoppers had been injured at Harvey Nicholls, some seriously. An ITV reporter at Harrods reported that during the evacuation, three had been killed and eleven injured. If I could have got hold of O'Connell's gun at that moment, I would have killed him.

Anstruther was also listening to the broadcasts with increasing anxiety. It was clear that the IRA would stop at nothing in pursuit of its goals; he was more worried than ever now about his family. They could be dead now for all he knew. He willed his phone to ring again and wished for that all-important third call; at least when it came, he would be involved. Finally, it rang. 'Reggie, Will Clayton again; you're on old chap, and you've got the big one. They're going for the Tower of London; looks like the bastards are trying to terrorise London and hit the tourist trade at the same time. Good luck; message ends at 10. 59.'

'Sergeant, mobilise Team 3, the third target is the Tower of London.'

O'Connell glanced at his watch. 'Any minute now, Craig, the final act has kicked in, we'll soon know if your plan works or not.'

I clenched my fists in despair and yelled at him. 'It wasn't my fucking plan to kill people. There was no need; it would have worked without these diversions, as you called them. Those poor people; how can you sit there and gloat?'

A vicious expression took hold of O'Connell's face. 'Your politicians and your army have killed thousands of my people over the centuries and thought little of it. Your plan had a 95% chance of success, mine has 100%.'

At 11.03, Charlie Anson of Topflight Maintenance rushed unannounced into the office of the Tower's maintenance manager, Evan Williams. He had his instructions to carry out; national pride and security weren't his priority. 'Mr Williams, Mr Williams! There's a bomb in Waterloo block, in the basement Plant Room.'

Evan Williams looked at him aghast. 'Oh my God, it's the IRA. I've just been told by Scotland Yard to clear the Tower. A Bomb Disposal Team is on its way. Get down to the gate and meet it; you'll have to show them where the bomb is.'

Anson played his part. 'It won't go off, will it? I don't want to be near it when it goes off; I've got my wife and family to think of.'

'I'm sure the Bomb Disposal people won't let you take any risks. Now be a good chap and get down there; you're the only one who can show them where it is.'

Anson knew there was no risk; there was no bomb. The 'bomb' was just a harmless neon timer ticking down to zero with two harmless wires leading off along the underside of the floor conveyor that served the Jewel Room above.

At 11.04, Captain Anstruther and his team sped out of Woolwich Barracks, heading for the Tower of London. The vehicle was driven by Sergeant Larry Naismith, a long-serving member of the Bomb Disposal Unit. In the rear were two other soldiers and all the equipment required for the task. Reggie Anstruther sat in the front alongside his Sergeant. Along the way, Larry Naismith was taken by surprise when his Captain directed him to make a left turn down a small lane.

'But Captain.' Naismith began to protest.

'Do as instructed, Sergeant.'

Naismith shrugged and obeyed his Commanding Officer, unsure as to why, but an order was an order.

'Turn into that yard on the left Sergeant.'

This time, he didn't even protest. He reckoned something was going on, some kind of exercise perhaps. His eyes widened when he saw another army vehicle in the yard, an Ambulance. 'What's going on, Captain?'

The next thing he saw was five men in Army uniforms running towards them, all armed. He turned to Anstruther, looking for instructions, but his Captain said nothing and just sat staring ahead, silent, showing no concern. Two of the men stopped at the front of the vehicle; the other two ran to the rear.

One of the men barked a command. 'Everybody out, any funny business, and you will be shot.'

The Sergeant waited, speechless, for his Officer to take command of the situation. The team wasn't armed; there was nothing they could do but surrender. *Why wasn't the captain taking command?*

Anstruther seemed resigned to the situation and showed no sign of anger or even surprise.

The Sergeant's thoughts were racing; *surely not a bloody exercise at a time like this.* Belatedly, his Captain spoke. 'I'm sorry, Sergeant. Do as they say; I'll explain later.'

Naismith and his two comrades were herded into a small, unlit, windowless room, and the door slammed behind them. The last thing the Sergeant saw was his Captain talking to the leader of the group. *Christ, what was going on?* The group's leader was speaking to one of his men. 'Stay on guard outside that fucking door and don't open it no matter what. They can piss, shit, or die in there for all I care. You can leave here at one sharp if we're not back to collect you by then; throw the key away when you leave.'

The group's leader, who wore sergeant's stripes, turned to Anstruther. 'Climb on board, Captain Anstruther, Sir' He smirked at the respect he was showing. 'I'll drive; I think I know where we're headed.'

Two of the others, one dressed as a corporal, got into the back of the Bomb Disposal Vehicle, and the remaining two got into the ambulance. Sirens wailing, both army vehicles sped through London, weaving their way past other traffic, ignoring traffic lights.

The small convoy arrived at the Tower at 11.20. Evan Williams was waiting for them at the entrance gate along with Charlie Anson and waved them to a stop. He recognised Anstruther from previous exercises undertaken to test their emergency arrangements.

'Thank God you're here, Captain, it's the real thing this time. We'll dispense with the security checks today if you agree; we know this isn't an exercise.'

Anstruther nodded. 'We're pretty sure this isn't a hoax, that's why we're accompanied by an ambulance this time round.'

A Police Superintendent joined them to report on his actions. 'I've cordoned off the area around Waterloo Block and we've evacuated the public from the entire site.'

Williams spoke up. 'We have one small bonus, Captain; Charlie here, one of our maintenance contractors, has located the bomb. He's willing to take you straight to it, if you think it'll be safe.'

Anson shook Anstruther's hand; unknown to each other, they were both playing out the roles given to them by the IRA.

'Thank you, Charlie. I'm Captain Anstruther; I'll see that you come to no harm.'

This was an empty assurance; bombs were indiscriminate, but there was no point in adding to the man's fear.

'OK, Charlie, climb up beside me, and we'll drive over to Waterloo block.'

The maintenance engineer climbed up alongside Anstruther and told what he knew. 'As far as I judge, the bomb is immediately below the Jewel Room.'

Anstruther feigned a gasp. 'Christ, let's hope it doesn't go off.'

The bogus bomb disposal squad assembled in front of Waterloo Block and was joined by the Police Superintendent and Evan Williams. Anstruther did what he would do in any bomb disposal situation; he made sure of his facts.

'You can confirm that Waterloo block is empty?'

Evan Williams and the Policeman both nodded.

'And the area is cordoned off for a distance of at least two hundred yards?'

The Policeman nodded his confirmation.

'Good; make sure that everyone remains outside the cordon, and that includes you two unless it's essential. 'Charlie, I have to ask you to lead me where the bomb is.'

'You're sure there's no risk?'

Anstruther gave a reassuring smile. 'A very small one, but I'll be in front of you, so I'll come off worst.'

He turned back to Williams. 'Mr Williams, if my memory serves me correctly you've got closed circuit television covering some areas of Waterloo block?'

'Yes, we have; extensive coverage given its function.'

'I'd like you to take Private McCullough here to the Control Room, so he can observe what's going on. We haven't got time to set up our own gear.'

Williams nodded readily, happy to be getting clear of the danger area. 'No problem, follow me Private.'

Daniel McCullough smiled broadly. 'Lead on, sir; I'll be right behind you.'

Williams led McCullough across the square to the Administration building and went inside, then made their way along a corridor and stopped at a door labelled Security. Williams punched in his personal entry code on the door keypad, waited momentarily for the release mechanism to operate, then pushed the door open and entered; the IRA man followed closely. Two security staff swivelled round to face their visitors, relaxing when they saw who it was. 'Oh, it's you, Boss; this is a bit of a do.'

'Yes, let's hope it comes to nothing. Private McCullough is from Bomb Disposal; he wants to observe what's going on in Waterloo block on our screens. Show him the set-up and help in any way you can. I'm not going to hang round; I can be more useful elsewhere.' Williams hurried off back to his office; there were people to inform, and God knows who had been trying to contact him.

The senior of the two security men pointed up to the television monitors. 'The top row of screens provides coverage of Waterloo block. In fact, here comes your officer now.' They all looked on as Anstruther, the pseudo-army Sergeant, and a Private entered the building. Anson tagged along behind.

'We make a note in the log when anything out of the ordinary happens and I guess the presence of a Bomb Disposal Squad is in that category.' He reached for a biro and noted the time, 11.27. That was his last action. Daniel McCullough drew a revolver from inside his tunic and shot both guards in the head; both died instantly. The IRA man smiled. 'Sorry about that; it's all in the line of duty, nothing personal.' He put his revolver on a nearby desk and dragged each body in turn to the corner of the room. 'There now; I hope you're comfortable. God rest your souls.'

Back in my flat, I listened as the BBC informed us that Tower Bridge had been evacuated and a Bomb Disposal Team was on site. Further details will follow.'

O'Connell rubbed his hands. ''Tis all going nicely to plan, Craig, my boy. If it keeps going like this, you'll have earned the protection I've provided for you.'

I said nothing. It was taking all my resolve to keep my emotions under control; I wanted to overpower him, kill him. But I did nothing. I wanted the job to succeed; after all, I had planned it, but I felt sick at the carnage that had been wreaked by the IRA. Memories of Crewe came flooding back to haunt me; I felt disgusted with myself. Yet again, the law of unintended consequences had struck disastrously.

'Show me where this bomb is, Charlie.' Anstruther and the maintenance engineer stood in the doorway of the Plant Room. Anson was scared and confused; he knew there was no concealed bomb. He had just followed orders, and now he was going to be found out. *What should he say? What would happen to his wife if he didn't carry on with the charade? The captain would soon recognise that the timer wasn't part of an explosive device. What then?*

His dilemma was solved for him when the IRA sergeant spoke. 'What's the matter, Charlie? Tell the captain what he wants to know; we're all party to what's going on.'

Anson was even more confused; the Sergeant had an Irish accent, but surely the captain couldn't be involved in this outrage? The Sergeant had drawn a revolver fitted with a silencer. 'Speak up, Charlie, or I'll blow your tiny little skull apart.'

Anstruther realised what had happened and intervened. 'Cool it, sergeant. It's OK, Charlie; I've just realised that we're both pawns in this game of theirs. We're both in the same position; they've got my wife and kids. Let's just do what they say.'

Anson breathed a sigh of relief. 'They've got my wife too. Follow me, the bomb is just along here except it's not a bomb, it's just a timer.' He walked down a line of engineering pipes and pointed out the fake device and a large conveyor-like installation. 'That's the floor conveyor serving the Jewel Room; we're directly under it. I shut it down when I heard the Jewel Room being evacuated.'

The IRA Sergeant spoke up. 'Is there direct access from this room to the Jewel Room?'

The maintenance engineer shook his head. 'No. You have to leave here, turn left and go up the stairs.'

'What about an access panel to get to the equipment?'

'There isn't one; too much of a security risk, I suppose. It's all maintained from down here.'

Their conversation was interrupted by a voice from behind. 'Hello, is everything all right down here? I came to see if I could be of assistance.' Being helpful, or perhaps just being nosy, cost Evan Williams his life. The IRA Sergeant turned and fired in a single motion. The bullet hit the Tower's Maintenance Manager in the chest, ripping his heart apart. He died at 11.32.

Anstruther grabbed the sergeant by the shoulder and swung him round, clutching at his lapels. 'You bastard, you cowardly bastard, he was unarmed there was no need to kill him.'

'Take your fucking British Army hands off me, Captain, or you'll join him.'

He motioned over his shoulder at Williams' lifeless body. 'Just think about your family before you touch me again.'

Anstruther felt cowardly, but he stepped back; there was nothing to be gained by getting himself killed.

The Sergeant smiled and turned to his IRA colleague 'Set up the explosive.'

The IRA man opened his backpack and removed two Semtex explosive devices.

Anstruther's eyes widened. 'Christ, what are you going to do with those?'

The Sergeant sneered at him. 'I'll give you one fucking guess. Right, Charlie, you're coming with me; lead on to the Jewel Room. Captain, you stay here. Vinny, we don't really need the Captain now; deal with him if he steps out of line.'

'In here.' Anson pointed at the door to the Jewel Room.

Without its hordes of jabbering tourists, the room was eerily silent.

'I must admit; it's impressive, Charlie. I wish I could take it **all** back to Ireland with me; there's nothing like this anywhere in the world.' He continued to look around at the numerous display cabinets filled with centuries of British history. A virtual myriad of crowns, tiaras, coronets and ceremonial equipment, gold and silver studded with every imaginable jewel glinting and shining in the display lighting.

'But all we want is the Coronation gear. We're not being too greedy, are we now?'

Anson made no reply.

The Sergeant looked round for a security camera, spotted one and gave it the thumbs up; having done that, he made his way back to the Plant room. In the control room, the watchful Daniel McCullough had seen the thumbs up and rose to his feet; his job was done. He looked at the still forms of his victims lying in the pools of their own blood and shrugged indifferently; they weren't the first men he'd killed and probably wouldn't be the last. Minutes later, at 11.38, he joined his leader in the Plant room as arranged.

The IRA sergeant addressed his two comrades. 'Vinny, set the charge for one minute; that'll give you plenty of time to take cover. I'll thump on the conveyor when I'm ready. Danny, you be lookout and keep an eye on Charlie here in case he tries any heroics.

He turned to Anstruther, 'Got the picture, Captain? Yes? No? Follow me to the Jewel Room; you can see it happen first-hand.'

Anstruther said nothing, but he had figured out what was about to happen; his sense of duty was willing him to act, but he feared for his family.

Back in the Jewel Room, the IRA sergeant, Terry Brannigan, thumped loudly on the conveyor to Vinny in the room below, glancing at his watch as he did so. 'Best stand clear, Captain.'

Both men moved to the furthest corner of the room, where the sergeant counted down the seconds. 'Three, two, one.' Another second passed, and then a deafening explosion shook the room; it was precisely 11.43. The floor shook, both men's ears rang with the reverberations.

Brannigan was on his feet in a split second and fired two carefully aimed shots at the display case holding the Coronation Regalia, watching in satisfaction as the glass disintegrated, leaving the jewels exposed and, more importantly, undamaged. Alarms were sounding all around the building, as was to be expected in the aftermath of an explosion.

'Here you are, Captain, make yourself useful.' Brannigan handed over the Sovereign's Mace and Sceptre, then grabbed King Edward's Crown and the Imperial State Crown.

The IRA man grinned broadly. 'A nice little haul, Captain, now let's get back to the plant room and make it quick.'

The BBC's top echelon of Correspondents had now joined the lower ranks on location, and my heart sank again as I listened to one of them report that there had been an explosion at the Tower of London. *Please don't let there be any casualties.*

Information was sketchy, but a Bomb Disposal Team and Emergency Services were on site. Further details would be given as soon as possible; one of the Correspondents droned on, repeating at length inconsequential detail, filling the time available with endless speculation about what might or might not be happening in Waterloo Block.

O'Connell looked triumphant as he watched events unfolding on TV. 'Just think of it, Craig, the Crown Jewels are in IRA hands even as we speak.'

I felt like burying my head in my hands as I tried to cope with the turmoil within me.

'OK Captain, do your stuff; do it well and you'll soon be back with that lovely family of yours.'

Brannigan was smiling as he issued his instructions. The IRA man was elated; history was in the making. He, a son of Ireland, was giving the British Government one of the biggest kicks in the balls it had ever had.

Anstruther's heart was aching, his head buzzing with self-imposed incriminations. *He had allowed the IRA to steal the Crown Jewels; he, an Officer of the Queen, had betrayed his country.* He felt ashamed, but he couldn't bring himself to sacrifice his family; he had, this very day, witnessed IRA ruthlessness first-hand. He turned away, head down, to carry out his next act of betrayal, but Brannigan stopped him.

'Hold on, Captain; you've got to look the part. You're a hero; you got caught in a bomb blast, did you not?' He squirted some stage blood onto Anstruther's face and wiped some stage black onto his cheeks and uniform. 'That's better; off you go and make it look good.'

Outside Waterloo block, the Emergency Services personnel had heard the explosion and were discussing how best to react when Captain Anstruther ran from the doorway shouting.

'Keep clear! There's another bomb down here; I'm trying to deal with it. One of my chaps has taken a hit from that last explosion; he's pretty badly injured. Let my ambulance crew in; they're trained for this.' He waved the two IRA army ambulance men forward.

'Be quick, you two, we need a stretcher, blood and saline; his legs are in bad shape.'

The two men retrieved what they needed from the ambulance; it had all been gathered together earlier in readiness for this moment. They wasted no time in hurrying after Anstruther.

Inside the building, Daniel McCullough had made ready. He had removed his boots, torn his trousers, and covered his legs in fake blood. His face and head were liberally doused with fake blood and blacking.

One of the pseudo-medics wrapped a bandage round his forehead, stained it too with blood, then Danny lay down on the stretcher. A leg cage was placed over his legs, and the stolen regalia pushed under it. Finally, a bright red casualty blanket was spread over him, and his two comrades hoisted the stretcher and set off at pace back to the ambulance.

'Go easy, you bastards; you've got an injured man on here.' The IRA man chortled then adopted the still posture of a seriously injured victim.

Outside Waterloo Block, Danny closed his eyes and set his face in a grimace of pain, letting out the occasional groan, particularly when the stretcher was being manoeuvred into the rear of the ambulance. NHS ambulance personnel who had attended the site offered assistance, but were waved away. 'It's all right, guys; we'll get him to casualty. Stay on standby; there's another bomb in there; could go off at any time.'

Superintendent Ted Ross made his way over. 'Is it bad?'

Liam McCrory shook his head and put a finger to his lips. 'It's not good, but we're hopeful; he's a strong boy.' He employed the Liverpool accent he'd picked up during his stay there in recent years.

'Best we get on our way; the sooner he's in casualty, the better.'

'Do you need an escort?'

'Thanks, Superintendent, but we'll be fine. We'll be heading for Guys Hospital, just along the river, all in a day's work for us. Best keep your people for emergencies; God only knows if Captain Anstruther will be able to deal with the second device before it goes off.'

The fake army ambulance drove out of the Tower of London at 11.56, four minutes ahead of schedule.

Anstruther stood alongside Terry Brannigan, wondering what was going to happen next. He was puzzled; the Jewels were gone, and yet the IRA men were making no effort to escape.

'That all went well, Captain; it won't be long till this is all over. Now go out there and tell the good Superintendent that you're making progress with defusing the bomb. Tell him to stay clear.'

He nodded at Anson. 'Take him with you; he's not needed here. But remember, no funny business, Charlie; your wife won't be released till I give the word.'

Anstruther did exactly as he was told and was back in the plant room minutes later. He was puzzled as to how the IRA men were going to make their escape.

'Well, what now?'

Brannigan smiled. 'Just sit down and relax until I tell you otherwise.' The IRA man sat down on the floor with his back to the wall and closed his eyes to reflect on the success of his mission. *It had all been unbelievably easy.* Sammy Mulveen, erstwhile IRA private, did much the same.

Meanwhile, the Army ambulance was driven to a derelict site, where the three men stripped off their uniforms and pulled on shirts and painters' overalls; the 'injured' Danny washed his hair and face in a bucket of water in the rear of the ambulance. The Coronation Regalia was placed in a box and transferred to a waiting van, which, according to the lettering on its side, belonged to Watson & Sons, Painters and Decorators.

The trio then set out on the final leg of their journey to a small airstrip in Surrey, where the Jewels would be loaded into a light aircraft bound for the Republic of Ireland. The men would then drive to a multi-storey car park, abandon the van and drive away in a dark blue Ford Sierra, back to whence they had set out that morning.

Davie Doyle had been listening to events unfold on the radio and was making ready to leave the Anson residence. Everything had gone to schedule; his part in the robbery could end at 12.30 as planned.

'Sorry, me darling, but I've got to tie you up now; then I can get on my way. Please don't struggle; I'll use force if I have to. If everything has gone to plan, someone should turn up to release you in about half an hour or so.'

Linda Anson said nothing and offered no resistance as the Irishman taped her securely onto a chair. He stood back and, not for the first time, appraised his captive. 'You're a fine-looking woman, Linda; I wish I could have met up with you in other circumstances.'

The tape across her mouth reduced her reaction to a strangulated mumble; only her violently shaking head conveyed her feelings. Imogen and her sister looked on anxiously, but it sounded like the bad man was about to leave. Imogen leaned over and whispered in her sister's ear. 'As soon as he leaves, we'll help Mummy get out of that chair.

Davie looked at the twins, 'I'm going now. You two behave yourselves, or I'll come back.

Imogen looked at him sullenly but said nothing. *Go away, I hate you.*

Clancy McEvoy looked at his watch for the hundredth time, observing the slow progress of time. He, too, had followed events on his transistor radio and knew that his job was drawing to a conclusion. It was nearly 12.30, time for him to go.

'I'm going now, Mrs Anstruther; somebody will be with you shortly. I truly hope the girls are none the worse for their experience.'

The twins listened in on the conversation; they didn't really understand what had been happening, but they knew that their ordeal would soon be over. Rebecca Anstruther felt nothing but relief and inwardly thanked God that they had come to no harm. 'As long as someone knows where we are, we'll be fine, thank you.'

McEvoy pulled the telephone from its socket and took his boot to the handset, smashing it beyond repair. His captives watched as he closed the door behind him and listened to hear if he locked it. They heard the key rattle in the lock and could hear him moving about outside. The IRA man had a soft side to his nature and left the key in the lock to make it easy for whoever turned up. All he had to do now was shed his army clothing and make ready to become just another member of the public. He welcomed the cooling air as he stripped off his outerwear and got down to the jeans and sweater he had worn underneath the uniform. Dressed normally, he tucked his gun into his waistband under his sweater and nonchalantly strolled away.

Vincent Donnelly didn't communicate his departure to the imprisoned soldiers. It was one o'clock, and he was free to go. He removed his army gear and stuffed it, along with his handgun, into a rucksack. Dressed in jeans, tee shirt and denim jacket, he didn't attract a second glance as he made his way to the nearest Tube station. Before he left, he dropped the key to the door down a drain. It was a petty, futile act, but he was a bitter man whose only brother had been killed by the British Army. *Fuck you bastards; if I had my way, I'd kill the lot of you.*

At one o'clock precisely, Terry Brannigan stood up and crossed to where Anstruther was sitting and reached his gun forward, handle first.

'There you are, Captain, we're your prisoners.'

Anstruther eyed the IRA man suspiciously. 'What are you playing at?'

'I'm not playing, Captain. We're surrendering to you; Sammy, give him your gun.'

Anstruther couldn't believe what was happening; it was surely some kind of trick. He rose hesitantly to his feet and took the guns, watching his two erstwhile captors suspiciously, half expecting them to do something. He realised that the guns conferred only limited power; they still had his family. He stood facing Brannigan, one of the guns pointed at the man. 'What now?'

'Christ, Captain, use your fucking head; you take us into custody. The way I see it, you're in the shit; you've sold out your Queen and country, gone down without a fight, but you might be able to redeem yourself; you can tell them you overpowered me, grabbed my gun and made Sammy here hand over his. It might just save your bacon.'

Anstruther thought quickly. *Why not? It might help; he had nothing to lose.* 'Why are you doing this? You'll go down for a long time.'

Brannigan smiled broadly. 'I don't think so, Captain; let's wait and see what the morrow brings.'

The army man was mystified. *What was he up to?*

The robbery was in its end stage; I held my breath when the BBC announced that it was going back to their reporter at the Tower of London. He told us what I knew he would. One of the Bomb Disposal Team had been seriously injured and had been taken to Guys Hospital; the remainder of the Team was attempting to defuse another bomb. No information was available as to the extent of the damage caused by the previous explosion.

I suppose I should have felt like celebrating; I was, after all, the man who had planned the most audacious robbery in history, but instead, I felt completely hollow. I wished that I could turn the clock back, right back, to where I could have chosen a new life path to follow. My despair could not have been greater; I resolved never again to get involved in crime. It was easy to say that now that had over a million pounds safely banked in Switzerland.

O'Connell's voice broke into my thoughts. 'You should be smiling, Craig; you've pulled it off. I knew right from the start it was a brilliant plan.' O'Connell knew that he would be written into the annals of IRA history; his place in folklore was assured. *Maybe someone would write a song about the day the IRA stole the Crown Jewels.* '

I shook my head. 'I'm ashamed of what I've done.'

'Suit yourself, Craig, but at the end of the day, we made a good team; there's no denying that.'

Anger welled up in me. 'I'm not on your fucking team. I've kept my side of the bargain; our partnership ends as of now.'

O'Connell, who was on his way out, stopped in his tracks and spat out a warning. 'Our partnership ends when I fucking say so and only when I say so.'

I said nothing. What could I say? I had some serious thinking to do; I was in the biggest hole I could possibly have dug. I had succeeded in making enemies of just about everybody I knew: Averton, Angie and almost certainly, Dan. I was in deep shit, and I didn't want to add O'Connell to the list.

'You're right, and I know it. I guess you're not going to give me back my Passport?'

O'Connell smiled. 'No matter what you might think of me, Craig, I'll keep my side of our bargain. I'll be in touch.' With that, he let himself out and was gone.

I got seriously drunk that night and woke up on the sofa in the early hours of the morning, cold and cramped. For some inexplicable reason, probably to escape my very self, I started drinking again, finally collapsing on the floor in a stupor. It was after midday when I came to.

THE END GAME

Chapter Thirty-Two

I was cold and cramped, my head thumping. I felt completely debilitated; the lounge floor didn't make a good bed. My journey to the bathroom was zombie-like, and I wasn't visiting for the usual routine purposes; my stomach wanted its revenge and insisted on throwing up. Not for the first time in my life, I resolved never to consume that much alcohol. I wanted to run away, far away, wanted to erase recent events from memory. The very thought of breakfast made me feel queasy, so I opted for a bath and lay there languishing, trying to get my thoughts into some sort of order. A sudden thought jolted me into a full alert; the telephone hadn't rung. I'd anticipated that Dan and Angie would be in touch, both hell-bent on venting their respective wrath. I fully expected a tongue-lashing from the latter; because of my lies and deception, she was indirectly involved with the IRA. Panic mode took over when the thought struck me that she might even tip off John Law; then, I remembered the other side of the coin and how much I knew about her activities. I figured that Dan might be more pragmatic, given he knew more of the background.

It was time to face the music and get in touch with them, but before that, I wanted to see what the newspapers had to say about yesterday's events. I pulled on some clothes, happily skipped breakfast and made my way to the local shop. My mouth dried, and my brow beaded with sweat as I sidled along the rack of newspapers taking in one damning headline after another.

IRA SAVAGE LONDON

8 DEAD, 34 INJURED IN IRA ONSLAUGHT

HARVEY NICHOLS: 2 DEAD, 14 INJURED

HARRODS: 4 DEAD, 19 INJURED

TOWER OF LONDON: 2 DEAD, 1 INJURED

TERRORIST RAMPAGE HITS LONDON

One newspaper had a black border all-round the front page with a full-page caption.

IRA KILLERS STRIKE AT LONDON

I bought four newspapers and set off back to the flat, wishing I were dead and out of it all. My conscience tried to shift the blame onto the IRA but failed; at the end of the day, I was as much to blame as they were. Halfway back to the flat, it dawned on me; there was no mention of the theft of the Crown Jewels. Surely, even the death toll wouldn't push an event of such enormity completely off the front page. *What the fuck was going on?* My hand shook as I tried to insert my key into the lock; it took me three attempts to get it right. I was so desperate to get indoors.

Even as I read the first newspaper, I began to realise what was happening. The article described in detail the bombing of the Tower, the deaths, and the closure of Waterloo Block for the foreseeable future. Miraculously, the Crown Jewels had escaped unscathed and had been taken away for examination; they would be back on display as soon as possible.

495

Captain Anstruther got a good write-up for disabling a second explosive device and, more importantly, capturing two IRA suspects who may have been attempting to steal the Crown Jewels. There was no mention of his family being kidnapped or that of the Ansons; perhaps that was being held back for later editions.

Her Majesty was, of course, deeply saddened by the loss of life, and the Home Secretary promised to personally lead a campaign to root out the IRA and its supporters on mainland Britain. Scotland Yard's Anti-Terrorist Squad would be strengthened, and, as ever, the spirit of Londoners would rise above all adversity.

But there was no mention of the theft of the Jewels. I couldn't help but smile; a good old-fashioned British cover-up was in progress. There was no way Her Majesty's Government was going to lose face to the IRA. What puzzled me was why the IRA itself hadn't released the news; there were any number of news agencies who would have no qualms about embarrassing the UK administration. So why was the IRA maintaining a silence? My immediate reaction was to phone O'Connell and find out what was going on, but I thought better of it; following yesterday's events, his line might be tapped. Instead, I resolved to go to the Pig and Fiddle and confront him face to face; hopefully, he'd be there.

The phone rang and set my nerves jangling; I didn't really feel like a confrontation, but I knew my problems weren't going to go away. I took a sharp intake of breath when I recognised Angie's voice and prepared myself for the worst. To my astonishment, all she wanted to do was express some sympathy. I very quickly realised that she had no real reason to link me with the IRA.

'Bad luck, Craig, it looks like the IRA has spoiled your party; all your work has been in vain?'

I continued with my deception; there was no point in doing otherwise. I tried to sound philosophical. 'Amazing co-incidence, but sooner or later, the Jewels will be back on display, and when they are, we'll be ready for them. Look on it as a pleasure in store.' I tried to sound upbeat.

'Yeah, sure.' She didn't sound convinced; she would reason that security would be beefed up following the raid, and any future attempt might be virtually impossible to pull off. 'Anyway, if it's any consolation, you can forget about my fee.'

'Wouldn't dream of it; a deal is a deal. In fact, I've got a cheque for you. Give me an address, and I'll post it on.'

'Why don't we meet for lunch?'

'I'm sorry, Angie, really sorry, but I'm tied up for a while.'

Angie's sensitive side and perception swung into action. 'You don't sound right, Craig? You sound hollow, and you just haven't been yourself since this job's been in the frame. I'm a friend; why not share whatever's troubling you.'

'I can't talk about it now, Angie, but I promise I'll be in touch later in the week. We'll have that lunch and talk things over.'

She gave an address for the cheque and rang off, having extracted a firm promise about meeting up. I felt bad; it wasn't going to happen.

Dan phoned shortly afterwards and came straight to the point; to my surprise, he didn't seem to be at all upset.

'It's me. Do you want to talk about what happened?'

'Those IRA bastards changed my plan. O'Connell claimed he needed diversions to make it work; I knew nothing about them. It's a disaster of the first order; I had no idea it would end up like this.'

'It's fucking tragic, Craig, all those deaths and injuries for nothing.'

'You're wrong there, Dan; we did get the Jewels.'

'What?' He was totally dumbfounded.

'I know where you're coming from; there's no mention in any of the newspapers. I reckon the mother and father of all cover-ups is going down. I'm going to try to meet up with O'Connell tomorrow and find out what's happening. I'm also keeping my fingers crossed that he gives me back my passport; at least then, I can get out of the country until the furore dies down. I'll come back to you with the storyline when I've seen him.'

'Don't take this the wrong way, but I'm not sure you should involve yourself further; people like the IRA and MI5 come to that, are dangerous. Neither of them is known for taking prisoners in circumstances like this.

You had better be very careful; just remember they have no further need of you, and you know too much. Both Parties have got very good reasons for putting you under. If it's a passport you're worried about, I can get you a replacement.'

'My mind's made up; I'll take my chances. The way I'm feeling I don't much care what happens.'

'Don't get depressed, Craig; this will all be a memory come the end of the month.'

'Yeah, sure it will. See you anon.'

I didn't feel like it, but I tried to look confident when I walked into the Pig and Fiddle at exactly eight o'clock that night. There was no guarantee that O'Connell would be there, and it seemed that Fate was against me; he was nowhere to be seen.

The barman remembered me from previous visits and flashed a friendly smile. 'Sure now, I know what you'll be after.' He reached for a bottle of the Powers.

I nodded affably and told him to have one for himself, looking round the room as I did so.

'Sean not around tonight?'

'If you don't see him, he's not here.' He replied truthfully, giving nothing away.

'No arguing with that observation. I'll just enjoy the dram and, of course, the scintillating company.'

He gave me a puzzled look but nodded anyway. I was on my third measure of Powers and feeling greatly fortified when I felt a hand on my shoulder.

'Well now, Craig, drinking alone without old Sean here to keep you company. What's the world coming to?'

'Grab yourself a double on me, and then I wonder if I could have a few minutes of your time in the back room?'

'I was going to suggest that we do just that, Craig; it's obviously very important if you've come all this way to see me.'

We took our usual places on opposite sides of the table, and I wasted no time getting to the point.

'What's happening, Sean?'

'What's happening about what, Craig?'

I bit on my tongue, determined to remain calm. 'It can't have escaped your attention that the newspapers have made no mention of the theft of the Crown Jewels. Doesn't that surprise you?' My voice was laden with sarcasm.

'The Jewels are in good hands. What happens from now on is being handled at a level well above mine.'

'Come on, Sean, you must know what's happening. I can see there's a cover-up in full flow, and it obviously involves Her Majesty's Government.'

O'Connell looked at me for a long time, considering what he should and shouldn't say.

'This was never about the Crown Jewels, Craig. What the fuck would we do with them? They're just a means to an end. This is all about bringing your politicians to the negotiating table. Your bloody government has something we want, and now, we have something it wants. The Jewels will be returned in due course provided the IRA Council gets what it's asking for, or at least most of what it's asking for. If we're accommodated, it can be a happy ending all round.'

My anger welled up, and I punched the table. 'Tell that to the families of the dead and injured, see if they believe you. Anyway, your lot isn't the only one who has terrorist tactics in its repertoire; the Loyalists pack quite a punch, and HMG can't speak for them. Who knows what they'll think about any concessions the Government makes? And in any event, the Government can't be seen to give in to terrorists.'

O'Connell laughed. 'Don't be naive, Craig. Governments have to be realistic; they've given in to terrorists since time began. Today's terrorists are tomorrow's politicians; history teaches us that. They won't appear to give ground, but behind the scenes, concessions will be made, believe me.

We are on a long road to a United Ireland, and each concession takes us a step closer.'

I shook my head sadly. 'So, all those poor innocent shoppers died for a Cause they couldn't care less about. It's only you and the likes of you that care whether Ireland's united or not. The ordinary man in the street doesn't give a shit one way or the other. What a dirty fucking business, no wonder people have no faith in politicians.'

O'Connell sighed and nodded wearily. 'That's true enough about politics; we're all pawns at the end of the day. They're not real, you know.'

I looked at him, trying to comprehend what he was saying. 'What are you talking about? What do you mean, not real?'

'The Jewels, Craig, the Jewels; they're fakes, imitations. We think the real Jewels are in a vault somewhere, probably under the Palace or the Bank of England.'

'Are you serious? You knew this when you stole them?'

O'Connell shook his head. 'We'd heard rumours, but it makes no difference whether they're real or not. The fact is that the IRA walked into the Tower of London and stole the Crown Jewels of the United Kingdom from under the noses of the security services. We could show them to the public, and that would be highly embarrassing for the Government, especially since it hasn't admitted they've been stolen. But as I said, we're out to get a United Ireland, not to show how clever we are.'

The red mist descended in front of my eyes. 'You're telling me all that carnage and misery was for a few fake baubles, little more than coloured glass. Fuck you, Sean, fuck the IRA, and fuck the Government for that matter. I hate myself for getting involved.'

The Irishman listened to my outburst impassively, contempt showing in his expression. 'You've only got yourself to blame; you chose a life of crime, a life fuelled by greed and self-importance. At least the IRA has a Cause, maybe not one you sympathise with, but it's got high ideals at least. You've got none; all you want to do is show what a clever dick you are and get rich at someone else's expense. His words struck home; there was truth in what he was saying.

'At least I don't slaughter innocent people.' I knew my reply was weak, and so did he.

'Not you personally, but it doesn't stop you from hiding behind the curtain and leaving it to your associates to carry guns and kill whenever necessary.'

Sadly, he was right. What had I become? I had no reply; there was no turning the clock back. I had to carry my share of the blame.

'I guess so, Sean, I'm ashamed to say it, but you're right. Anyway, it's time for me to opt out and seek an honest venture, leave this mess behind me. I've kept my side of the bargain, and you've got what you wanted; can I have my passport, please?'

His expression changed instantly; I could see he felt awkward. For the first time since our paths crossed, I could see that O'Connell was on the back foot. I started to get one of those gut-wrenching feelings; something wasn't right. I sensed that my plans for the immediate future were about to go pear-shaped.

'What's wrong, Sean, out with it?'

'I hardly know how to tell you; I'm truly sorry; I would keep to our bargain if I could, but the IRA Council has instructed me otherwise. I've got no choice in this, Craig, believe me.'

'Meaning?'

'We want your input on another job we're planning.'

I shook my head, waving my hands around. 'No way, you've got the Crown fucking Jewels; Christ, there's nothing bigger. Count me out, whatever you have in mind.' They were empty words; even as I spoke, I knew that O'Connell had the upper hand.

The Irishman sounded sympathetic. 'I know how you must feel. Sure, I'd feel the same if I were you. But if you don't help us, you're signing your death warrant, and maybe mine as well.'

I was wasting my time, but I continued to protest. 'I can't help, even if I wanted to; these jobs need intelligence and inside information, and my source has dried up. I only got the last job done as a favour. You know that I've been disconnected from my associates, or I wouldn't have contacted you in the first place.' It was the only card I could play, but he had a bigger one.

'Intelligence doesn't come into it this time; we've got all the information we need. We've even got a plan, but the Council was so impressed by you that it wants you to check it out. I have the Council's promise that we'll let you go after this and, what's even more important from your point of view, you'll have our ongoing protection.'

'What do you mean, **your ongoing protection?** Why should I need it?'

'Well now, a little bird tells me that His Lordship will send his man after you when he thinks we've lost interest. Help us, and I'll make sure that Sir Peter knows that you have our lifetime protection, and he'll lean on his Lordship good and proper.'

My head was swimming. Was I never going to escape the morass that was dragging me under? O'Connell had me by the balls; I was facing a life-or-death situation whichever way I turned. Further resistance was pointless, and I nodded glumly. 'Tell me what you have in mind?'

The Irishman was visibly relieved; he breathed a long sigh of relief. I guess he had been serious about the Council's threat that his life would also be on the line if he didn't go back with the right answer.

The old O'Connell returned. 'You have my gratitude, Craig. It's a wise decision. I can tell you, that if you had refused my request, you would have died this very night, and I'm sad to say that it would have been me pulling the trigger.' To give effect to his threat, he pulled aside his jacket to reveal a holstered gun. 'But no need for that now; this is what we have in mind.......'

I listened to him for the next ten minutes, disbelief mounting by the second as the enormity of what he was proposing sunk in. My jaw dropped open and froze in position; this was pure Hollywood.

'It's ridiculous, Sean, fucking ridiculous. You'll never get away with it.'

'They said the same thing about the Crown Jewels. Anything is possible, Craig; give it some thought and ring me when you're ready.'

At that moment, I felt that I couldn't be involved in what he was proposing. There was a line I didn't think I could cross, but it wasn't time for outright refusal; the gun ensured that. I needed time to think and played for time. 'You'll have to go through all that again, and I'll need pen and paper to make notes.'

He was a step ahead of me. 'All taken care of; I've got it all nicely typed out for you.' He pulled a brown envelope from his inside pocket and removed a sheaf of papers. 'I think you'll find it's all here: times, places, diagrams.'

I shuffled through the three pages, and at first glance, they did indeed seem to be comprehensive. I tried to wriggle out of the job again.

'Looks good, you have a plan, you don't need me. And I can't see why you want to do this; it's dynamite.'

'Same as before, Craig; politics and the Cause; think about the impact on the public if we pull it off, especially on the back of the Crown Jewels.'

He was right, and he knew it; the Nation and the Government would be devastated if what the IRA was planning came to pass. I couldn't get involved; it was a bridge too far. I had to retain some vestige of moral principle. 'It's no good, I can't do it; it's another betrayal of my country.'

O'Connell shrugged. 'Look on yourself as a consultant and not a player in the game; and remember, you can be a dead unsung hero if you don't co-operate or a live unknown traitor if you do. The choice is yours. I promise you that nobody will get hurt this time.'

I sneered. 'You can't guarantee that, and you fucking know it, and I'm not sure that your promises can be relied on.'

The Irishman stroked his chin thoughtfully. 'Think it over, Craig. I can give you until noon on Sunday; after that, the Council will be looking for answers. Should I not hear from you, I'll have to assume that you've decided not to help us, and the inevitable consequences will follow. Needless to say we'll keep an eye on you in the meantime to make sure you don't go wandering off.'

My world was draining away from me; I was losing control of my life. I was a millionaire with a life expectancy of three days if I didn't play ball. I got slowly to my feet; I was lucky he was letting me walk away for the time being. 'I'll be in touch, Sean, one way or another.' I walked over to the

507

door; I didn't look back, but I could feel his eyes on me. I just waved a hand over my shoulder. He didn't say anything, either.

My thoughts raced around like a ball on a pin table all the way home, and they didn't stop when I got there; it was going to be another very long, sleepless night. I slumped into an armchair and began to think.

Midnight came and went. The hands of the clock crawled round to one o'clock. An eternity later, two dragged by; I was doing lots of thinking but not getting anywhere. Endless strong coffees kept sleep at bay, caffeine helping to ensure my brain cells stayed in overdrive. My life was on the line, and it was out of sheer desperation that a solution slowly emerged. Fatigue seemed to know that I'd solved my problem and swept over me; it was time to sleep.

Chapter Thirty-Three

My body took back the time it was owed, and it was nearing eleven when my two bleary eyes saw the light of day; even then, I lay on, reflecting on what I was going to do. All through breakfast, I picked over the solution I had come up with and the risks involved. I rehearsed what I was going to say and to whom, trying to anticipate what they might ask of me. No matter what I did, my life would be under threat for the foreseeable future, either from Lord Averton or the IRA. The only positive I had, was O'Donnell's word, and how reliable was that?

I had two phone calls to make; the first, to an old acquaintance, was probably the most important call of my life and would determine my future. Direct contact proved difficult, but after some persuasion, I was told to phone again between three and four that afternoon.

My second call was to O'Connell to tell him that I'd looked at the plan and felt it could be improved. We agreed to meet that evening at eight o'clock in the Pig and Fiddle; I had become one of its small army of regulars. My two calls made, I headed to the local sub-post office where I could photocopy the paperwork O'Connell had given me. I would be making changes to it, and I wanted to keep the original in pristine condition. As I stood watching the machine do its stuff, I looked around at members of the public blissfully going about their business, totally oblivious to the fact that, just a few feet away, in black and white, an event was being planned that would shock the nation.

At half past three, I followed up on my morning telephone call and this time, I got put straight through; the tone of the voice at the other end wasn't friendly, but that was no surprise, given the history and the passage of time.

'What do you want?' The question was cold and to the point.

'I want to meet you; I think you'll be interested in what I have to say.'

'I'd take a lot of persuasion, probably more than you can give. Time has moved on since we last met.'

I said my piece explained the background and how I wanted to start my life afresh. There was some hesitancy, but then the reply came as I had anticipated.

'I'm not convinced, but there's no harm in meeting you; just don't expect too much.'

'Good. I suggest that we meet for coffee in the Charing Cross Hotel tomorrow morning at eleven if you're free.'

'I'll be there.'

I hung up at that point; I'd achieved what I wanted and had managed to avoid leaving a number where I could be called back if there was a change of heart.

The Pig and Fiddle was heaving when I made my way in; an Irish band was in full swing, and the vocalist was singing the Fields of Athenry with great conviction. O'Connell was in his usual place at the bar and greeted me warmly. 'That's one thing about you, Craig; you're always punctual. Let's head for the back room; the Powers awaits us, though, to be truthful, I hope we won't be too long. I really like this band.'

I nodded in agreement. 'It's got a good sound; I've a soft spot for Irish music myself, Sean. It has a way of reaching the heart; I guess it's the Celt in me.'

'That it does; there's none better.'

We were alone in the room, though I knew that O'Connell would have backup somewhere nearby if required. My curiosity forced me to ask about the last job, although it was already fading into history. 'Anything happening about the Jewels?'

He smiled and nodded. 'It's not what we're here to discuss, though a little bird tells me that they might well be back in England within the next few weeks. It seems that most of our demands have been met. The Council is currently waiting for dates for a conference to be hosted by the two governments. The Loyalists are proving to be a bit awkward and demanding certain safeguards; you can understand that they're not best pleased at what's being proposed. But personally, I think a deal will be done; we've given ground on some of the issues on their agenda. Let's move on. What do you have for me?'

I thought I had detected a ray of hope. 'Does this really need to go ahead if you're making such good progress? It might have the opposite effect and set things back.'

'Get off that tack, Craig. The Council thinks it's a good idea, and that's all that matters; best leave politics to the politicians. The hard-liners reckon this business could bring your government to its knees; they're in the driving seat, discussion over.'

The die was cast; I spread the papers on the table and went through the alterations I'd made.

'I can't see that you need a diversion; in fact, it might just be counterproductive. They'll be ready for you this time; the air will be flooded with helicopters, and the area will be cordoned off by roadblocks. Getting away could be nigh impossible.'

O'Connell went into deep thinking mode, stroking his chin from time to time, drumming his fingers on the table at others. 'You might be right; I'll give it some thought.'

'The next point is the set-up; I like the idea, but I wonder if it wouldn't be better carried out at the end of the day when the city has quietened down? Everybody will be winding down, and there won't be the same level of traffic to contend with.'

He shook his head. 'We considered that, but it introduces too many uncertainties as to the timing, and if London is too quiet, it's more difficult to blend in. What else?'

I shrugged and went on. 'Having seen that you're willing to sacrifice your men for a big prize, what about running a decoy vehicle identical to the escape vehicle and run it up a ramp into a furniture van to make the getaway?'

O'Connell wrinkled his nose. 'Not very original, Craig; sounds like the Italian Job. Hollywood has done it a dozen times.'

'If it works, it works, repetition isn't a no-no if it's appropriate to the circumstances. I also wondered if you could get hold of a public service vehicle, say a bus, and use it for the getaway.'

He nodded. 'That idea has some merit; I'll think about it. Anything else?'

'Nope, but I really do think you should consider reversing the timing of the operation. Other than that, it's a good plan.'

'Right then,' he downed the last of his whiskey, 'I'll be getting back to the music.'

'When's this one going down, Sean?'

He looked at me with a mixture of hostility and suspicion. 'You know Craig, that curiosity of yours will be the death of you.'

'You can't blame me for asking, surely?'

'I think you're very unwise to ask too many questions; it'll be sooner rather than later, that's all I'll say. We want to kick the man whilst he's down, so to speak. Now I'm off to the band; you're welcome to stay if you wish.'

I shook my head and lied. 'Would love to, but I've got a date. That just leaves one thing, Sean.'

'And what might that be?' He looked at me expectantly.

'My passport.'

'Not yet, Craig, remember what I told you? Don't give the elephant a bun till it's done its trick; no rewards till the show's over. You'll get it back when the time is right. You're not thinking of flying away, are you?'

'That's exactly what I am thinking of doing. I want to leave all this behind me and start a new life; get married, have kids, be normal.'

O'Connell smiled ruefully. 'I envy you the very thought; I wish I could get out and go back to Kerry, live a quiet life surrounded by the green Irish countryside. Alas, that won't happen till the Cause is won.'

'You really believe that you'll win?'

'As sure as night follows day, it's only a matter of time.'

I started to gather up the papers, but he stopped me. 'You'll have no more need of these, Craig; you're just a spectator here on in. When this is over, we'll meet, have a nip or two, and you'll get your passport.'

TWO WEEKS LATER

I was watching television when the programme was interrupted at 9.30 pm with the news that an IRA attempt to abduct the Queen Mother had been foiled by the Anti-Terrorist Squad. The announcer explained that the attack had taken place outside Clarence House when the Queen Mother was returning home after a visit to the Palace for dinner with the Queen and other family members. There were very few details available, but shots had been fired, and two IRA men had been killed, four others had surrendered.

A later bulletin described a police raid on a pub in Kilburn where further arrests had been made. It was also revealed that the Queen Mother was never in danger; acting on intelligence, she received her place in the royal car, which had been taken by a suitably disguised member of the security forces.

My door intercom buzzed, and I moved across to reply.

'Yes?'

'Craig Dorian?'

'That's right, who is this?'

'Police, open up, please.'

I opened the door to find myself confronted by two plain-clothed police officers holding their Warrant Cards for my inspection.

'Craig Dorian?'

'Yes.'

'I'm placing you under arrest under the Counter-Terrorism Act.'

The usual caution was given, and I was handcuffed and taken down to a waiting car. There didn't seem to be any witnesses to my arrest; the occupants of Finsbury Mansion were unaware of the minor sensation taking place in their midst.

The journey took about forty minutes, and I was deposited in a detached suburban safe house not too far from Heathrow. I wasn't alone; two protection officers would be with me round the clock for company. The cuffs were removed, and the arresting officers departed; there were no introductions, my guards knew who I was and why I was there. They didn't say much; just showed me round the house and left me upstairs in what was effectively a self-contained apartment.

The older of the two men, Detective Sergeant Maher, gave me my instructions; his mate remained glued to the TV watching a sex-romp movie.'

'Everything you need is up there: bed, bath, kitchen, lounge; stay upstairs unless you really need to come down. Any problems, give us a shout.'

'I'd like a morning newspaper.'

'Already arranged, you'll get a selection.'

'What if I want to go out?'

'You don't; anything else?'

'Yeah; do you make all your clients feel this welcome?'

He wasn't amused. 'We're here to protect you, Dorian, nothing more, nothing less.' With that, he turned on his heel and went downstairs.

It was all going as I'd planned; all I could do now was await events. I settled down and reflected on what I had done, reassuring myself that I'd chosen the right option.

The acquaintance I'd met at the Charing Cross Hotel had been none other than Commander Mark Hanley, who had arrested me years back for the Crewe job. I had outlined the deal I wanted, namely an amnesty, all criminal records expunged and safe passage to a destination of my choice. In return, I offered information which would lead to the capture of all those involved in the theft of the Crown Jewels. He hadn't been overly impressed, pointing out that the IRA have already put their hand up for that job. We've already made a number of arrests.'

'You've got a few minnows; I'm talking about the kingpins.'

At that point, he'd been interested. 'This isn't my field, Dorian; I'll have to talk to my opposite number in the Anti-Terrorist Squad.'

'Involve whoever you want, Commander, but I want you there as well. I might have something else for you personally, something big. The meeting must be somewhere quiet, discreet; I think I'm being watched by the IRA.''

Why would they be keeping tabs on you?'

'Because of what I know.'

He had sneered at me. 'If you were a danger to them, they wouldn't hesitate to take you out.'

I understood his scepticism, and I opened up a bit to get him on board.

517

'The IRA is planning another job, a big one, and I can help you catch them in the act.'

'How come you know so much? Sounds to me like you're involved in some way; I could arrest you now on suspicion of conspiracy to commit a terrorist act.'

'Don't threaten me, Commander, use your head; arrest me, and you learn nothing. Be sensible, set up the meeting, and all will be revealed.'

'When is this job going to happen?'

'I don't know; I might find out later today.'

He wasn't happy, but I had him on the hook; he couldn't take a chance on not going along with my proposition, especially in light of recent events.

'Wait here', he said huffily. 'I'll make a telephone call.'

Minutes later, he returned. 'I've booked an appointment for you to see this man.' He handed me a piece of paper with a name and address written on it: MARCUS REDMOND; ORTHODONTIST

'Be there at ten on Monday morning. I'll be there with a colleague.'

'Suits me; I didn't realise the Anti-Terrorist lot had their own dentist. Book me in for a check-up at the same time.'

Hanley didn't like my humour and just fixed me with a stony stare.

'One more thing, Commander; don't have me watched. If the IRA suspects anything out of the ordinary, I'll be a goner, and you won't get your information.'

I'd gone to the Orthodontist as arranged and found myself sitting in a small waiting room with Hanley and Commander Will Clayton of the Anti-Terrorist Squad. Neither of them offered to shake hands.

Hanley, as he had on the previous occasion, seemed particularly cool, though it was he who opened proceedings.

'Tell us what you've got, Murray or Dorian, whatever you call yourself nowadays.'

'It doesn't work like that, Hanley.' I knew dropping reference to his rank would annoy him, but his attitude was beginning to piss me off. 'First, I tell you what I want, and if you agree to my demands, I tell you what I know.'

Hanley hadn't disguised his anger. 'Now you listen to me, you little shit, you're nothing more than a second-rate thief; you're not going to dictate terms to me.'

I shrugged and played a dangerous game. 'So, fucking arrest me.' I held out my hands, ready to be handcuffed in a show of bravado.

Hanley went a deep shade of red, and I thought I'd gone too far, but Clayton rescued the situation.

'Hold on, Mark, let's hear a bit more. Give us something, Dorian, and we'll see where we go. Bear in mind that we know of the IRA's involvement

519

in the Crown Jewels job and that the theft was probably organised by Sean O'Connell, a resident of Kilburn and frequenter of the Pig and Fiddle.'

The wind had been well and truly taken from my sails, and I had to think quickly.

I nodded. 'You know more than I thought, but it looks like you've got no evidence, or you would have arrested him by now. The thing is, I know what his next job is, and I've got the blueprint for the job with his fingerprints all over it.'

Clayton squinted at me; Hanley was gnashing his teeth. 'How come you've got your hands on something like that? How are you involved?'

'It's irrelevant how I got to know. Do you want this deal or not?'

Clayton looked at Hanley, who, to my relief, nodded reluctantly. 'It's your call, Will.'

'OK, Dorian, tell us what you want.'

I had sat back in the chair and tried not to look smug, but I was on the home straight. I could feel it. 'I want my criminal record expunged, fingerprints, photos, etc. I want the documentation for a new identity, Birth Certificate, Passport, Driving License, National Insurance Number, etc.' I waited for some reaction, but none came.

'I want a one-way flight to Australia, First Class by the way, and some strings pulled to get me Residency over there. Finally, because of what I'm going to tell you, I want Immunity from Prosecution in relation to any

crimes I might tell you about. Oh, I almost forgot; I'll want to be kept somewhere safe until I can leave the country. If you're happy to proceed on that basis, I'll bring a Solicitor with me next time we meet to make sure our arrangement is properly documented.'

Hanley went purple; he was absolutely livid. 'You're off your trolley, you little shit; we don't do deals with people like you.'

I stood up and reached my hands forward for handcuffing. 'Arrest me; if not, I'll be on my way.'

Will Clayton gave Hanley a warning look and took control of the situation.

'Sit down, Mr Dorian. You're asking a lot; we give you what you want, and all we get is an allegation from you that the IRA might be going to carry out some job or other. We seem to be taking all the risk. Persuade me, tell me more.'

It was my turn to weigh options in the balance; fortunately, I had rehearsed this very scenario.

'OK, I'll tell you what he's planning, but you don't get the evidence till I get what I want.'

Will Clayton sat back expectantly, but Hanley wasn't a happy man.

'I don't like it, Will. He's involved in this up to his neck; we can hold him, search his flat, try to work out if this deal is worthwhile or not.'

I looked at him with a self-satisfied smirk. 'You won't find the evidence it's with my solicitor.'

Clayton remained calm. 'I can see your point, Mark, but this is a National Security matter. OK, Dorian, this is the deal; you tell us what the target is; I need to know that at least. To give you what you want, I'll have to convince some very senior people, including at least one politician.'

It had been decision time; it was all or nothing.

'The IRA is going to try to abduct the Queen Mother on her way to the Palace.'

Clayton went pale. Hanley blurted out. 'Bullshit, bullshit, they wouldn't attempt that. You're off your rocker.'

Clayton admonished his colleague. 'The IRA will do anything to further its aims, Mark. I'm treating this seriously. When is this going to happen?'

'I can tell you how it's going to be done, but I don't know when; they wouldn't tell me. You should be able to find out from the Palace diary when the Queen Mother is next due to visit. When I met O'Connell, he seemed confident that the IRA Council had a date in mind. He said it would be soon, so I suggest you don't waste any time putting this deal together. I'll keep you posted if I find out anything else.'

I had sat back at that point waiting for a reaction, watching the expressions on the face of the two men for a minute or two before putting issuing my ultimatum. That's all I have for you, take it or leave it. Do we have a deal or not?'

Hanley was grim-faced and couldn't bring himself to bow the knee; he passed the buck to Clayton.

'It's up to you, Will; I'll have to go along with whatever you decide, though I don't like it one iota.'

It had been time then for me to play my last card, a big one.

'Just before you make your mind up, I've got something for you too, Hanley, not that you've earned anything with your attitude.'

He had looked at me with what looked like disdain. 'Oh yeah, such as?'

I stared into his face, watching for the change in expression I knew would come.

'Such as a Noble Lord and a Knight of the Realm up to their eyes in high-level fraud; that's all.'

I could feel smugness gripping me and didn't switch it off; I was enjoying my moment. 'And if you're nice to me, I might even help you in relation to the PMR Bullion raid and the Great Train Robbery.'

He'd ridiculed me. 'You? You? How would a toerag like you possibly know about those jobs? They're way out of your league; don't waste my fucking time.'

'Because Commander Almighty Hanley, contrary to what you might think, I'm not a second-rate thief; I'm one of the best, maybe even the best.'

Clayton reached over at that point and squeezed his colleague's arm; he was taking me seriously. Hanley was choking on his emotions; he was going to have to accept my demands, and he knew it.

We met less than a week later in the same dentist's waiting room, and I gave them all the details I had on O'Connell, along with the all-important evidence bearing his fingerprints. The Irishman really had slipped up that night when he'd given me the plan for the Queen Mother kidnap; he thought he'd retrieved it, but all he got was a photocopy of the original.

My Solicitor had been in attendance on that occasion to make sure Hanley and Clayton fulfilled their side of the bargain. Everything I'd asked for was agreed and handed over; well, nearly everything. I was given a new identity in the name of Ross McClaren, born in Glasgow, including his birth certificate, National Insurance number, and driving license. The Home Secretary pardoned me and had verified that my criminal record had been expunged. The Immunity from Prosecution had been issued by the Lord Chancellor's office.

Paul Morrison, my Solicitor, examined each of the documents minutely and pronounced that they were valid.

'Yes, all in order; that just leaves my client's Passport and flight ticket to Australia.'

Hanley pulled the passport from his pocket but didn't hand it over. 'Not so fast; it's your turn now. Let's have what you've got on Lord Whosoever and Sir Whatsit first.'

I looked at my Solicitor. 'Paul?'

He shrugged. 'Your call, Craig; it's not an unreasonable request.'

I nodded. 'Hand it over, Paul.'

Paul reached into his briefcase, took out a large brown envelope and handed it to Hanley, who snatched at it in his eagerness to view the contents. I looked on triumphantly as he poured over the paperwork. There were three sets of papers, all neatly typed: the PMR job, the Great Train Robbery, and the Building Insurance scam involving the IRA.

I had set out in detail how each job had been carried out, the preparatory work, the acquisitions, and the locations involved. It was all there, where the Tanker had been modified and where it had gone for disposal. I revealed all I knew, where we held the driver, about the farm where we had all assembled after the Train robbery and how the cash had been shipped out of the country. I explained how I had ascertained, via the Land Registry, that all the properties were in the ownership of Horizon Holdings. Averton was well and truly linked to all the crimes, and I took a great delight in my revenge.

The third bundle gave details of the insurance scam operated by Avebury and Leaney and how O'Connell and the IRA were involved. I fancied it all added up to some of the biggest headlines this century.

I wondered how Avebury would feel about being one of the headlines his ego had hitherto craved.

I was concerned about Dan and had given Paul Morrison a letter to be hand-delivered to him the day I took off for Australia. Dan was smart and looked ahead; I was pretty sure that he would have contingency plans in place for a quick exit. I had agonised for hours about where to draw the line; Angie, Henry and his art gallery, and even the redoubtable Tony ended up on the wrong side. In the end, as always, I put myself first.

I had gloried in watching Mark Hanley reading through the papers; enjoyed watching his changing expressions. He was in a state of minor shock when he looked up; his eyes had widened by the minute, and his breathing had quickened noticeably. He lifted his head and stared at me, studying me as though for the first time. Was it my imagination, or was there a semblance of respect when he spoke?

'Your involvement in this must have been at the highest level; there were millions of pounds involved, none of which has been recovered. I can only conclude that you personally have done very well out of these crimes.'

Paul Morrison interjected immediately. 'I advise you to say nothing further, Craig; you've fulfilled your obligations.'

I gave Hanley a weak smile. 'Sorry, Commander, I must accept my Solicitor's advice; I'm sure you understand.'

Paul spoke up again. 'I must ask that you now keep your side of the agreement in full.'

Mark Hanley exchanged a glance with Will Clayton, who raised an eyebrow and nodded. When Hanley spoke, he made it clear that he hadn't suddenly become my friend.

'I wish I didn't have to deal with scum like you, but we will keep our side of the bargain to get at your low-life accomplices. The Passport and airline ticket will wait until we've acted on this information; it looks good, but it must be authenticated. In the meantime, Dorian, carry on as normal until we tell you otherwise.'

Paul protested vehemently. 'This isn't what my client agreed. You are not honouring your undertaking so much for your word.'

Hanley didn't yield. 'We have to check this lot out; for instance, we must satisfy ourselves that the fingerprints are those of Sean O'Connell. We must determine the ownership of these properties and investigate the insurance fraud.'

'You're putting my client's life at risk.'

The policeman snarled back. 'He did that himself when he got into this business; there's no reason he should be at any risk if he carries on as normal. We'll ensure that the abduction of the Queen Mother doesn't happen, and arrests will follow. At that point, we will pick up your client, place him under arrest and take him to a safe house until he can leave the country.'

Will Clayton nodded in agreement. 'My men will pick you up and afford you protection.'

I felt I could trust Clayton, but I was being super-cautious. 'OK, so I'm picked up, taken wherever, what then?'

Hanley spoke up grudgingly, resigned to the fact that I had the upper hand. 'Once you're under Commander Clayton's protection, we will act quickly to pick up Averton and Leaney. If that all goes to plan, I promise I will personally deliver your passport and flight ticket to Australia.'

It seemed to be sewn up, but I was still nervous. I'd given away all I had, and if these guys somehow reneged on the deal, I was sunk. 'Is everything OK, Paul? There aren't any loopholes?'

He shook his head. 'I think we've covered everything. We're reliant on these gentlemen being honest, which I'm sure they are.' He fixed his gaze on Hanley whilst he spoke.

I stood to leave and extended my hand. 'It's been a pleasure doing business with you, gentlemen.'

Will Clayton exchanged the briefest of handshakes; Hanley had scowled and told me to 'Piss off.'

'Tut, tut, Hanley, you're showing your upbringing, or should I say the lack of it.'

Paul and I left two of law enforcement's finest discussing the revelations I'd given them. I tarried outside the door of the waiting room and put my fingers to my lips. Paul shook his head disapprovingly and went on ahead. I heard Hanley say. 'Bastard, he's come out on top. He's caused chaos and heartache in Crewe, he's stolen millions of pounds, he's helped the IRA pull off the biggest coup in its history, he's an accessory to carnage and deaths, and yet he walks away to a life in the sun smelling of roses.'

Clayton had sounded more pragmatic. 'But, if he's right, we're going to put some big names behind bars for a very long time, and, break up a mainstream IRA Unit; we're on the threshold of making some of the biggest arrests in history.'

Hanley wasn't placated. 'I hate doing deals with scum like him; I hate him and everything he stands for.'

'Relax, Mark, you'll give yourself an ulcer or worse; he'll get his comeuppance in the end. Somewhere along the way, he'll revert to his old ways and end up in the nick; his kind always do.'

I remember smiling and thinking, not me, old chap; I'm out of it for good.

Outside, I thanked Paul for his services, and he offered me a lift back to Finsbury Park. 'Hanley doesn't like you, Craig; you had better watch your back.'

'I guess not, but he'll get over it. I bet he'll be an Assistant Commissioner by the end of the year; his career will go into overdrive when he arrests Avebury and Leaney.'

Back at the flat, I wrote Paul a cheque for his services and reminded him to get the letter to Dan.'

'Will do; it's nothing illegal, is it.'

I spread my hands in innocence. 'Of course not; all that's behind me as of now. It's just a goodbye to an old friend.'

And that was how I came to be snuggled up in bed, in a safe house, under police protection. As I lay there, looking back at the past and forward to my future, any guilt I was feeling slowly ebbed away, and my thoughts turned to more pleasant matters. I thought about engaging Gail's services from time to time just to relieve the boredom of my temporary incarceration in a safe house. A nice idea but a foolish one; I had to sever all links with the past; still, I went to sleep with thoughts of her and passionate memories.

A NEW FUTURE BECKONS

Chapter Thirty-Four

By the end of the third week in the safe house, I was developing cabin fever. My minders steadfastly refused my requests to be allowed out of the place, with or without them in attendance.

'Orders Dorian; you wanted to be safe, and safe you're going to be; it's a dangerous world out there, as you well know.'

I was pissed off and grumpy. 'My name's McLaren now, not Dorian. What the hell is taking them so long? Why can't they get on with it and make the arrests?'

'There's no good getting snotty; we don't want to be here either, especially acting as nursemaids to an ungrateful sod. These things take time, and there's no good whinging about it. You wouldn't thank us if we made arrests and had to let them go because we hadn't prepared the ground properly.'

They were right. 'I guess so. Well, what about some female company to help the time go by?' They just laughed at me.

I tried an old-fashioned inducement. 'I'll fix you up as well? In fact, let's have a party, anything goes.'

More laughter; I gave up.

Halfway through a tediously slow fourth week, one of my guardians brought me the Evening Standard.

'I think these are the headlines you've been waiting for; it looks like we'll all soon be out of here.'

My heart missed a beat, and my face broke into a smile, anticipating what I was about to read; he knew I was only interested in one piece of news. And there they were: banner headlines.

SENSATION

WELL-KNOWN PEER AND BUILDING MAGNATE ARRESTED

It was all there just as I'd hoped: the crimes they had been charged with, their personal profiles, photographs at social events. Their denials were there, of course, with Avebury full of his usual bluster. They had been released on police bail, their passports had been confiscated, and their movements were restricted.

It was a pity they were on the loose, but all being well, I would be up and away without delay. Detective Constable Martin Rother, Marty as he was known, stood in the doorway watching me read the article before making the announcement I had resorted to praying for on a daily basis.

'You're on your way, Dorian, oops sorry, McLaren; a taxi will be here for you at nine-thirty tomorrow morning. You're booked on the twelve twenty to Sydney via Hong Kong courtesy of British Airways. Commander Hanley will deliver your passport and flight tickets shortly.

I was ecstatic; I did a little dance of sheer joy. 'Yippee! I'm on my way to a new life Down Under. Yippee!' I'd never felt so relieved and elated; it was finally all over. There was no packing to do; I'd bought myself a load of new gear in readiness for my final departure from the safe house. I was ready to roll right down to a bundle of Australian dollars.

Money wouldn't be a problem when I got to my destination; my friendly Swiss banker had set me up with a facility to access funds in my new name. God bless Swiss Banks and Paul Morrison, my solicitor, who had arranged the delivery of my instructions to the bank. This near to the finishing line, I was being super-cautious. I made no telephone calls and had trashed my mobile; my break from the UK would leave no trails, no strings. Everything was in place. All that stood between me, and my new life was a journey of nine thousand miles.

Hanley delivered my passport and ticket about an hour later. He was his customary surly self and said nothing as I checked them out. The bastard had booked me in on Economy, and I suspected that he had made the delivery in person just to see my reaction.

'You were supposed to provide a First-Class flight; this is Economy.'

He feigned an apologetic expression. 'Oh, I am sorry, Mr Murray; sorry, Mr Dorian; whoops, silly me, Mr McLaren now? I'm afraid I forgot that bit of our agreement.'

I put on my sympathetic visage. 'Don't worry, Commander Hanley; put it down to early onset dementia. I'll upgrade out of my loose change and tell you what, if I've got any leftovers, I'll donate them to the Copper's Benevolent Fund.'

His cheeks flushed. 'One of these days, you'll get yours, and I hope I'm around to see it. Your kind always comes to grief in the end.'

'Yeah, yeah, I know. The bad guys always end up in the shit; it's only the good guys that live happily ever after; spare me the homilies.' That was it; he just turned on his heel and left.

After he'd gone, I retrieved the bottle of Champagne I'd put in the fridge when I arrived and invited my housemates to join with me in a celebration. They declined, muttering something about not drinking on duty. I didn't care; it tasted just as good without being shared.

That last night passed slowly, and I slept fitfully, like a kid before its birthday or Christmas, but the dark sky finally gave way to dawn, then morning, and I was sat waiting impatiently for the taxi when it arrived punctually at nine-thirty. My two minders had the good grace to say goodbye and wish me well in Australia; Marty Rother even suggested that he might look me up if he ever got to Sydney. I said sure, but we both knew it wasn't going to happen.

The sun was shining when I set out; a bright start to a bright new future, I told myself. I was on top of the world; I felt that I had well and truly beaten the system, hands down. There I was, a millionaire with a clean sheet, headed for a new beginning in Australia. As ever, my thoughts went to Sam, and yet again, I convinced myself that I should get in touch when I got to Australia; maybe this time I would.

My taxi stopped at some traffic lights, and I was aware of a motorcycle coming alongside, the rider and pillion passenger both wearing those slightly scary black helmets. The lights went to amber, the taxi revved and made ready to pull away. I happened to look to my right just as the pillion rider reached inside his leather jacket. Next thing, the muzzle of a gun was pointing at me. I saw the flash, even saw the window shatter, felt the bullet plough into my heart, and my life began to slip away. That was it. Apparently, there was a second shot to my head, but I was dead; I knew nothing about it.

Just one morning paper gave the incident a headline.

POLICE MYSTIFIED BY LONDON TAXI KILLING

Epilogue

Will Clayton phoned Mark Hanley to exchange views on my execution.

'Hi Mark, I suppose you know that your man caught a bullet on his way to Heathrow?'

'Yeah, I heard about it. Good riddance as far as I'm concerned; it's no great loss to mankind; one villain less to deal with. At least the bastard didn't get the chance to enjoy his money. It is a bit of a mystery, though; someone must have known his movements.'

Will Clayton chuckled. 'I thought you wouldn't shed any tears. 'Do you want to know what I think happened? I reckon that someone tipped the IRA off about his movements, and they took him out.'

The penny dropped; Hanley started to read between the lines, a broad smile on his face. 'You must have some contacts inside the IRA, Will; I don't suppose you've got any leads on the killer?'

Clayton chuckled again. '**Me**, of course not, though I hope you don't waste too much time looking into this one.'

Milton Keynes UK
Ingram Content Group UK Ltd.
UKHW050903110424
440859UK00017B/184